A Sense of Duty

Dark Horse Guardians, Book 1

Written by Ava Armstrong

Edited Version II

A dark horse is a little-known person or thing
that emerges to prominence,
especially in a competition of some sort
or a contestant that seems unlikely to succeed.

~ Prologue ~

Lara's attacker never knew what hit him in a dark alley outside of the restaurant where he worked as a dishwasher. Carefully stalking him for months, she memorized his patterns. She shot out the one street light the night before using a pellet gun. There were no security cameras in the alley. Canvassing the area one last time, she made certain there were no lights or people in the passage where he enjoyed his smoke break at precisely 9 PM every night.

Dressed in a dark hooded sweatshirt and black pants, she crouched in the shadows across the street hiding behind a row of trash cans. A rat scurried near her foot, but she focused on the task. He deserved what he had coming. He had raped and nearly beaten her to death. He altered the course of her life. Because he was a minor he received a slap on the wrist. She's the one that had the life sentence. She had to live with the aftermath.

He arrived at the appointed hour. She watched him with revulsion. His hand shook as he lit the cigarette. Now a drug addict with rotting teeth, he hunched over and inhaled his first draw.

That night she watched the late news. He was found by one of his co-workers. The police weren't saying much. Over the next few days, she heard on the radio the victim died from two bullet wounds—one in the head and one in the heart. She imagined death was instant.

Lara read about the incident later that week in the newspaper. The police suspected the double tap with hollow points was the mark of a hired killer. Later, authorities concluded it was a drug related gang execution. He became a statistic, another dead junkie.

Lara folded the newspaper with no emotion. She just celebrated her 21st birthday.

~ End Prologue ~

CHAPTER 1: *Scars*

The brutal rape changed her in a way she could never explain. Often the scene would replay in her mind like a movie she wished she'd never viewed. The humiliation of the act was bad enough, but the beating she suffered brought her to the point of no return. She feared for her life as she was savagely pummeled with his fists. He was much bigger than her and once he was on top, he had the advantage.

"I will never forget that feeling... of being totally powerless." she told the licensed clinical social worker in the counseling session. "I didn't realize what he was doing until he flipped me over and pulled my hair. It hurt, and I screamed. But, the more I screamed, the more he hit me. The harder I fought back, the worse it got. But I could not stop fighting. I thought I was going to die."

In the small suburban town, everyone at school knew about the violent incident. She spent three nights in the hospital and missed six weeks of school. She was bleeding internally for several days. The doctor said it was her kidneys. Her eyes were blackened and many bruises on her body remained for weeks afterward. At one point during the attack, she was slammed with such force into the pavement that she picked pieces of rocks out of her knees for months. Road rash, they called it. Reddish purple scars remained as a grim reminder. She escaped from death, barely. The only thing that saved her was the fact that he was exhausted from raping her twice and released his grip slightly. That was the moment she lurched away and ran like the wind, taking the shortcut home. But, the feeling of vulnerability after the violent attack changed her. There was a simmering rage within Lara.

Although her parents reported the assault to police, little was done to punish her attacker. He agreed to attend a "violence against women" program. He served a reduced sentence in a youthful offender's program. Because he was a minor, seventeen years old, and his parents were wealthy donors to the private school she attended, her rapist was given a second chance.

Lara wanted to move away or attend another school. Her parents moved her to the local high school and she got a new social worker.

But every so often, she saw him somewhere in the small town. He grinned once, as if to say, *I won, you lost -- get over it.*

 Lara's nightmares continued. The social worker called them night terrors.

"Why do I keep reliving this over and over?" Lara asked in one session.

The counselor explained, "You were traumatized. This will take time." It's a totally normal reaction. Eventually, with time, other memories will push those bad ones out. That's what we need to focus on now, Lara, making positive memories."

Lara sensed this counselor had no idea what it was like to be beaten and raped. How could she? She was probably twenty-eight years old.

"Did you hear what happened to Fiona?" Cloe, one of Lara's classmates leaned over before class started.

"What?"

"She was raped at that party—you know, the one at

Bethany's house."

"Oh God." Lara shivered and glanced away. "That's horrible. Who?"

"Hugh Boyd, you've heard of him, haven't you?"

"Oh yeah. Him. He's a creep." Lara's eyes met hers. There was no sign that she knew he was the one. "Did Fiona tell the police?"

"No. He told her he'd kill her. Fiona didn't dare to report it."

Other kids sat at the lunch table and Lara listened silently with disgust. Some of them even laughed about the vicious attack. Again, the monster walked away, unpunished, while Fiona was going to a counselor to exorcise her demons. *He got away with it again.*

Lara ran into him at the library, then at the corner store. Was he following her? He always had a sickening smirk when he looked at her. As he continued to intimidate her, the anger within Lara simmered. She began looking him squarely in the eye—and, as she did so, an intense fury began to replace her sense of fear. It wasn't a simmering anger any longer; it had become uncontrollable rage.

At her new school she kept her head down and found a niche as a top student. By the time she turned fourteen, Lara realized the counseling wasn't helping. In fact, it seemed to be making her have headaches. She ended the sessions and focused on school. Over the course of the summer, it seemed she turned into a woman. Tall and lean, she never slouched to appear shorter nor avoided wearing heels. She stood out being tall and enjoyed towering over the boys in her class. Being tall somehow made her feel more powerful. But being pretty had its cost. Girls were jealous; boys hated her because she refused their advances.

High school was the worst four years of her life. Groups formed, and she didn't fit in. She shoveled cow manure on a dairy farm and worked at a fast food restaurant while in high school. She didn't wear make-up like the other girls and was ostracized because of it. So, Lara wore funky shoes and brightly striped knee socks. Her clothing was a riotous statement of mismatched patterns and colors, picked up in thrift stores. The way she dressed and carried herself kept many boys away. Most boys did not understand her, and if they did, they feared her. She was not a follower. Lara did not respect anyone who half-heartedly did anything. Life, for her, was an all or nothing proposition.

She began to embrace her life as an outsider. She read voraciously, all the classics and modern literature. She memorized poetry and Shakespearean sonnets. She wrote her own poetry on napkins and in notebooks. Lara's passions were art, history and architecture. She was an aficionado of jazz at a time when rap music was in vogue. She watched classic movies at a time when her peers were going to raves and experimenting with drugs. She was in the art club, played no sports and had two friends who occasionally stopped by to do homework. At times, it was difficult for Lara to even relate to them. Their lives were so alien to her. Strangely different from her generation, Lara had strong values that never wavered. She had always been against abortion, the use of illicit drugs, and casual intimacy with men. That was the real irony of it all. *Lara had ethics and morals, yet she was the one that got raped.*

She started to work on an emotional force field to protect her. But, it did not protect her completely. The force field disappeared one hot summer night when her attacker drove up to the fast food window to give her a personal message. She heard the voice on the crackling speaker inside, not knowing it was Hugh Boyd. When she saw his face at the drive-thru window she ceased breathing. She was suddenly face to face with the monster. He sneered as he looked her straight in the eye, "I'm not through with you..." He grabbed the food and sped off.

She felt a mixture of panic and anger as it overtook her. *But, finally she gained a coldly rational sense of mind.* And, the strategy started to formulate. It might take years to put into place, but it became her secret duty. That's the year she met Don and Rusty and, without their knowledge, she devised a detailed plan. She would kill the guy who ruined her life and make it look like someone else did it.

"Where are you going now?" Lara's mother asked too often.

"To my Krav Maga class, you know, mother. We talked about this."

She found coping skills in Krav Maga. She used the incident of the attack as a learning tool and earned a black belt by age twenty. Martial arts taught her breathing control, concentration, meditation and how to take a large person off their feet instantly. Don Henderson, her Grand Master at the dojo, and a Viet Nam vet, became a trusted mentor. At the same time, Lara became fascinated with firearms and developed a passion for shooting ranges, 9mm Glocks, and the smell of spent ammo. Target practice took the place of church. With training, she became a marksman. At age sixteen, Lara bonded with her concealed carry instructor, Rusty McManus, an older man, a former FBI agent who trained FBI and secret service agents in his later days. Rusty showed her how to hide weapons in her home, carry a variety of concealed weapons on her person, how to shoot from a seated, prone, or supine posture. As Rusty said, *you never knew what position you would be in when your life was threatened. You needed to be prepared for anything.*

Lara found her conversations with Rusty, Don and Olivia Henderson incredibly helpful. They became a crucial lifeline for her. Occasionally, she called in the middle of the night after an episode of night terrors. Don and Olivia were both kind and reassuring. She spent hours on the phone with Rusty. In six months, they helped to bring Lara more peace than all the counseling sessions that went before.

Chapter 2: The Encounter

It was the night of the piano recital. Her favorite professor happened to be an accomplished pianist and had just finished his performance. No matter how busy her life was, she never missed one of Professor Harris' recitals. In the last year of her master's program, she was eagerly looking forward to graduation in the spring. The cocktail party was packed into a small space with too many people. Dealing with her claustrophobia, Lara's careful guard was down the moment she first set eyes on *him*.

Who was this stranger with blue eyes following her as she moved through the throng of people? He made her uncomfortable with his sudden and intense eye contact. That was the first sign of trouble. Lara had never met a male that she could not stare down. She prided herself on being able to make any man turn away. She had always been in control of every situation, every conversation, even eye contact. Lara's life was orderly, planned and controlled, until she met *him*.

Dressed in a long pink sweater, black pants and boots, carrying a bulky leather sack, she doubted she looked attractive. Lara's long dark hair was loosely pulled to the side in a ponytail, with black curls escaping. Being germ phobic, she wore pink leather gloves.

When Ben approached Lara, he extended his hand and introduced himself with a welcoming smile. "Hello, Lara? My name is Ben".

She left her gloves on and felt awkward doing so as she shook his strong broad hand. "Lara, I have heard so much about you from Professor Harris." He pronounced her name correctly – he said *Lara*, the way it was *meant* to be pronounced. She did not immediately respond. She couldn't. Her heart was racing; was it the claustrophobia or was it him? A moment passed. She smiled at him afraid he was imagining she was deaf or mute or both. She felt unprepared and started sweating. Lara did not know who he was, nor did she know why he was speaking to her.

Feeling self-conscious, the only thing she could utter was, "Professor Harris? Yes, he is my history professor. How do you know him?"

"He is my uncle." When Ben smiled, it was with his whole face. There were laugh lines and dimples. His deep blue eyes lit up as he held Lara's gaze. She noticed he hadn't shaved for a couple of days, but the scruff looked good on him—a symbol of masculinity, as if he needed it. As she scrutinized him, she couldn't help thinking, *this guy was just too handsome.* She detected a slight Irish brogue and she surmised: he's black Irish, like me, black hair, fair complexion, blue eyes. Even though Ben was a stranger to Lara, she was not feeling her usual sense of paranoia. She was standing unusually close to him in the jam-packed room. He smelled of lavender and sandalwood, wore a button-down shirt with a sweater vest and corduroy pants. Lara smiled. *Good he is a fellow geek.* She scanned the room quickly looking for an exit.

Ben stayed close to her. "Did you enjoy the performance?"

"Oh, yes," she was now pushing through the crowd speaking to Ben as he moved alongside her, "I have spent many hours listening to Harris practice in his office. He has the baby grand in there, and I often go in after class to sit on his couch and visit with Einstein — that's his dog."

"Actually, Einstein is *my* dog."

Einstein was the most beautiful black and white English Bull Terrier Lara had ever seen. She visited her professor's office partly because she so enjoyed the company of Einstein and walking him had become part of her daily routine. He was young with a lovely egg-shaped head and black Mongolian eyes and built like a bulldozer, about forty pounds now, but would grow to fifty pounds of solid muscle. The canine was devoted to her. Einstein looked forward to Lara's visits as she showered him with attention and carried organic dog treats in her pocket.

Ben touched her arm as they moved toward the exit. "Would you come with me to walk Einstein now? I'm sure he's ready to get outside for a bit." His eyes met hers.

Lara surprised herself, "Sure."

The office of Professor Harris was one of her favorite places in the world. The large wood paneled room faintly smelled of cherry pipe tobacco and expensive brandy. The professor's slippers were tucked under the baby grand. There were books everywhere. Built-in shelves were filled with rare first editions and curious artifacts from faraway places. Professor Harris taught world history and, in her opinion, was a genius. He also played that baby grand piano in a way that could bring tears to her eyes.

When Ben opened the office door, Einstein was eagerly waiting. Ben slipped on his leash and the dog powerfully pulled them both outside. Ben and Lara walked at a brisk pace in the cool mid-September air. She detected the aroma of a wood fire the moment they stepped outside. She tried to avert her eyes from Ben's attractive face, especially his mesmerizing blue eyes. It was easier for her to communicate with him if they walked side by side.

She couldn't help but notice all six-foot two inches of his rugged frame was composed of solid muscle. This guy even had muscles in his neck. His wide shoulders tapered to a well-defined waist and he had a sense of confidence about him. It wasn't a swagger, but close. He also had a particular walk, a cadence that was distinctive. She couldn't put her finger on it. Maybe he was an athlete. There was a quiet power in his body and the way he carried himself with a sense of purpose. Lara and Ben strolled on the brick sidewalks passing by the lovely historical buildings of the campus lit with period street lamps.

"Have you lived here long?" Ben asked her.

"All of my life." She replied. "This campus has been my home away from home for the past six years."

It was one of the rare places she felt truly safe, but she didn't say that. The 1800's buildings were familiar to her. She knew every inch of the campus, even the basements and hiding places for the custodians. The original buildings were also of historical significance, her favorite being the four-square brick building next to the library. That structure was the original university established in 1845. Back then it was known as Maine Secondary and was the oldest coeducational boarding school in the country.

"I was drawn to the small town feeling here." Lara explained. "Even though Portland is a bustling city, the campus is quiet and filled with green space."

Ben glanced at her as they walked, "It is beautiful..."

***

Walking next to her, Ben was stunned by her beauty and tried to keep his eyes forward, so he would not make her feel uncomfortable. Staring was rude. But his curiosity was insatiable when it came to Lara. Initially she was friendlier than he imagined she would be. It had taken two years to get this close to her. But he knew he had to proceed slowly. He had carefully prepared his story and wanted it to unfold gradually, as planned. As the conversation developed, Lara learned that Ben had recently moved to Maine because he was hired for a teaching position at the university. He watched her expression soften and detected a positive reaction when he told her.

She was more beautiful than the photographs. Although it was difficult to see her figure through the layers of clothing, Ben estimated she was tall, five feet nine inches maybe, and muscular. He guessed her weight to be around one forty and he noted she had large feet for a female. Surely, they provided good balance, especially in martial arts. Her physical traits were strikingly beautiful, and he understood why she had problems with guys pestering her. Lara's long thick hair was dark, shiny and slightly wavy. He wanted more than ever to reach his hand out to touch it, but only imagined doing so. Her eyes took his breath away. He was unprepared for the spark he felt when he looked into her hazel green eyes. No woman had affected him like this, *ever*. And he had been with many beauties in his thirty-one years.

He began to formulate a plan to meet with her again. He knew he had to be careful about personal boundaries. Instead he tried to keep her talking. "Tell me about yourself, Lara."

Usually at the ready with her standard story, Lara suddenly felt tongue-tied in the presence of this handsome mystery man with the slight accent.

"I'm a student here at the university. I live a short distance from the campus in a one-bedroom condo in an ancient pink Victorian." Lara impulsively blurted out just about everything to Ben on that stroll. As their feet rustled in the falling leaves, she continued. "I love art, architecture, history and I'm finishing up an internship with a local architectural firm."

By the time the thirty-minute walk ended, Ben knew her favorite food was lobster and her favorite ice cream flavor was ginger. He knew the colors she loved and, more importantly, he knew her address and phone number. Trusting him this soon was very uncharacteristic for her. She had never opened up to an unfamiliar male so quickly. Maybe she felt comfortable with him because he was the nephew of Professor Harris. No, there was something else about him that made her feel safe and secure.

The tiny yellow lamp on the piano lit the professor's office, casting a warm glow on the room and its lovely antique furnishings. Professor Harris was still busy with his fans at the reception. Lara automatically prepared a big bowl of fresh water for Einstein. As she carried it to the dog's corner of the room, Ben asked, "Would you share a cup of something hot with me before heading home tonight?"

She paused as she carefully placed the dog's dish on the floor and watched Einstein drink like he had never seen water before. She weighed the decision in her mind momentarily. Then she looked into Ben's blue eyes and said, "Yes, let's get hot chocolate."

When Ben smiled, Lara got lost in his eyes. She knew she was throwing caution to the wind but felt a strong need to discover more about this handsome stranger—he definitely intrigued her. The café on campus was busy for a weeknight. Newly renovated, it was designed to fit the character of the original building that housed it. It was an L-shaped room with wood paneled walls and wide pine floors. The antique sconces along the walls lit up the wooden booths. The place smelled of cheeseburgers and freshly brewed French vanilla coffee.

Ben led her to a small corner booth and ordered hot chocolate with marshmallow for both of them. Lara noticed he was a take-charge type of guy. "Let's talk more," he said sitting across the table as he looked directly into her eyes. His gaze was intense.

"Well, what would you like to talk about?" she asked with an innocent tone. Lara thought she sounded coy, not her style. Ben obviously wanted more personal information about her. Usually, this would raise her danger antennae. She had been known to give guys fake information to throw them off. However, with great enthusiasm she told Ben all about her life in Maine, graduating top of her class in high school, earning a scholarship to the university, her master's program, sprinkled with waiting on tables and working as an assistant for various professors on campus. She even told Ben about the untimely death of her father, something she rarely spoke about with anyone.

"My father left a small inheritance that allows me to live a comfortable life in the pink Victorian, until I can work full time as a designer." she told Ben. She left out the fact that she was a black belt, obsessed with weaponry and personal safety and filled with anxiety and phobias. These things she held close to the vest. She did not want to frighten him away.

***

Ben felt fortunate to have gained Lara's trust so soon. As he listened with rapt attention he took mental notes. Occasionally, he would interrupt and ask a quick question to clarify something. Ben felt certain he had gauged her correctly. She was already feeling comfortable with him. Lara seemed compelled to be a willing participant in Ben's informal interrogation of her. He was pleased that she was more than happy to give him the most personal and private information without restraint. She stopped speaking for a moment, pausing as if she sensed she was giving Ben too much.

He anticipated Lara would now turn the questions toward him, and she did with an engaging smile, "Ben, you know everything about me and I know nothing about you…"

Ben smiled and spoke softly, "Well, you know Professor Harris is my uncle and you know Einstein is my dog." He watched Lara as she leaned toward him.

She was eager to know more. "Where did you grow up?"

Ben took a deep breath, as if he was about to dive under water. He knew it was necessary to share some details with her, but he couldn't be too wordy. He would stay with the sketch of his life that he wanted her to know, for now. He slowly let his breath out, "My story is a bit sorted, Lara."

She touched his hand lightly as he looked down at the empty mug of cocoa, "Tell me, please." she requested softly.

Ben fell silent for a moment and felt his smile disappear. He spoke deliberately, "My family emigrated from Ireland before I was born. I'm the youngest of seven children. We lived in the suburbs of Boston, first Waltham, and then Newton. I've always been a bit of an over achiever and competitive. I pushed myself to graduate at the top of my class in high school, something we have in common. I often visited my brother, Patrick, in New York and marveled at the majesty of Wall Street, the financial epicenter of the free world. Although Patrick was keen on the idea of me attending a top-rated business school, I chose a different path. I was fortunate enough to be accepted to the U.S. Naval Academy in 2001. I spent four years in Annapolis, then after special training, I was deployed to Iraq and Afghanistan. After serving six years in the Middle East, I retired from the Navy. In 2012, I started a small consulting group, and now work as a contractor for the government." Even though he made it all sound mundane and normal, he instinctively knew she intended to dig up every detail about him.

***

Ben's career path was impressive; he was a self-made man in every sense of the word. The first moment Lara met him she perceived that he was driven, but she never thought he was a former Navy guy. "Ben, you have told me about your professional life but what about your *personal* life?"

She noticed Ben paused when she asked that question. He cleared his throat. "That part," he said, "is the sorted bit."

"What do you mean?" Lara asked quizzically. Ben's face grew tense. He looked at the table avoiding her eyes. In a low voice he began. "I got married shortly after graduating from the U.S. Naval Academy. It wasn't a good marriage. I have myself to blame for marrying so young. I have a son."

There was an awkward moment of silence. Lara wondered if Ben was still married and where his son was now. She wondered if she should even *ask* these questions. He seemed uncomfortable talking about his private life. A group of students in the café became rowdy.

"Let's go," Ben whispered.

They walked solemnly out of the café onto the brick sidewalk. "I'll walk you home," Ben smiled. Taking charge again, he was now her escort. Everything about Ben gave her the impression he was a gentleman. There was still something about how he carried himself. Maybe it was because he was a Navy man. He was different from any guy Lara had met before. She felt safe as he tucked her arm under his and enjoyed the tone of his voice with the subtle Irish accent.

Lara wanted to know more. "Have you had any experience teaching?"

He glanced at her, "I did quite a bit of teaching in the Navy, but nothing in a formal setting, like the university." He spoke with enthusiasm about his upcoming position as a modern history professor. Ben told her he was eager to teach the modern history of the Middle East and the events that led up to 9/11.

It was a short walk from the university café to Lara's Victorian apartment. Diagonally across the street from the campus there was a side street that led down a hill and connected to Maple Lane, the dead-end road where Lara's pink Victorian sat in all its glory. The neighborhood was filled with old Victorian homes and sprinkled with bungalows from the 1920's. The larger Victorian homes were divided into condominiums or apartments. The ocean was a couple of blocks further down the hill and the breeze was refreshing. The streets were tree-lined with big oaks and maples, with well- manicured lawns. Most of the homes had flower gardens, but they were in the last throes of summer. It was a star-filled night perfect for walking.

The building Lara lived in was on the historic registry. It was loaded with gingerbread trim and charming details. Ornate with over-the-top paint colors, built in 1899, it was the quintessential painted lady. Ben spent a moment taking in the design of the front of the house. His eyes lit up as he explored the pink and white details, the slate blue doors and the ornate arches and cut-outs of the large wrap-around porch, complete with a comfortable metal porch glider painted white. The roof shingles were designed to look like slate. The side entrance was lit with period gas lights now modified for electricity. His voice was excited.

"This is absolutely breathtaking! I must see the inside, if you don't mind..."

The moment had arrived for Lara to make a big decision. Should she invite a stranger into her apartment whom she had just met that evening? *No, too dangerous*. She needed to Google him and do a thorough background check before that would happen. So, she made an excuse. "My place is a mess right now, Ben, tonight would not be a good time for you to see it. The architectural details of this place show better in the daylight."

"I understand." he said quietly. "See you tomorrow then?" She loved listening to his voice. Ben was understated. He looked down at her and winked. He proved to be an imposing figure to her five foot nine-inch frame. They planned to meet in Professor Harris' office the next day late in the afternoon to walk Einstein. Ben smiled, his dimples adding to his charm. He took her hand, lifted it to his lips and gently kissed her palm. A warm sensation ran through Lara and she blushed. She had never had a man kiss her hand. Ben had been flirting with her all evening.

As he turned to walk toward the campus, Lara fumbled with the lock, opened the door and stepped into the hallway. As she closed the door, her face flushed, her heart hammered. All her senses were heightened as if she had just encountered someone dangerous yet exciting. For a moment, she leaned against the wall as she listened to Ben's receding footsteps. Then she walked up the short creaky staircase to her apartment door. Ben's face was etched in her memory as she replayed the conversations of the evening over in her mind.

The entry lamp cast an inviting glow upon the parlor as she dropped her keys into the candy dish. Her tiny apartment had three rooms and a bath. The kitchen, once a butler's pantry, was modern but tiny. White marble counters and subway tile contrasted with the sleek stainless-steel appliances. There was a small bistro table with two chairs in the corner near the window. Her bedroom held a queen-size bed with a carved Mahoney antique frame, a white velvet settee, a small marble-topped night table, and a small crystal chandelier. There was also a boudoir lamp on the night table, plus a tall Victorian lamp for reading near the settee. An antique vanity held her personal items. The draperies were a soft green silk with a subtle pattern of leaves. A large arrangement of fresh white roses stood in the corner on a plaster pedestal, a gift from Eliot Stone. They infused her bedroom with the wonderful scent of summer. The white chenille bedspread had a circular pattern of swirls with fringed edges. Floral throw pillows with peonies depicted on them covered her bed. The parlor was the largest room with a huge window, sofa, chair and ottoman, and several side tables. There was also a working fireplace that had been converted to gas. A small space near the doorway was sectioned off by a half wall. Lara had an entry table there and an ornately carved Victorian wall unit complete with hooks, storage bench, and mirror.

Her heavy pink leather sack slid to the floor as she kicked off her boots. She was immersed in thought. It was late, and she was usually exhausted at this hour, but she could not sleep. Lara needed a cold ginger ale and her computer, in that order.

As she opened her laptop Lara googled *Benjamin Aiden Keegan* and her breath quickened. Sifting through the hits that came up, she found an article about him. Then she found a copy of his high school yearbook on Google, so he was the top graduate of 2001 of his high school class. She was impressed. But she was more impressed when she saw his U.S. Naval Academy photo. He looked so young; Lara guessed he was twenty years old.

The articles she read about Ben described him as a successful and highly paid consultant, owner of Dark Horse Guardians, LLC. In a Canadian news article, she came across a picture of Ben with his wife, Sienna, and his son, William, and her heart raced. The photograph was taken three years ago, in Vancouver. They had attended a star-studded charitable event.

Zooming in on the photograph, Lara scrutinized it on the screen. A former model, Sienna was a skeletal blonde with big brown eyes. Ben's son, William, looked like his mother, blonde and gaunt, five years old in the photo. *Oh no, Lara thought - is Ben still married?* Immediately she searched government websites in Canada to find out if there was any record of his marriage or divorce. She spent hours on-line searching for articles about him, and only found a few details. But no divorce record was found. As she closed the laptop, Lara had only served to whet her appetite for more information about Ben. She took a hot shower and fell asleep exhausted with Ben's blue eyes the beginning of her dream.

Chapter 3: The Good, The Bad, and The Terrible

As he walked back toward the campus, Ben examined the beautiful Victorian houses in the neighborhood, hoping that one would have a vacancy. He made a mental note to canvass the landlords in the area. He needed to be near the university for his teaching, and to set up shop for his consulting business. The night air was refreshing. Earlier, he noticed Lara admiring the flower gardens as they passed, naming each type of plant. He got the sense that she loved flowers, and nature, overall. She especially loved the peonies in the flower bed in front of her Victorian porch.

He had many details to turn over in his mind now that he had physically met her. Ben smiled to himself as he reviewed the finer points of tonight's meeting. The initial introduction went much better than he had expected. She was more beautiful than he had imagined her to be. He kissed her hand. She agreed to see him tomorrow. He was walking on air. He pictured her searching right now on-line to learn as much about him as possible. Lara would discover the information that had been selected and planted on the internet about him. His public persona had just enough detail to satisfy the average person but would be enough to kindle a desire in Lara for more.

The things she would not know about him was that he was in the middle of his own holy war, but it wasn't called a jihad where he came from. He was a consultant for the CIA and served other foreign intelligence agencies. Lara would discover Ben's history gradually, as he placed the bread crumbs for her to find, one by one. He was no ordinary guy; he had to be certain that she could handle the lifestyle he had chosen. No other woman could, and he hated the corner of stark loneliness that he had painted himself into.

As he walked into the weight room at the campus, he forced himself to spend ninety minutes doing push-ups, lifting weights and running on a treadmill. This was part of his daily routine wherever he happened to be. As he exercised, he marveled at how differently he had lived the thirty-one years of his life compared to Lara's twenty-four.

Literally, Ben had traveled the world while Lara had remained in Portland Maine. But, as he pondered this difference, he also felt a strong, almost magnetic, pull to her. She was naïve, and he could be her teacher, if she would let him. And, he knew Lara could domesticate him. There was one nagging issue that lingered in the back of Ben's mind. He needed detailed information on Eliot Stone. He knew Lara was seeing the owner of Stone and Associates outside of work occasionally, but had been informed that it was not a dating relationship, per se. He would run a background check on the guy and decided not to put it off.

He found the name of Rusty McManus on his phone and asked him to take care of the background check. "Sure thing, chief." Ben hesitated, "Oh, and one more thing. Find out, if you can, if Lara O'Connell is seeing anyone else...dating or otherwise." Rusty said he would and hung up.

Ben clipped on Einstein's leash and got into his 2004 Dodge Ram pick-up truck to drive to his temporary home at his uncle's house. Professor Harris was sound asleep in the recliner when Ben entered the living room of the old colonial. The place smelled of pipe tobacco and roast beef. Not wanting to wake him, Ben walked upstairs to the second floor and put his laptop and phone on the table next to the bed. He ran his hand over his face as he peered at his reflection in the mirror over the old bureau. He definitely needed a shave.

The bedroom was spartan. There was only a bed, nightstand and bureau with an antique mirror hanging above it. The wallpaper was faded and peeling. Ben moved into the bathroom and got his shaving mug and straight razor. As he methodically shaved the black stubble from his face, he thought about the complexities of getting into a relationship with Lara. What if she didn't like him? What if Sienna would not give him the divorce? There were many important issues to be sorted out.

He would put his training to good use and turn this into his private mission. But the nagging doubt was there in the back of his mind: *could he make any woman happy?* His life as a consultant was filled with upheaval and travel. As a SEAL, he'd been a nomad living out of a duffle bag, forgetting to shave, fanatically dedicated to physical fitness, exploring newly designed weaponry and staying on top of his training. He knew he had to eventually embrace a normal life, but he needed a strong woman who could take on the daunting task of taming him.

He brushed his teeth and examined the dental implants. They still looked good. The oral surgeon had done a great job. His mind pushed away that difficult period in Afghanistan. It was a minor thing compared to the broken bones and gunshot wounds he had repaired, and the beatings. Still, as he looked at himself in the mirror in the unforgiving fluorescent light he realized the mileage on his body was much higher than a typical thirty-one-year-old.

When alone like this, his mind would wander to his SEAL brothers, Sam, Javier, Gus, Nate, Elvis, Tom, and Jake. He missed them so much his heart ached. Even though five were still with him as operatives, it wasn't the same. The devotion he felt toward them took the place of a romantic relationship for most of his life. They were more than brothers; they were warriors bound together by the same philosophy. They slept, ate, and lived together in the dust-filled air of Iraq and Afghanistan for six years. They laughed and suffered together and saved one another's lives on more than one occasion. The reality was ever present: each day lived with them could be the last day, a life lesson imprinted on his soul.

He lived every day with deliberation, fixated on the smallest details, noticing things that ordinary people overlooked: the sun glistening on the water, the stillness when the wind stopped, the sound of bird song, the beauty of the beginning of a rain shower. He had become extremely grateful for things that most people took for granted.

In solitude, Ben's thoughts drifted back to the men he so admired in his unit.

The ones he missed the most were not among the living. When alone he thought of them, remembering every little detail. They were a part of him that he never wanted to forget. Tonight, his mind wandered back to Sam, a soft-spoken young man from Oregon, who was a state finalist on his high school swim team. Ben enjoyed competitively swimming with him while in SEAL training. Sam did not return from their last deployment and Ben thought about him often—wondering why things happened the way they did. He had no answers. An IED took Sam's life on a routine recon mission. It was instantaneous. Sam was the lead scout and it was usually Ben. That night Ben was sick with a parasitic infection wreaking havoc with his gastrointestinal tract.

Weak and unable to do much, he stayed in the middle of the stack, trying to stay hydrated. When he heard the blast, he knew what it was. He ran to Sam, but it was too late. The memory of that night would haunt him forever.

Everyone on the team had played competitive sports and all were in the groove as far as reaching and maintaining the highest level of physical fitness. The group of eight bonded and helped one another through BUD/S and later Seal Qualification Training. Of all his brothers, the one Ben missed the most was Javier, his swim buddy. During Hell Week, they especially supported one another mentally, physically, and psychologically. Their strong bond carried into deployment.

In theater, each SEAL had coping mechanisms to break the boredom of missions. Memorizing passages from literature was Ben's specialty and he was often known to recite poetry, albeit dark stuff. The other guys had their own ways to break the boredom in order to stay awake on long recon missions. Ben was often on top physically, due to the fact he was a bit more ritualistic about exercise. He felt as Lieutenant he should be in top shape, as he was the role model. Ben was the navigator and specialized in sensitive site exploitation. He also took the lead in technical surveillance and was a highly qualified sniper.

Although each man had a specialty, Ben constantly honed their skills cross-training them in all areas. Ben was the first lieutenant, the unit leader, but no one would ever have guessed it. The way he interacted with his brothers was different than a normal officer with a subordinate. He loved them in a way that could never be explained. This was a family akin only to the one he had at home and, sometimes he thought, much stronger than blood ties. It was not uncommon for SEALs to be closer to one another than to family members. They came together and suffered the same brutal and unique training, then took the same oath. Their relationship was forged of love, honor, commitment, loyalty. He knew it would take a special woman to understand his uncommon life.

Ben never talked about Javier Mendoza or how he ended up with his 2004 Dodge Ram pick-up truck. Some subjects were too emotional and defied explanation. The plain fact was: Javier died with a bullet in his head in Ben's arms in Afghanistan during a recon mission that had gone sideways. It was toward the end of the last tour of duty. It was most common for mistakes to be made at the beginning or the end of a tour. In the beginning, the unit is just getting their legs under them, getting the lay of the land. Toward the end, fatigue and a little bit of complacency creeps in.

When Ben had to make the visit to Javier's widow, Marissa, he did not expect events to develop as they did. Javier's uniforms and personal effects were neatly folded along with his medals and an American flag. Stoic and professional, Ben rang the doorbell on that beautiful sunny June afternoon in Santa Clarita California. The air was light and full of summer's promise, but Ben's sunglasses concealed his blood-shot eyes. He had made these visits to fallen heroes' families before. But there was something about his relationship with Javier that made this deeply personal.

Javier Mendoza was a California kid, the son of immigrant farmers, one of twelve children. He lived in extreme poverty all his life. A six-foot-two mountain of muscle, he sported gang tattoos that he had to remove before joining the Navy. The tattoos had become blurry faded images on his neck, back and arms, but a serious reminder of the course his life could have taken.

As Ben's swim buddy, Javier was a fellow BUD/S graduate and had a brilliant mind. In training and in battle the two men could finish one another's sentences. They had the same political leanings, the same sense of humor, enjoyed the same books, movies, video games, even the same taste in food and women. Ben spent more time with Javier than with anyone. If they walked into a bar and both were attracted to the same dark-haired beauty, Ben deferred to Javier. Ben often laughed saying that he and Javier might have been brothers in a former life. And, to that Javier would say, "Let's not get to the Nirvana part just yet, buddy..." But that blistering hot day in Afghanistan they had a fire fight on their hands and Javier was going to Nirvana in Ben's arms. The Taliban somehow got to their flank and made a clear shot and it was Javier who paid with his life.

Dragging him behind cover in the unforgiving desert heat, Ben immediately knew the shot was fatal. Javier's blood poured out and Ben had his hand over the wound trying hopelessly to stop the bleeding. But he did not let Javier know it was hopeless. He stroked his hair and begged him to hang on. Javier was sweating profusely and dehydrated. Ben gave him a drink as he watched the life drain out of his brother's young healthy body. It was Ben who wrapped the warrior in a blanket and carried him away from the scene. It was Ben who stayed with Javier's body as he was cleaned and examined, even though his commanding officer asked him to leave. Ben watched as the medical team put Javier's body into the icy cooler.

Usually the calm, cool, collected soldier, Ben lost it that night. He gathered Javier's blanket and personal items before the officials could do so. He slept that night on Javier's bunk and silently wept. He blamed himself for losing Javier. Ben was the commander. He was responsible for their position and the mission planning. It simply should not have happened. They had been running night missions and the enemy, an extremely dangerous and sought-after Taliban leader and drug lord had become familiar to their pattern. It was Ben's idea to do a daytime mission while the Taliban slept. Ben's planning proved to be a fatal mistake.

Knocking on the door waiting to see Marissa's face on that June afternoon, Ben wished he had taken the bullet. Marissa, knowing what was coming, wailed uncontrollably. Thank god, Javier's three young children were away with their grandparents for the day. It was Flag Day, June 14. Ben handed the sacred folded flag to Marissa along with Javier's personal effects. He held Marissa in his arms for what seemed like an hour. Ben remained calm and helped her regain composure. His eyes were drawn to the dented white Dodge Ram pick-up in the driveway. He and Javier had spent many nights in that truck in dive bars in the vicinity of Coronado. He wanted to do whatever he could to help the family financially. He offered to buy Javier's truck and paid Marissa cash, much more than it was worth. It was priceless to him. He also respectfully asked for one of Javier's shirts and Marissa tearfully complied.

He had all he could do not to break down in front of Marissa. He spoke lovingly to her of Javier and his valiant fight. Ben remained in California to attend Javier's military funeral. He did not shed a tear at the service. He held Marissa and the children in his arms and comforted them, paying tribute to Javier, the brave warrior.

Ben remained stoic until he started driving Javier's pick-up truck from California to Prince Edward Island. Driving for hours on end alone, he sobbed uncontrollably some days. Staying at cheap motels along the way, he ate, slept, and cruised for sometimes ten hours at a time listening to Javier's favorite CD's found in the storage compartment of the truck. They both loved country music. Ben knew he had to look forward and not back. Somehow, he felt planning a new life would dishonor Javier. But, over time Ben came to the realization that he would never forget Javier and the special bond between them. Javier's soul had permeated Ben's like an irremovable tattoo.

As he spent time at the Prince Edward Island retreat, he started Dark Horse Guardians. He threw himself into the project working morning, noon, and night. However, Ben was wrestling with demons that would not leave him. He could not stop looking for IED's. This was a particularly annoying habit from his time in combat. It took transcendental meditation classes, but he was finally looking for IED's less frequently. At one time he thought he might never conquer the obsession. But as everything in his SEAL training taught him, it was mind over matter. What made it so difficult was the fact that he had to go against the training he had been immersed in for the last ten years. The mind of a naval man, especially a SEAL, was purposefully programmed to assess threats twenty-four hours a day. This was not something he could turn off like a switch. He had to force himself to deep breathe and focus his mind away from the frightening thoughts that periodically invaded it.

The other major problem he suffered from was chronic insomnia. However, with many months of meditation and counseling, he was now able to force himself to sleep most of the time. The deep breathing and a unique form of visualization helped, and if he did it for about ten minutes it most often brought immediate slumber upon him. He learned he could also manage his dream state focusing on detailed visualizations just before drifting off. This made his dream state more pleasant, especially when the thought of holding a female body close was involved.

The technique didn't always work, however. There were still night terrors. But he was gradually seeing improvement in his sleep pattern. And, he found Einstein. The moment Ben laid eyes on the tiny English Bull Terrier pup, he felt his heart melt. As he sat on the floor in the breeder's mud-room, the small black and white dog with a head that seemed too big for his body came directly to him, tail wagging.

Einstein forced Ben into a regular sleeping and waking cycle, gave him unconditional love, and brought him back into the world he once knew. The breeder hooked him up with a dog trainer, John Rolfe, who also was a counselor. For nearly two years, the twice weekly session for dog training turned into a psych session about his service. Without being aware of it, he was healing. The magic of a kind human being and a puppy gave him the hope he needed to carry on.

CHAPTER 4: *Getting Acquainted*

Upon awakening, Lara followed her morning ritual. As any good obsessive-compulsive would, she opened her daily calendar and checklist on her phone. Her careful life was ruled by lists and appointments, running from one task to the next, while living off portable food in her pink leather sack. Protein bars, apples, bananas, yogurt, granola, and the occasional sandwich or salad, was what her diet consisted of on a daily basis. She rarely had time to cook a meal.

Everything in Lara's life was neat and orderly, even her relationships. After classes she drove to the architectural firm of Stone and Associates to perform the duties of her internship. About a six-mile drive from campus, the Fiat wound through Portland traffic getting her there by 1:30 PM. She always wore business attire at school because she would go directly to work after classes.

Eliot beckoned her into his office as soon as she entered the reception area of the historical stick-built 1902 building. Stone and Associates inhabited a magnificently restored structure with huge floor to ceiling windows filled with wavy glass.

She smiled and swiftly moved into Eliot's lavish office and closed the door. "What's up?"

Eliot was standing next to his desk. "I just wanted to know if you would be available tonight for a work-related chat."

"I have an appointment late afternoon and that could drag on...." She knew Ben would be waiting for her to walk Einstein and she was secretly hoping she could stretch the walk into something more.

Eliot seemed disappointed with her answer. "Maybe tomorrow then..." he dangled the invitation tentatively. Lara said she would think about it and get back to him. She knew what he wanted. He was chomping at the bit to go over a project she had just picked up from him.

For the last two years, Eliot Stone had been her mentor, of sorts. Although, Lara knew almost as much about renovation and restoration as Eliot did at this point, she went along with his little game of being her tutor. She trusted Eliot. He had always been a gentleman and she genuinely enjoyed his company. He was a clean-cut man, mature, intelligent and often humorous. She enjoyed the good-natured sparring they sometimes carried out regarding design elements. Eliot visited salvage yards with her in the quest to discover the perfect elements to finish historical restorations and they called it *treasure hunting*.

As she turned to leave Eliot's office she heard him say, "Lara, there's one other thing. Someone delivered flowers to you today...they're on your desk."

Lara's breathing quickened. She opened the door and stepped into the hallway filled with anticipation. *Who sent her flowers?* Usually it was Eliot for a project well done. The firm was a bustling hive of activity. She slipped into her small office which felt like a fishbowl of glass. Only eight by ten, her office contained an antique desk and an office chair. One other chair for visitors was next to her desk. A long narrow table ran the length of the windowed wall, its purpose to view design plans with clients.

Lara's eyes were immediately drawn to fresh pink peonies in the middle of her desk. Her favorite flower filled her tiny office with the aroma of summer. She snatched the card from the bouquet and tore it open, aware that several eyes in the office were upon her.

"Hope this brightens your day, Ben." was handwritten on the card. She instinctively slipped the tiny card into her pocket. She sat at her desk and inhaled the lovely aroma as she closed her eyes. Out of the corner of her eye she saw Eliot pacing by the plate glass window. She waved to him through the glass while on the phone with a client. She ignored Eliot as she busied herself with the work before her.

Lara dutifully returned client phone calls and went through the afternoon absorbed in architectural design, consulting with co-workers and talking with contractors. Having a touch of obsessive-compulsive disorder actually made her life easier. She was rigid with schedules and rarely missed a detail. With a client list of wealthy individuals, the Portland architectural firm of Stone and Associates was well known and widely sought after. Grant Stone, Eliot's 80-year old father and the founder, personally selected Lara as an intern for the firm. Thirty-five other students applied for the coveted position, but Lara was chosen.

The internship was a benefit to the firm and to her. She provided free labor for them and the work experience was great for her portfolio. She was now at the end of her two-year commitment. Although everything she did was overseen by Eliot, Lara was in charge of a team of contractors on six medium-sized renovations. She delighted in pulling permits, meeting with supervisors, and searching architectural salvage yards to find the perfect items for each project. Her days consisted of sorting through painstaking details, site visits and attending meetings that lasted hours. The most difficult part of the position was proving her leadership skills to a group of Neanderthal men. She was the project manager and every person who reported to her was male and older than she. However, every moment of *this* afternoon was spent consumed with the thought of one man, the one who sent her Peonies -- Ben Keegan.

Her chaotic day ended abruptly as she felt the vibration of her phone. She observed a text from Ben. *"Where are you?"* He was waiting for her at Professor Harris' office to walk Einstein.

Lara sent a text, *"Coming."* Then packed up her leather sack and parked the Fiat at home. She quickly strode toward the four-square brick building that contained the most exciting man she had ever laid eyes on. She imagined Ben standing in her professor's office awaiting her arrival. Lara's heartrate quickened with the thought of seeing him again. Poised before the carved wooden door, she paused to take a deep breath and gained her composure. She opened the door and stepped into the wainscoted hallway that led to her professor's office. It was cool, dark and quiet inside. Her boots moved quietly across the ancient mosaic tile floor. She caught the distinct fragrance of Harris' pipe.

Professor Harris was playing the piano softly as Lara walked down the hallway and she barely heard their voices. As she moved toward the office, she overheard part of the conversation. "Have you told her?" Harris pressed Ben with an insistent tone. Lara wanted to hear more. But Einstein noticed her familiar footsteps and bounded through the door that was slightly ajar.

Lara kneeled in the doorway and took his bull dog face in her hands, "Oh, I love you, too!" She slipped a dog treat to Einstein and his tail wagged.

She felt Ben's eyes on her and he said jokingly, "Thank goodness you came. I thought you might stand me up."

Harris relit his pipe and bellowed, "She would never do that, not this one. She is very responsible, never late. She would never be rude."

Lara smiled at this impromptu compliment from her favorite professor. She watched as Ben grabbed Einstein's leash, then felt his touch upon her arm. They started out for their walk, bidding goodnight to Harris.

"Why don't you leave your knapsack here?" Ben asked her.

Harris answered for Lara. "She will never leave it, Ben. She always has it with her."

The door closed behind them and Ben teased her, "You never set your leather bag down. It is almost as big as you are. It must be heavy by the end of the day."

Lara lied to Ben telling him the sack contained her make-up, cell phone and wallet, all things she needed to carry. It wasn't *completely* a lie. She had just omitted a few other items that she carried in the bag, like her loaded 9mm Glock, pepper spray, a stun gun, and a five-inch fixed blade. Carrying weapons made her feel less vulnerable. Telling Ben that right now might be too much information.

***

Ben could not suppress his excitement to be with her again, and he felt a warm rush of happiness as he tucked Lara's arm under his during the walk. He observed everything she was wearing in a matter of seconds. He knew she just came from her work at the firm. Her full lips were slightly stained with lipstick. Her long dark hair was pulled to one side and secured with a clasp. He made a note that she liked vintage jewelry.

Her hazel-green eyes lit up when she spoke, "Thank you for the lovely flowers today, Ben. How did you know peonies were my favorite?"

He had to force himself to stop staring at her exquisite face. He was taken by her sheer beauty, and the fact that she was seemingly oblivious to it.

"Glad you enjoyed them." Ben smiled, and felt her eyes examining him... "You mentioned peonies last night when I walked you home from the café."

She was nothing like the women Ben had been with in the past. The females he had bedded were sultry temptress types with too much make-up, more like pole dancers, wearing too much perfume. He was usually drunk and close encounters were considered stress relief. He took what he could get in that department.

Lara had a fresh innocence about her. There was depth and intellect. He decided he had to see her tonight. The autumn breeze chilled the air. "How about dinner tonight?" Ben asked with his subtle Irish inflection.

"Sounds great."

"Seafood," Ben winked, "I love it, especially in Maine."

Lara nodded. "Where do you want to meet?"

Ben stopped short and loosened his grip on the dog's leash. He turned and looked directly into Lara's eyes. "I don't want to *meet* you at the restaurant. I want to pick you up and bring you home, like a proper gentleman...if that's all right with you." He noticed Lara's surprise.

He sensed she hadn't been in dating mode lately. Most of the guys she spent time with probably met her at the restaurant or movies. Lara wasn't the average young woman. He knew she was more than careful. Except for that Eliot character, it was his understanding she didn't go out much at all.

He got the feeling it was difficult for Lara to leave the plans for the evening in his hands. Lara smiled, "It's just that I'm used to paying for my own meal and driving myself. No one ever comes to my apartment to pick me up." Ben listened carefully as she continued. "But, it would be a nice change. Okay, Ben, I'll be ready at 7 PM?"

Ben nodded, "Perfect." He allowed himself to relax and smile. He could not take his eyes off her as they resumed walking. Making small talk on the walk back with Einstein, he noticed that Lara thoroughly enjoyed simple things like the natural beauty of the campus surrounding them as the late afternoon sun moved toward the horizon. The brick campus buildings framed a large courtyard of green space filled with mature maples, oaks, and elms. The leaves rustled lightly in the ancient trees as a light breeze blew through them. Autumn had been fair and warm thus far, with a few cold snaps at night. He watched as Lara marveled at the beauty of the bright red and gold leaves. He was immersed in her appreciation for the smallest details as she held a bright red leaf in her hand marveling at its design.

***

Pausing to sit on the granite steps at the professor's building as the late afternoon sun warmed their faces, Lara slyly scrutinized Ben from head to toe. Even with the sunlight directly on his face, Ben was handsome. Lara detected no flaws. He had attractive laugh lines in just the right places from many hours in the sun. His teeth were flawlessly white and without fault. His features had perfect symmetry and proportion. Lara appreciated his physical beauty as she would a magnificently handcrafted antique. She charted every detail, the shape of his brow, his chin, his nose, and those blue eyes: a beautiful pale blue in the sunshine. And, those dimples when he smiled melted her.

She was sitting on the granite stairs next to him. Einstein was enjoying the warmth of the sun, too. Suddenly, the wind died, and the courtyard became silent and empty for that moment. Ben stood in front of Lara and grasped her hands to help her stand. As he did so, they were face to face in the warmth and silence of the courtyard.

His eyes met hers and she felt his hand as he tentatively touched her dark hair.

"It's beautiful.... I'm sorry, I just needed to touch it."

Her heart raced as she felt his fingers. Lara smiled and removed the clasp, then shook her head slightly and her dark mane surrounded her.

"I've been thinking of cutting it. It's time consuming to wash and dry every day."

She was shamelessly flirting with him and knew he was

mesmerized.

"You can touch my hair...Ben." she whispered.

His face was so close to hers, she felt he might lean in for a kiss. But he restrained himself from doing so. Lara realized he would not push her boundaries. Gazing into her eyes, he accepted her invitation and delicately touched her silky hair, enthralled with the mass of waves.

"Don't ever cut this," Ben said softly, "I think it suits you."

Blushing, Lara gently pulled away as she heard students approaching. "Oops!" She suddenly glanced down, and she felt her nervousness return.

"I'm sorry, Lara. I should keep my hands to myself." Ben apologized. "Can I pick you up at 7:00 PM?"

She touched his arm politely and smiled. "See you at 7 PM."

Lara briskly turned on her heel and headed in the general direction of her condo. Her mind was mixed with excitement and fear at the same time. She needed to take a long hot shower and process what just happened. Marching toward her apartment, Lara could not stop smiling. She was having dinner with Ben tonight and he had sent her flowers.

Chapter 5: Anticipation and Anxiety

As he made his way back to his office Ben hoped he hadn't been too bold with her. He knew she was introverted and shy. She had been known to kick guys to the curb for being too forward. The sudden intimacy would either intrigue her or put her off entirely, but it was a chance he had to take. He suspected she enjoyed the touch of his hand much more than she let on.

He found her delightful, but knew he had to walk a fine line to win her over. Lara would be smitten with him once he worked his boyish charm on her, or at least he hoped. He was getting into this relationship for the long haul. He had to be on his best behavior—no easy task for him. Since his failed marriage, he had been in and out of the sack with plenty of women. Some were pretty, but they were one-night stands or lasted a weekend. He did not consider them relationships. He cautiously used protection and never lingered after the physical enjoyment was over. He didn't want more unplanned children or, worse, life threatening diseases. It had been a very long time since he had touched a woman's hair and looked into her eyes longing to kiss her. He wanted everything with Lara to be perfect. He was willing to wait until she was ready.

Standing in his stark new campus, office void of any furnishings except for an old mahogany desk and a leather chair, an idea occurred to Ben. He would hire Lara to renovate his office. His phone vibrated, and it was Rusty McManus with the background information on Eliot Stone.

"Yeah." Ben grunted.

"Here's the info you requested. Eliot was now the owner

of the architectural firm started by his 80-year old father, Grant Stone. Stone just turned thirty-eight and was recently divorced from his former wife, Bridget. He had no children. Bridget received a large divorce settlement, ten million to be exact, to go away and leave him alone. He did not have a criminal record, not so much as a speeding ticket. He lives in the family estate located on Casco Bay in Falmouth Foreside. It's six acres directly on the ocean and includes a small spit of sandy beach. The 1925 estate is a Tudor Style home with 6,000 square feet of living space, a pool and extensive botanical gardens."

"Hmm…" Ben ruminated. "That's it?"

"No, there's more. Eliot Stone is also a member of the Falmouth Yacht Club and dines there often. He owns a 40-foot Hinckley sailboat moored at the club. He prides himself on winning sailing competitions and earned several prestigious cups. Ten months ago, he dissolved a relationship with Elizabeth Wellington, a wealthy widow in his small circle of friends. There are reports of his Bentley picking up Lara on a regular basis and delivering her to the yacht club or to his home in Falmouth. The Bentley also makes frequent trips to the symphony and the art museum in the city, and Lara has been seen with him on occasion. Nothing major. From what I can discern, it's strictly a platonic relationship."

"Yeah, right." Ben grunted. "Platonic."

"That's all I've got for now, Chief."

"Thanks." Ben ended the call. His attention turned back to his stark office. He had plenty to do in preparation for his teaching duties and to run his operation for Dark Horse. He hit the campus gym for a sweaty hour and a half; then drove to his uncle's old colonial to shower and change for dinner tonight. He felt like a teenager, hungry with anticipation to see Lara again.

Ben had been watching Lara Reagan O'Connell from afar for two years. At first, she was brought to his attention by his uncle, Professor Harris. Fond of Lara, Harris told Ben she was a genius, albeit a bit anxiety ridden. Harris even shared some of Lara's coursework with him. Ben found Lara's intellect far superior to many he had vetted for military purposes. Then their mutual friend, Rusty McManus, discussed the dark-haired beauty one day. He said Lara had come to him to obtain a concealed carry permit and their relationship blossomed from there. Ben asked for photos of her and a dossier, which Rusty readily supplied. Even more intriguing, however, was the fact that she had killed a man and never been detected, well, not by the local authorities. When Rusty gained her trust, she explained what happened to her. She didn't come right out and say she offed the guy—but, Rusty was pretty sure.

Ben knew she was a black belt and highly proficient with guns and other weapons. The more he learned about Lara, the more obsessed he became with meeting her. Their first encounter had been carefully arranged through Harris. Ben had to relocate to the Northeast quadrant of the United States for his consulting work anyway, so the job at the university was conveniently arranged. Although a practical person, Ben sometimes wondered if fate played a hand in some of the events of his life. He sensed Lara was a special woman. He felt drawn to Portland Maine and to her.

CHAPTER 6: *Interrogation*

Sipping cold spring water, Lara sank into the down-filled sofa in her parlor and turned on the lamp. Her apartment was quiet, and she only heard the ticking of the wall clock in the background. It made her think about the clock ticking inside of her. She was twenty-four years old, almost twenty-five, and never had a *real boyfriend*, and she didn't count Eliot Stone as such. Eliot was strictly a friend, nothing more.

But, this Ben Keegan was different. He ignited something in her that she had never felt. She was worried about the hunger she felt when Ben kissed her hand and touched her hair. There were two reasons she was worried about physical contact with him. First, he might be a married man. But, her second concern was regarding her own uneasiness with physical touch.

For years she had been embarrassed by what happened to her in middle school. She had not been able to get close enough to a man to have a physical relationship. Over the past few months, the excursions with Eliot had served to help her understand what going on a date might feel like.

She still suffered from night terrors and sometimes found herself in the middle of the attack, reliving it. The nightmare was always the same. She would wake up screaming and sweating, fighting the covers on her bed, punching her pillow. Then, breathless from exertion, she would turn on the light and steady herself. She usually could not go back to sleep. The only solution was for her to find a distraction. Sometimes she would watch television or talk with Rusty on the phone. From the moment she met him, he seemed to understand everything about her.

Anxiety began creeping into her mind as she became consumed with the coming evening. What would she wear for Ben tonight? Then thought: this must be what happens to women when they have fallen for someone. Lara had never thought this way about Eliot, or any guy for that matter. She never cared what she wore of what men thought of her. She took a long hot shower and washed her hair, all the while thinking of Ben taking a shower and washing his hair.

But was he married? That was the question. And, she simply had to obtain the answer. It was against her rules to date a married man. Tonight, she would be the interrogator and he would be the one answering the questions. Black pants and a pink wool jacket finished her unexpectedly feminine outfit. Boots, pink leather sack, and the doorbell buzzed. It was an old-fashioned doorbell and it startled her for a moment. Lara's doorbell rarely buzzed. She knew it was him.

As Lara unbolted the three locks on her apartment door, she skipped down the stairs to slide the two dead bolts on the outside door to the porch. Fumbling with the bolt, she paused briefly to gaze at Ben through the wavy glass of the door. He stood patiently in a well-worn brown leather jacket and khakis. His face had color from being outside and his blue eyes seemed filled with anticipation. She held her breath for a moment, then opened the door and he stepped inside to the small hallway. Lara caught a trace of his masculine scent, sandalwood mixed with leather. *Oh, did he have to smell so good?*

Ben stepped confidently into the hallway and looked into her eyes.

"Hi, Lara...ready to go?"

She wanted to reach her arms around his neck in a warm embrace, but instead she awkwardly smiled and mumbled. "Hi, Ben."

"Your chariot awaits, my lady."

He spoke with an exaggerated Irish accent and made a grand gesture as he bowed before her, which made her giggle. Ben opened the porch door and she ran to the driveway to admire Ben's "Chief". Brand new, it was a 1940 vintage inspired Indian motorcycle with shiny black paint and beautiful curved fenders. The machine seemed to be the perfect symbol for Ben's masculinity. He handed her an antique helmet and goggles.

He slipped his gear on and flashed a dimpled smile with tinge of mischief in his eyes. "Are you ready for this?"

She nodded and wrapped her arms around him and they were off. Lara was terrified. She had never been on a motorcycle in her life.

For a moment, she was filled with anxiety as she mounted the motorcycle with Ben. She feared the loss of control, as Ben started the bike, the motor roared and vibrated against their bodies as he slowly rolled onto the roadway. As the machine picked up speed, the power became a primal blast of excitement. She felt her hair flying from under the helmet as the air whipped by. When they stopped at traffic lights, people pointed and stared at the beautiful cycle. Ben planted his feet firmly on the ground until the light turned green. She relaxed into his body trusting his instincts as he laid into the curves. Ben was at one with this machine. It was obvious to Lara that when it came to riding motorcycles, he was very experienced.

**

Hopeful to make Lara's first motorcycle ride enjoyable, Ben took the longest route to the restaurant. He lived on the bike, except for when it was in the garage for the winter. He'd been riding since the age of sixteen when he had a real 1940 Indian Chief. He worked on that bike lovingly restoring it for too many years. The new motorcycle was a treat he allowed himself once he started Dark Horse.

He especially enjoyed Lara clinging to him. He knew instinctively she had never been on a motorcycle before and sensed her anxiety. But as the ride continued, he felt her relaxing into his back. Her cheek pressed against his jacket and her arms were tightly wrapped around his chest. Careful not to exceed the speed limit, he wanted her first encounter with his Indian motorcycle to be enjoyable. People always waved at him on the bike, but today it seemed they were not only noticing the beautiful lines of the cycle, but the dark-haired beauty with her arms around him.

***

Arriving at the waterside restaurant parking lot, Lara was breathless with excitement from the ride. Several people had gathered to examine Ben's motorcycle. Dazzled by its performance and curvaceous lines, Lara smiled at him.

"It's simply beautiful."

"Especially with *you* on it." he added. His gaze was on Lara, not the bike.

A cool autumn breeze from the ocean blew past them as they walked into the Seafood Palace on the waterfront in Portland. Lara felt him tuck her arm under his as they walked into the building. She felt an exhilaration whenever Ben touched her. The motorcycle ride was filled with pleasures she hadn't expected: the air rushing past, the vibration of the motor, inhaling Ben's scent, her arms cinched around his solid waist, her face against his broad muscular back. She had never experienced twenty minutes packed with such overwhelming physical delight. It was the first time she enjoyed being close to a man, ever.

Like diamonds, the reflection of the city lights sparkled on the water. Downtown Portland was bustling with urban dwellers seeking good hot food. The restaurant was a Portland favorite. It was an older one-story oceanfront building that housed one of the best seafood restaurants on the planet. The interior was filled with huge windows giving views to Portland harbor. As Lara and Ben made their way to a table, she spied someone near and dear to her. Don's eyes connected with hers and he waved to get her attention. She pulled Ben in that direction and Don stood, all six-foot-four inches of him, as he extended his wide hand to them.

"Come—sit with us. We just got here." Don was exuberant to see her, and she could tell he was curious about Ben.

Lara tried to read Ben as he smiled and made a cordial introduction. They sat across from Don and Olivia. Lara had known Don longer than anyone else, at least ten years. They met after her attack, when she turned fifteen, he was her martial arts instructor. Don said she was suffering from PTSD, but Lara would not accept his diagnosis. Instead of arguing with her, Don patiently talked her into immersing herself into Krav Maga. Lara assumed Ben had no idea of the nature of her special kinship with Don and his wife. She politely introduced Ben.

Charming and polite, Ben extended his hand to both and sat down. Nervously, Lara chatted about the weather and work projects. She spoke with excitement about her upcoming spring graduation. She couldn't wait to be in the working world.

"I think you might get a job offer from the firm." Don pondered.

"Maybe…" Lara's eyes met his.

"Something you want?" Olivia smiled.

"Could be good." Lara responded.

Then Don turned his attention to Ben and proceeded to interrogate him throughout the meal. *Good, Lara thought. Don is doing my dirty work for me.*

"Married or single?" Don asked.

"Separated" Ben replied.

"Do you have any children?" Don asked.

"One"

"How old? Boy or girl? Don was pushing.

"A boy, eight years old."

"Where do they live?"

"In Vancouver Canada."

"What do you teach?"

Ben gave a brief description of his Navy background and spoke enthusiastically about his new teaching position. Lara could tell, Don was sizing up Ben, making judgments and decisions as to whether or not he was a stand-up guy.

Finally, Olivia broke the tension. She remarked on the white ruffled shirt Lara was wearing. "What a lovely blouse you have on tonight, Lara."

Even though Ben was answering questions, Lara felt his eyes on her throughout the entire meal. In fact, he rarely moved his gaze from her, except when answering Don. But when he gave an answer, Lara noticed he looked him squarely in the eye.

"I never see you in feminine clothing. It's usually business suits." Olivia smiled. "I like it. It's a good look for you." Then Olivia teased Lara about her ever present, pink leather sack. But it was good-natured teasing, because Olivia knew all about the bag. She knew all there was to know about Lara.

After coffee, Ben was ready to sweep Lara away on the motorcycle and they took their chance to leave. As she stood, Lara thanked Don and Olivia for their good company. Don winked at Lara. She knew he would contact her later to discuss Ben at length; that was his modus operandi.

Don Henderson was the big brother every woman wished she had. Lara felt fortunate he was in her life. He was one of the very few people in the world who really understood Lara's obsessive-compulsive problems, phobias and anxieties. He knew why she had panic attacks and nightmares. Don Henderson had big shoulders and Lara frequently used them to shore herself up. He was always there to listen and offer his advice.

Leaving the noise of the restaurant and stepping out into the fresh ocean air, Lara inhaled the familiar salty air of the harbor. Ben held her hand as they walked toward the motorcycle. Although he was smiling at her, Lara was not so sure if Ben enjoyed Don's interrogation.

"Best lobster I've ever eaten." Ben quipped. "And that water view is incredible."

A small crowd had gathered around the outside of the restaurant eyeing Ben's 1940 Indian Chief. As she mounted the motorcycle, Lara savored the closeness to Ben. Wrapping her arms around him, she delighted as she reached her hands underneath his open leather jacket and felt his muscled chest. She smiled to herself as she put her cheek against his back inhaling the aroma of the leather, thoroughly enjoying this secret thrill.

Winding their way home, Lara realized she could have ridden for hours holding Ben. As they stopped in her driveway, he kicked the stand out from under the bike as if he had done it a million times. His strong arms encircled her waist and he lifted her off the machine effortlessly, then drew her close to him for a split second.

"I hope you're not put off by the talk about my private life tonight," he whispered.

"Why should I be put off? It's the unvarnished truth and I would rather hear it now." Lara said logically trying to sound void of emotion.

Ben seemed pensive for a moment. "You're not upset that I am still legally married?"

Lara swallowed hard and tried to remain neutral. "It's not the best situation.... however, you *are* separated..." She did not continue. She knew there would be a lengthy discussion about this subject. Feeling his blue eyes upon her, Lara said casually, "Coming in?"

The porch light was on and Lara opened the antique door to the creaky staircase and closed it awkwardly latching both locks. When Ben caught her hand, she ceased breathing. He kissed the back of her hand and his blue eyes gazed into hers. She turned and lightly held his hand behind her as she led him up the stairs. Then, slowly she opened the three deadbolts on her apartment door.

Inside, she dropped the keys into the candy dish. The small lamp was casting a warm glow on Lara's charming apartment. She kicked off her boots and Ben removed her jacket, then his boots and jacket.

"Why do you have five locks on your doors, if you don't mind me asking?" Ben queried.

Lara ignored his question. "Would you like something to drink?"

"Water, please, and I'd love a tour of your apartment."

Walking him through each room, Lara showcased the original features of the condo, pointing out the plaster moldings, and lovely period furnishings she had carefully selected from architectural salvage yards and auctions. She now had Ben in her private domain. The level of intimacy Lara was sharing with him had not been permitted for any other man, except Rusty, Professor Harris, and Don Henderson.

Lara felt herself relaxing as she gave Ben the little tour.

"The owner hired me to decorate the entire house."

Ben seemed to love the parlor and kitchen. Lastly, she brought him into her small bedroom with a lovely stained-glass window and original fireplace. Turning on the petite bedroom lamp, she sensed he was longing to lie down on her bed and get comfortable. Lara watched as his eyes focused on the female items atop her vanity. He picked up her perfume bottle and playfully read the label aloud, "Sexy No. 9"...then smiled. His blues eyes were filled with mischief as they met Lara's.

She rolled her eyes, "You sound like you've just solved the mystery of the sphinx."

"Maybe I *have*." Ben laughed.

Lara moved toward the kitchen to retrieve a cold bottle of water for Ben and he followed. She opened the fridge.

"Here you go. I think I'll have one, too." She dangled the

bottle in her hand. As she turned to get another, she felt Ben's body brush against her back and she nervously flinched. He gently removed the clasp holding her hair and it fell loose. As she turned to face him, he slowly pulled her into his chest. He ran his hands through her loose hair. Lara relaxed into his arms as the water bottle slid to the floor.

She felt his face buried in her hair and he whispered. "You smell so.... good." He was invading Lara's boundaries and usually she would slap a guy for less. But this time she did not withdraw. She was, however, becoming uncomfortable with the response she sensed in her own body. She did not want to recoil from his embrace. However, after a brief moment she gently pulled away.

Feeling the need to be honest with him, Lara looked him in the eye.

"Ben, I'm sorry, but I have a strict rule about dating married men." she declared with an air of authority. Mentally, she had been making a checklist of questions about Ben. *Where was he living? Why was he sniffing around her if he wasn't yet divorced?* There were still questions to be answered and the unknown gave her pause regarding a relationship. Truth was, she knew very little about him.

Ben sat in the kitchen chair looking defeated.

"I need to clarify something. Would you date me if I *wasn't* married?" He was putting her on the spot. Lara did not want to let him know that she was already attracted to him. She had to take control, no matter how difficult.

"Yes, Ben. I would date you if you were not married."

He stood and took Lara's hand. "Would you consider having meals with me dating?"

Not wanting to stop seeing him, Lara replied. "Having meals or hanging out together would be fine, but no intimacy." She tried to sound firm in her conviction, but sounded timid, she thought.

"One more question." Ben pressed her softly. "Do you consider kissing to be intimate?" Lara thought for a long moment as Ben's beautiful blue eyes awaited her reply.

She wanted to kiss him so much, her own desire made her fearful. So, she made up a rule.

"I think we *shouldn't* kiss, Ben, as it could most likely lead to more...intimate acts...possibly..." Her voice trailed off as she felt her cheeks flush.

His face looked like he just took an arrow to the heart. Ben hesitated, then spoke softly.

"I want to respect your wishes. That's what a gentleman would do. But, to be honest with you, I don't see the harm in kissing. I'm not the typical guy. I have a great deal of self-control."

Lara did not respond, but looked away, her mind racing.

Then, Ben uttered a quiet request. "Tomorrow for breakfast?"

"Yes." She smiled. She lifted his leather jacket off the hook for him in the entryway and said goodbye, properly thanking him for dinner. She watched as he bounded down the stairs toward the motorcycle.

***

Ben turned his body slightly as he zipped his leather jacket and prepared to climb onto the cycle. He did not look directly at her parlor window; that would have been too obvious. But he sensed she was watching. He instinctively knew the intimate moment in the kitchen excited Lara. She *wanted* his touch, and he was certain she *wanted* to kiss him. Plus, it wasn't his style to back off when he wanted something. He turned from the bike and purposefully strode toward the porch and knocked on the door.

As he stood there waiting, Lara stepped out. "Forget something?"

No words were spoken. Leaning her against the house, he touched his lips to hers. Slowly and deliberately, Ben enjoyed the lush sweetness of her mouth. A tender caress that exploded into a warm, sensual, intimate kiss. She did not resist. He stood back and lightly touched her long dark hair, gazed at her for a split second, then walked away.

As he mounted the motorcycle, he headed straight for the campus gym to work off the heightened sense of desire he felt for her. Physical exhaustion always helped him sleep. But tonight, that kiss only served to bring to mind a much more desirable work-out than the one he would burn through at the gym.

This time physical exertion did not take his mind off Lara. The campus gym was empty at the late hour. As he lifted weights, he wondered what Lara would think when she knew all there was to know about him. When alone, he wondered if *any* woman could love him. Benjamin Aiden Keegan was a counter-terrorism operative. His clients knew him simply as "chief" and transferred large amounts of money to his bank accounts in the Grand Cayman Islands and Switzerland, which he emptied little by little putting the cash into an underground waterproof vault in a secret bunker. Ten million was now piled in the safe, but he wanted much more before retiring from his chosen profession, if he ever did. He needed to have enough to provide Lara with everything she wanted—a home, a family, a comfortable life, along with the sense of safety she so needed. Plus, he had many missions that he needed to complete.

As he arrived at his uncle's colonial, he saw the kitchen light on. Harris was making a cup of tea before retiring for the night. As Ben came through the kitchen door, Harris glanced up.

"How did it go?"

Einstein did his happy bull dog dance to see him. Ben lovingly rubbed the dog's ears, then took a cup out of the cupboard to join Harris for tea.

"She's perfect. You should be in the matchmaking business."

"Have you told her yet about Dark Horse and all that's involved?" Harris waited. There was a momentary silence between the two.

"I've only told her that I'm consulting for the government. I haven't given her the gory details yet. I'm afraid it may drive her away. I need to be patient with her. I know she has been through a lot."

"I'm turning in." Harris rubbed his head and walked down the hallway to his bedroom.

"Goodnight, uncle." Ben said.

CHAPTER 7: Worries and Fears

Lara was examining her relationship with Ben on the phone with Olivia Henderson.

"I don't know about this, Olivia. Ben and I are just friends. Did I bring him to my apartment too soon?"

Olivia was Lara's sounding board, especially in matters like this. She was always calm and rational. "Well, Lara...I don't think Ben is like any guy you have met in the past."

This was true. Ben wasn't trying to impress her. He wasn't concerned about how he looked or the acquisition of things. He never boasted about his accomplishments, although she suspected there were many. He had a quiet dignity about him but was personable and friendly.

Olivia added. "He seems comfortable with himself. I like this guy, Lara."

Ben exuded responsibility, maturity, masculinity. These were the qualities that drew Lara to him. "What about the fact that he's married? Well, separated, actually. Oh damn, Olivia, I am so fearful of getting involved and having it fall apart. It's going to take so much to get close to him, and if it doesn't work out..."

"Nothing ventured, nothing gained." Olivia replied.

Lara continued with her self-analysis. "As happy as I am to be with Ben, I also realize we are polar opposites in many ways. I'm a nine-to-five person; Ben has always been a globe-trotter working 24/7. I want marriage and a family; Ben is already married and has a child. I have lived a life of organization, checklists, schedules; Ben has a spontaneous impulsive personality."

"But opposites attract."

Lara was silent for a moment, then whispered, "True."

Olivia added one last comment. "He's had quite a career already, Lara. I think he is looking for someone to share his life with. There is a maturity about him. I think he knows what he wants."

Lara thanked Olivia for listening to her anxious ramblings. When she hung up the phone, she realized there was one thing that she had in common with Ben: both had a need to be in control. That might present a problem. Lara smiled to herself imagining what a pair they would make, two control freaks with obsessive compulsive disorder. The real fear Lara was wrestling with was losing her own self-control with Ben. Yet, ironically, she experienced an incredible sense of peace and safety when in his presence. She completely trusted him.

Lara had a long list of fears. Her greatest fear was remaining alone for the rest of her life. She did not want to miss the experience of being married and having a family. She feared living alone forever, never knowing real love with a man. Her second greatest fear revolved around her physical safety. Constantly aware that another attack could take place, Lara wanted to be prepared for it—if and when it happened. She worried about losing her phone, her internship, her potential job, her best friends, and her safety net. She feared flying in a plane, was germ-phobic and had claustrophobia. She worried about not being able to bear a child.

Lara's anxieties were endless and caused her exhaustion at

times. She had created a seemingly safe little bubble in which to live and feared stepping out of it. She wanted certainty in her life, but Ben filled her with uncertainty right now.

The next morning, she woke early. Lara pulled on a soft white cotton robe and brewed a fresh pot of coffee. While in the shower she heard her phone chime with a text. Wrapped in a towel, she glanced at the message. Ben texted her a photo of him waiting on the front porch with freshly baked blueberry muffins. She knew they were having breakfast but didn't expect him to be there at 6:00 AM. *Be right down.* she messaged back. Towel drying her hair into a damp mass of waves she slicked on lipstick and dressed in jeans and a faded blue T-shirt. She ran down the staircase barefoot with two cups of coffee.

* * *

Ben was thrilled to see Lara as she opened the wavy glass door to his freshly shaved face. He smiled, hoping she was as happy to see him as he was to see her.

"Coffee?" she asked as she handed him a hot steaming mug and he thanked her. They sat together on the white porch glider enjoying the sunshine, eating freshly baked muffins on a tranquil September morning.

Ben felt transported to another world with Lara on the porch. The pink Victorian had arches and curly decorative cutouts all around the top and sides of the porch. It gave the illusion of sitting in an outdoor room. The view from the porch was particularly pleasing. Directly in front, framed by the arches and cut-out was a lush flower garden. It was planted so the occupants of the porch could relax and watch the birds and flowers from the vantage point of the glider.

"Lara, I had a great time with you last night."

"It's a perfect setting for breakfast, isn't it?" she smiled. He loved how she looked just rising from sleep. Ben studied her hazel-green eyes fringed with thick black eyelashes and how they contrasted with her fair complexion. He watched as she ate the blueberry muffin with her fingers, delicately breaking off bits and slipping them between her rose-colored lips. He had already eaten his muffin in two bites. As they sipped coffee, their discussion flowed easily.

"Where do you live now?" Lara asked.

"I am staying at my uncle's house temporarily. But, Harris

has the house for sale and I feel uncomfortable imposing. I'm actively looking for a rental right now. He's been charitable, however. He gave me space on the second floor. It's a bed and a bath. I'm thankful for his hospitality as it allows me to have Einstein with me at night."

"Tell me about Einstein, where did you get him?"

Ben observed her every move. She was feminine, innocent and charming. He was so wrapped up in watching her, he could barely continue talking.

"I got Einstein as a pup when I finished my last deployment two years ago. The moment I saw him at the breeder's in Canada, I knew he would be a great companion for me. I've spent a lot of time alone, Lara. Einstein is my best buddy."

Ben sensed the big question was coming. It seemed Lara finally got up enough nerve to ask what she was most curious about. "What is the status of your divorce?"

Ben became somber for a moment.

"I have a legal divorce underway, but my wife is fighting me. I want custody of my son, William. I feel Sienna is an unfit mother. With my son living in Canada, my time with him has been limited. That has been the hardest part, not seeing William for long stretches."

"Do you think your wife will eventually be cooperative in the proceeding?"

Ben felt his brow furrow. "She has to agree to the divorce, that's all there is to it." He did not want to continue the conversation about Sienna. He felt certain the divorce would get through the negotiation phase soon. Or, at least he *hoped* it would. He could tell by the way Lara brought up the subject, it signified concern on her part. He did not want the issue to be a roadblock to their relationship.

***

Ben turned to Lara with intensity in his blue eyes.

"Now, what's this rule about not dating married men...technically, I'm *separated*, not married you know. And, I will soon be divorced."

"It protects me from getting my heart broken."

"Has someone broken your heart in the past?"

"No. I generally do not allow anyone close enough to accomplish that."

Ben asked softly, "Do you think you can trust me, Lara?" He continued in his subtle Irish brogue. "I want to see you, just be with you. I know it sounds pathetic, but I am lonely here in Maine knowing only Harris and Einstein. Being with you, having dinner with you, walking Einstein, talking with you the past few days has been so much fun. I would like to continue seeing you, if that's all right. I don't want to become a pest or bother you in any way."

If only he knew how much he bothered her already. She couldn't stop the butterflies in her stomach every time she was in his presence. He touched her heart with his words.

She paused for a moment pretending to contemplate an answer; she had made up her mind the moment he kissed her hand.

"You can see me, Ben, as often as you'd like. I think you are fun and exciting." *Oh no, she sounded like a stupid gushing schoolgirl head-over-heels in love.* But, her answer made him smile and his blue eyes lit up. His dimples melted her cool façade.

As soon as Ben left her porch to sign paperwork at the university, her phone rang. It was Don Henderson. Lara was surprised it took this long for him to call her; she expected him to phone last night after meeting them for dinner.

"You had him in your apartment, didn't you?"

Lara ignored his question. "What did you think of him?"

"I like the guy. I like him a lot. He's a man of substance, a self-made man, and I have a deep respect for that. And, it's obvious he's intelligent. The only small detail that bothers me is he isn't divorced just yet."

Lara told Don everything, including the excitement she felt when she was with Ben. But, most importantly, she told him that Ben did not know everything about her either.

"He will find out soon enough about you. I think he's a great guy, Lara. I mean, take it slowly. I think the divorce will be a requirement. But, get to know him. My goodness, people get divorced every day. Some of them get divorced two or three times. He's a grown man; he knows what he needs to do before he can enter into a serious relationship with you." She heard voices in the background. "Hey, I've got to run, see you at the dojo." and he hung up.

Looking at the time reminded Lara of her standing appointment with Rusty at the shooting range at 10 AM every other Saturday. He would be waiting for her. She picked up the leather sack and a bag of extra ammo and scrambled to the back of the house to get into the red Fiat. It was a twenty-minute ride to the range in Casco and she did not want to be late.

Arriving just in time, Lara waved to Rusty. He was a solid man, five feet ten, but the way he carried himself made him appear larger. He greeted Lara with open arms and a bear hug, as usual.

"I have some cool stuff to show you today." he said with eagerness.

Rusty always had new and interesting weapons to show her, long guns, automatics, revolvers of every size and type. He also loaded his own ammo. Today he had some new targets, which he staggered throughout the range, and they moved and looked like bad guys. A licensed firearms dealer, Rusty had his own private shooting range and taught classes on gun safety. Enjoying the challenge of the new moving targets, Lara and Rusty fired guns of all types for two hours. Finally, Lara's hand shook from holding the gun so long.

Rusty laughed. "That's normal. I ran you hard today."

"I'm starving, let's go get lunch." Lara wiped her brow.

Rusty nodded and she helped him unload all the weapons, clean each gun and put each in its proper case. As they worked together side by side, Rusty seemed to be examining her closely.

"Lara, there's something different about you today."

"I met someone; his name is Ben Keegan."

"We need to have a talk at lunch today, about Ben Keegan, young lady."

Lara stopped moving for a moment. The way he uttered that statement filled her with curiosity. Eager to get to lunch and talk with him, Lara followed Rusty to their usual lunch spot, a tiny hamburger joint with hand cut French fries. The antique neon sign above the place simply said *Lunch*. The building looked like a dive from the outside. A simple rectangular box made of wood covered with aging clapboards; it had a huge plate glass window in the front. In a former life it must have been a 1940's diner. Now cleaned up and slightly modernized, it was their favorite burger joint. And, that was the entire menu, burgers and fries, but they were the best because the beef came from a local farm. They placed their order and received a ticket with a number, then walked to the back of the room to their usual corner table. The place was getting crowded.

Lara was riveted to Rusty as he delicately brought up the subject of Ben. He asked Lara if she had done a background check on him. Rusty said he had connections and would call in a favor to gather as much information as possible for her.

"How do you know him?" Lara asked.

Rusty looked serious. "Anyone in the intelligence community knows of Ben Keegan. He is a well-known hero, a former Navy SEAL Lieutenant. He was captured in Afghanistan not once, but twice. He served six tours and virtually invented new ways to run recon. The stories about this guy are amazing. He just retired from the SEALs a couple of years ago and started his own company. Hell, Lara, he contracts with the CIA. What Ben does is commonly referred to as black ops. Do you know what that term means?"

Lara nodded her head but was filled with apprehension as she listened to Rusty.

"Is he trustworthy, in your opinion?"

"He's a great guy, but I believe he's married. Just be careful you don't end up with a broken heart."

They had finished eating. Rusty hugged Lara in the parking lot and he promised to call her later with more information about Ben.

Driving home, Lara had the déjà vu feeling of being forewarned and not listening once or twice in her life before. There were the warnings she received as a young girl from her mother to be aware of her surroundings at all times. Don't walk alone. Be wary of men, especially those you don't know well. If Lara had really listened to those warnings, she wouldn't have left herself vulnerable to her attacker. In retrospect, Lara was acutely aware of everything she did to give the attacker the advantage. As a result, she listened carefully to her intuition in matters involving trust. Don and Rusty told her they thought Ben was a great guy. These two men were Lara's closest allies. She had tremendous respect for them and confidence in their opinions.

As she pulled into her driveway, Lara noticed she had received two phone messages—one from Eliot asking her to return his call. The voicemail from Ben was his simply, *How about dinner?* Then, as if reading her mind, he added, *No pressure.*

He knew how to make her laugh, but she wondered if this was his way of manipulating her to get what he wanted. She decided to take the chance and called Ben back. It was now late afternoon and if they were going to have dinner, a reservation might be needed. Having never called Ben on the phone, Lara was a bit surprised to hear him answer, "Keegan." His tone was abrupt, and it seemed an odd way to answer the phone.

"Hi Ben, its Lara."

Immediately, Ben's voice softened. "Thanks for getting back to me. Are you available right now? I'm looking at an apartment and would appreciate your expert opinion. It's in a nice building, a short walk from campus." Ben sounded breathless. "The best part is—I can have Einstein with me if I pay an extra deposit. I don't want to miss this opportunity. What do you say?"

Wrapped up in his enthusiasm, Lara said, "Sure, I'd love to walk through the flat with you."

"I'll be there to meet you in a few minutes." And he hung up.

Just back from the shooting range, Lara dashed to the bathroom to wash her face. She pulled her unruly hair into a loose pony tail. Her clothing was dirty and stained from the shooting range and lunch. As she tried to decide what to change into, her doorbell buzzed. It was Ben already. The 1940 Indian Chief was in the driveway.

Lara ran down the stairs to meet him on the porch. Ben was beaming as if he couldn't contain himself. Out of nowhere, the landlord, Mr. Walsh, came around the corner of the porch. "Do you two know each other?"

"Yes!" they both said simultaneously.

Ben was cheery. "Lara showed me her beautiful condo and when I discovered the one next to it was available, well, I just had to come and view it. It's exactly what I have been looking for and it's walking distance to the campus."

Mr. Walsh took them to the other side of the porch and they walked to the back of the enormous house, up a small stairway. The landlord opened the door to the beautiful two-bedroom apartment, completely furnished, more ornate than Lara's humble condo. Lara knew the place well. She had decorated and furnished it. Familiar with the unit, she took Ben through every detail. The kitchen was a work of art, complete with restored cabinetry painted a dark green, with leaded glass windows lit from within. A black slate sink and slate countertops contrasted the stainless appliances. An octagon shaped dining room held a unique original plaster medallion that fixed a vintage chandelier to the ceiling and a fireplace painted white. The expansive parlor had floor to ceiling windows and another fireplace with an ornately carved mantle. The furnishings were period.

Ben was thrilled and immediately wrote a check.

"It's move-in ready." Mr. Walsh said. "And remember to keep your dog quiet and have him do his duty outside."

Ben nodded. The landlord had to leave, but before he did he handed Ben two sets of keys.

Once alone in the apartment, Ben smiled and said. "Hello, neighbor!"

He handed her the extra set of keys. This seemed to be a stroke of good fortune for Ben. For a moment Lara was in awe of the events of the past week. She had only met Ben a few days ago and couldn't stop thinking of him. Now they would be living in the same house.

"We should have dinner tonight to celebrate." Ben said beaming. "Would you help me get Einstein and move my toothbrush in?"

CHAPTER 8: Getting Closer

Moving into the condo next to Lara's was an unexpected coup. Ben couldn't stop the joy that ran energized him as he raced the motorcycle back to Harris' home to remove his few belongings. Several duffle bags and a box held everything he owned, and he tossed them into the back of the old Dodge truck. He also collected Einstein's dog bed and bowls and brought the happy canine with him to the pink Victorian.

Ben plotted and planned the time he would now have alone with Lara to get to know her better. Although he would be traveling more in the next few months, he had specific plans to spend as many hours as possible with her. Living in the apartment next to hers would afford him that luxury. He could visit her morning, noon and night and eventually she would fall in love with him. *That was the plan.* The worst thing that could happen right now would be to have some guy get between them, like Eliot Stone. He would do his best to make sure that would not happen. Winning Lara's affection became Ben's personal mission. He was one step closer to his goal.

***

Lara knew tonight's dinner would be different, more intimate. Ben was all moved in. Einstein bounded up the stairs in his bull dog manner, sniffing every inch of the new place. He already had his afternoon walk and was ready to settle for dinner and a nap on his dog bed, which was tucked in the corner of Ben's kitchen near the radiator. The dog followed her to her apartment as she showered and changed. Ben sped off in his truck to pick up their celebratory dinner at a nearby restaurant.

Einstein curled up at her feet and she rubbed the dog's ears affectionately. Ben's beloved Einstein was now here with her, as she waited for her mystery man to return to his new home. Lara filled a bowl with fresh water and placed it on the kitchen floor. Lara's hair tumbled over her shoulders onto a faded green T-shirt. She was comfortable, barefoot, wearing jeans. For a moment, she sat in Ben's dining room in silence, wondering what it would be like to live in the same building with this secretive man. The very thought of it gave her butterflies.

Lara heard his truck roll into the driveway. He appeared in the dining room and his mood was joyful. She arranged the take-out food on his antique table in the formal dining room, something she did not have in her tiny apartment. The meal consisted of beef tenderloin, rice, broccoli, two slices of cheesecake, and a bottle of ginger ale, and, of course food for Einstein. They both were ravenous, and dinner was gone in a matter of twenty minutes.

"Let's put things where they belong." Ben winked at her and smiled.

Together, they rinsed the plates and put them into the dishwasher, bumping into one another a few times. Holding one of the plates in her hand, Lara noticed Ben watching her.

"I remember picking these plates out for this unit. They're lovely."

"You have exquisite taste." Ben nodded.

Lara marveled at the fact that Ben had moved the entire contents of his closet and bathroom in about an hour into his new place. Very few people she'd ever met could make something happen that quickly. And, Lara was astonished at how *little* Ben had in the way of stuff. As he put his clothing in the closet, she started to unpack Ben's duffle bags and found some beautiful candles. She was surprised to discover they were Blackberry Vanilla Musk, Sexy No. 9. Huh. She set them on the table intrigued they were among his possessions. She wasn't aware this scent was sold in candle form, and it surprised her even more to find them in Ben's duffle bag. It seemed odd, but she didn't say anything.

***

"I need to wash up; I'm a mess. I'll be right back." Ben uttered. He noticed Lara was unpacking his duffle bags and glanced up and smiled. Immediately, Ben stripped off his clothing as he entered his charming Victorian bathroom giddy with excitement to be having dinner in his new place tonight with Lara. White marble floors and tiles covered every surface of the bath. Ben examined his face in the large white antique mirror. He didn't have time to shave, but he turned on the hot water and lathered up from head to toe, quickly rinsing.

Drying his naked body, he wrapped the towel around his waist and found Lara in the kitchen. "Hey...Lara." She seemed surprised Ben appeared draped in a towel with hair dripping. "I just wanted to tell you I will be right out." Ben felt her eyes on him as he turned to leave the room. He smiled as he pulled his clothing on in the bathroom. He had intentionally walked into the kitchen with only a towel to gage her reaction. She seemed tolerant, not fearful. He still couldn't believe he had Lara in his new apartment. He felt like a kid at Christmas. Dressed in a white T-shirt and faded jeans, Ben padded barefoot into the dining room softly lit by the antique chandelier.

"This is perfect." he said sitting at the table and looking into Lara's eyes. "Dinner with you."

Time stood still as Lara handed him a glass of ginger ale and they toasted his new home. Ben did not drink alcohol, at least not any longer. He didn't tell Lara, he'd had his run with it in his early-twenties. As he got older, he witnessed the destruction it did, especially to many good military men. He knew this was an important attribute in Lara's book. It spoke volumes about his level of self-control. Ben didn't need alcohol, he wanted to tell her. He was drunk with happiness. His eyes swept over Lara. He'd not seen her dressed casually except for breakfast on the porch and his eyes took in her figure in the faded T-shirt and jeans. He noticed her hair was loose and fought the urge to embrace her. He restrained himself mentally and physically—knowing this would be the only way to gain her trust.

* * *

Lara had never seen Ben so relaxed and happy. Dying to ask him about the candles that bore her scent, she posed the amusing question.

"Where on earth did you get these candles?"

Ben appeared to be at a loss for words... for a moment. When his eyes met hers, she thought she saw him blush. Then he confessed.

"It's your scent...it's a Navy guy thing. When guys are away from their girls, well...they like to keep something with her scent on it. When I met you for the first time, I thought it would be awkward to ask what perfume you wore. You'd probably think I was a weirdo. I noticed the bottle of perfume on your vanity in your bedroom when you gave me that little tour, remembered the name and Googled it. I bought the candles and lit them in my room at night, when I was alone... thinking about you. You don't want to know the rest..."

She noticed for the first time he had a bashful, boyish smile.

"Oh Ben, that's creepy." Lara said with hint of embarrassment.

"No, it's normal for a guy to do that, Lara. You asked, so I told you the truth. But, believe me, this is what a guy does when he's attracted to a woman."

Lara felt her face warm slightly. *He was attracted to her.* She was absorbed in thought and a bit shocked Ben spoke so openly about his physical attraction.

***

Ben led her to the comfortable sofa in his parlor and they sat together with Einstein at their feet. He wanted nothing more than to take her in his arms and overwhelm her with pleasure. But he knew that would be too much, too soon. His iPod sitting on the marble top table near the sofa had been playing during dinner. Tim Halperin came up on the playlist. The title of the song "Think I'm in Love" started.

He so wanted to hold her.

"I like this song...I've always wanted to dance but I'm clumsy. Would you give it a try with me?" He waited for her answer, but she didn't speak.

He turned the volume a bit louder and swept Lara into his arms slowly leading her as they danced. It was an older love ballad, and a perfect excuse to hold her in his arms close to his chest. The antique wool carpet felt soft on their bare feet. Both smiling and awkward at first, Ben slowly pulled Lara closer to him as he nuzzled her neck. Their bodies moved as one. He was intoxicated with her everything about her, the feel of her hair against his skin, the warmth of her shapely form against his. He sensed that Lara enjoyed the intimacy.

He never wanted the song to end. But once it did, Lara gazed into his eyes and said excitedly. "There's a super moon tonight!"

It was a cool autumn night, so they wore fleece jackets and sat on the white porch glider holding hands, with Einstein at their feet. The pair sat in silence as they watched the full moon rise above the tree tops. It was enormous and there was something primal about viewing it together.

"It's beautiful." Ben whispered in Lara's ear as he wrapped his arm around her. He felt something stir inside him every time he touched her. They sat for a long time enjoying the night air and the moon. Ben savored the warmth and intimate embrace as Lara curled up underneath his strong arm pressing her cheek against his chest.

"I can't believe how lucky I am to have found a condo right next door to you." He whispered, then turned to her in the glider. His blue eyes searched Lara's in the moonlight. Ben gently placed his hand beneath her chin and lifted her face slightly. She was incredibly beautiful, and he took the chance—to steal a kiss.

She was dying for Ben to kiss her. Normally, she would have pushed such an advance away. Lara felt she was in dangerous territory, but she couldn't stop herself. His lips brushed her cheek lightly then he gently kissed her. Ben's lips were full and soft; his kiss lingering and sensual. Her heart was pounding. It was the only time Lara ever *liked* the feeling of being powerless. Ben tasted like mints.

Then she realized *he had planned this moment*. Lara imagined few women had ever resisted Ben Keegan's charm. Ugly thoughts intruded into the romantic moment: *Oh damn, why does he have to be married? How many other women does he do this with? Why does he have to be so handsome?* She turned away and Ben dropped his face into Lara's hair as he heaved a dramatic sigh.

"I'm sorry. I shouldn't have done that." She felt his breath on her neck. She was frightened things were progressing too rapidly with Ben.

Lara stood and took his hand as she encouraged him out of the porch swing, "Goodnight, Ben."

As they parted on the porch to walk up separate staircases, Lara was dazed by his kiss. Every cell in her body was alive with a wild feeling she was not accustomed to and it terrified her. She wanted to kiss Ben more than once and felt if she did, she would not be able to stop herself. He was incredibly handsome, but more than that, he had character and substance. Lara respected him. But, she had to know more about him. She was becoming preoccupied with everything about Ben and didn't want him to know how strong her feelings were becoming. She needed to keep her emotional force field intact.

She lay in bed that night knowing he was only a wall away and could not sleep. The intense light from the super moon came directly through her stained-glass window in the bedroom creating a kaleidoscope of color on the wood floor. She stared as if in a trance reliving the details of Ben's sensual kiss in the porch glider. Her reverie was interrupted by her ringing phone. It was Eliot.

"Hello..." Lara said sleepily.

"Why didn't you call me this afternoon?" Eliot sounded slightly annoyed.

"I had something to attend to first." Lara said vaguely. "What's up?"

He was being evasive. "I just wanted to see you. That's all. Will you be available tomorrow for dinner?"

"I don't know. Give me a call tomorrow. I have a busy day lined up."

The phone call ended, and she contemplated why Eliot called her at such a late hour. But, she drifted off to sleep thinking about Ben's kiss in the porch glider and could hardly believe he was now sleeping on the other side of the wall.

In the morning, Lara's ringing phone woke her. Rusty's insider government friend came through.

"Hey, you awake?" It was Rusty with a few more details about Ben.

"Yes. What's up?" Lara spoke sleepily.

"I'll not sugar coat any of this stuff about Keegan. He's an adjunct history professor, not a fulltime faculty member, small detail. Everything he told you about being a Navy SEAL is authentic. Ben is now a well-known military consultant with clients in high places. He's working on cases for the CIA involved in a shadowy counter-terrorism task force. Ben's consulting group is called Dark Horse Guardians. All the work Ben does is classified, black ops. I have no way to obtain specific details. The bottom line was: there's a real risk of danger in his line of work."

"Wow, tell me more..." Lara sat up and listened.

"As for his personal life, he *was* married, and there's a divorce pending in Vancouver. Ben is financially responsible to support his wife, Sienna, and his son, William, until the divorce is final. His earnings from consulting are substantial. His clients are not only the U.S. government, but also international: Israel, Saudi Arabia, Dubai, Turkey, to name a few."

"Okay—what else?"

Rusty continued. "The most difficult information to dig up was Ben's property ownership and financial information. The Dark Horse group does not own any property. Only one piece of real estate was on the books and it was held jointly with his wife; the home they share in a wealthy gated community in Vancouver Canada. His wife and son, William, currently live there. William attends a boarding school. I had to go through several sources to find the other properties held by Ben. This shit is top secret. One is a rustic cabin off the grid on Prince Edward Island and there's a mystery property in the U.S. Virgin Islands. The Prince Edward

Island cabin was utilized primarily by Ben for respite from his work and was purchased long before he married Sienna. In other words, it's was the place he lived before the Navy and he went back there when he ended his Navy career. He had some problems when he left the Navy—I won't go into that right now."

"What do you mean—*problems*?"

"Ben's had a rough time in combat. Suffice to say, he's been captured—twice—tortured. Nearly killed, but he managed to get away. He has PTSD, sleep problems. You know what I mean."

"I do understand, somewhat."

"You would understand, I think..." Rusty hesitated, then he went on. "Sienna did not work outside of the home. She came from a privileged background and had her own wealth. The marriage was never happy. Ben married Sienna because she was pregnant, not because he wanted to. As a SEAL, Ben was married to his career and spent a great deal of time deployed. Sienna's family is very powerful in the province, and she has access to their money and influence. Sienna contested the divorce at first but seems to be cooperating now. According to reports from the school, she coddles William excessively. Sienna exhibited unstable behavior when Ben told her he was leaving the marriage. A former model, she suffers from anorexia and has been hospitalized several times throughout the marriage. This was a union that was not made in heaven."

"That's it?" Lara queried.

"That's it." Rusty pronounced. "He's handsome, loaded with money, successful and brilliant, runs the secretive Dark

Horse Guardians and has a crazy wife."

There was a period of silence on the phone. Rusty knew Lara was in a state of momentary disbelief. "Got to go, have an appointment for a gun permit arriving." He hung up the phone.

She thanked Rusty for the report, but he was gone. Lara sat in stunned silence in her parlor on a beautiful Sunday morning absorbed in thought. Who *was* this guy?

Her silent reverie was interrupted when she received a text from Ben asking her to meet him at his unfurnished university office that afternoon. His text was upbeat and there was a happy face embedded in it. Folding laundry and cleaning her condo, Lara jumped at the chance to make the brisk walk across the street to the campus to see the dark-haired stranger who had captured her life lately.

Sundays on the campus were peaceful, as many students left for the weekend or were recovering from hangovers. The building was quiet, and she found Ben in his stately, but somewhat empty, office with his eyes riveted to a computer screen, one of three in on his desk.

"Hello, beautiful." He smiled and jumped to his feet to greet her. Lara noticed he minimized the screen quickly. "I need your decorator's touch to help me with this office, please." She glanced into Ben's blue eyes and could not seem to break her gaze for a moment. There was so much about him she didn't know. But, in order to find out more, she would need to get closer to him. Lara decided to take the job to renovate Ben's office.

Scrutinizing Ben instead of his office, some of the pieces were beginning to fit together. Occasionally he slipped, and she got a glimpse beyond the façade that he wanted her to buy into. She was noticing Ben's consulting work was much more involved than he had initially led her to believe. He was secretive and evasive regarding his work for the government. Standing in Ben's empty office, Lara was slightly amused with his plea for her decorator's touch. With ulterior motives, she agreed to help. She expertly sketched Ben's newly designed office on a piece of photocopier paper.

"There!" she announced proudly. "We just need to find the proper furnishings and get some painting done. What is your budget?"

Ben told her to go forward with the project. He stated there was no budget. He wanted to personally pay for her services. At the moment, Ben's office looked pathetic. The stark room was quite large, had three computers with huge flat screens, a beautiful antique mahogany desk, probably original to the place. There was a well-worn large black leather chair. With all the technology in the office, it had more of a stock broker feel than a professor's office. Einstein's bed and dog dishes were moved in, along with Einstein snoring softly in the corner.

Ben sat in the worn leather chair and gestured to Lara and she lightly perched on the arm. "What color would you paint in here?" Ben asked as if he was interested in the décor.

"Oh, it needs to be a deep red." She said with certainty.

Ben's eyebrows rose; then he furrowed his brow. "Red, really?" he flinched. The walls were now a stark white with dirt marks on them.

"We need to warm this room up." Lara said expertly.

At that, Ben pulled her in one swift move with incredibly strong arms off the edge of the leather chair into his lap. They were suddenly nose-to-nose and Ben was examining her closely.

"Let's warm it up, then." He whispered, gazing directly into Lara's eyes with a playful look. The office door was closed, and she suddenly felt nervous sitting in his lap. She jumped up quickly, silently chastising herself. She should not have sat so closely to him on that chair. Lara had never thought of making love in a leather chair. But as she looked at Ben sitting there, the thought ran through her mind. She sensed he was thinking the same.

"Oh, one more thing, Lara." Ben said, as he reached into his pocket. "Here is the key to my office. I know you will need it to renovate the place. And, I need to give you some money to get started." He reached into his pocket and peeled off five thousand dollars in cash and handed her a credit card. "You're authorized."

Thanking him for the key and the cash, she got back to business quickly. She smoothed her hair nervously and smiled. "I will draw up the plans and get shopping."

She made a hasty exit knowing her face was flushed. Lara could sense Ben was happy about making her blush. He was smiling as she closed the door and she imagined he was focused on his computer the moment she left.

Today was no different than any other Sunday, except when Lara walked in the door and sat on the arm of the leather chair. She brought him back to the normal world for a few moments. He wondered if he could ever live a life that was ordinary. He had to find a way to blend the two. He needed to fulfill his mission and he needed Lara by his side. But would she have him? Every advance he made seemed to set him back a step.

Sundays Ben dedicated a great deal of time to communicating with overseas clients and local informants. He lined up conference calls, Skype chats, and used a secure encrypted satellite phone. He was in the business of gathering intelligence and performing sensitive reconnaissance work. Most of his confidential informants were well paid by him in cash through personal meetings or via FedEx or UPS. The recon work was now being done by a team of thirty operatives that he had gathered in the last two years. There were lots of soldiers coming back from Iraq and Afghanistan who needed work and he found things for them to do. It was cash on the barrelhead, but it paid the bills. If they passed his vetting process and produced results in the field, he was happy to have them. It had taken a lot of work over the last two years to assemble the team he had now. Jake, Tom, Elvis, Nate and Gus were first on board. The payroll for these top guys, plus his, came to one million.

The most distasteful part of his contracting business were the required meetings with those in power in Virginia who employed him. He had to wear a suit and make nice to jackasses he sometimes disliked intensely. But, he knew being persuasive and social was part of the job, and he took care to win the trust of those who hired him. Ben listened more and talked less whenever he was around the Central Intelligence crowd. The less he said, the better, as far as he was concerned.

The bulk of his work, in the beginning, consisted of mundane security jobs all over the globe. He took on the task of building a defense team for the King of the United Arab Emirates. Then he started on a project that grew in scope and time: surveillance of suspected terrorists in the Boston area. He was kept busy supplying intel to the CIA and the FBI and taking out well-known terrorists without any fanfare.

His missions were becoming more complex and dangerous, and he became known as *the problem solver*. They gave him the gist of the problem, and they really didn't give a shit as long as he solved it and their hands did not get dirtied in the process. He had taken out a few terrorists living in the New England area, plotting attacks on soft targets. Ben made sure to use the least violent course to resolve problems. He made absolutely certain the target was a real-life terrorist, with a violent record, before he put his plan into action. But it wasn't difficult to prove these things. If he set up surveillance on a target and found bomb-making materials inside, it was a cut and dried case.

There was a lot of recruiting of American citizens going on in the Middle East and right in this country. Plots were being formulated each day to do great harm to the United States. Ben had taken a few jihad recruiters out of business. Some of them went missing. Their bodies were never found. Many of them were living in the United States illegally to begin with. Many came on a legitimate visa and simply overstayed. He had great disdain for the lax administration that made it impossible for law enforcement agencies to actually *enforce* immigration laws already on the books. Thus, the Department of Homeland Security was a paper tiger; they were puppets. Immigration and Customs were often prevented from doing their jobs. There were good men and women working in the field, but even if they apprehended criminals, the suspects were never prosecuted. They were turned loose, and innocent Americans were often the victims.

Even worse, by executive order, terrorists were now being granted asylum in America. Only the United States could be this liberal, trusting and foolish. Ben was filled with frustration as he watched American institutions embracing terrorists giving them welfare, food stamps, free housing, health care and other amenities, while these very people plotted to kill innocent Americans: all paid for by hardworking taxpayers. If only the veterans returning from Iraq and Afghanistan were treated with such hospitality.

Ben hoped to someday, somehow change the minds of the lawmakers who made these critical decisions. But, right now he had to protect the American people from their own foolish government. He had to fight a war on terrorism in his own backyard.

The communiqués Ben had on Sunday were around the clock, uninterrupted, and usually filled with details, coordinates, times, suspects, and the results of months of surveillance. This was Ben's holy day. It was important for him to get everything right. He was the chief, and the burden was heavy on his shoulders. Failure was not an option. He did this for love, honor, devotion and a sense of duty to the United States of America, a country he loved more than life itself.

***

Lara tried to remain focused on the renovation of Ben's office, but she kept thinking about how blue Ben's eyes looked today when he pulled her into that leather chair. The sun was shining, and she couldn't stop smiling, recalling how he wrinkled his nose when she said she would paint his office red. That confirmed it. It would definitely be red. But she was determined to make it a masculine office, representative of Ben in every way.

Her phone chimed while walking home. Eliot Stone again. She answered, and Eliot's voice boomed over the speaker. "Lara, let's have dinner at the club, talk business, and watch a movie at my place this evening, what do you say?" He seemed to be in an upbeat mood.

Lara had gone to dinner with Eliot before and they'd always talked business. However, employees at the firm noticed the attention he showered on Lara, sending her flowers and delivering lunch to her desk for a job well done. Sometimes she was uncomfortable being in the limelight. However, Eliot had always been respectful and was, in fact, quite entertaining at times.

"Sounds good." She heard him exhale. "I'll arrive with the Bentley at 6:00 PM then."

She agreed and ended the call.

As she continued walking, Lara plotted the décor of Ben's office. But more importantly, she hoped by decorating his office, she would learn more about Ben. She knew he shared her love of original architectural features in the 1800's buildings and she planned to make his office a showplace, the envy of all the other professors on campus. It would also be a great excuse to be with her beloved Einstein every day. Renovating Ben's office was going to be a long, drawn out project. It would go into Lara's portfolio. But, more importantly, it would give her an up close, personal view of Ben's working and personal life.

She looked at her phone before getting into the shower. It was a text from Ben.

Dinner tonight?

She messaged back. *Sorry, have a meeting.*

Ben sent back an icon of a sad face and she smiled. She knew Ben was disappointed, but she reminded herself again, *he was married*. His pursuit of her was futile until he got a divorce. She had to remain firm on this point. Or at least try to.

CHAPTER 9: *Eliot Stone*

Eliot Stone was a well-known Portland native and his family dripped with old money. There was a rumor that his ancestors traced back to the Mayflower. The money surely did. He was a tall good-looking man with a penchant for sailing. Eliot would describe himself as refined and masculine. His thick brunette hair was usually a bit unkempt and his dark brown eyes brightened whenever he spoke with Lara. Eliot was careful to rein in his feelings toward her, acting as her mentor at the firm.

Most of the women at the firm, single or married, were drooling over him. He was divorced two years ago from his ostentatious wife, Bridget. Looking back on that relationship, Eliot couldn't understand what he ever saw in Bridget. She was an artificial person in every sense of the word. She had artificial lips, artificial breasts, and recently had a Brazilian butt lift, all paid for by him. Bridget's days consisted of changing her hair color, having her nails done, shopping or working with her personal trainer. Eliot decided he really didn't trust anyone that wore false eyelashes and whatever physical attraction there was initially faded away quickly. Thank goodness, he only saw Bridget infrequently during their marriage. He spent much of his time at the firm or sailing. It used to be particularly uncomfortable when Bridget would stop by to see him at the firm. He always made sure the door was closed when she visited because he was embarrassed to have anyone overhear their banal conversations.

Eliot was the polar-opposite of Bridget. Maybe that's why their marriage lasted only five years. But, in retrospect, he hadn't tried very hard to keep the marriage together either. He was now thirty-eight and single. Bridget never wanted children, so there were none. The rumor mill at the firm was correct; he had just ended a relationship with Elizabeth Wellington, a wealthy divorcee with two children he had been dating for six months. She was nice enough, but Eliot did not feel the fireworks with her that he felt in Lara's presence.

Being a multi-millionaire and living on the ocean in the small town of Falmouth, Eliot had a limited circle of friends and not many opportunities for dating. He was a long-time member of the Falmouth Yacht Club and that defined his social connections. He tried to hide the fact that he was smitten with Lara from the moment he laid eyes on her. He talked his father, Grant, into hiring the twenty-two-year-old as their intern two years ago. Eliot privately schooled Lara in architectural restoration and design. She was a natural and he admired her work ethic and extraordinary intelligence.

Although he was beguiled with Lara from the first moment he saw her, he built a solid professional relationship with her at the firm. But secretly, Eliot couldn't wait for her arrival each afternoon and made excuses to meet with her. Her attire was always professional and conservative, but he could see the long legs and shapely figure beneath the suits. Every day he tried to catch a glimpse of her without her jacket, but it was rare for her to take it off. She usually did so only in her office on a hot summer day.

Lara wore a seductive fragrance, of warm vanilla and sultry musk, and it drove him crazy. He remembered the exact moment that he knew he could longer repress his feelings for her. It was the night she attended the Christmas Eve open house at his home last year. At the party, he finally got her alone away from the crowd to talk privately. Out of the work setting, she was even more alluring, especially that night. He remembered her enthusiasm as she asked for a tour of his Tudor style home on the ocean. Of course, he was more than happy to oblige. Leaving his party guests on their own, he paid attention to Lara and her questions. She was feminine and sexy that night. He remembered every detail. She wore a red silk dress that hugged her curves. Her long dark hair was pinned into a loose twist, revealing the supple nape of her neck. She had no idea how difficult it was for him to focus on the tour of his mansion and not her lovely features.

Eliot knew asking Lara out for personal excursions was risky. She could possibly say his advances were unwelcome and this could put the firm at tremendous risk. But he was careful not to make their meetings outside of the office too intimate. He had yet to kiss her and would not do so without her express approval. He always had servants present or met her in public places. He was no fool. He protected himself. He had a specific agenda for tonight's dinner. He knew that Lara had high standards and saw few men. That's why he was a bit surprised when he learned about her seeing the new professor at the university, Ben Keegan. What did she see in him? Eliot wanted to get the details from Lara herself.

* * *

Dinner with Eliot was always at 6 PM, always at the club, and he always arrived in the white Bentley. *Predictable.* That's what Eliot Stone was. Tonight, Lara wore a little black dress, a patterned green silk scarf, and a moss green cashmere cardigan. She twisted her long hair into a low, swirl and pinned it. She grabbed her green leather gloves as she bounced down the stairs. The Bentley had just pulled up in front of the pink Victorian. Only Eliot Stone would own a 1956 Bentley limousine. It was pure white, seated three passengers and had a champagne bucket centerpiece with two glasses.

Eliot was cheerful, and he took her hand as she slid into the backseat as the driver closed the door.

"You are beautiful, Lara." He said in his soft deep voice. Lara noticed Eliot seemed to be more casual tonight. He wasn't wearing a business suit, for one thing. But, she sensed something different about him. He seemed more personable, friendly, and there was a warmth in his eyes when they met hers.

He could not take his eyes off her. Eliot loved her eyelashes, thick and black, when she looked down they contrasted with her flawless complexion. She often looked down when speaking with him and he read Lara as being shy, especially when lavished with compliments. Her hands were in green leather gloves and he gently placed his hand over hers on the seat. He imagined removing her glove and feeling the warmth of her skin and wanted nothing more than to lean over and kiss her in the backseat of the Bentley. But he knew that move would be catastrophic for their relationship at this juncture. If he moved slowly, he thought there might be a chance with her. *But, he had to be patient*. Touching her gloved hand was the only pleasure he could allow himself right now...that and his eyes drinking in every detail of her person. He wore a brown tweed jacket over a crewneck and chinos, casual tonight. He wanted nothing more than to embrace her and feel her long lean body close to his. It seemed Lara was oblivious to his growing attraction to her, and that was a good thing.

***

The building that housed the Falmouth Yacht Club dated back to the 1920's. It was a shingle style beauty perched on a bluff above a protected cove. The building was charming as it had the appearance of a very large summer cottage complete with decks and large sweeping porches. There had been several additions since its inception, but they were so close to the original design only a well-trained eye could discern them.

Chef Pierre L'Abbe made his dishes from scratch often using local Maine items. To say he was a masterful chef would be an understatement. At the door, their coats were taken, and the head waiter whisked them to their favorite corner table ensconced in privacy with a lovely water view. Arriving at the yacht club with Lara on his arm, all heads turned to view Eliot as he walked across the luxuriously appointed dining room filled with floor to ceiling windows facing the ocean.

Lara sensed they really weren't looking at Eliot, but at her. Everyone knew she was his intern, fourteen years his junior. The men at the club seemed envious of Eliot; the women angry that their husbands turned to watch them.

"Pay no attention to them, my dear." Eliot smiled and ordered a bottle of champagne and a plate of antipasto to share with Lara. She always trusted his taste in food and drink. In fact, she had fun exploring new dishes with him at the club. He had expanded her palate in food as well as architectural design, and she felt indebted to him for his kindness. Tonight, however, she sensed Eliot had something else on his mind besides food and design.

"So, what have you been up to, Lara?"

She wanted to say she just met the most handsome man in the world a few days ago. But, instead she said, "Oh, you know, I've been doing the usual, finishing up coursework, walking Einstein for Professor Harris, martial arts, the gun range, and wrapping up projects at the firm."

Eliot wrinkled his brow ever so slightly and his brown eyes were intently upon her.

"I've heard you have met the new professor, Ben Keegan...."

Lara sensed he was fishing.

"Yes, we met at the piano recital and he invited me to walk Einstein with him that night, that's his dog, you know."

Eliot was rapt with attention. The antipasto arrived, and he speared little pieces encouraging Lara to continue. "You didn't call me back; did you see Ben for dinner the other night?"

Lara felt she had to be honest. "Well, yes, Ben asked me to have dinner and picked me up on his motorcycle. We actually had dinner with Don and Olivia Henderson. We bumped into them at the restaurant and they insisted we join them."

She noticed Eliot's eyes flashed when she said the word motorcycle. She could tell he was making assumptions. Lara continued, "Actually, I've never been on a motorcycle in my life."

Eliot was watching her closely, "Well, that must have been fun." He said it flatly without emotion.

As Lara enjoyed the antipasto, Eliot prompted her, "Tell me more about Ben, this motorcycle man, where is he from? What's his background?"

Eliot was all about someone's pedigree. She continued with a brief sketch of Keegan.

"Ben is a former Navy SEAL Lieutenant. He owns his own consulting firm now. Plus, he is a professor at the university."

Eliot shifted his eyes away from Lara's. "He sounds like he is much too busy to be riding his motorcycle with you."

Lara sensed Eliot already resented Ben. She then dropped the big news, "Ben just moved into the condo next to mine in the pink Victorian. You know—the one I decorated as a school project. So now, we are neighbors."

Eliot's face went from mildly ticked off to genuinely surprised. "He moved into *your* building? How did that come about?" He was now sitting at attention, very interested to hear more.

Lara shrugged her shoulders. "I don't know. It was the strangest thing. He was looking for an apartment where he could keep Einstein with him, and I guess the condo next to mine opened up and he jumped on it."

"I'll just *bet* he did." Eliot had a smug look on his face.

Soon the meal came, and Lara moved the conversation to the architectural project Eliot originally brought her there to discuss. As usual, Eliot was an enjoyable dinner companion and helped her explore the culinary delights that the yacht club had to offer. It was common for the chef to make dinners for him upon request, and tonight Chef L'Abbe served Chicken Scaloppini. The lemon and capers went perfectly with the soft champagne Eliot had chosen. It was the best Lara ever tasted.

As Eliot and Lara moved toward the exit, the head waiter snapped his fingers and the doorman expertly slipped their coats on. The driver had the Bentley waiting outside and sprang into action opening the door for them. Lara asked to be dropped off at home. She did not feel like a movie tonight. Eliot complied, as always.

As was his habit lately, he held her hand in the Bentley on the way back to her house. Lara had the sense didn't want the evening to end so abruptly. Shocking her, Eliot leaned over and gazed into her eyes as they pulled in front of the pink Victorian.

"A penny for your thoughts?" He whispered.

Eliot didn't seem to want to let go of her hand tonight. She lingered in the back seat of the Bentley with him. "I'm sorry, Eliot. I'm tired and probably not good company tonight."

"Lara, I enjoy your company immensely, you know that. I'm sorry you won't come along to keep me company tonight. But I will be thinking of you." Eliot sighed with a dejected look on his face, his dark brown eyes imploring her. "Are you sure you won't change your mind?"

He was trying to sway her, but it was 8:30 PM and she really felt like being alone. She thanked Eliot for a wonderful dinner and slid out of the vehicle as the driver held the door. The Bentley slipped silently away into the blackness of the night.

Lara thought about Eliot as she mounted the creaky stairs

to her tiny condo. He was definitely getting a little too friendly with this hand-holding business. She was a bit unnerved by his interest in her relationship with Ben. How did Eliot know her every move?

As soon as Lara stepped into her entryway, her phone vibrated with a text from Ben.

Too late to visit?

Lara was surprised. She knew he had probably seen her emerge from the Bentley moments before.

She replied. *Okay.*

He answered back with lightning speed. *Be right there.*

Lara kicked off her boots and heard Einstein snorting at the bottom of her locked door. Opening it, she looked into Ben's smiling face and felt Einstein as he wiggled around her legs with joy.

"Come in."

"I hope we're not intruding, Lara." Ben started. "But I thought you'd not be going to bed this early and Einstein and I were sort of lonely."

As he spoke, his blue eyes met hers and she felt her heart melt. And she couldn't ignore Einstein. She dropped to her knees and rubbed the dog's smooth body as he wagged his tail excited to see her.

Lara always took Einstein's face in her hands and whispered in his ear. "You're my good boy." She noticed Ben was dressed in pajama pants and a T-shirt.

She heard Ben murmur. "Lucky dog."

As Lara examined Ben he appeared to be covered in sweat and had obviously been doing something physical.

"You're soaked." Lara laughed. "What have you been doing?"

"Just training, you know, keeping fit."

Lara observed his biceps, chest and torso in one glance. Ben looked uber-masculine in the T-shirt. She tried not to be too obvious as she studied the details of his form, noticing he had a particularly nice rear in those pajamas. She had the fleeting thought: what might it feel like if she lightly skimmed her hand over his muscle-laden chest and arms. Lara wasn't accustomed to seeing guys that looked like Ben. In reality, Lara wasn't used to seeing *guys* –period—at least not guys her age. She was staring at a real live American soldier in a T-shirt and pajama pants mesmerized with his handsome features and perfect form. The butterflies started again.

CHAPTER 10: *Enjoying the View*

Ben was thoroughly enjoying Lara's lingering stare. He purposefully wanted her to see him in a T-shirt and pajamas, and she displayed the exact reaction he hoped for. As she emerged from the bedroom, she invited him to sit on the sofa.

"Let me get you some water, you must be thirsty after all of that exercise."

Ben knew she had been out with Eliot because he saw her getting out of the Bentley minutes earlier.

"How was your meeting?" he asked innocently. Lara gazed at him with her beautiful hazel eyes hesitating before answering. Ben sensed she was performing some sort of mental Kung-Fu. The subject of Eliot appeared to be a sensitive one.

She finally spoke. "I had dinner with Eliot Stone. He is the president and owner of Stone and Associates."

Ben took a long drink of the cold spring water then said provocatively. "Ah, the boss dating an employee, a bit risky don't you think?"

Lara narrowed her eyes and stared at him. "We are *not* dating. It was only dinner and we discussed business." Just the way she said it made Ben realize he was right on target. Lara was uncomfortable about the relationship with Eliot. Good. He felt he had a chance with her.

"Hey..." Lara smiled, "You're in your pajamas. If you'll excuse me, I'd like to slip into mine."

With all his senses, Ben drank in the feminine trappings of

Lara's apartment. Her condo always smelled like freshly baked gingerbread. She was a talented decorator and created sumptuous surroundings meant for a comfortable life. She had an eye for antiques and recycled objects and creatively utilized them in her designs. The fabrics, patterns, and textures were perfect, just like Lara. Sitting in her parlor, he felt immersed in her world—the normal world he so missed. She was beautiful, brilliant, and fun. He wondered what it would be like to live with her. Everything about her was cultivated and sophisticated. He felt at home when he was in her presence. As he pondered her beauty, Lara swept into the room wearing a pair of cotton pajamas with blossoms on them.

Ben's immediate thought was: she even looks feminine and beautiful in pajamas. She sank into the sofa with Ben and turned on the television. A show came on that featured funny videos and they both giggled and relaxed sitting at opposite ends of the sofa. Lara had her feet propped up on an ottoman in front of her as she glanced Ben's way.

"Would you like some popcorn?"

"That would be great."

He watched her get up and move toward the kitchen and studied her figure through the floral cotton fabric. She moved with the elegance of a dancer. She had a swimmer's body, long and lean but strong. She disappeared into the kitchen and returned with a large bowl of micro-waved popcorn. She sat close to Ben on the sofa to share the popcorn with him. Pretending to be absent-minded, Ben's hand frequently touched hers every few minutes as he reached for popcorn. His mind was not on the kernels, however. Ben could not stop gazing at her as she watched television. He tried not to be overt and observed her from his peripheral vision. Her profile was delightful, her nose delicate and feminine. He loved her laugh. She turned and smiled at him frequently. The scent she wore wafted by him.

Twenty minutes into the show, he stretched his arm out behind her on the sofa. Ben inhaled her scent and felt as if he was under a spell. All he could think of was finding creative ways to touch her. She reached into the bowl and Ben brushed her hand again, but this time he held her hand and did not release it. Lara's eyes met his and the popcorn bowl slid to the floor; she giggled as Einstein gobbled up the last of it.

With incredibly strong arms Ben playfully pulled Lara into his lap. She was still laughing from watching the funny show. He ran his hands gently through her silky dark hair as it spilled down onto his face and chest. Lara was now straddling Ben and they both fell silent at the same moment.

His hands moved down slowly to the small of her back, it was an instinctive move. He sensed Lara was enjoying the moment. Ben felt her breath on his face and her lips were an inch from his. She was in the driver's seat. If she wanted to kiss him, he was more than ready. His hand progressed slowly beyond the small of her back and he felt the curve of her shapely bottom. Lara's hands were now in Ben's thick hair. She had never touched him like this and he held his breath. Her lips lightly brushed his forehead, his eyes, the tip of his nose, his cheeks; she showered his face with soft kisses. Ben thought he would lose his mind when her mouth finally found his. He couldn't believe this was happening. Her kiss became passionate, her breathing irregular. Ben sensed her arousal.

But as unexpectedly as the sensual moment started, it ended. Lara moved off his lap onto the sofa. She pulled her hair back and Ben noticed her face was flushed.

With great reservation, her eyes met his.

"I'm sorry, Ben. I didn't mean to play around like that."

Ben had been breathless with anticipation during the minute she was on his lap. He wanted to make mad passionate love to her right there but could only fantasize such a thing.

"Lara, I enjoyed every second of that minute." The moment, however, had passed and Ben sensed it was time to make an exit, sparing her feelings of embarrassment. It was the gentlemanly thing to do. He stood and pulled Lara to him and embraced her like he might never let her go. She relaxed into his chest as he nuzzled her neck.

"I will go now and take a cold shower. I'm all sweaty and gross."

Ben pulled away and kissed Lara on the forehead and she smiled sweetly. He gazed at her face as his hand lightly touched her hair. Then he was gone.

Tonight, she had been a combination of devil and angel. But Ben did not view her actions as teasing. It was obvious to him that she was terrified to get physical with him. He knew this stemmed from the gruesome attack she experienced as a young girl. He was fairly certain Lara had not been with a man since that brutal indoctrination. But tonight, she felt relaxed enough to kiss him and he loved it. He was slowly gaining her trust. That told him all he needed to know for the moment.

＊＊

Lara listened as Ben softly closed the door and made his way down the creaky staircase with Einstein. She wanted him to stay but knew in her heart that she had come dangerously close to losing control again. It was not like her to sit on *any* man's lap, let alone kiss him. Ever since she met Ben, she found herself doing things spontaneously—and she didn't like that feeling—but, then she had to admit, she did like Ben. He was funny, sweet and thoughtful. Every text or phone call made her heart skip a beat. No man ever had this effect on her and she liked it—but she feared it at the same time. She wanted nothing more than Ben in his pajamas on her sofa kissing her. She replayed the events of the evening acutely aware of how differently she interacted with Ben than any other man.

The sticking point was—Ben was still married. If he wasn't, she would take a chance on him. But he *was* married, and she was afraid she might end up with a broken heart. If she allowed herself to fall in love with Ben, the ramifications could be serious. He was not the type of guy a woman got over. He was the once-in-your-lifetime type of man that a woman dreamed of loving. There was no question in Lara's mind, she *wanted* Ben. But the relationship had to be on her terms. Was she willing to compromise? That was the question. Sometimes when she thought about the wonderful qualities he possessed, and how incredibly handsome he was, she wondered if any one woman could ever keep him for long.

Lara slept fitfully that night. The night terrors returned, and she woke screaming in the middle of the night. The ringing alarm clock seemed too loud as she pulled the blanket over her head. No classes this morning. But, it was time to go to the architectural firm to have an important project meeting with the contractors. Opening her phone, she scrutinized her calendar and checklists that would dictate the events of her day. She paid particular attention to an e-mail from Eliot. He wanted to meet with her late in the day in his office to talk about a new client.

Showering and eating quickly, she studied the details for the contractors meeting. She mentally prepared for the meeting as she dressed in a black business suit with a white silk scarf and twirled her hair into a French twist. Then she was off in her car.

A long rectangular space, the conference room at the firm had one full wall of windows. Water bottles sat in an ice-filled bucket upon a credenza. Large photographs of the firm's top projects lined the walls in sepia tones. Walking into the conference room, Lara shifted her attention to the final phase of her current projects and put her checklist before her.

Men, of varied sizes, shapes, and ages were all talking at once as they filtered into the conference room. Plumbers, carpenters and electricians poured over Lara's punch lists delivered to them the day before, complete with budgets and tiny details yet to be finished. She knew all the contractors and had a good relationship with most of them. A couple of the men overtly flirted with her. But, she knew when to put her game face on to exert authority. Plus, Eliot was always her back-up. This time he asked her to run the meeting on her own and she knew it was a test.

The room fell silent as Lara called the meeting to order. She was given a huge task by Eliot Stone as project manager and she took her responsibilities seriously. Lara worked through the timeline of each project to make sure they were on time and on budget. Throughout the meeting she would call out a contractor's name and ask a question or two. The plumbing was behind schedule and Lara called out.

"Simmons, can you get the bathrooms and kitchens done on Williams Street by the end of this month?"

From the sea of men, Simmons surfaced and replied, "We are taking a few men off another job to help out. Yes, it will be completed by the end of the month."

Only one contractor was veering way off course on the Williams Street Project. Lara called his name out and he was sitting in the corner with a baseball cap pulled down over his eyes.

"Stephens...I need to meet with you on site at Williams Street 4 PM today. We need a walk-through." It was an order more than an invitation.

Some of the men in the room chuckled as Bill Stephens saluted and mocked her.

"Yes, ma'am!"

Lara was concerned about Stephens. He was a new electrical contractor and she didn't like his attitude or his electrical work. In the last few discussions she had with him, he became belligerent and used the F-word a lot, sort of letting her know he wasn't taking orders from her. Lara was surprised he had the audacity to make design changes without running them by her. He was not following the specifications Lara was required to adhere to for the client. Bill Stephens had not only changed some of the lighting fixtures but placement, as well. He made decisions on his own that really ticked her off. As a result, the electrical work had to be redone. This ate into the contingency budget and pushed the completion date out. Lara could not tolerate contractors who made decisions without consulting her. She thought it would be best to meet him on site in person to walk him through each detail to make sure it sank into his thick skull.

Bill Stephens' face at the meeting looked more like a scolded child than a professional contractor, and Lara sensed he was suffering from a bruised ego because their conversation took place in front of the others. She watched him out of the corner of her eye as his surly face turned red; he spat a gob of tobacco juice into a paper cup. The rest of the meeting went smoothly, and the meeting ended. A few of the men stopped to shake her hand on the way out.

"Thanks, Miss O'Connell."

"Pleasure working with you on this one."

Lara was pleasantly surprised with their comradery and packed her bag to meet her electrical contractor at the project.

Located in the West end of the city, the Williams Street condo project was the biggest job Lara had undertaken during the two years of her internship. This would be her master's thesis. The building was originally built in 1885. The Mansard roof was hipped with two pitches and had dormers set in. With patterned shingles and deep eaves, the building had decorative brackets, two over two and the windows had elaborate pediments. The style was close to Italianate, but the Mansard roof characterized it.

The first half of the year, the outside of the building was restored with painstaking detail and it oozed charm which contributed to the project selling out quickly. The condo interiors were a combination of lovingly restored ancient details, mixed with ultra-modern features. The floors, ceilings and windows were 1885, but the lighting, appliances, and surfaces were sleek in design.

Lara was now filled with anxiety and impatience as she paced the oak kitchen floor of the unit. *Where was Stephens?* She glanced at the time on her phone. The condo was in the throes of renovation. The kitchen was almost completed, but the walls in the rest of the rooms were still being taped and sanded. The electrical work was just wrapping up. There were tools and materials everywhere.

Stephens was to meet her at 4 PM. Lara looked at her phone again then set it on the counter. He finally rushed through the door at 4:30 PM.

"Thanks for coming, Bill." she started. "We need to go over a few things."

He stood there seemingly mute, his face red, and his hat covering his eyes. No response. Lara thought it would be a good idea to continue.

"This project is a mixture of old and new. The building is antique, but the interior of these condos were to be modern in design, and that's why *these* lighting fixtures were chosen."

She had the catalog open on the marble countertop and pointed to the correct fixtures. She sensed that Stephens was ignoring her. But then he spoke, and his voice was filled with indignation.

"I really don't think this meeting was necessary, boss

lady." He had somehow moved much closer and was staring at her now. She got the impression he was not paying attention to anything she was saying. He was a big man, six-foot-four and probably weighed well over two fifty.

Without warning, Stephens slammed Lara up against the kitchen counter hard. Grabbing both of her arms with his huge hand, he pinned her against the marble countertop with his hulking body. It took her a second to realize what was happening. His other hand reached up to her throat.

"You need someone to put you in your place, bossy lady."

Bill's face was now red as saliva flew from his lips, he yelled obscenities.

"Fuck, yeah! I'm gonna show you who's in charge here, right now, missy!"

He grabbed Lara's body with tremendous force attempting to push her to the floor. Her whole body was alive with adrenaline. The building was vacant, and no one would hear her scream. She instantly knew she couldn't let him get her on the floor. She would not have the body strength to shove him off. He used a leg to spread Lara's feet apart. She inhaled deeply. Moving her legs as he did, gave her the opportunity she was seeking. It allowed for a clear, unobstructed path between Lara's right knee and his genitals.

When Lara's kneecap struck him, it didn't drive his testicles next to his colon, it smashed them against his pelvic bone. The pain made him double over, his upper body moved past Lara. She heard his head as it cracked against the countertop. Her Krav Maga skills became automatic at that point, Lara saw the opportunity to jab her elbow into the back of his neck causing his head to bounce off the counter. Lara moved away from him quickly thinking only of a way to use her most powerful muscles— her legs. Once she had distance, she drove a kick into the side of his knee, bringing him down to the floor. Heart racing, Lara's rage intensified, and she proceeded to stomp on him a few times. Two kicks to the ribs, one to the liver, and one for each kidney. Stephens hit the floor hard and stayed there moaning. The pink leather sack was on the counter behind her and she grabbed it. With only a split second to think, she grabbed the 9mm Glock and trained it on him as she moved toward the doorway. He was writhing on the floor, red-faced and angry.

She pointed the Glock at him and yelled. "Stay on the floor you bastard or I'll shoot you!"

She recognized a glimmer of fear in his crazed eyes, but Stephens complied. Lara took a deep breath and dialed 911 with shaky fingers. It was only a matter of minutes and she tried to catch her breath as she waited for police to arrive. Stephens remained prone. She threatened to kill him if he moved. He shouted a few profanities, but he did not move toward her. She would have pulled the trigger if he had.

As soon as police arrived, Stephens was handcuffed and taken away. Lara made the police report; she wanted to press assault charges. The police officer asked if she felt she could drive to the station. They wanted to photograph her injuries. Lara said she could drive. But she noticed her hands were trembling slightly as she walked to her car. Adrenaline, she thought. It would soon subside. She had been through this before.

The police officer was waiting for her at the station and

quickly brought her to a private interrogation room and closed the door. Officer Randall Bettencourt told her he would bring a female officer to the room to record her statement and take photos. Lara looked into his soft brown eyes. He was young, and stood straight and tall, about six four. There was an air of authority about him. He removed his hat in Lara's presence and she noted the shaved brunette haircut. In under a minute, Lara's eyes swept over him and she sensed she could put her life in his hands. She told him she was fine with photographs, she just wanted to get it over with.

The officer stepped out of the room briefly and returned with a petite blonde woman in a navy-blue police uniform. She shook Lara's hand and introduced herself as Officer Rebecca Benson. Officer Bettencourt took great care to make Lara feel comfortable and secure. He brought her a bottle of water and spoke in a deep soft voice as if trying to soothe her. He sat in on the interview as Rebecca Benson asked questions. At one point, Lara didn't answer some of the questions, and Bettencourt looked up from his notes. When his brown eyes met hers, it was as if he knew this was not the first time this had happened to her.

"Take your time." he coaxed her gently. She focused on the details of his uniform and his person. His arms were well developed and his hands big. She detected a slight southern accent. Through her blurry eyes, she finally became conscious of the fact that he was exceedingly handsome. But, he never once smiled. He was somber, efficient and professional.

After Rebecca Benson recorded her statement, she got out a camera and set it on the table; then handed Lara something that looked like a hospital gown.

"We'll step outside while you put this on, ma'am. Just open the door when you're ready."

Randall Bettencourt and Rebecca Benson left the room. Lara stripped down to her underwear, then put on the gown. She could not stop shivering as she opened the door and Rebecca Benson returned alone.

"This will just take a few minutes, Miss O'Connell." she said. "It's important to have this evidence for your case."

Lara closed her eyes as the bruises on her arms and neck were photographed. Then she shifted the garment opening it in the back. She heard the camera click and whir as Rebecca Benson zoomed in on the purple bruises on her back where Lara was driven into the marble countertop with tremendous force. Her bare feet felt cold on the tile floor. She couldn't stop shivering.

Officer Benson left the room and Lara got dressed. She dialed Eliot's phone number but there was no answer. She sent him a text saying she could not see him tonight, but she needed to talk to him about a serious incident that had just occurred at the Williams Street work site.

Randall Bettencourt walked Lara to her car. Her whole body shook uncontrollably as she drove home. Once inside, she ran to the bathroom and vomited. She took a hot shower and brushed her teeth. As she made her way to the kitchen for a cold ginger ale, her phone vibrated, and it was Ben. His voice sounded happy and excited.

"Hey Lara, I am cooking one of my specials tonight. I would love you to join me and Einstein for a light dinner and a walk."

She was silent. Ben said, "Lara, are you there?"

She replied in a concise manner.

"Yes, just give me some time to shower."

They agreed to meet at 7 PM in Ben's apartment. Lara robotically dressed to have dinner with Ben. She suddenly wanted nothing more than to be with him.

CHAPTER 11: *Something in Common*

When Ben hung up the phone, he immediately sensed something was wrong. He already heard Lara take a shower thirty minutes ago. So, why would she say she was going to take a shower when she had already taken one? Her voice sounded strange on the phone. Lara arrived at Ben's apartment door precisely at 7 PM. Before she even tapped on the door Einstein scrambled from his dog bed. His nose pressed against the threshold and he made a snorting sound. Then he whined with delight knowing Lara was on the other side.

Ben opened the door and took her into his arms. The embrace was long, and he held her tightly.

"I missed your afternoon visit today." Ben whispered as he held her.

Lara pulled away gently. "I had that contractor meeting..."

Ben noticed her eyes were red and she avoided eye contact with him. He thought she may have been crying earlier.

"Are you okay?"

"Sure, I'm fine." Laura quipped. Slipping a dog treat to Einstein.

"What's for dinner?"

Ben smiled, in an attempt to cheer her, but she didn't seem to notice.

"My special mushroom and Asiago cheese omelet and a salad. Here, sit and have a glass of ginger ale while I finish cooking. I'll put the television on for you."

He noticed her hand was shaking as she held the glass of ginger ale. He watched as she gently placed the glass on a side table. As she sat near the window, he noticed she nervously twirled a tendril of hair around her index finger and was staring into space. Lara wasn't smiling or talking, and Ben knew something serious had happened today.

He placed the food into the oven to keep it warm and moved toward her as she continued her absent-minded trance. When he approached her near the window, he noticed the deep purple bruise on her neck and immediately knew someone had hurt her. She looked into his eyes and no words were spoken. Ben held her in a tight embrace and felt her body shake involuntarily as she heaved and sobbed. Fifteen minutes passed. Ben stroked her hair as Lara's tear-stained cheek was pressed against his chest.

"Do you want to tell me about it?"

Lara's voice was muted. "It was the electrical contractor. He's a big bastard, but I took him down. I was scared, Ben. I kicked him and got him on the floor. I left my bag on the countertop and almost couldn't reach it. I thought about it afterward and realized how lucky I was to have escaped. I pulled my Glock out and came very close to using it."

Ben held her tighter. "So that's what you carry in your leather sack. I thought it was a little heavy to be make-up, seeing as you hardly wear any. Now I get it."

Ben felt Lara relaxing in his arms. The sobbing stopped as he stroked her hair and continued holding her close. If anyone knew the experience of violence up close and personal, it was Ben Keegan. And, he was very familiar with the adrenaline rush and its crash afterwards. Human beings were wired for flight or fight and no matter how much training or preparation, the letdown was a series of involuntary bodily reactions that were not very pleasant. He was glad Lara had come to him tonight. He wanted nothing more than to soothe her. She felt like a broken bird in his strong arms. He was suddenly overwhelmed with the feeling of being her protector. He could think of nothing now but Lara and helping her through the aftermath.

As she splashed cold water on her red eyes in Ben's bathroom, Lara took a deep breath knowing she had barely escaped this afternoon. What was she thinking leaving her bag on the counter? What was she thinking, meeting a man she did not know at a job site after hours? She couldn't believe she had been so careless. She blamed the whole incident on herself.

Meanwhile, she had an uncontrollable urge to beat the crap out of Bill Stephens. She felt the old anger rising in her again and fought to regain control. Lara's primal fear had flooded back when Stephens shoved her against that countertop, and for the first time in years she experienced raw, unrelenting panic. She decided to learn from the incident and move on. The dark purple bruises would fade away. Breathing deeply, she lowered her blood pressure. She emerged from the bathroom feeling exhausted, but she managed a smile for Ben.

It was a tender moment when Ben held her and soothed her raw nerves. She was grateful for his compassion. The smell of butter heating in a frying pan wafted through his apartment. Unlike Lara, Ben was a skilled cook and dinner was delicious. After eating they walked Einstein in the cold night air and came back to his apartment discussing the news events of the day. It was getting late, but Ben was preparing his favorite dessert. He removed the fresh strawberries and whipping cream from the fridge.

Lara watched him in the kitchen desperately wanting an excuse to linger in Ben's apartment. For the first time in years, she didn't want to be alone. While Ben sliced the strawberries, Lara studied the graceful form of his body. She suddenly experienced the strongest urge to embrace him. She rose from her chair in the kitchen and stood behind him, gently encircling his chest with her arms. She laid her cheek upon his muscular back inhaling his clean soapy smell. It was the same position she had on the motorcycle. She closed her eyes for a moment remembering the sensation of trust and safety she felt so strongly with him that day. Ben stopped moving and Lara suspected he was reading her mind.

***

Ben recognized Lara's feeling of vulnerability and sheer exhaustion. He had to persuade her to stay with him for the night. He knew she was shaken by the attack and needed his companionship. However, he did not want her to think he was trying to exploit her in any way. He would need to restrict his physical urges and pay attention to her emotional needs.

"Lara, that hug reminds me of the motorcycle ride, and how thrilled I was to take you on your first ride."

He turned toward her and brought her lovely face close to his. He endearingly kissed her cheek lightly and whispered into her ear.

"Stay with me tonight—please. I'll be on my best behavior, I promise."

He felt Lara relax into his embrace.

"It's settled then. I have a spare toothbrush. That's all you need. You can wear my robe." She clung to him now and Ben knew she needed nothing more than his tenderness and compassion at this moment. Although the tremors had stopped on the outside, Ben knew she was still reeling inside with the aftermath of the attack. He knew exactly what she was feeling.

He led Lara back to the sofa and they enjoyed the strawberries and freshly whipped cream. He turned on the television and distracted her by feeding her strawberries with his fingers. She smiled and curled up in his lap as he fed them to her one by one. The television was distracting her and the close contact with Ben was helping, too. Her head was now lying against his chest and he knew she was fighting off sleep. Ben would sleep on the sofa tonight and Lara would have his comfortable four-poster bed. He grabbed his robe off the hook and gave it to Lara in the bathroom. He listened by the door as she quickly slipped off her clothing and got into his robe. He led her to his comfortable bed and turned the covers down. Lara looked so beautiful and fragile at that moment. He embraced her as she wore his robe.

Then he moved her into the bed without words and covered her up as he leaned down to kiss her cheek.

"I'll be right there on the sofa in the parlor. I'll leave the door ajar, if you want."

Ben sat on the edge of the bed as he watched her fall asleep. With her lovely dark hair sprawled upon his pillow she looked like sleeping beauty. He wanted nothing more than to climb in beside her and hold her body close to his, and to whisper, *I'll protect you.* Instead, he moved off the bed and left the door half-open, so he could hear her if she needed anything.

Turning off the television, Ben grabbed the blanket off the back of the sofa, found a pillow, but sleep would not come. His SEAL training kicked in. He reviewed Lara's incident focusing on every detail she told him. He made a mental note to start working with her at the shooting range and at the dojo, giving her some SEAL self-defense techniques. It was imperative for her to gain her confidence back. Plus, he would find out who this Bill Stephens character was and planned to pay him a visit.

Once during the night Ben heard Lara crying. He jumped off the sofa and ran to her. She had a nightmare and needed to use the bathroom. He brought her to the master bathroom and waited outside near the door. When she emerged, she was disoriented, and he wrapped the robe snugly around her and tucked her back into his bed. He lay beside her on top of the covers and stroked her hair. In a few moments, he felt her drift back to sleep. Although he wanted to stay with her on the bed, he didn't want her to feel uncomfortable. Once Lara was soundly asleep, he moved back onto the sofa and slept.

***

As the sun came up, Lara opened her eyes and realized she was in Ben's bed wearing his robe. Ben's sandalwood scent was on it and she wanted to stay wrapped in it forever. Her eyes took in the details of his sumptuous bedroom. It was a masculine room, red, green, gold and ivory in its color scheme. The floor to ceiling windows had gold and ivory silk draperies covering them. She had no idea what time it was.

Recalling the events of the night before, she felt a strong feeling of gratitude sweep over her. Ben instinctively knew what she needed. There were no words spoken. He looked into her eyes and just knew. She could never imagine the violence Ben had experienced in Iraq and Afghanistan. Not once had he spoken of his years in battle, but she somehow knew he experienced horrors that could not be described with words. There was so much more to Benjamin Aiden Keegan than she had originally thought. He had shown tenderness and kindness when she most needed it. Ben was a man of mystery, yet she longed to know everything about him.

Lara's phone rang, it was Eliot Stone. He returned her urgent call from yesterday.

"Lara, I got your message. What's going on?"

"Eliot, something terrible happened at the condo project yesterday, I was attacked by Bill Stephens. He's in the county jail, and I don't know if he's been bailed out yet. But, you need to fire him officially. The incident occurred at 4:30 PM yesterday and the police hauled him away." She heard Eliot perk up on the other end of the phone.

"What exactly happened, Lara, are you hurt?" She explained the details to him.

"I am so sorry, Lara. I will personally take care of it. I'd like to meet with you to hear about this. I think a quiet dinner might help. Can I send the driver tonight?" Lara decided Eliot should hear her firsthand account, so he could understand the gravity of the situation. She told him to have the driver arrive at 6 PM and she would come to his house.

Ben appeared in the doorway.

"Coffee, tea, breakfast?" He smiled with dimples as his blue eyes lit up.

"I'll take a quick shower and be right there." Lara replied. As she moved to get out of the exquisite bed, she closed her eyes briefly thinking how wonderful it would be to sleep in this bed with him.

Showering, she examined the black and purple bruises on her body. They were particularly dark across her lower back where she was shoved against the countertop. Although ugly, she felt lucky as she scrutinized them, knowing it could have been much worse. She left her hair damp and loose and slipped into her clothes from the night before. She brushed her teeth with an extra toothbrush Ben left on the counter for her.

Ben was waiting in the kitchen with his frying pan ready. He had fresh coffee, juice, toast, and bacon. He asked her how she liked her eggs.

"Once over." Lara replied smiling. Things seemed to be normal again.

"Lara, I'd like to join you to practice my shooting skills, can I tag along to Rusty's on Saturdays?"

Lara was thrilled with the idea and added. "Would you tag along to the dojo, too? I have a feeling you could teach me a few moves." Ben nodded. "Consider it done."

The events of the past twenty-four hours only served to solidify her respect for Ben. He wasn't just another married guy trying to get her into the sack. He knew Lara better than she knew herself. He was sincere and honest, and she trusted him.

Watching her eat breakfast, Ben was assured that she felt better. He could tell by the glint in her hazel eyes and she smiled twice.

"Ben, I'm so grateful for last night..." her voice trailed off.

"You needed someone to lean on, and I'm happy you chose me for the job." He never took his eyes off Lara as she ate. Not wanting to push her, but also not wanting to let her go just yet, Ben asked if he could see her in the evening. He offered to cook dinner for her.

"I just got off the phone with Eliot. I think we need to have a chat about this Bill Stephens guy. He's got to be removed immediately. Eliot suggested we meet to go over the details, for the record."

For the record, Ben thought, Eliot wanted nothing more than to see the bruises on her lovely body. He cringed as he thought of that worm gawking at his sweet innocent Lara. He hoped Lara knew she was going into a spider's web.

"I'll text you when you return?" Ben persevered.

"Sure." Lara's eyes met his. It was decided, then.

Ben felt uncomfortable about Eliot Stone and his clandestine relationship with Lara. He didn't trust the guy.

"Call or text me if you need anything. I'll drop everything-- and, I mean that." Ben said sweetly.

Lara hugged him and thanked him for the robe, his bed,

the good food, but mostly for his kindness. Ben listened as she made her way back to her apartment. Einstein whined to go outside. He took his faithful dog out and sat in the porch glider sipping a lukewarm cup of coffee. He had two classes to teach today and lots more work involving Dark Horse. However, he would find it difficult to concentrate completely on work. Today Lara would occupy his thoughts.

CHAPTER 12: *Paved with Good Intentions*

Lara dressed quickly in her apartment and had difficulty concentrating in class. The gray suit she wore seemed to match her mood. At 1 PM, She was all business as she walked through the front door at Stone and Associates. The rumor mill had already been bubbling with various versions of what happened to her at the Williams Street project. She held her head high and spoke to everyone she met as if it was just another day. Waving to Eliot, she entered her glass office and closed the door leaving the din of the workday and gossip behind her.

She was surprised to see an arrangement of flowers sitting on her desk. Opening the sealed envelope, she read the note. *Thinking of you, Ben.* Two dozen long-stemmed pink roses nearly took up all the space on her desk, but definitely served a purpose—they brightened her day. Ben was on her mind as she returned phone calls and e-mails to clients. Eliot had his secretary bring in the forms to fill out regarding the incident—standard operating procedure. Lara painstakingly recalled every detail and made reference to the police report and Officer Bettencourt.

At the end of the day, she was drained. As the other employees started to filter out of the building, Eliot tapped on her glass door. She looked up and waved him in.

"Lara, I want you to know I have spoken with the police and I have a pretty good idea of what happened yesterday. I am so very sorry..." His brown eyes were filled with concern. He sat in the chair across from her and touched her hand.

"I survived it, Eliot, and that's all that really matters in the end, isn't it?"

Eliot withdrew his hand and stood, "I'll see you later for dinner then. Charles will prepare something delicious for us." Lara saw his eyes sweep over the flowers in her office; he was curious but didn't mention them. She watched through the window as the white Bentley picked him up in the parking lot. Then she finished going through the next few days' design folders. Finally, she drove to the campus to meet Ben for Einstein's walk.

***

Einstein heard her first. He bolted toward Ben's office door to welcome Lara. Ben was pleasantly surprised she kept her informal dog walking appointment today. He knew she was meeting with Eliot Stone and he hadn't expected her. He missed Lara even though he last saw her in his kitchen that morning.

Although smiling, she was subdued. "Thank you so much for the gorgeous roses today—they made me smile." Ben was surprised when Lara embraced him. She appeared to be tired and hungry.

"You didn't eat today, did you?"

Instinctively, Ben set out a can of mixed nuts that he kept in his desk. They shared a few handfuls and two cold bottles of water. She changed into a T-shirt and yoga pants in his office bathroom. He knew she was seeking normalcy. They made small talk about the events of the day.

Ben talked about teaching. "The students are a refreshing change of pace, not yet filled with cynicism. I think I'll enjoy working here at the university. It's important for me to communicate the significance of 9/11 and all that led up to it. My challenge as a professor will be to keep the subject matter interesting. I don't want students falling asleep in my class."

***

Lara imagined there would be no one falling asleep in Ben's class. The females would be eyes forward, riveted on the handsome dark-haired Irishman with the gorgeous blue eyes. The guys would look up to him, especially with his military honors. Ben would be a role model for all his students.

Lara had a final design element to ask Ben about.

"I almost forgot, what would you like hanging above your new fireplace mantle?"

He answered without hesitation. "A portrait of you."

There was silence as Lara pondered Ben's request.

"That would be impossible. Ben, you're a professor. It's against the rules. You know what I mean. I don't want people at the campus to think we're *involved*...in that way." Her words trailed off.

"Aren't we?" Ben was now teasing.

"We can't be involved, Ben, not until you're a single man, available, *legally*." Lara spoke with certainty, but her mind felt the slightest twinge of reservation. They were a couple – a couple of friends. She had already clarified her stance on this detail with him earlier. Lara would not be physically intimate with Ben until he was divorced. Even then, it would have to be within the confines of marriage. She had too much self-respect to have it any other way.

After a short discussion about the mantle, they both decided upon a few photos of his son, William, and the Prince

Edward Island cottage.

"You have a cottage at Prince Edward Island?" Lara feigned surprise, but it prompted Ben to talk.

"Yes, you've got to see it. You and I share the same love of nature. I think you would enjoy the rustic beauty of the place; it is tucked into a private cove with a sunset view—rural and remote; there are nine acres of privacy. I have daydreamed about you there with me, Lara, in that cottage. I can tell you the details of my dream, if you'd like."

Ben's blue eyes were on her and she smiled.

"Please tell me." She whispered.

He continued. "I see you there in my dream wearing shorts and a T-shirt standing in the kitchen drinking coffee. The windows are open, and it is a beautiful sunny day in July. In this dream, I am cooking eggs for you in the cast iron frying pan. Einstein is with us. The beach is warming up, and after a hearty breakfast we toss the ball around the water's edge for Einstein. Then we put a blanket on the sand and get comfortable."

Ben was flirting shamelessly with her. But as he confessed his most intimate daydream, Lara felt her heart melt. It was impossible for her to hide her growing affection for Ben, especially when he said things like that. If he was trying to get to her, he was doing a good job.

"I would love to visit your cottage someday, Ben."

Ben talked more about Prince Edward Island on their campus walk with Einstein. "It's not far from where I found Einstein as a puppy. It's a special place for me, Lara." She enjoyed hearing him talk about the place and watching the way the subject lit his face up.

Lara wanted to know much more about Ben, including his most private and personal thoughts about her. After walking Einstein, she excused herself as she had to get ready for dinner with Eliot. Lara reluctantly walked to her condo and took a long hot shower. She was hungry and looked forward to discovering what Eliot's chef, Charles, might cook for them. He was a creative artist in the kitchen. He could take the most basic ingredients, add a sauce and the right spices and voila, it was a gourmet meal. She marveled at such talent. Ben had that gift, too.

Wearing dark green slacks and a long-sleeved shirt, she slipped into her boots and brushed her hair. She wrapped herself in a deep purple cashmere cardigan and matching purple gloves. The driver arrived at precisely 6 PM and she hurried out to the Bentley.

As she slid into the seat, she thought she saw Ben in his parlor window. But maybe it was Einstein. She took a deep breath. The driver told Lara the champagne in the back was chilled for her. She had only sipped champagne once for New Year's Eve and didn't care for it. But tonight, she poured the bubbling concoction into a long-stemmed glass and sipped it slowly as the Bentley made its way to Falmouth Foreside and it tasted wonderful.

She was greeted at the stately Tudor's door by Raphael, Eliot's house manager, a small older Italian gentleman, he had many duties at the estate. Raphael led her to the library as he disappeared to fetch Eliot. Looking around the room, Lara noticed a large vase filled with fresh long stemmed white roses and leaned over to inhale the aroma of summer captured in the blossoms.

Eliot entered the room. "Thanks for coming...aren't those beautiful, Lara?" He embraced her warmly and encouraged her to remove her cashmere cardigan. But she insisted on keeping it on.

"I saw some beautiful flowers in *your* office today, Lara, – a secret admirer? Come, sit with me. I want to know about what happened with Stephens, although the police were quite graphic."

Lara joined Eliot on the settee and relived every detail of the attack at the worksite. He listened intently asking a few questions.

Finally, when she had recounted it completely, Eliot asked, "Are you badly bruised?"

He gasped when she removed the cardigan and stared at the bruises on her neck and arms. "Oh Lara, he must have hit you with tremendous force. The police officer said you had bruises on your back, too. I'm so sorry this happened. Are you in pain?"

Eliot's hand touched hers.

"Yes, it does hurt, but I feel lucky to have gotten away from him when I did."

Raphael announced dinner was ready.

Eliot took her hand and led her to the dining room. Charles did not disappoint. The meal was wonderful, consisting of Maine lobster pie and warm apple crisp for dessert. She took a few drafts of champagne and felt the tension of talking about the attack wash away.

Eliot's brown eyes looked deeply into hers.

"I was so worried when I heard what happened. You mean so much to me, Lara. I can't wait to see you every day at the firm. Working with you on projects has filled me with a renewed energy. I'd like to see more of you, in a personal sense, if you'll let me."

Lara remained poised and polite but felt a chill.

"I didn't know you felt so strongly, Eliot. I enjoy your company and appreciate all that you have done for me. But in regard to a personal relationship with you, I thought we already had one. I consider you a friend." She watched as disappointment registered on his face.

Then he seemed to reframe the question. "I was hoping you would join me for dinner and more social events. I'd love to take you sailing this spring."

Lara smiled politely. "I would accompany you to dinner and any social event, as a friend. And, yes, I'd love to go sailing."

Eliot seemed pleased with her answer and smiled. "Charles made us a wonderful dessert. Would you like to sit by the fire in the parlor?"

She thought for a moment, hoping she said the right thing and averted his gaze. "That sounds great."

Lara knew women rarely, if ever, said *no* to Eliot Stone. For the first time, Lara realized he wanted more out of life than being a wealthy playboy and sailing. But she also knew her relationship with him would remain as it was—friendship—period. It occurred to her that Eliot Stone was a lonely man.

They retired to the parlor and enjoyed the roaring fire. Eliot asked Raphael to bring them champagne and dessert. When Raphael left the room, Lara stood in front of the fireplace enjoying the warmth.

"I'm glad you came here tonight, Lara, and had dinner with me. I so hate eating alone."

"I knew you'd want to hear about Stephens directly from me. It was an awful day, really, and I hope I never encounter anything like that again."

Lara moved as Raphael returned to the room and she found a comfortable spot on the settee. While they enjoyed dessert and champagne, Lara put her feet up, and Eliot encouraged her to have another glass of champagne. As she stood to leave, her cardigan loosely wrapped around her shoulders, slipped to the floor. Eliot retrieved the sweater and helped her back into it.

"Thanks, Eliot."

"I'm sorry, Lara, and I'll scrutinize all of the contractors again. I don't want anyone like Stephens working for Stone & Associates. I'll walk you to the car."

The white Bentley awaited; the driver started the engine. Eliot kissed her cheek as she slid into the leather seat. "Goodnight, Lara." his brown eyes were fixed upon her. Surprisingly, Eliot slid into the backseat with her. "I'll ride along with you. I owe you that, at least, after all you've been through." In the backseat of the Bentley, Eliot held her hand and she felt him squeeze it through her purple leather glove. "I'm sorry for everything, Lara." His eyes were filled with concern. "Will you let me take you sailing this spring?"

"Sailing sounds lovely, Eliot, but I'll only be ballast at this point. I know nothing about it, really."

Eliot laughed. "Well, at least you know what ballast is. I think you know more than you're letting on." Then he paused. "Dinner tomorrow night? Oh, there's this little bistro that just opened in the city—food's marvelous..."

"Sorry, I'm busy, Eliot. Thanks for dinner tonight."

Before she got out of the car, Eliot leapt out before her. He took her hand as she emerged from the Bentley and hugged her. He'd never done that before and she wondered if it was his way of showing empathy. He seemed genuinely concerned for her wellbeing.

Lara pulled away. "Eliot, thanks for everything. Goodnight."

Eliot got back into the car and disappeared into the night. Lara climbed the creaky stairs to her condo and stripped off her clothes. She brushed her teeth and washed her face in the bathroom, knowing Ben was a wall away. Slipping beneath the coolness of the covers felt wonderful. She was asleep within five minutes. It had been an exhausting, tumultuous day. Her dream was a hazy vision of Ben and Einstein eating breakfast in his kitchen.

***

He watched the white Bentley come and go and noticed Eliot's frantic attempt to embrace Lara when they parted. This was something Ben felt he could not compete with. Eliot Stone was a rich trust-fund brat who was single, good-looking, and could offer Lara everything that he couldn't. The main point being Eliot was single, and Ben was not. Eliot could offer her wealth, and one hundred percent of his time. Ben could offer her financial comfort, but his time would be split between Lara and Dark Horse, always.

Ben wondered what her evening had been like. Eliot undoubtedly pampered her. The thought ran through Ben's mind: was Lara having intimate feelings about Eliot Stone? Was she planning to work for him at the firm upon graduation? Was he calling her and texting her every day? Suddenly, Ben felt the ugly sting of jealousy.

It was quiet in Lara's apartment. He assumed she had gone directly to bed. He knew she was exhausted from the events of the past two days. He felt that Lara would only be happy with him. If only he could get Sienna to sign those divorce documents. The divorce could then proceed through the complex Canadian court system and that could take months. Only then would he be free to make progress with Lara. He made a mental note to call Sienna again tomorrow. He needed to somehow convince her to sign the paperwork. He rolled onto the floor and proceeded to do push-ups for the next twenty minutes. Then he did pull-ups for a while. Finally, he left his condo to go for a long run. But when he returned, he dropped into his beautiful four-poster bed still unable to sleep. Breathing heavily from his five-mile run, Ben couldn't stop thinking of Lara. Last night she slept in his bed. He held her in his arms as she wept. He wanted nothing more than to run to her apartment and knock down the door. He lit the candle in his bedroom and closed his eyes.

CHAPTER 13: Renaissance Man

The renovation of Ben's office was now fully underway, and Lara was getting an intimate glimpse into Ben's life. She was in and out of his office on a regular basis. Einstein loved the extra attention and enjoyed the workmen who came in to paint or make deliveries. The budget was substantial. Lara kept the décor period, yet more opulent than all the other offices at the university. Other professors stopped by to watch the progress. They seemed envious of Ben, even though they tried to disguise it, except for Harris. He was excited and pleased. Lara made sure there was a special space for Einstein.

After the walls were painted a warm soft red, Lara filled his empty office with expensive down-filled furniture, and craftsman style stained-glass lamps. She purchased a luxurious hand-made wool rug to cover the middle section of the floor. The fireplace was no longer functioning, and she arranged to have the flue repaired. There were permits and insurance riders to sort through, but she got the work finished with the permission of the campus capital committee, so the fireplace could function once again. The mantle was original and full of scrolls and ornate carvings, thus became the focal point of the room.

She expertly organized the built-in bookcases with Ben's impressive collection of books, interesting objects and unique pieces of art. She interspersed the books with found items from his travels around the world. It was to be a masculine office.

She began learning more about Ben Keegan and what he really did for a living. One day she noticed a newspaper folded to an article about a house that imploded in Portland. The news story reported that investigators thought a couple of bomb-makers had blown themselves up accidentally. She finished reading the article, wondering if it was the handiwork of Dark Horse.

Going through the boxes Ben asked her to unpack, Lara searched for clues about his past life. She needed to incorporate modern devices into Ben's office as he was a high-tech guru. He had a flat screen television and several Apple devices that needed to be worked into the design.

In Ben's personal belongings, she came upon an unusual primitive sword and mounted it in a glass case in front of Ben's desk, so he could see it whenever he looked up. She noticed flash grenades, a stun gun and high-grade pepper spray stored in the locked top drawer of Ben's desk. She found something he referred to as his *kit*. When she opened it, she noted a few items; a stainless steel mini multi-tool with pliers, a wire cutter, a file, and an awl, a button compass and a suspended navigation magnet, LED Squeeze Light with a red bulb, Ferrocerium rod and four tinder tabs in a resealable bag, 2-liter water container, 40 water purification tablets and 2 electrolyte tablets, a signal mirror, thermal blanket, Kevlar line and thread, 4 safety pins, can opener, steel wire and green duct tape, a magnifying lens, waterproof paper and an ink pen. Who was this guy—MacGyver?

Ben had boxes shipped to his office and he instructed Lara to sort through all of it. A shipment came from Prince Edward Island and appeared to be his personal mementos. Opening one of the boxes she found photographs in a large envelope marked SAVE in bold letters. There she found pictures of Sienna, her large brown eyes had a doll-like stare. She was dressed in haute couture evening wear worthy of the red carpet. Her collar bone protruded from her gaunt body. Her arms were so thin they looked like bones loosely covered with skin. Her hair was bleached blonde and thinning. Sienna's lips were drawn into a straight line.

Ben had a massive collection of books and Lara knew she could garner a great deal of information about him by studying what he read. He had a full complement of Classic literature. She was surprised to discover that Ben was a lover of poetry. He had volumes of Keats, Shelley, Byron, Wordsworth, Shakespeare, Yeats, Tennyson, Browning, Kipling, Whitman, the list was endless. One poem, in particular stood out to her. It was a page torn out of a book stained and wrinkled. The sheet of paper had what appeared to be multiple nail holes at the top. The poem was *Invictus*.

Invictus

Out of the night that covers me,
Black as the Pit from pole to pole,
I thank whatever gods may be
For my unconquerable soul.

In the fell clutch of circumstance
I have not winced nor cried aloud.
Under the bludgeonings of chance
My head is bloody, but unbowed.

Beyond this place of wrath and tear
Looms but the Horror of the shade,
And yet the menace of the years
Finds, and shall find, me unafraid.

It matters not how strait the gate,

How charged with punishments the scroll.
I am the master of my fate:
I am the captain of my soul.

William Ernest Henley

Lara caught her breath as she read the words. This poem was about Ben and his personal war. She took the ragged page, smoothed it out with her hands and slipped it into an envelope. She would have it framed and placed next to the sword in his office. It had to have deep meaning to him as he'd taken it with him to the far corners of the globe.

Ben also had a substantial history library, in fact it rivaled Professor Harris' in its scope. She turned over hundreds of books written about ancient battles and many about the Spartans of Greece. There were also volumes about Native Americans. Lara smiled to herself; Ben was a Renaissance man.

Then she stumbled upon an old burnished leather briefcase. It was locked. She searched through his desk drawer and found a pile of keys, but no luck. As she turned the case over in her lap, she noticed a small pocket on the outside. Her finger explored the pocket and inside was a brass key. She put the key into the slot and turned it. The case was heavy and the moment it opened numerous magazines and news clippings poured out, which made a huge pile on the floor. As she sifted through each one, she noticed there was a theme; an accident or natural disaster, or the death of someone. She noted that all the articles were fairly recent, within the last two years. She jotted down some of the names of the victims, then quickly put the case back in order and locked it, then put the key in the pocket where it was.

"Wow, Lara! You've done a great job here putting things away! Ben popped in just as she put the valise back as it was. He noticed she seemed a little jumpy. Maybe he just surprised her.

"You have so much. I love your book collection."

"Great. Well, feel free to borrow whatever you want. I've got to run to my next class. See you later."

He imagined Lara going through all his belongings. It had to be a treasure trove of information for her, and he pictured her sitting there wondering what some of the items were. Eventually, she'd piece together who he was. He knew it was better to make this a gradual process, because otherwise it might overwhelm her. And, he also knew he'd have to tell her everything eventually. Lara seemed like a normal young woman who wanted a husband, a family, a home. If she knew everything about him right now, she might turn away in revulsion. He never wanted that to happen, but it was always the chance he took, doing the work that he did—living this unconventional life. He wanted her to see him as a potential husband, but would she *want* him when she knew the truth?

While Ben taught classes, Lara worked in his office whenever she had a free moment, listening to the soft music, Einstein's breathing as he slumbered, and the ticking of the stately clock she found for the wall. She selected several photos of William as a young child and had them enlarged. Lara carefully placed the photographs of William on the mantle. Also, she found a special photo and placed it in the middle. She found a stunning photo of the cottage on Prince Edward Island. As with any client, Lara wanted Ben's office to represent his taste. As she stood back to make a final edit of the room, she hoped she had represented what was near and dear to Ben's heart in the choices she made for his office. Today Ben would see it in its finished state.

After teaching his second class of the day, Ben arrived at his office as usual for his lunch break. Lara had covered the mantle with a drop cloth planning a dramatic unveiling for him.

"What's this?" he smiled as he strolled into his now beautifully renovated office.

"I hope you like it." Lara said tentatively. With excitement, she pulled the drop cloth away and watched Ben's reaction to the renovated fireplace and mantle. His eyes quickly took in the photographs. She knew he hadn't expected the enormous photo of Einstein. He appeared to be particularly touched that Lara knew how much his dog meant to him.

"It's perfect. Lara, you've done such an incredible job. I don't know how to thank you."

Lara smiled with satisfaction. "Oh, you paid me very well. I would say that was adequate compensation. I'm thrilled that you like it."

Ben swept Lara into his arms, buried his face in her hair and whispered, "Have dinner with me tonight. I'll pick you up at 7 PM."

Lara received a text from Ben letting her know it would be a casual night, steaks at a roadhouse. With care, she chose comfortable jeans, boots, and a fitted T-shirt with an American flag on it. The word *roadhouse* to her meant loud music, cowboy hats, and beer. She had recently purchased an old leather jacket to top off her outfit. She had stumbled upon it in a thrift store and, as if it was meant to be hers, the jacket fit her perfectly.

Brushing her hair, she decided to leave it loose tonight. There was a knock on her door. Opening it she looked directly into Ben's enthusiastic face. He smiled.

"Wow, gorgeous." He whistled softly. "Let's go."

She watched as he climbed onto the motorcycle and hopped on behind him. After securing their helmets, she reached her hands around his powerful body and felt the cycle rev and take off. They drove through several small towns before arriving at the roadhouse. Lara was enjoying the ride more than Ben could have imagined.

This time Ben took her to a place that he loved to frequent with his SEAL brothers whenever they were in town. It looked like an old barn converted to a dance hall. Inside, the place was dimly lit and there were peanut shells on the floor. The name of the place was *The Comfort Zone*. Everyone wore boots and jeans. Flat screens were filled with sports of all types. Country music played in the background as the smell of grilling steaks wafted through the air.

Lara measured Ben's level of comfort as he walked in the door with her on his arm. She instantly knew he was at home in this place. As her eyes swept the huge room, there were decidedly more men than women. Several guys tipped their hats, nodded, subtly waved or made eye contact with Ben as he walked to a table with Lara. Before sitting, Ben slipped off Lara's leather jacket and his own and hung them together on a peg near their table.

"Are you okay with this?" He asked his blue eyes filled with hesitation.

"Yes, this is fine."

Ben smiled with dimples and she sensed his relief. He leaned back in his chair and explained the agenda. "After dinner, they open up the dance floor around 9 PM. Maybe you will enjoy the music."

Their meal was simple and delicious--salad and steak. As they finished eating, one by one, a parade of men stopped by the table. Not one of them had a real name. They were all military guys and had nicknames like Torque, Trace, and Hutch. There were marines, rangers, pilots, and SEALs. Their conversation would be brief and always a bit humorous and they had a special handshake thing. They all called Ben "Chief". In Lara's mind, it appeared to be a ritual of sorts to greet her and make her feel welcome. And, each one of them made her feel comfortable, as they smiled and shook her hand.

Just as Ben indicated, at 9 PM the music started. It was a simple set-up. A disc jockey played music from a corner of the room. During the dinner hour requested songs were sent by those in the audience, along with a five-dollar tip. She felt unsure of herself as Ben took her hand and led her to the dance floor. Lara had never danced with a man except for once at a wedding; she was a bridesmaid and it was required. The roadhouse had filled with a large crowd. Ben pulled her into his chest as they slow danced and Lara felt her heartbeat quicken.

"Here's my request—you remember this one?" He whispered in her ear.

Lara recognized the Tim Halperin song *Think I'm in Love*. He drew Lara so close she could hear his heartbeat as they danced. The words were beautiful, soulful. Ben was an excellent dancer, agile and light on his feet. Slow-dancing with Ben was a tender and sensual experience. Tonight, there were no shadows across her heart. She felt blissfully alive, and incredibly safe in his strong arms. She never imagined dancing could be so pleasurable.

Surprising Lara, Ben also knew how to two-step, something she was completely unfamiliar with. But, being a patient teacher, Ben took her through the moves, slowly at first. Then she got the hang of it. Twirling in Ben's arms with her body snuggly nestled against his muscular form was heavenly. They danced for an hour, then finally took a water break.

"It's a bit of a work out." Ben smiled as he slaked his thirst.

Several couples winked or nodded at him on the dance floor in acknowledgement.

"You seem to know most of the people here." Lara remarked.

"Yes, it's a hideaway for me when I get some downtime." Ben smiled. "You probably guessed there are a lot of military guys here." He looked particularly young and innocent tonight, especially with those dimples. Because he brought her to his hideaway, Lara somehow felt closer to him. It was as if he invited her into the most private sphere of his life.

They left the roadhouse at 11PM to ride home. Behind Ben on the motorcycle, Lara was exhilarated. The night ride was different. She felt she had given herself over totally to Ben once she pressed herself into his back. The aroma of his leather jacket mixed with sandalwood and the natural scent of his body was masculine and pleasant. The ride with Ben was breathtaking and she arrived home more stimulated than relaxed.

Wanting to invite him in, she realized it would make more sense to turn in for the evening because tomorrow would be a busy day. She lingered on the porch with him as he embraced her. Then he lightly brushed his lips against her neck causing a shiver of delight to run down her spine. Ten minutes passed; no words were spoken until he whispered.

"Thank you for a really fun night." He gently touched his mouth to hers. She kissed him, lingering, savoring the warm wetness of her mouth with his. Then, pulling away, she said, "Goodnight Ben."

Lara moved up the creaky staircase to her apartment, revved up and unable to sleep. She sent a text to him. *I had a great time tonight.* Lara took a long hot soak in the tub before bed. She played the details of the night over in her mind. Ben was such a gentleman compared to anyone she had ever met before. She never thought she would ever feel this relaxed with any man—truly a milestone for her.

***

As Ben dropped into the huge four-poster bed he realized tonight was a breakthrough for him. He had never brought a woman into the tight knit group of ex-military guys that he hung with. But he knew this brief introduction for Lara was critical if she was going to enter his world. He assessed her reaction tonight as positive. She was open and receptive to everyone she met, flashing her beautiful smile. She laughed at all the right jokes. He was so proud to have her on his arm. Every guy in the place indicated their tacit approval. She looked gorgeous in those jeans and a simple T-shirt. She needed nothing to add to her beauty. In Ben's eyes, she was perfect in every way.

He also thought about how different an evening with him was from a night out with Eliot Stone. No matter how much wealth Ben acquired, he would not flaunt it like Eliot. The two men had different priorities. Ben would *always* go to the roadhouse to be in the company of his brothers. His net worth would never change who he was. He would continue to donate a large percentage of his income to the families of his fallen brothers and those disabled in the line of duty. Ben had a difficult time spending money on himself. The 1940 replica Indian motorcycle was a big splurge for him when he bought it, but he was thrilled tonight to have Lara on the bike with him. He could tell the night ride was exhilarating for her. Few things in life gave him such pleasure. He already knew he was going to have difficulty sleeping tonight. He slipped into his sneakers and jogging pants to take a long run. He needed to drain the excitement that filled him whenever he was with Lara, especially when he was pressed against her lovely figure for several hours on a dance floor.

CHAPTER 14: *Observation Leads to Admiration*

Lara continued to visit Ben's office every day for late afternoon walks with Einstein. She sat cross-legged in Ben's office on the beautiful hand-made rug as she rubbed Einstein's egg-shaped head. She listened intently whenever Ben received a phone call. When he spoke, it was sometimes in a foreign language, and when he did speak English, the conversations were filled with military jargon and orders, of sorts. She knew his work was classified and he was careful to protect his data. His office door remained locked except for when he was there. Lara began to realize how much he trusted her.

Occasionally, students made appointments to visit with him. Some of the adult students would meet with him on his lunch break. Lara noticed that Ben always made time for them. He would sit in the overstuffed chair in the seating area and listen intently to their questions or concerns. He took his teaching duties seriously. Lara suspected some of the female students made an appointment just to talk with him. Ben treated each student with patience, dignity and respect. She was gaining more insight into this mysterious man and with it came a longing to be with him, whenever possible.

***

Ben was now teaching the first civilian classes of his life. In the Navy. he frequently took the role of teacher with his men. But this atmosphere was completely different. His lesson plan had to be approved by the dean of the university. He knew well in advance what would be acceptable to those in power at the university and what wouldn't be acceptable, so he carefully crafted the lessons around those unspoken rules and regulations. There was a lengthy history lesson regarding the countries in the modern day Middle East leading up to the events of 9/11.

The first day he walked into the classroom, Ben instinctively picked out the students who had a family member serving. They paid attention when he spoke and actually took notes. There were also several soldiers returning from the battlefield. These students, in particular, memorized every detail of his presentations. Many of them had *lived* it. Many students in the classroom were not completely aware of his entire background. If asked, Ben would simply say he was a former Navy man, that's what the syllabus stated. He didn't want the subject matter to be about him being a SEAL or the gruesome details of his missions—that was classified. His teaching material focused on 9/11 and the Iraq and Afghanistan conflicts, and he taught the events leading up to the battle with accurate details. Most of the students in his classroom were seven years old when 9/11 happened. As for the overarching theme of his presentation, he stuck with *his* definition of patriotism. Patriotism was devotion to your country, even though you may not necessarily agree with your government, a patriot did his or her duty.

He was surprised that he enjoyed the role of professor. It was nothing like his preconceived notion. The university itself was an extension of the government, however, the student body was much different than he had imagined. Maybe, in some small way, he really was getting through to his students, making a small difference in the world. Having this diversion from his usual work made him feel a glimmer of hope.

***

While walking Einstein one afternoon, Lara asked the big question.

"How is the divorce proceeding?" She watched Ben's face grow solemn.

"Sienna is not being cooperative. Lara, you don't know her. She's not a normal person. She has money, power, and influence and she may use it to hurt me in any way that she can."

Becoming more insistent with her tone, Lara pressed him further.

"When do you think the divorce will actually be finalized?" She searched his face for a response. Ben narrowed his eyes and his gaze remained fixed on the ground in front of them.

"I am hoping she will soon realize the pure logic of taking the deal I offered her."

Lara and Ben's lives seemed irrevocably connected. The afternoon walks with Einstein had become a comfortable habit for them. Although Ben insisted on varying their daily route, Lara often asked him to walk by a stunning purple and blue Victorian a few blocks from the campus. Majestically, it sat on a hill with ocean views and a perfectly landscaped lawn with a flower garden. Whenever they passed by the purple Victorian they always paused to admire the details of it.

Ben appreciated the lines of the architecture as much as Lara, "Someday, I will buy that house for you." he said unexpectedly in his soft Irish brogue.

For a moment Lara allowed herself to enjoy the wild fantasy of living there with Ben, having his children. Then, she returned to her sensible self, realizing how irrational that scenario would be. Ben was some sort of secret agent and he was still married. But she couldn't help imagining herself being there, living with him. What would it be like to be his wife? Suddenly, she realized she was living in an imaginary world. How many other women felt this way about Ben? Every female student must have been infatuated with him. He was, after all, the handsome new professor on campus. Was he working with other women in his Dark Horse group? How many exotic women had he slept with in his travels? Some of these questions she didn't want answered.

Ben was seven years older than her, but he seemed mature beyond his thirty-one years. Lara imagined other women were also taken with his witty humor, spontaneous personality, and striking good looks. He was the complete package. She sometimes wondered if he was human, he seemed *too* perfect. Ben's life was so different from hers. He lived what appeared to Lara as a life unstructured, unplanned, spontaneous, while Lara's was neatly packaged. Had she always lived this ground-hog day existence? Had she always been so boring?

***

Like clockwork, every other Saturday, Ben and Lara drove to Rusty's shooting range in the morning. Lara was a willing student and Ben taught her advanced tips and techniques. She learned how to carry two weapons in case one failed. She was schooled in taking weapons apart and putting them back together in record time. She learned how to get a jammed cartridge out of the chamber quickly and safely. Speed, accuracy, and threat assessment was taught to Lara in each session with Ben.

As for him, Ben secretly loved the extra time with her, especially standing behind her to watch her aim, or teaching her how to use a new laser or scope. He found creative ways to be physically close to her. Touching her hand, inhaling her scent, brushing against her, listening to her laugh—just being in her presence brought him joy. The more time he spent with her, the more he believed she was his. As a result, his expert guidance improved Lara's shooting skills dramatically. Rusty delighted in watching them and sometimes participated in the shooting competition. But most often he would set the targets up for them and sit back to enjoy the show.

Honing Lara's Krav Maga skills at the dojo on Wednesdays, Ben worked with Don Henderson on a regular basis. The two men showed her submission techniques that were valuable and deadly. Ben went a step further demonstrating a complete anatomy lesson on how to kill a person with her bare hands. Don would go through the session with her and Ben would repeat it. With each man, Lara learned useful skills.

Instead of a thirty-minute martial arts practice, it became a grueling hour-long grappling session. Ben emphasized that Lara's body was always her most important weapon. He taught her how to move in silence before an attack. And, he taught her the most helpful hints: how to *avoid* physical confrontation altogether.

More importantly, he taught Lara how to use her senses, all six of them. He trained her to utilize peripheral vision and to notice the smallest details. Ben played a game with her in which she needed to ferret out things that didn't seem like they belonged. He coached her to use hearing, taste, touch, and smell. But of utmost importance, he emphasized attention to that nagging little tactile feeling that says something is not quite right: hackles. That uneasy feeling is an early warning, the prelude to the fight-or-flight instinct.

***

Meanwhile, as Lara enjoyed Ben's companionship at the shooting range and the dojo she was learning more about him as a person. He was incredibly patient with her and had a sense of humor that sometimes caused her to collapse on the floor in a fit of uncontrollable laughter. Ben was a practical person with no pretension. He acted swiftly and decisively. Her physical attraction to Ben was growing stronger as her respect for him grew.

She relished the moments when he moved in close and she felt him against her at the dojo or shooting range. When she passed him in the hallway at the university he would wink at her. Ben sent her texts all day. He had become the most pleasant part of Lara's daily life, and when his work took him away his absence was noticeable.

Lately, Lara sat in her classes but could not concentrate on the subject matter. She often closed her eyes and envisioned Ben's face, heard his voice with the slight Irish accent, felt the touch of his strong broad hands. Then, she would sit up and focus on the task at hand. She impatiently waited for graduation a few short months away. She looked forward to the promise of spring, hopeful that Ben might soon tell her more about his secret life and become a free man. There were times when she thought that naïveté could be her Achilles heel.

CHAPTER 15: Observation Leads to Frustration

The next day, watching from his window, Ben observed Lara as she got into the white Bentley with Eliot Stone. He noticed Eliot was dressed to the nines and imagined he was trying to look younger. Well, he did. He looked like someone right off the cover of GQ. But, he was a girly-man in Ben's book. But, maybe that's the type of guy Lara liked—or not.

He sensed Lara had been putting Eliot off as she poured her attention into renovating his office and spending time with him at the gun range, the dojo, and walking Einstein. In fact, Ben had managed to monopolize a good deal of Lara's time since meeting her. He phoned Rusty McManus and asked for more information on Eliot.

Rusty sighed. "She's not seeing that guy again, is she?"

Ben probed further. "What is it about this guy? I want to know *everything*." Rusty answered. "He's her mentor, nothing more. I don't think you have much to worry about. If Lara was going to be interested in him—in that way—she would've shown signs of it long before now."

"But, she's young—and inexperienced—you know what I mean." Ben pondered.

"She is young and inexperienced, but she's not easily swayed. Hell, you must know that by now. Ha!"

"Yes. She sticks to her guns on all fronts, let's just say. No big deal. Let her enjoy the art museum with Eliot Stone—I've got some business to attend to anyhow." Ben exhaled.

Meanwhile, Ben had a private rendezvous of his own

tonight. The thorough background check on Bill Stephens brought up multiple aggravated sexual assaults on his record. Why Eliot Stone did not discover this in a simple background check before hiring him was a mystery. Ben planned on making sure Stephens would be paid a little visit. He knew the pub he frequented and exactly what time he would be leaving to drive home. He stopped by the police station to make sure a few officers were waiting to pinch him for driving while intoxicated.

Ben spent the better part of an hour tossing Stephens' filthy apartment in a seedy section of town that night. He discovered a raft of child pornography on his computer and made an anonymous tip to the local sheriff. And to create the perfect trifecta, a particularly nasty homicidal maniac named "Tiny" was waiting in the local prison for Stephens to arrive. The laundry list of charges would put Bill Stephens away for a lengthy period and Ben wanted to ensure his time behind bars would be wretched.

Although he would have preferred to have put a bullet through Stephens' head, he knew the wisest course was to trip him up with his own rotten deeds. He always used the easiest method to undercut an evil person. He chose the safest and least lethal means possible, *this time*.

When Lara returned, Ben heard her walk up the squeaky stairs, and within ten minutes, he was standing at her door with Einstein.

"Sorry to bother you, but do you have some coffee I can borrow?"

"Yes, sure. Come in." Lara smiled.

He waited as she found some coffee in the cupboard.

"Hazelnut, right?"

"Yes, please. Oh, by the way, Lara, I heard that Stephens is behind bars, without bail, awaiting trial and sentencing."

"Oh good—that's a relief." She handed him the coffee. "Coming in?"

"Only if you're not busy."

"I'm not busy—just went to the art museum to see a new collection."

"Yes, I saw you leaving in the Bentley. Eliot, is that his name?" Ben feigned ignorance as he sat on the sofa.

"Yes, he's the owner of Stone & Associates—you know that's the architectural firm where I'm doing my internship."

"Seems like a nice guy." Ben muttered.

"He's a good boss—and mentor—always teaching me new things. I can't wait to graduate and be on my own."

Einstein whined to go outside. "I've got to take him out for a bit. Thanks for the coffee." Ben moved across the room and took her into his arms and took hungry possession of her mouth. He couldn't help himself. "Sorry, I just had to do that."

Lara watched him open the door and disappear down the staircase with Einstein at his heels. She smiled to herself and touched her wet lips with her finger. She whispered, "Don't be sorry, Ben. Don't *ever* be sorry."

Finished for the day at the architectural firm, Lara could not wait to get to the pink Victorian. She planned to meet Ben for Einstein's usual afternoon walk. The late November sun was setting earlier now. Her final site visits for most of her architectural projects went smoothly and the clients were extremely pleased with the results. Arriving home, she put the Fiat out back. As Lara walked onto the porch Professor Harris was there to greet her.

"Hello..." she said with surprise. "Come in, please." Lara unlocked the door and Harris lumbered slowly up the stairs.

"Coffee, tea, or brandy?" She asked.

"Brandy, if you have what I like." he smiled. Harris knew Lara had his favorite brandy on the entry table ever at the ready for him. He had made a few visits to her place, usually with serious intention. The last time he came he talked about his wife, Greta. She had recently died, and Lara knew he was depressed and lonely. His wife was the love of his life and he enjoyed telling stories about her.

But today she sensed he was not here to reminisce about his wife. Harris had always been a good friend and a favorite professor. Lara poured brandy for him as he sank into the down-filled armchair. "I could sleep in this thing." he joked.

She pulled up the ottoman and sat close to him. "What have I done to deserve a personal visit from my favorite professor?" Lara queried. He fumbled with his pipe. She pulled the ashtray toward him. This was going to be a long conversation if the pipe was involved.

"I miss your visits to my office late in the day, my dear, but I know you've been visiting Ben and Einstein, just down the hall." He began slowly. "Lara, I want to talk with you about Ben..." Here it comes. She was expecting this. "You know Ben is married and has a child."

Her heart skipped a beat, but she sat still and listened.

"But, more importantly, you need to understand that Ben is married to his work. He is a unique individual; a bit obsessive, maybe even compulsive, in regard to his chosen profession. I think he finds his consulting cases to be a safe-haven from his personal problems. I never had a son, but Ben has filled that void. I brought Ben here to Maine and arranged for him to bump into you at the reception. I had a strong sense that the two of you needed to meet. I'm not playing matchmaker, mind you." He puffed. "But, I think you make a unique couple."

Lara stared into her professor's dark eyes. Oddly, she had sensed Harris was instrumental in her meeting Ben.

Harris went on. "Lara, over the last few weeks it has become obvious to me that Ben is taken with you. This is not a casual type of thing; it's the love that comes along once in a man's lifetime. He has spent countless hours talking with me about you, plotting to make you his wife."

Trying to maintain composure, Lara knew she could not disguise the joy that must have lit up her eyes.

"There's only one wrinkle. Even though Ben is getting a divorce from Sienna he will always be required to travel to Canada to see William, and these visits may be difficult for your relationship. Sienna is an evil woman. Under normal circumstances Ben never would have married her. But he did marry her at a very young age because she was pregnant. He tried to make it work but now he is divorcing her. But, here's the rub: by divorcing Sienna, Ben is losing William."

Lara thought for a moment. "But, won't Ben have parental rights? Ben would be sacrificing his relationship with William to be with me?" It was as if Lara had to repeat the sentence to fully understand its magnitude.

Harris looked down at the floor, "Yes, this is the choice Ben is wrestling with. If he has the strength to make the choice, I hope he has the fortitude to live with the results." He shifted in his chair and took a series of puffs on the pipe before he spoke again. "There is another thing about Ben that you need to know, Lara." She watched his demeanor change. He was no longer looking in her eyes, but now focused on the pipe in his hand. "Ben's consulting group does secret government work and you must never speak of his work to anyone. He is a professor here at the university, but the bulk of his time is dedicated to consulting. Whenever you speak of Ben, you need to talk about him being a professor, nothing more. I am not at liberty to tell you more than that, except to warn you, the consulting work Ben does is risky. It will take a special woman to understand him and tolerate his unstructured life. I just want you to know what you are getting into."

"What am I getting into?"

"Has Ben told you about his life as a young boy?"

"No. Why? What was his childhood like?"

"Ben was the last of seven children who grew up in the

suburbs of Boston. There were four girls and three boys in the Irish Catholic Keegan Family. Having emigrated from Ireland, his father, Jonathan Keegan, is a well-educated man. He started off as a stock broker, then later became a successful hedge fund manager. His mother, Catherine—my sister—is half English and half Irish. She made a fulltime career out of housekeeping and cooking for all seven children taking especially good care of her husband."

"That seems perfect."

"It is, really. There's a love between Jonathan and Catherine Keegan that every man hopes to experience once in his lifetime. My sister, Ben's mother, dotes on his father, caters to his every whim. She cooks his favorite foods, washes his shirts just the way he likes them, and there's a raging love affair between them—even now. His mother is an incredible beauty with blonde hair and brown eyes. Ben's father worships the ground his wife walks upon. He never forgets their anniversary and many times I've walked into a room when they were embracing. After many years of marriage, they still kiss and hold hands. Maybe that sounds corny..."

"No, it's *beautiful*—go on."

"Ben's father is a stern and serious businessman, but a loving supportive father. He taught Ben to go for what he wanted without holding back. He did not believe in doing anything half-way. Ben *lives* for his father's approval. He would throw himself into any project with full force. This enthusiastic approach worked for Ben as a young man in high school. He swam and ran long distance competitively and placed first consistently. He got into weight lifting and marathons in the last years of high school, gaining more muscle. Senior year, he met a personal trainer at the gym. That was the turning point for him. His trainer, a former marine, encouraged Ben to become a marine. Ben's parents were in their late thirties when they had him, thus the least attention was paid to him. His older siblings have carved out comfortable lives for themselves and most of them live in New England, except for one. His older brother, Patrick, had moved to New York City and gained employment on Wall Street with a well-known brokerage firm. Ben often spent time with Patrick in New York. When 9/11 happened, his brother Patrick perished, and Ben's path was clearly set before him. He felt a sense of duty."

Lara expelled a deep breath. "Oh God, I didn't know this."

"After four years at the U.S. Naval Academy in Annapolis, Ben knew he had found his calling. Once he arrived at boot camp in Great Lakes Illinois, he threw himself into the harsh environment. Ben understood that what he learned at basic training was an appetizer; Ben's entrée would be earning his trident as a Navy SEAL and he poured his heart and soul into that one singular goal. His dream was being given the chance to use on the battlefield all that he had been taught. He was deployed with his SEAL platoon to Iraq, then Afghanistan: Tom, Elvis, Nate, Gus, Jake, Sam, and Javier, they were together for eight years. However, Sam and Javier never returned."

"Oh no, I'm sorry to hear that..." Lara whispered.

"If there was one thing that Ben could change, it would be making the drunken decision to sleep with Sienna without using protection. Sorry to be so blunt, but it's true. He met her at a club a few nights after completing basic training in Illinois. Sienna was trolling with a group of her modeling friends and she was all over him that night. He was a young man filled with too many beers and way too much testosterone, and he enjoyed Sienna's attention. She was a tall blonde runway model from Canada, three years older than him, with big brown eyes. She threw herself at him and he ended up in the sack with her that night. He saw Sienna a couple of times before he left for a trip to Ireland, then back to the states for the challenge of his life: Navy SEAL training. He had no way of knowing he had impregnated Sienna."

"Oh, he *didn't know*?"

"No. He had no idea." Harris took a puff on is pipe. "Becoming a Navy SEAL requires extreme physical and mental agility and the sense of mind to make rapid decisions, while carrying out operations as part of a team under the most stressful conditions. I asked him about SEAL training, and Ben was at a loss for words to describe the horrendous, exhausting, demanding, sometimes torturous experience. He knew it would be the challenge of his life. For starters, the odds of even completing SEAL training were not high. Only 25% even make it to SEAL training. The drop-out rate is high."

Lara stared at Harris. "Yes. It sounds difficult."

"Ben could not have chosen a higher bar. The mental acuity required was mind-boggling, but he threw himself into learning foreign languages, mathematics, science, mechanics, electronics, and physics. He is an avid speed reader with the ability to retain every detail. Ben is gifted with the ability to recall images, sounds or objects in memory with great precision. The physical training tests were beyond tough: push-ups, pull-ups, sit-ups, competitive 500-yard swims, and runs wearing boots and trousers, often with no rest periods. Blisters, bleeding skin from sand abrasion, exhaustion—all of this was prior to the most intense boot camp in the world at Great Lakes, Illinois."

"Oh gosh."

"Once at boot camp, Ben had more physical endurance tests and mental challenges that pushed him to the breaking point. It was during the grueling second phase of BUD/S in Coronado California that he found out in a phone call that Sienna was pregnant. He arranged for their marriage to take place in hospital over a weekend while he nursed a pulled muscle. The ceremony was brief and handled by a judge. He never had a honeymoon with Sienna because he was immediately dispatched back to Coronado California to finish his basic underwater demolition training. BUD/S, a 24-week challenge pushed him further into mental and physical hardness. He swam with his legs and hands bound, survived surf torture, cold water exposure for lengthy periods of time, performed endless calisthenics and ran miles in cold, wet clothing. *And that was just the beginning.* The physical conditioning ramped up to a 7-week course where he ran four miles in boots, swam two miles in the ocean, participated in obstacle courses and learned small boat skills."

"Wow...amazing."

"The frosting on the cake was the fourth week, fondly referred to as Hell Week, where Ben trained for five and a half days with four hours of sleep. This is the ultimate test of any human being's physical and mental stamina. Although he fought hallucinations, Ben found that he could do much more than he ever thought possible. He also learned how critical it was to depend upon and work within a team. He moved into the land warfare phase for the next 7 weeks learning land navigation, patrol techniques, rappelling, marksmanship and military explosives. Parachute Jump School was exhilarating and took place at Tactical Air Operations in San Diego. He started with the basic static line jump and accelerated to free falls. Soon he found himself jumping out of moving aircraft with sixty pounds of combat equipment from 9,500 feet. Another twenty-six weeks of (SQT) SEAL Qualification Training ensued. Although most grueling, this was Ben's favorite phase as it included survival, evasion, resistance, escape school, and tactical air operations, where he honed his physical and mental abilities. The final leg was filled with tactics, techniques, and procedures. He was put though cold-weather survival, marine operations, advanced combat swimming, close-quarter combat and land-warfare training. Sienna had the baby as Ben finished BUD/S. He was unable to visit her as he spent the next 26 weeks in SQT. He only laid eyes on his infant son, William, once before his first deployment."

"Oh, no. He only saw his son once?"

"Yes. Ben became part of a platoon and a valuable team member. When he finally earned the prestigious Navy SEAL Trident at graduation, he knew it would only be the beginning for him. He felt as if he had been trampled to death and literally brought back to life. Ben's area of expertise is asymmetrical land warfare, tactical non-conventional combat, with a specialty in explosive ordinates. He is also a skilled sniper. His time in theater was spent capturing high-value enemy targets in Iraq and Afghanistan. Setting up drone attacks, Ben also secretly worked with countries bordering the region. He collected intelligence through special reconnaissance missions, as he scouted both enemy installations and enemy movement, setting up air support in battles."

"This is fascinating, Harris. Ben never told me this." Lara leaned forward.

"I know he hasn't. But you need to know—twice Ben was captured by enemy forces. Once he suffered severe beatings, cigarette burns and mutilation with a rusty razor blade. He escaped. Another time in captivity he was saved by his tactical team, guided by an Israeli operative named Moshe. Gus, Elvis, Javier and Nate found him thanks to Moshe's pinpoint accuracy. Ben was minutes from being beheaded. In fact, the sword that was to be used was packed in his belongings. It's an unusual piece, hand forged and heavy. *He never wanted to forget the barbaric enemy he was fighting.* The beheading sword serves as a reminder that his enemy did not adhere to rules of engagement. They are brutal, savage animals. He never wants to forget how close he came to death. It serves as a constant reminder to live life to the fullest every day because it could be his last."

"That's the sword—oh yes, I held it in my hands—it's mounted on his wall in his office."

"Ben is just now beginning to conquer the nightmares and insomnia. He understands the medical explanation of his night terrors. They're due to the gruesome nature of his missions and going for years without a normal sleep pattern, fueled by caffeine and adrenaline. And he's accepted the sleep problems for what they are—physiological, not mental weakness. Ten years of Ben's life consisted of irregular schedules and sleep deprivation for long periods of time, which threw off his Circadian rhythm. It merely proves he's human."

Harris rose and stood next to Lara. "I want you and Ben to be happy together. But I also want you to go into this relationship understanding everything there is to know about Ben. If you need to talk, you know you can always find me in my office, my dear."

The faint smell of his pipe hung in the air. He touched her arm lightly before closing the door behind him. This conversation was very difficult for Harris to carry out. He prepared his words carefully. Lara quickly rewound back to the part where he said Ben was *taken* with her, wanted to make Lara his *wife*.

Sitting back on the ottoman Lara took a long deep breath and attempted to collect her thoughts. She knew she could not stop seeing Ben now, at this juncture. She felt compelled to be with him. This type of relationship with a man, for Lara, had always been elusive. She had never been taken by surprise in this way. Her relationships, her life, every tiny detail, was planned and put on a daily checklist. Lara's dreamt of being married and having children by the age of thirty. She was now twenty-four, almost twenty-five. Was Ben the one? He seemed to appear in her life overnight. There were moments when Lara was terrified by the intensity of her feelings for him. Then there were moments when she felt exhilarated and completely alive in his presence. Professor Harris had arranged the meeting and thought she was the perfect woman for Ben. *If only Ben wasn't married.*

CHAPTER 16: *Thanksgiving ~ or Bust*

Excited to have Ben in her life for Thanksgiving and Christmas, the holidays took on special meaning for Lara. Being an only child, Lara typically visited her mother and closest friends the week of Christmas. The holidays always magnified her grief of her father's sudden death. Lara's widowed mother, Lillian, at the age of fifty-two, moved into a condo community on the coast of Maine. She had friends, played cribbage, and traveled extensively. Lara kept in touch with her and visited whenever she could. She usually invited her mother for Thanksgiving and drove up to visit her for Christmas.

Lara had a special feeling about the holidays. If she had to define the spirit that filled her, she would describe it with one word: *hopeful*. She was optimistic that someone might come into her life to alleviate the aching loneliness in her heart.

Lara planned a Thanksgiving feast for Ben that Martha Stewart would envy. Not accustomed to cooking, she followed recipes and tackled meal preparation with the careful study of a scientist. She wanted to impress Ben. Stuffed turkey breast, roasted vegetables and gingerbread muffins with cream cheese frosting were prepped to near perfection. She invited her mother, Don and Olivia Henderson, Rusty, and Professor Harris to join them. The dining table could easily hold a party of eight.

Everything seemed to be in order until she received a last-minute phone call from Ben.

"I'm sorry. I'm at the airport and I need to get on a plane right away."

"What? Why?" Lara tried to remain calm.

"It's my son. There's an emergency. He's in hospital, that's all I know right now. I can't tell you how sorry I am that I will miss that wonderful meal. Once I get more information, I'll text you." Then, he paused, "Can you take care of Einstein for me?"

"Sure. I hope everything's all right, Ben."

"I've got to run. I'm so sorry, Lara. Really, I am."

Ben sounded exhausted and hung up in a hurry. Lara's heart sank. She would have Thanksgiving dinner, minus Ben. As planned, it was in Ben's lovely dining room. Lara glanced down at Einstein. "They're due to arrive any moment, buddy."

Lara was longing to see her mother. Lately, she had become a slower driver and didn't like to drive at night. Don and Olivia called last minute and asked if they could add their nephew, Eric, to the guest list. He had just arrived from Boston unexpectedly. Lara said, yes, of course.

Don, Olivia and Eric arrived first. Lara helped them put their coats away in the entry. Rusty and Professor Harris arrived moments later. Harris politely asked if he could light his pipe and all agreed it would be fine. The aroma of cherry tobacco wafted through the room. Lara's mother, Lillian, arrived last and Lara introduced her to each person.

Lara noticed Rusty's demeanor change the moment he laid eyes on her mother. Lara sensed her mother was unaware of Rusty's keen interest in her. Once all had assembled, Lara took the guests on an informal tour of Ben's large beautiful Victorian apartment and they marveled at the beauty of every little detail. It was obvious to Lara that Rusty had taken a special interest in her mother, and it was sweet how he intentionally sat next to her at the table. Their conversation was quiet and steady. Lara paid close attention to their body language.

Thanksgiving was a dreary, rainy day, but the fresh flowers brightened the room bringing fragrance and life. Lara had filled Ben's apartment with flowers, knowing her mother would love them. White roses in the bedroom and bath, a mixture of mums and sunflowers placed in low glass containers on the dining table and buffet mixed with miniature pumpkins and gourds. Peonies brightened the kitchen. The food was perfection. Don sat in the seat at the head of the table and expertly carved the turkey. Einstein was delighted to have a house full of people petting him.

Lara felt Eric watching her throughout the meal. He sat directly across from her at the table and in between bites, kept up a running conversation about his life and work.

"The meal is delicious. You're quite a cook!"

"Well, not really. This is only the second turkey I've ever roasted."

"So, my uncle tells me you're going to be an architect?"

"Oh no. Not an architect. Maybe a designer. I don't have the skills to be an architect."

"Ah, don't downplay your talents…" Harris spoke up as he overheard them. "She's brilliant. She'll probably run her own firm someday. That's what I'd guess. You should see what she did with Ben's office at the university—incredible."

Lara felt her face turn pink. She finished her meal as she listened to the others chatter. She wondered if it was obvious that her heart was aching for Ben. The conversation around the table became about Ben. Her mother looked up. "What's this? You did Ben's office?"

"Um, yes." Lara dabbed her mouth with a napkin. "It's my master's project. I have a few photos, I'll show you later."

"Sounds intriguing." Olivia smiled.

"That's how you two met?" Eric asked.

"Well, I met Ben at Professor Harris' concert. But, yes, you could say I got to know Ben quite well renovating his office. And, walking Einstein everyday together. He's a former Navy SEAL, you know. He's brilliant. I love talking with him."

Lara could not seem to stop herself from babbling on with admiration for Ben. Suddenly, the room became silent.

Lara's mother announced. "I was so hoping to meet Ben today. It's too bad he was called away suddenly."

Harris chimed in. "Ben is like a son to me. I so respect his service to the country."

Don and Olivia talked about meeting Ben at the restaurant. "He's an impressive young man—how old is he, Lara?"

"Thirty-One, I think." She suddenly realized everyone in the room was fascinated with Ben.

Rusty put his two cents worth in, in his own inimitable way. "Here's my take on this guy: if he makes Lara happy, then I *like* him. If he makes Lara unhappy, ever, then, I will make him pay." The guests laughed.

After dinner everyone sat in the parlor enjoying gingerbread muffins and fresh coffee. Sitting next to Lara as he finished off dessert, Eric talked non-stop, bragging about his latest bonus and promotion at the financial firm where he worked. Eric helped Lara collect the empty coffee cups to put them into the dishwasher, allowing them to be alone for a few moments in the kitchen.

The guests were busy finding their coats when Eric said, "Go say goodbye to your guests, I'll fill the dishwasher and wash these pans."

Lara nodded. "Okay. Thanks."

One-by-one, the guests left early, as a snow squall was threatening. Lara's mother gave her a hug. "Thanks, honey, for including me tonight. It was great fun. I'll meet Ben next time."

"Drive carefully, Mom."

Rusty gave Lara a hug and a wink. She stood in the window watching them all drive away. Only one vehicle was left—a black Infinity. She startled when she felt a tap on her shoulder.

"Oh, hey—I didn't know you were still here. Didn't you come with your aunt and uncle?"

"No, I followed them here—I'm heading out to see a friend. Thanks for the great dinner. I really enjoyed this."

"Well, thanks for loading the dishwasher. I've got to clean this place up and take the dog for a walk." She grabbed Eric's coat off the hook in the entry and handed it to him.

"Lara, would you join me for lunch tomorrow? I'm not

going back to Boston until Sunday." Eric was now imploring her with his eyes, putting her on the spot.

"Thanks for asking, but I've got plans for tomorrow, actually the whole weekend." Lara lied as she moved toward the door. Eric took his coat, slipped it on, and exited to the stairway. He turned and waved goodbye and Lara closed the door.

Thanksgiving was over, but Lara was not feeling thankful; she was missing Ben. The house was quiet with guests gone, and she worked expertly cleaning Ben's dining room, the kitchen counters, and took Einstein outside for a few minutes. Back inside, she decided to linger until the dishwasher finished. As she waited, she spied Ben's laptop on his kitchen counter. That's odd. She remembered moving it to the pantry earlier when she was cooking. She didn't want his laptop to get messy. As Lara stacked the dishes into the cabinet, she wondered if she just thought she moved the laptop; lately she'd been absentminded, thinking about Ben. Finally, she locked Ben's apartment door and brought her canine companion to her parlor. The dog seemed to sense her loneliness and he cuddled against her as she turned on the television. Exhausted, she must've fallen asleep on the sofa. The hour was late when her phone rang. It was Ben.

"Happy Thanksgiving." He said in a muted voice. It was midnight, but he was in Canada in a different time zone. She was happy to hear his voice, but not the news he had to share.

"My son, William, had a seizure and the physicians at the hospital are not able to determine what caused it. A number of tests have been conducted to rule out various possibilities." Ben sounded dreary. "It's unbearable."

"Oh, I'm sorry, Ben."

"It's not William who's unbearable, it's Sienna."

"How long do you think you'll be there?" Lara asked, afraid to hear the answer.

"William is stable. It's Sienna who is making this into a circus. She's fighting with the doctors and she has William frightened. A seizure is no small thing, but it could be the result of William's hockey game two nights ago. He was roughed up badly and suffered a mild concussion. Sienna pulled him off the hockey team and William is now furious with her. I am not a father but a referee between these two. I'll try to catch a flight home tomorrow morning."

Lara said goodnight but hung up the phone with a feeling of apprehension. Would this be Ben's life—running to Canada at Sienna's beck and call—leaving at the drop of a hat to travel to faraway lands for his consulting work? She trudged to her bedroom with Einstein close behind. He slept on the foot of her bed and she was comforted with his presence.

Eric felt he might at least get a lunch date with Lara, but she wasn't coming under his spell as he thought she would. He knew the moment he spoke with her in person at the Thanksgiving table she was infatuated with Ben Keegan. He was intent on forging a relationship with Lara. To do so, he would need to drive a wedge between Lara and Ben. He knew as long as this Ben was around, no other guy would have a chance. He had to find a way to make the former Navy man less appealing or unavailable.

Ideas were brewing. He had a few flash drives in his pocket from work. He was constantly downloading financial data and moving it from one device to another. When he attached it to Keegan's computer, he didn't even realize the machine was running. It came out of sleep mode without needing the password, which made his download quick and easy, a bonus he hadn't expected. He'd planned to take the laptop without Lara's knowledge—but, now he didn't need to.

Alone in his room, he plugged the flash drive in and planned to dive into whatever he'd captured. *Damn!* Everything was encrypted. He scrolled through pages and pages—finally giving up. However, he noticed some photos of Lara on there—not just her, but the two of them together. These were more valuable. He had an idea that someone might be interested in them.

How could Lara refuse him—just like that? He was accustomed to getting his way. As an only child, Eric had been showered with attention. His parents sent him to the finest schools and provided a sheltered childhood in one of the best neighborhoods in Boston. He liked the feeling of being the guy on top. Many of his dates were from on-line services. He had a penchant for the most beautiful women, models, actresses, singers and dancers—and the ones on this dating service seemed to be void of intellect. Until now, that lifestyle had suited him. But lately he noticed his college chums and colleagues at work had wives and homes and families. They were far ahead of him in the world of acquisition, and this didn't sit well with Eric.

Tagging along for the Thanksgiving feast gave him the chance to meet Lara. Uncle Don had mentioned her a year ago, saying what a wonderful young woman she was. At that time, Eric was engaged to Nicole and was under the impression he was going to be married. But that never happened because she ran off with his best friend. So much for loyalty.

Eric really didn't trust anyone after that. People were good at saying one thing and doing another. He was still resentful about Nicole walking out and had found ways to compensate for his emotional wounds. Sleeping around and using alcohol helped take his mind off Nicole. But he still harbored the anger he felt being discarded with such indifference.

Lara was the type of trophy wife he wanted, and he would go to great lengths to gain her trust and affection. The one thing that disturbed him was the fact that Ben Keegan had moved into a condo in her building, right next door to her. Even though she was infatuated with Ben, Lara had to know he was married. From conversations with uncle Don, he knew Lara had strong principles when it came to guys. Ben Keegan being a married man was off limits for Lara—or *was* he?

Eric had left his cashmere scarf at Ben's place—he knew it

was the perfect excuse to stop by the next night. He had also installed an app on Lara's phone; whenever she got a phone call or text, he'd get a notification. The app recorded everything. Eric slept fitfully and woke late the next morning, then showered and decided not to shave. He thought he looked older with a bit of facial hair. He checked the app on his phone. She had a phone call from Keegan—it was late, around midnight. Keegan sounded frustrated—he was going to be gone for a while, or so it sounded. He still had some time.

He went to the dojo where his uncle worked and hung out for a while, but Lara didn't show there. He also drove through the campus where Keegan worked. The pictures of Keegan's office that Lara redecorated showed three computer screens on his desk. He wondered how he could gain entry but noticed security guards were making their rounds on a regular basis—and there were cameras everywhere. He slipped the brass key out of his pocket that was marked *office*. He'd found it in Keegan's coat in the entry when he had dinner there. That was almost too easy.

He stopped at a little jewelry shop in the city and found a perfect necklace for Lara.

"Wrap it, please—I'll take it."

***

Late in the day, Einstein stood by the door, then whined. Lara leapt off the sofa realizing it was time for his walk. She swore Einstein could tell time. Lara wondered what Ben was doing in Canada. When she glanced at her phone, she noticed she had missed a brief text saying something about possibly being home the next day. The time zone was different—and she tried to guess what time it might've been when he sent that text. Lara donned her warm coat and gloves, then clipped the dog's leash onto his collar and took Einstein for a long walk. They passed by the beautiful ornate purple Victorian, the house that Ben said he wanted to buy for her.

"We have the same taste in houses." Lara whispered to the dog, thinking of Ben. Einstein stared back at her, then tugged on his leash. They resumed walking down to the ocean; then several blocks back to the pink Victorian. As Lara approached the porch, she noticed the figure of a man standing beneath the porch light. When he turned around, she recognized Eric.

"What brings you here?" She stayed on the walkway for a moment and stared up at him. She wasn't about to go inside until he was gone. The sun was setting as Lara stepped up onto the porch, her hand moved over the Glock beneath her coat.

"I'm sorry, but I think I lost my scarf. It's green, cashmere, I just noticed it wasn't in my car."

"You're just noticing this now?" Lara suddenly felt uncomfortable. "If I find it, I'll give it to your uncle. I see him often."

"Listen, I'll wait here—you can go inside and check." Eric

suggested. "I'll stay here."

She waited there for a split-second, then decided she'd check Ben's apartment quickly. She just wanted him to go. "Yes, you wait here."

After bolting the door, she dashed upstairs to Ben's condo with Einstein on his leash and found the scarf underneath one of Ben's coats. Maybe the coats got jumbled when everyone left on Thanksgiving. It was green cashmere as described. She stepped back out onto the porch, kept her distance and handed the scarf to Eric.

"There you go."

"Thanks, I appreciate this. It was a gift from my aunt Olivia." Eric turned and descended the stairs, then got into the black Infinity—waved, and sped away.

Lara let out a sigh of relief. She hated surprise visits from strange men. If only Eric knew how close he came to...*oh, stop obsessing*. She tried to let her anxiety dissolve. *He was gone. Nothing happened*. Once inside, she removed her coat and snuggled on the sofa with Einstein. Lara's phone rang five minutes later. She recognized Ben's number.

"Lara, I'm here and I need to talk with you."

"What do you mean you're *here*? So soon?" Lara was surprised. She was expecting him tomorrow morning. It was late, but Ben was insistent on seeing her at that moment. She sensed something ominous happened on his urgent trip to Canada. Within two minutes Ben appeared at Lara's door. Einstein was ecstatic to see him, but Ben looked weary and wasn't smiling. He briefed her on the medical situation with William, recounting his angry concerns with Sienna's overly dramatic behavior. Ben's blue eyes did not contain their usual spark; he looked beaten. Lara sat with him on the sofa and took his hand.

"I'm sorry, Ben, that this was so difficult."

Once his anger with Sienna subsided, Ben apologized again for his absence during Thanksgiving. "Harris sent me an e-mail praising your cooking abilities and even attached a picture of the turkey dinner. He also mentioned Eric's attendance at the table. Was that *him* on the porch?"

"Yes."

"What was *he* doing here? He seemed a bit friendly with you. I mean you just met the guy. I was parked in the truck— hadn't gotten out yet, was checking my phone for messages."

It became impossible for Lara to look at Ben's face at that moment. He seemed hurt, angry, and tired, and now experiencing the same insecurity Lara felt about his wife. It was unsettling for Lara when Ben told her he was going off to where Sienna was, where they shared a home and a son. She had concerns about what Sienna might do next to manipulate Ben back to Canada.

"Ben, we're both tired and need to get some sleep."

However, Ben was not ready to let go of the subject of Eric. He continued to question Lara about her relationship with him.

"Who *is* this guy, Lara? And, what is he doing with you on the front porch? Was he here with you tonight in your apartment?" Then, when he realized she was not responding, he abruptly changed course. Ben whispered. "Oh damn. I'm sorry, I shouldn't be saying this. Yes, I'll go."

Lara watched as he closed the door in slow motion, then listened to his footsteps as he receded down the creaky staircase. Lara's heart was in her throat and she fought back the urge to run after him as a tear trickled down her cheek. As she snuggled into bed, she realized how that probably looked—her on the front porch with Eric. It was just a misunderstanding.

Ben silently berated himself for losing control with Lara. How could he have been so foolish? She was smart, single and beautiful. She probably had a line of potential suitors a mile long. He felt a sense of urgency to secure a relationship with her now before another guy stepped in. He couldn't explain what came over him. No matter how tired, angry, or frustrated he was in the past, he had always maintained control. Suddenly he realized— he'd never been in love before. He never felt such a wave of raw jealousy sweep over him as he did when he witnessed Eric standing on the porch with Lara. Who *was* this character? She'd just met him, for God's sake. Ben sensed that he overreacted about Eric.

Filled with frustration, Ben was truly exasperated from the emotional trip to Vancouver to see William. He took a deep breath as he stripped off his clothing and started doing pushups slowly on the bedroom floor. Before taking a shower and hitting the sack he decided to work off some steam. He needed the exercise and the oxygen seemed to help him think more clearly. But after an hour of physical activity and a shower, Ben tossed and turned in bed. Lara was a wall away from him and she was on his mind constantly when he wasn't thinking about work. Ben's work had always been his substitute for a relationship, but not any longer. His priorities changed the moment he met her. Lara was now his main focus, and work was his distraction. Ben knew he was in love with her and his frustration was due to the fact he had to be a free man to win her heart.

***

Eric was pleased he'd managed to create a rift between the two. Now, if only he could expose Keegan for the fraud he was—a married man trying to act single. He had to learn more about Ben's wife. Then, once he knew enough about Keegan— he'd somehow expose him to Lara—maybe even anonymously. Or, did he want her to *know* he was one step ahead of Keegan? That might impress her. He wasn't sure yet how that would work out. But, he sensed that Keegan was playing Lara—leading her on. He was married and trying to engage her in his sordid little world. How many women had he done this with?

If he was unable to impress her, Eric had to appeal to Lara's sympathetic side, which he knew she had—but how? His mind worked furiously as he imagined ways to need her expertise. Driving through the neighborhood, he spotted a beautiful old Victorian—not far from her residence. He got out of his vehicle and walked around it—and noticed it was empty. No furniture inside. While he was parked in the driveway, another car pulled up and a middle-aged guy stepped out.

"Can I help you, sir?"

"This house—it needs a lot of work. You're a realtor, I see."

"Yes, I was just going to install this sign. This beauty is officially for sale, it's going on the market today, in fact."

"Well, I'm interested. Can I look inside?"

The realtor eagerly shook his hand, "I'm Steve Corey. Yes, I'll take you inside. I didn't catch your name. Are you from around here?"

"Eric Peterson—and I'm from Boston. But, I'd like a summer house in Maine. This one has a nice ocean view. It might fit the bill."

Saturday morning found Lara at the dojo with Don, punching and kicking her pent-up anger with him. When she arrived, she warmed up with the punching bag, she envisioned it was Bill Stephens. Then, she imagined it was Sienna, even though she had no idea who she was or what she was like. It was a wonderful diversion that served to defuse some of her frustration with Ben from the night before. After thirty minutes of pure concentration, sweating, and finally meditation, Don called it quits.

"You are distracted today, grasshopper. It's time for pancakes, let's go."

Lara changed and tossed her bag into the Fiat. They met at their usual brunch spot. Don had a concerned look on his face; Lara knew him well enough to sense they would be having a long conversation about something.

Pancake Heaven was clearing out. Don and Lara slipped into a quiet booth.

"Tell me what's going on with you ..." Don started. He seemed to have psychic abilities when it came to her. "Are you sure you're all right? You seemed really frustrated today. You kicked the crap out of me for the last half hour."

Lara smiled into his concerned eyes. "Ben saw Eric standing on my porch yesterday—picking up his scarf—you know, the one Olivia gave him."

"What scarf?"

"You know, the green cashmere—wait a minute—Olivia

didn't give him a scarf?"

"No. I don't think so. I'd have to ask her. That's not important. What happened?"

"Ben was angry. I didn't say anything. He questioned me. Ben was exhausted from the trip to Vancouver and just seemed irritated."

Don listened as concern filled his blue eyes. "Lara, I know Ben. He has spent a lot of time here at the dojo working with me to hone your martial arts skills. Did you say he was upset with you?"

"No, he didn't yell. In fact, he was quiet. But, he asked me about Eric, said something like *I'd just met the guy—what was he doing there*?"

Don leaned toward her. "Ben cares about you, deeply. He'd just spent twenty hours flying to and from Vancouver, was exhausted, had to deal with his soon to be ex-wife, and probably said some things without thinking."

Lara knew he was right.

"About Eric—he asked me to go out with him. He helped me in the kitchen on Thanksgiving." Lara stated with certainty. "I'm not interested."

Don laughed. "He asked me about you, Lara. I told him about your relationship with Ben. But I also told Eric it's not in your DNA to get involved with *married* guys."

Don was searching Lara's face for a reaction. She was never able to lie to him, not even a white lie. "Don't talk about me with Eric. I'm serious."

Don furrowed his brow. "If Eric gives you any shit, he's my nephew and I'll personally kick his ass."

There was silence for a moment as they finished eating.

"I do feel funny about Ben being *married*. How can I commit to a relationship with *him*? How can I be *sure* he will divorce Sienna?" Lara exhaled sharply. "Why doesn't he just divorce Sienna and get it over with?"

Don's eyes narrowed. "Maybe it's not that simple, Lara. There's a child involved in Ben's divorce, not to mention assets. These things can get messy. Give it some time."

As Lara drove home from brunch, she thought about Don's words. She needed to exercise patience, but also some good common sense.

Meanwhile, Christmas shopping was on Lara's to do list. She usually visited her mother for the Christmas holiday and it was rapidly approaching. The holiday break was a welcome reprieve from exams at school and several days off from the architectural firm. She picked up a few gifts for her mother. Then she walked into a unique clothing shop and contemplated buying a curve-hugging red sweater. As she tried it on, she daydreamed about Ben as she stared at herself in the full-length mirror. This sweater was provocative for her, but she felt bold today. Her holiday bag was almost packed.

Once her shopping was completed, Lara strolled into Rudy's Chowder House, a block away. Snow was lightly falling. As she opened the door to the pub, she suddenly felt a body bump into her from behind and quickly turned around.

"Hello, beautiful." Ben whispered.

Lara hadn't seen him since the rant he gave her about Eric on the porch.

"Ben, what are you doing here?"

He smiled. "Having lunch with you." They sat at the table by the window and a light of desire illuminated his soulful blue eyes. "I'm sorry—for last night—for interrogating you. I acted like an idiot. This has been frustrating for me, Lara."

This has been frustrating for me, too, Ben. Lara thought—*but* she didn't say it.

His eyes seemed to undress her. "I will miss you." He clutched her hand on the table with both of his. "I'm leaving for Virginia, and then out of the country early in the morning and I'll be gone until Christmas Day. I sent a text earlier, but you didn't reply. I thought you might be angry with me."

Lara quickly looked at her phone and noticed she had silenced it. "Oops, sorry, I was shopping, and had my phone off..."

He leaned forward and lowered his voice. "Yes, I saw your car pull away. I followed you to the clothing store. By the way, the red sweater you bought looks fantastic on you."

"Ben, have you been spying on me?"

A mischievous smile played upon his face. "I saw you walk toward Rudy's and thought I could catch lunch with you here. That's it!" He threw his hands up in the air with that dimpled smile she loved.

"I'm sorry if I embarrassed you." Ben was now the one blushing. He took her hand again, lightly. "Lara, I want to see you for Christmas." He had color in his cheeks, was unshaven, and smelled incredibly good. He was wearing the leather jacket and a black V-neck sweater. His pale blue eyes filled with intensity when they met hers. His smile was intoxicating; Lara suspected Ben was well aware of the effect he was having on her.

"Will it be okay if I keep in touch with you while I'm gone?"

"Yes, sure. Is this trip something to do with your secret agent life?"

"I guess you could say that. It sounds silly, though, doesn't it?" Ben smiled. He stood and slipped her coat on. She felt his lips against her neck as he whispered, "I'm gonna miss you, darlin."

Lara started missing him already as they parted and left Rudy's. She could sense Ben's eyes upon her as she walked toward her parked vehicle. Unlocking the door, she brushed her hair aside. She looked up and saw him leaning against a telephone pole staring at her. He smiled and waved. Then walked to his truck and got in. He sat in the truck as it idled, and she realized he was waiting for her to drive away first. Lara's mind turned to how she would fill the empty days without Ben. She phoned her mother on the way home and planned her Christmas visit.

CHAPTER 17: The Spirit of Christmas

Driving back to the apartment, Ben wished Lara could stow away on the plane with him. For the first time in his life he did not want to travel abroad for his consulting work. Even though the face-to-face visits would net him a great deal of information in a short period of time, he knew he would miss her. The thrill of the chase used to be the intel, now it was her. He had never been captivated by a woman like he had been with Lara.

Ben memorized every detail about her and brought her image to the forefront of his memory. While away, he would turn the details over repeatedly. Her eyes were a shade of green that took his breath away; they gave away her deepest secrets. He felt he belonged to her when his eyes met hers. He would replay slow dancing with her at the roadhouse, and how she embraced him on the motorcycle. The memories of Lara would sustain him in the long days ahead.

Trying not to think about Ben, Lara packed Einstein up and brought him with her to visit her mother, Lillian O'Connell. Although every time Lara stared into Einstein's eyes, she knew he missed Ben as much as she. The drive would be good for both of them. Lara's mother lived in an oceanfront condo a two-hour drive from Portland. As Lara approached the building, she noticed it was decorated with multi-colored lights for the holiday. Lara opened the door of the main lodge and saw her mother placing freshly cut boughs on the mantle in the community room and decorating a huge evergreen tree. She was serving hot chocolate to all who came by the table. Her hair was in a French twist and was now a lovely shade of pewter.

As she looked up and saw Lara approaching, her mother threw her arms into the air. "Hey! You're early!"

With a springy bounce in her step, Lara's mother moved toward her, beaming. The two sat in the atrium for a while and spoke about the coming holiday season. An avid gardener, her mother helped prepare the flower garden for the coming winter. Her interest now turned to oil painting. This was new.

Lara retrieved Einstein from her car and walked to her mother's cottage to have tea. A dog lover, her mother was delighted to see Einstein and petted him with affection.

"Oh, he's adorable. I met Einstein on Thanksgiving. That's a cute name. He's Ben's dog."

"Yes." Lara gazed at some of the sketches her mother was working on. "Hey, these are really good, mom!"

"Well, I love doing it. But, I sketch everything first on the canvas. Then, I start painting. For all my well laid plans, I can never decide until the last minute how I want it to look."

"I love the subject matter, mom, seriously—you're good!" She stared at landscapes, fruits, flowers, and garden scenes. The flower petals in her paintings looked so real—it was as if Lara could smell them.

In her private cottage her mother turned the conversation to Lara's life. Lara knew she had to fill her mother in about work, school and Ben—especially Ben.

"He teaches at the university—oh, you know that part. You didn't get to meet him at Thanksgiving, and he's away now until Christmas on business. But, I have a few pictures of him here on my phone. He hired me to decorate his office."

"Oh my—he's handsome, Lara!"

"Yes, he is—but he doesn't come off that way. I mean, he seems sort of unaware of how good looking he is."

"Where's he gone off to? Visiting his family for Christmas?"

"Well, this trip is business..." Lara hesitated. "But, there is one sticking point...he's married and has a son."

"Oh, okay."

"But, he's in the process of getting a divorce..."

"Well, if it's meant to be—it will happen. Your father was engaged to another girl when he met me. Meeting your father was just sort of accidental, he brought me some gasoline in a can—I was stranded on the side of the road. Falling in love was totally unexpected. That's how life is. Lara, I will only tell you this: when you marry, choose the man you are madly in love with--the guy that makes you feel secure. Marry the man you trust, who makes you laugh, who wants to be with you every minute of every day. That's how it was with your father. I have been so lonely since he died. Even though I have friends, it's not the same. It's like part of me died with him."

Lara paused for a moment, for the first time realizing how much her mother missed male companionship.

As her mother served tea, she nodded to Lara. "Come on—out with it. Tell me everything that you know about Ben."

"He's been calling and texting me ever since we met. He is not only handsome, but a man of integrity. He's a Navy officer, actually a Navy SEAL Lieutenant, retired now. He spent six years in the Middle East. He's teaching at the university. He owns a consulting firm and travels a lot."

"When you speak about Ben, your face lights up. Your eyes dance with excitement. I think he sounds like a wonderful person." For the first time, it dawned on Lara that her relationship with Ben could be the once-in-a-lifetime type of love that she yearned for.

Lara stayed for lunch and gave her mother a cashmere sweater for Christmas, a beaded necklace, a lovely pair of silver starfish earrings, and some new books to read. Her mother gave Lara the beautiful painting she had just finished, the roses with dew drops. Lara wrapped it in tissue paper and packed it into the

Fiat.

It occurred to Lara, although her mother had plenty of busy activities, her mother needed a male companion in her life. Her thoughts immediately turned to Rusty McManus. "Do you remember Rusty at Thanksgiving?"

"Yes, he said he would like to see me again. I really enjoyed his company." It had been a long time since Lara had seen her mother smile like that. Lara told her she was having a New Year's Eve soiree and wanted her to come and spend the night. Her mother eagerly agreed.

Lillian O'Connell was now a young widow, only fifty-two. Lara's father passed away two years earlier at the young age of fifty-six in an auto accident. Both women missed him terribly. Living in the house alone was not a good option for her mother as she was a social butterfly, the total opposite of Lara. Mom was in her element here. Even though there were lots of people and activities, and relatives nearby, there was something missing.

Lillian was too young and beautiful to be alone. Rusty McManus would be a good match. Lara knew she needed to work out the details. She added this task to her checklist. Lara hugged her mother and kissed her goodbye. The next stop was Rusty's cottage on the pond. She started driving late in the day planning to be there by early evening. Rusty was expecting her. Einstein snored in the passenger seat as she hummed along with Christmas songs.

The woodpiles at Rusty's cottage were neatly stacked. This was standard procedure for him. Usually, by December, he had his woodpiles assembled neatly on the West side of the cottage to help keep the wind and snow drifts down. His sturdy, rustic home was on the water on Panther Pond in Raymond, beautiful and secluded; it reminded Lara of the cottage in the movie *On Golden Pond*. The windows were energy efficient; he had a wind mill, a generator, and a sophisticated solar grid to keep everything running if the power went out.

Rusty was widowed several years ago, and Lara met him at a point in her life when she missed her father tremendously and he conveniently became her father figure. Rusty McManus had just celebrated his 58th birthday, but you'd never know it to look at him. He was in fantastic shape, constantly physically working.

Rusty warmly greeted her at the door with his usual bear hug.

"Come right in and join me by the fire." Einstein bounded out of the Fiat and Rusty affectionately rubbed the dog's ears. The cottage was toasty warm. She removed her coat and placed it on the peg in the mudroom, then slipped off her boots. It was natural for Lara to visit Rusty at his cottage. It was a short drive from Portland and she spent a great deal of time with him on the pond, swimming, boating, fishing, and just plain talking. Whenever she had free time, the two would be together at his shooting range.

Immediately, Rusty began to ask questions about Ben. Lara explained Ben flew to Virginia, then would be abroad consulting; she would see him on Christmas Day.

"Divorced yet?" Rusty asked.

"No, not yet." She exhaled and noticed how his brows knit together as he listened intently. He nodded as she spoke occasionally adding a word here or there. After Lara's delivery of events there was a lull in the conversation. She sensed that Rusty was about to share his deepest thoughts with her.

"Well, Lara, I'm aware there are other guys who would like your attention. For example, this Eliot Stone guy. Don't trust him. And, Eric Henderson, he's a big phony. But you need to know I am familiar with Ben. And, even though he is still married, I know he's a good man. And, knowing you as well as I do, I'm sure you have set some boundaries with him. I knew right away that he would pursue you. Being a good-looking guy, he has plenty of women throwing themselves at him, but he's not interested in those types. But I knew the fact that he was married would be a roadblock. I knew you would set limits with Ben to protect yourself. You are an independent woman with strong values and a good head on your shoulders. I'm proud of you." Lara's heart swelled with the praise he lavished upon her. His opinion really mattered.

Lara probed Rusty for more information about Ben and Dark Horse. She asked if he had ever heard of the group before Ben's background check.

"I knew of it. Dark Horse is well known in the intelligence community."

Lara trusted Rusty more than anyone. She shared her most intimate thoughts of Ben. "He's different from any guy I've ever met. I have tremendous respect for what he does for a living. Although he doesn't share details with me, I feel as if Ben is making a positive difference in the world."

As Rusty listened, Lara spoke with unbridled passion. He knew she was hooked. *He made a mental note to push Ben about getting the divorce wrapped up as soon as possible.*

Rising from his chair, Rusty retrieved two cold ginger ales from the fridge. The pair sat on the three-season porch overlooking the lake. Even though it was a cold December evening the porch was heated by the fire roaring in his wood stove. He always thought they did their best thinking looking at the water, sitting side by side, drinking ginger ale.

Rusty sat in silence next to Lara for a long time. Then, he spoke.

"Lara, I understand why you want to be with Ben. It's normal to want that. It's not normal for a man or a woman to live alone. There are some days I get mighty lonely up here by myself. It's not that I want a woman to take care of me—it's just that I miss female companionship. I wanted to ask about your mother. We had a great time at Thanksgiving, and I have been thinking about her ever since."

Rusty detected a smile, then she surprised him.

"Rusty, I think it's high time you had a date with my mother!"

"Do you really think she'd be interested in an old guy like me?"

"I *know* she would be. I just came from a visit with her and she mentioned how much she enjoyed your company, funny thing, eh?"

Rusty shared a simple dinner with Lara and they had their usual burping contest after drinking too much ginger ale. Laughing with Rusty was the relaxation Lara needed. They made s'mores and talked well into the night. Finally, Rusty hauled the sleeping bag out of the closet and laid it gently on the sofa for her as he had done so many times before.

"Goodnight, Lara. Get some rest. You will need to be at the top of your game to beat me at target practice tomorrow."

The next day was sunny and warm, which was unusual for December. They rose early and hiked to the back of his seven-acre property to the shooting range. They shot at targets for hours. He won for a while, but Lara finally bested him. He was a good-natured loser, and sometimes she wondered if he actually allowed her to win.

Rusty bought Lara a big breakfast before she drove away that morning. Lara gave him a new 9mm Glock for Christmas with a laser sight. He was thrilled. She told him to reserve New Year's Eve for dinner at her place, and said it was a sleepover. Rusty couldn't stop smiling.

Lara was happy with the little plan she was scheming to put Rusty and her mother together for New Year's Eve. As she pulled into the driveway behind the pink Victorian, she remembered she had left a book in Ben's office. She had a night or two to work on her master's thesis and decided to retrieve it. There was no one on campus except a skeleton security force during the Christmas break. She went into her condo and turned on the lights. Then, she fed Einstein and put on his leash for a walk to Ben's campus office.

As she strolled out of the driveway, she wondered where Ben was and what he was doing. The campus buildings were dark with only a few security lights on. Few people had access to the professors' building, but Lara had an extra key made when she worked as an assistant several years ago. As she walked down the corridor toward Ben's office, she tried to remember where she left her books. Using the key to Ben's office, she opened the door and she slipped inside with Einstein. She flipped the light switch on and searched for her books. For a few moments, she hesitated and admired Ben's office. "It's beautiful, isn't it, Einstein?"

She looked at the beheading sword on the wall across from his desk with the framed poem next to it and instinctively feared for his safety. She knew he was overseas on a secret mission but had no details. Then wondered if she *had* details, would she worry even more? It was difficult to concentrate on her school project knowing Ben was on the other side of the world, possibly in grave danger.

Ben's fleece jacket was draped on his office chair. Taking it in her hands she brought it to her face and closed her eyes as she inhaled his scent. He would not mind if she borrowed it. She grabbed her books and turned off the light, locked the door, and ushered Einstein back out to the campus green, now covered with a light dusting of snow.

Arriving back at the pink Victorian, Lara settled in to make Christmas cookies for Don and Olivia. She would visit them the next day.

***

The black Infinity slowly pulled alongside a side street not far from Lara's house and he followed far behind her, so she'd not notice him. He watched as she let herself into the building where Ben's office was and caught sight of her through a sliver of light from the window.

For some reason this place reminded him of where he spent most of his life—boarding school. He smiled as he recalled the ingenious pranks he played on his classmates in his youth. Christmas was one of the few breaks he got to go home to be with family. All the other kids went home to parents who missed them, a home-cooked meal and Christmas gifts. At the boarding school everyone looked forward to going home for two whole weeks, except him. He truly would have preferred to stay on at school because he was used to the routine there; it was all the family he had.

His fondest Christmas memories were of driving to Maine to spend the night with his Aunt Olivia and Uncle Don Henderson at the farmhouse. He especially remembered the Christmas dinner they served and the real Christmas tree that filled the house with the aroma of the holiday. He enjoyed opening gifts with his cousins. Eric suddenly realized his life had been a solitary existence. He spent a great deal of time yearning to belong to someone or something but was always rejected.

He knew Lara would be walking home with the dog—and she'd find a small package on her doorstep. He got back into his vehicle parked on a side street nearby. He didn't have far to drive. He was sleeping at his uncle's house for Christmas week. His parents were in Greece for the holiday this year. He wanted to remain close to Lara, especially while Keegan was out of town. He needed to sabotage Keegan. It might take some time, but time was something he had.

He finished off the rest of the vodka in his room at the farmhouse and spent the evening on several dating sites. He chatted with prospective women and arranged to meet a few of them for coffee. The first meeting had to be quick because he got bored easily. This was just a substitution for Lara and he knew it. But, until he could have her, this was his tonic for the emptiness he felt inside.

CHAPTER 18 ~ Israel and Beyond

Ben's first stop was to meet with Moshe in Israel. Moshe outfitted him with the finest weaponry, ammo, knives, and a sleek HK416 rifle, as well as a canvas bag filled with disguises, robes, beards, varied styles of sunglasses - the works. Meanwhile, Ben was receiving fine details about sleeper cells setting up in the New England area from his trusted friend. For the past six years they had forged a close bond having both suffered personal losses on 9/11. Moshe's motto was *Kill them wherever you find them.*

He was the most creative operative Ben ever worked with, monitoring him with the most sophisticated drone technology on the planet all while he was in Iraq and Afghanistan. Moshe also had a situation room filled with computers and dedicated hackers that rivaled the best CIA cyber-com hacks in the world. Moshe knew the NSA and many other intelligence agencies around the world monitored his every move, therefore, any communication using a cell phone, or the internet was scrutinized by prying eyes. But that didn't prevent Moshe from communicating constantly with Ben.

During his first tour in Iraq, Ben discovered what an incredibly valuable asset Moshe was to the United States but was smart enough to keep the relationship under wraps. The two men coordinated intelligence often. With Moshe's help, Ben neutralized numerous high value targets. As Ben's unit rescued American military hostages in theater, Moshe helped gather information to assist him. Moshe was much more than a friend to Ben. In Afghanistan when Ben was injured by an IED then captured by the Taliban, Moshe literally saved his life. Minutes from being beheaded, it was Moshe's quick reaction that helped Ben's SEAL team track him down and extract him. It was Moshe's voice on a crackling radio to Elvis reading him the exact coordinates of Ben's location that saved his life. Today's meeting with Moshe was critical. They would have private, open and unedited conversations today.

The armored Humvee approached a remote adobe building in a southeastern corner of Israel. Dust clouds covered the vehicle in the late evening hour. The nondescript building was surrounded with several layers of razor wire and hidden security cameras everywhere. An impressive fighting force separated into several tiers protected the perimeter of the property. Moshe was waiting for him. Ben was dressed in black wearing a hat with a wig, sunglasses and a fake beard. His skin was darkened with make-up. As Ben entered what appeared to be a large warehouse, one of Moshe's men came out to greet him. Lots of precautionary measures were taken in this part of the world. Once Ben was cleared, he entered the building and Moshe embraced him and spoke softly in Hebrew. "Chief, we have details to work out; then you must get the hell out of here before daylight." Moshe and Ben had devised a careful communication system utilizing a gardening blog and an on-line encrypted game called Dark Horse.

Through the on-line encrypted game, Ben was going to be coordinating drone strikes in the United States on sleeper cells operating right under the nose of Homeland Security, the FBI and other law enforcement agencies. This meeting with Moshe was done with the secret blessing of the Central Intelligence Agency. Ben and Moshe found it ironic that Muslim Brotherhood members had infiltrated Homeland Security in America and were now setting up plots against the United States. Hell, they were even embedded in the Department of Defense. Moshe was all business. There was cheese and fruit to eat, bottled water and lots of strong coffee. The meeting lasted four hours and they were the only two people in the safe room. Ben was one of the few people Moshe completely trusted. He furnished photographs of the targets and exact locations within the United States.

After a long and detailed discussion, Ben left their meeting without delay in the dark before sunrise, just as planned. His notes were scrawled in Hebrew and written in a code so that only he and Moshe would understand them. Their encryption program would be virtually impossible for anyone to decipher. The heavily armored vehicle picked Ben up and whisked him away into the blackness of the night. He arrived at the airport and boarded a private jet.

The plane ride to Pakistan was comfortable. Before he fell asleep, Ben thought about the irony that most of his obstacles existed in the state department and congress. It was the coalition of politicians that fell into the category of liberal progressives with no real-world knowledge of how battle was truly fought and won. These blowhard politicians had one specialty, showmanship. They didn't read legislature consisting of thousands of pages, because they were too busy spending their time on television talk shows or standing in the well of the senate reading from a teleprompter. Most of them were nothing but brainless spineless idiots, especially the liberal elites. The CIA, FBI and Homeland Security were littered with incompetent people as well. The appointees in top positions were most often guys who made it through Harvard or Yale with a D-average and utilized crony connections to get into a position of authority.

The people in power had no real-world experience on the battlefield or as a commander. The sad reality was: the lives of the fighting men and women of the U.S. forces hung in the balance.

The jokers on the Senate Intelligence Committee or the Department of Defense and the Executive Office were the puppet masters pulling the strings. Each had their own political image as their top priority. They worried about focus groups, satisfying their campaign bundlers, the latest polls, their private jets, their $600 haircuts, lavish vacations -- these people made Ben sick.

Even though the United States government had pockets of corruption, it was *his* country. The United States was the only beacon of freedom and it was his home. When he first joined the military, Ben felt he belonged to the United States. But now, it was different. *He felt the United States belonged to him and he had a sense of duty to clean his own house.* He knew the cure for the greedy leadership in America would not be so easy. It wasn't a matter of just getting rid of the self-centered bastards in power; the task would be to change the system that rewarded them.

Ben boarded the twin turbine Piaggio P-180 Avanti appreciating the fine details of its Italian design. Faster than most jets, it cost a cool 4.6 million. Ben hoped someday he would be able to afford such a luxury. It was Ben's preferred way to fly, and he was thankful that Moshe provided transportation for his week-long trip.

***

Although it was midnight, Lara worked on her master's project for an hour and then her thoughts were filled with Ben. Knowing just bits and pieces about Dark Horse, Ben's consulting work was fascinating to her. What she knew so far was that Ben, with the help of other operatives, was tracking terrorists in plain view. For a moment Lara took a deep breath and closed her eyes; how could this be happening in Maine? But then she vividly remembered the September 11th terrorists boarded a plane starting their journey here in Portland, in this sleepy little corner of the country.

She wished she could chat with Ben on the computer, but that was not possible in this situation. One thing Ben and Lara had in common was neither of them used social media. Both used secure webmail accounts and texting only. She did, however, have pictures of Ben on her phone. She had taken several photos of him in his newly renovated office with Einstein. She also had a picture of him on the 1940's Indian Chief motorcycle. And, there was a particularly endearing photo of him sitting on her sofa in a T-shirt. She downloaded the photos onto her laptop and zoomed in. Just viewing Ben in the photos flooded her with memories. She wondered what it would be like to be married to someone who was gone most of the time. Could she handle the constant loneliness?

The next morning Lara woke to Einstein's bark. He needed to go outside. She slid out of bed and into her white cotton robe and slippers. She brought Einstein outside for his morning business. She wondered where Ben was. Who was he with? What he was doing? Two more days and he would be home. Lara showered and dressed. Then she took Einstein for a long walk past the beautiful purple Victorian house with the ocean view. She missed Ben, even though she received daily texts from him filled with tender words. She tried to imagine what he was doing, who he was with.

PAKISTAN

Ben wondered what Lara would think of him dressed in a burka. He was shuttled in a bulky armored vehicle in the middle of the night in Bhakkar Pakistan to meet with Nazmin. Her underground bunker was well concealed not far from the Afghanistan border. Ben's history with Nazmin dated back to his first tour of duty. Sympathetic to the cause for freedom, especially for women under the thumb of archaic laws in that part of the world, she frequently assisted Ben with intel for missions. It was imperative that Nazmin remain in the shadows regarding her work. Ben knew the drill.

He was disguised as an Islamic woman with full burka. Several other men, bodyguards, were dressed as women and surrounded him as he walked through the first layer of security. Concealed this way he was able to keep his body armor, HK416 and ammo strapped to his chest for this meeting. They met under the pretext of attending a women's prayer group. Nazmin played hostess to many such overnight meetings. There was always the chance that one of these gatherings would be crashed by radicals in the area utilizing gunfire or incendiary devices. Enemy patrols were ever present in the region.

Ben was thankful for the burka as it kept out the dirt and dust that seemed to permeate everything in this country. Although some areas of Pakistan were considered metropolitan, that description would not apply to Nazmin's property. This was a region of rural farmers and Nazmin kept a large poultry farm. The stench was sharp. Ben's sense of hearing was on high alert for anything that did not sound right. The men dressed in burkas spoke in falsetto voices in Urdu and occasionally giggled. Their kabuki theater had to be as real as possible.

The smell of this place triggered memories Ben preferred not to relive. Helmand and Kandahar came to mind. Ben had been captured in Helmand and savagely tortured. Some of his teeth were pulled out and fingernails ripped off. He was then burned with cigarettes and lacerated with rusty razor blades. Suspended upside down for hours on end, he said nothing. He urinated and defecated in the small cell, but he slept as much as he could. His plan was to wear them down and grab a weapon when the time was right. As long as he could sleep and get water, he could come back for more. His brothers doubled back and found him two days later with Moshe's guidance. He smiled as he recalled their reunion hours later in the safety of Camp Bastion.

Nazmin's building contained a safe room in a bunker for their private meeting. A small group of dark skinned paramilitary men were in front of the place and secondary group inside the farmhouse. Ben spoke to the men in Urdu and was admitted into the bunker without delay. Even Nazmin's people believed he was female. He always felt uneasy in this corner of the world. Life was cheap here. He wanted to get in and out as swiftly as possible without detection.

The group of men dressed in burkas stayed upstairs in the farmhouse for the prayer meeting. Nazmin took Ben down to the hidden bunker door and within a few minutes they were alone in a subterranean basement. Candles were burning. In the tomb, alone with Nasmin there were security cameras watching every angle of her property. Ben was amazed at the level of secrecy she kept in this underground vault. She read by candlelight while she kept one eye on the high-tech security cameras scanning the surrounding area. The information she was about to disclose could not be carried by a UPS or FedEx courier.

There could be no electronic contact with Nazmin for her own protection. She gave him detailed information about a terror group forming in the Western Massachusetts area. She gave him names, addresses, and photographs of the suspects. Ben put the information into an envelope and would burn it once utilized. The meeting lasted two hours. When finished, Ben handed her a sack containing two hundred thousand dollars for the information.

He made a swift exit with the group of burkas as a sliver of daylight started to edge above the desert horizon. He was on the private jet leaving the area by mid-morning and had packed his burka in the carry-on bag. Meanwhile, Ben's mind was working on how to take the terrorists out in Western Massachusetts and make it look like someone else did it. Ideas were already brewing.

These clandestine meetings were now the only form of overseas travel that Ben forced himself to undertake. These visits could not be handed off to anyone else. The contacts trusted him only. Ben knew how important the bond of confidence was and respectfully kept it sacred. He sent a message to Lara utilizing an encrypted satellite phone. *Missing you*.

He had several photographs of Lara on his phone and slowly scrolled through them before falling asleep. His favorite was the one he captured as they sat on the porch glider eating breakfast. Her hazel-green eyes were beautiful, and she was smiling. He closed his eyes and kept her image in his mind. As was his habit, he slept on the plane.

DUBAI

Ben's next meeting was to be with King Sahim. Dubai being the main city in the United Arab Emirates Federation, it was located on the southeastern coast of the Persian Gulf. As the jet landed in the blackness of night, a white armor-plated bullet proof limousine arrived and quickly swept Ben away. He was now dressed in white robes with a beard, dark make-up, wearing a turban with different sunglasses. The meeting place was an opulent skyscraper overlooking the Persian Gulf.

It was daybreak and the contingent that came out to meet Ben at the vehicle was dressed in white with AK's strapped to their bodies. The king had layers of security; body guards were expendable as there had been three or four deaths a year in those positions. Ben knew because he contracted for Sahim to set up an impenetrable security force when he started Dark Horse. The men swept Ben for listening devices and he surrendered his firearms and knives. He had been through this drill before and trusted Sahim.

Inside, the king and Ben embraced, and the two spoke to one another in Arabic. The king voiced concerns to Ben about the United States losing the counter-terrorism battle on their own turf. He had valuable intel to share with Ben. There were terrorists setting up shop in the Northeastern United States. Men and women living in America were traveling to Pakistan, Syria, Libya, Lebanon, Egypt and Yemen for guerilla training and returning to live seemingly normal American lives, blending into society in the United States.

In deep cover, King Sahim was taking a huge risk meeting with Ben. His information came from major players on the ground in the war-torn countries. Informants, it was amazing how they could be cultivated with revenge and the desire to take out their competition in the underworld they lived in. Sahim provided names, addresses, coordinates, and photographs of those living in the United States who had been to the training camps. The face-to-face meeting was important as Ben knew he was building Sahim's trust and support. The king handed an envelope to Ben. Its contents would be burned once he had utilized the details. There would be no evidence or record of this meeting.

King Sahim thanked Ben for his dedication to the cause. He joked about cloning Ben and hiring him to run the ground game in war-torn Syria. His concerns were grave regarding the savage violence that was spreading through the Middle East from Egypt, Lebanon, and Syria, and now pouring into Iraq and Jordan. All the good work done by the USA in Iraq and Afghanistan was being undone rapidly. Sahim thanked Ben. The two men embraced briefly, and Ben was given his weapons, then whisked back to Sahim's plane and taken away. At 5 AM Ben was at the Dubai airport. He immediately got into a fetal position and slept on the private jet. Before drifting into sleep, Ben sent a text to Lara, missing her more than ever. *Thinking of you tonight.*

***

Sensing that Ben could be returning with a Christmas gift for her, Lara called upon an old friend to provide a unique present for her handsome secret agent. She dialed the number for Rupert Jensen. When in his vintage shop several weeks ago shopping for a client, she had noticed a gold coin of the Parisii tribe of ancient Gaul, 100-50 B.C. There were few things she could buy for Ben that would have true meaning. He was a person who had a handful of possessions, but the small group of items he collected held significance.

The shop phone rang once, then she heard his voice and was relieved to hear him answer.

"Rupert, it's me, Lara. I need a favor. May I come by right away to purchase the ancient coin I was admiring a few weeks ago?"

Rupert was just closing the shop but said he'd wait for her. She jumped into the Fiat and drove to his shop in record time. Rupert's place looked like something out of a 1950's movie. It was a strange little building with bars on the windows and security cameras everywhere. At one time it had been a residence, but the Gothic style house had been modified for his business, *Jensen's Rare Treasures*. The outside light was on, but the door was locked. She rang the bell and Rupert appeared. He was a short round man in his 70's with a head of snow white hair.

"I have it all ready for you, Lara. I hope you remember what the item cost." He gave Lara a playful little smile.

"Oh yes, Rupert, I remember. It's a gift for someone special." She had the rare coin placed in a small box and paid Rupert the outrageous amount of money from her savings account.

"I didn't know there was a special man in your life, Lara. Glad to hear it. I am sure he will appreciate this. He will if he's an Irishman."

"Yes, he is." She smiled.

It would be worth it to see Ben's face when he held the rare coin in his hand. There were very few of these left in existence. Rupert had been haggling with a museum and Lara snatched it up before the deal could be done. It was karma.

Arriving in Bethany Jordan, Ben was well aware that this was the biblical place where Jesus wandered for forty days and started his ministry. Jordan was a country of contrasts, stark desert landscapes and towering mountains. Today at sunset he would meet Ismail in a safe house far into the desert. In Bethany, near the Jordan River, Ben was picked up by an up-armored Ford Expedition, strictly utilized for undercover operations. Ben was acutely aware that he was entering a zone that was militarily sensitive and Ismail arranged for his escorts. Since the influx of Syrians, Jordan had increased military patrols considerably. He was especially wary of passing through checkpoints. He knew there was one along the Dead Sea Highway near the sensitive border with Israel. He would be waved through the checkpoints today. He was dressed in the white robes, beard, and sunglasses; posing as a visiting dignitary from Iraq with a perfectly forged passport.

The visit with Ismail would be brief tonight. Ismail was the general manager of a construction company with clients in the energy business. The building Ben would enter was well secured and covered with cameras. There was valuable equipment inside along with a substantial cache of weapons. Any company doing business in this area of the world hired small armies to keep their investment safe.

Ismail met with Ben alone in a small private office in the center of the compound. The workers were off for the night and, except for the security guards, the place was eerily quiet. It was almost too quiet for Ben's comfort level, and he was glad he had weapons and grenades hidden beneath his voluminous robes, just in case. Information was given to Ben regarding an Al-Qaeda affiliate that was forming in Jordan. Since the Iraq war, and now with the Syrian conflict, there had been an influx of radicals organizing in Jordan with the intent to take over Jordan and to do harm to the United States.

In particular, there was a plot in the works for New Britain Connecticut. Ismail gave Ben the names and photographs of those at the top of the food chain and information regarding their movements in the past few months. Some of the information was word of mouth, but Ismail believed his sources were to be trusted. Ismail's motivation to help Ben was two-fold. His country was being overrun by radicals, thus the tenants of democracy were in great jeopardy. Secondly, he knew if the United States was infiltrated and weakened by these radicals, they could not respond, if and when, help might be needed in Jordan. Survival was a strong instinct and drove many of Ben's informants to help him. Ismail was worried about his own safety and the peaceful monarchy in Jordan falling apart. Ben understood. Leaving Ismail, he made a three-hour journey back to the airport and entered the private jet. Now, he prepared to meet with his confidential informant in Iraq.

Just the thought of going to Iraq caused beads of sweat to form on his upper lip. He was tired but forced himself to review the encrypted notes for the coming meeting. As he curled up on the plane, he thought about Lara and wondered what she was doing right now. His baggage and weaponry were securely packed. He immediately dozed off from sheer exhaustion once the plane was in flight. Startled awake, his hand automatically reached for his side arm; another bad dream. He woke sweating and drank a bottle of cold water just as the plane was making its descent to Adder, one of the last remaining U.S. air bases in Iraq.

Arriving home, Lara removed Einstein's leash and sat with him briefly on the back porch. The fresh December air was invigorating, and Lara could not stop thinking about Ben. Where was he now? Was he safe? Who was he with? A workout with Don Henderson at the dojo was always the best prescription to put her mind at ease. With frustrations to unleash, she got into the Fiat and drove to the martial arts center.

She had a raucous kicking punching, grappling martial arts work out. An hour later, she slid to the floor next to Don. Both were covered in sweat and panting heavily. She had taken him off his feet a dozen times in a dozen different ways. Don was either letting her win or getting older. Whatever the case, both wiped sweat from their brows as they tried to catch their breath.

"Meet me out here—after I shower." Lara said breathing heavily and sweating. She had kicked some of her frustration away.

Freshly showered, she met Don at the smoothie bar and drank heartily.

"Great work out." He said.

"Yes." Lara exhaled. "Thanks, I needed that."

"What's new? Have you heard from Ben?" Don's eyes, a clear Nordic blue met hers.

"I have a few texts from him—not much."

"You miss him, I can tell." Don took her empty glass. "Stop by the house if you're not busy—we'd love to have you join us for dinner."

"Okay—I have a few errands to run."

"See you later." Don glanced at his watch. "Another class coming up in a few—*beginners!*" he chuckled.

IRAQ

As Ben woke from night terrors, he was flying over Iraq in the early morning hours. Looking at the terrain below, he realized just how quickly U.S. military bases in Iraq had become deserted cities as America rapidly withdrew nearly of all the troops. The scene was like an abandoned movie set from an old western. There were very few military personnel, but the structures remained. Dust and weeds covered everything, giving an apocalyptic look to the strange scene. When first deployed in '06 for the Surge, Ben remembered the forward operating bases filled with the noise of thousands of soldiers working together to establish security in the war zone.

As his plane landed today, there were less than 6,000 troops remaining in the country, from a peak of 170,000 at the height of the war in '07. And, of the 505 military bases set up during the eight-year mission, only four continued to have a handful of personnel: Kalsu in Iskandariya; Echo in Diwaniya; Camp Adder near Nasiriya; and Camp Bravo in Basra, all reduced to a level of insignificance.

Adder, where Ben was landing today was once the largest base in Southern Iraq. It was the last to close and was now owned by Iraq and its struggling government. America gifted its seven-story control tower along with equipment too worn down or too expensive to ship out. In Basra, Camp Bravo was now barely inhabited. Huts constructed by the British, and later used by Americans, were empty. Rows of huge expensive diesel generators sat in silence and the only tracks in the mud now belonged to animals.

Camp Cooke, twenty miles north of Baghdad in Taji, had

few personnel left. Empty housing units were marked, and hundreds of tanks and other armored vehicles lay discarded on dust-filled fields. This was the end of the cyclical deployment of one million troops. About 16,000 people were working at the U.S. embassy in Baghdad, making it America's largest embassy in the world. The plan was to keep long-term access to military bases in Iraq. The four bases planned to keep open were to be the former Saddam International Airport outside Baghdad, Tallil air base near Nasiriyah, in the south, the air base known as H-1 in the western desert, and the Bashur airfield in northern Iraq, H-1, where Special Forces teams were based.

Once Ben was on the ground, he moved quickly to meet with Tayeb, his confidential informant in Nasiriyah, a city soaked with American blood from the '03 battles. Tayeb supplied an older up-armored Humvee to transport Ben to a safe house in the center of his date plantation. Ben drove through the newer parts of the town dominated by standard Iraqi cinder block buildings. But as he approached the plantation, he was in the older section where structures were built mainly from sun-dried brick and enclosed by mud walls.

The discussion with Tayeb was how the Islamic radical war was migrating to American turf. Tayeb briefed Ben on the latest actionable intelligence that had surfaced in the New England area. Ben knew the NSA had intercepted phone calls and other communiqués from one of several terrorist cells thriving inside Iraq. Suspects had traveled between Iraq and Portland Maine multiple times using indirect routes. Tayeb was connected to the underground terror groups through his cousin, Rami, who stayed plugged in by attending meetings and even supplying terrorists with small amounts of money and arms from time to time in order to keep their trust.

One of the most disturbing aspects was the usage of females and young children in the terror plots and the sophisticated nature of the bombs and tactics they were planning to utilize. Disguised as an Iraqi, Ben wore his usual beard and sunglasses and Muslim garb. The security guards at the date plantation gave him the once over, but knew a visitor was coming today.

Instantly, the sights and smells took Ben back momentarily to the hell-hole of Camp Ramadi, full of terrorists imported from Syria and Iran to join the fight in '06. He vividly remembered the bullet wounds and shrapnel he took as his platoon built one of the first combat outposts and took the fight to the enemy during the Surge.

Living on rooftops sniping large groups of insurgents all day or all night, sleeping only for four hours and going back to finish the job - *except they kept coming*. For a moment, he was there, working side by side with his brothers in the attempt to civilize the most lawless dangerous city in Iraq, risking life and limb every day, calling in air support, roping off entire city blocks, searching buildings, enforcing curfews, searching more buildings, arranging for training local Iraqi boys. *Urban combat, they called it*. Every day was a violent blood bath. Every night was filled with RPG's, grenades and bullets flying. Sleep was optional. Caffeine was required. He did his duty and never questioned his contribution: he was a small piece of a well-oiled machine.

Ben seldom consciously thought of Iraq. But as he left Tayeb and drove back to the air base to fly out, he took a deep breath and closed his eyes as he silently honored the fallen and wounded in this now abandoned country. Although Iraq was in the past, it was no less important or life-changing for him. Iraq was now in the hands of another government and his only concern was to honor his fallen brothers and to keep Americans safe.

His last stop would be Israel to say goodbye to Moshe, and to off-load his weaponry and disguises. He would also thank him profusely for the private jet. He would not see his good friend again for several months. As he curled up on the private plane back to Israel, Ben caught a nap and woke up sweating and shaking again. His thoughts drifted to Lara and how far away he felt from her. He wondered what she was doing. Did she miss his daily presence? It would be early afternoon in the states. He dialed her phone number, but it went to voicemail. He sent her a text. *Hope you're enjoying your Christmas break, miss you.*

***

"Merry Christmas, Lara, are you coming for the cocktail hour tonight, at least?" It was Eliot Stone the night before Christmas Eve. She had hastily answered the phone without looking at it, hoping it would be Ben.

"What time should I be there?" She knew Eliot would be greatly disappointed if his prize intern did not show up to be introduced to his most influential circle of friends.

"Drinks at 7 PM and dinner at 8 PM, and you are welcome to use the Bentley as a car service. In fact, I insist upon it."

"I appreciate that, thank you, Eliot." She sighed.

"I'll have the car pick you up at 6:45 PM—how's that?"

"Great. Thanks." She hung up the phone feeling lonelier than ever. Lara opened her closet door and wondered what to wear. She pulled out a green velvet cocktail dress that had an asymmetrical cut-out back. She wore the dangling vintage diamond earrings and pulled her dark hair into a twist, securing the mass with a jeweled clip. No leather sack tonight, but Lara took her small clutch and cell phone just in case Ben called.

The doorbell rang, and she dashed down the stairs. UPS left a package for her that had the words handwritten on it, *Do Not Open Before Christmas*. She shook the box slightly but couldn't seem to guess what it was or who it was from.

As Lara slid into the Bentley, she sipped a glass of Champagne just poured for her by the driver. "Thank you, Evans." She saw his hat nod and he proceeded to drive to the Stone estate. French Champagne, how delicious. As she arrived at the Tudor mansion, Lara's eyes took in the details of the place. She was accustomed to the opulence, but she had forgotten how lovely it was at Christmas. She was escorted inside, and Raphael took her coat. There were only a few people there and Eliot appeared quickly to greet her.

"My dear, Lara, let me look at you. You are lovely, as always."

Eliot barely paid attention to his other guests as he took Lara's arm and moved her toward the library.

ISRAEL

In Israel, Ben met with Moshe, touching down just in time for dinner. In disguise once again, Ben met with Moshe at the safe house. This time they laughed and talked as old friends for the first hour. Ben told Moshe about meeting Lara and shared photos of her with him.

"She's a striking beauty," Moshe remarked, "but is she ready to accept your lifestyle?"

Ben hesitated for a moment. "She understands me more than any woman I've ever met. There's something about her. She was attacked savagely as a young girl. I think that experience helps her to understand what I am living with, the night terrors and bouts of hyper-vigilance. We share many things in common, shooting, mixed martial arts. But, more importantly, she brings me back to the normal world, if there is such a thing."

Moshe smiled. "She sounds like a unique person. I hope I can meet her someday soon."

Ben gazed into Moshe's dark black eyes. "Oh, you will meet her, as soon as I can arrange it. I feel like I am incomplete without her, it's as if part of me is missing. I've only known her for three months. It's crazy."

"I felt the same way when I met Rachel. There was no question. I kissed her and that was it. I could not be away from her. She thought I was a mad man. That's what love feels like, Ben."

All of Ben's weapons and supplies were now in Moshe's hands. Ben got ready for his long commercial flight back to the

United States, now empty handed except for the documents and photos he had scanned into his laptop. He had encrypted the documents and carefully packaged the photos separately and sent them back to his post office box via UPS.

Moshe embraced Ben tightly. "Go in peace, my friend, and stay in touch. We have many complex problems to solve. I will pray for your safety."

Ben checked through Israeli security with minimal scrutiny at the airport in Tel Aviv. His face was a familiar one there, plus Moshe had entered Ben's passport on a list that granted him special privileges. As he boarded the plane, Ben's planning turned to Lara and how excited he was to be going home to her. He sent her a text with his estimated time of arrival. From sheer exhaustion, his eyes were closing. Just before he nodded off he scrolled through the photographs on his phone. He wished he could have been with her for Christmas Eve. He could not wait to see her tomorrow. He wanted nothing more right now than to call and hear her lovely feminine voice. But it was after midnight in Maine and she would be sleeping. He did not want to disturb her.

Although exhausted, Ben was charged with excitement. He had a surprise for Lara and he turned the beautiful item over in his hand observing the exquisite details of the piece. He wanted to make her smile for Christmas and knew the gift would be perfect for her.

***

More guests filtered into the beautiful mansion. Lara shook hands and politely introduced herself as she mingled and navigated around with hors d'oeuvres and glasses of champagne served on silver platters. Through the crowd she'd lost sight of Eliot. She studied the sailing photographs on the wall in the library and noted the cups Eliot had won. Newport to Bermuda, the Downeast Regatta, Eggamoggin Reach Regatta, Northeast Harbor Race, the Monhegan Regatta. The cups were prolific as were the photographs. Lara realized that Eliot Stone's sailing knowledge matched the magnitude of his financial proficiency. She could learn much from this man.

Eliot Stone was more than happy to have Lara in his home this evening for his annual holiday soiree. He particularly loved to see her at Christmas when she dressed in a feminine provocative way, for *her* anyhow. Tonight, she chose a green velvet dress that matched her eyes and showed the soft skin of her lovely back. He lost sight of her for a while as his house filled with guests—clients really. Once he found her, he moved quickly to bring her to his private sitting room off the master bedroom wing.

"I have something to show you in here and want your professional opinion."

Lara was propelled by Eliot's gentle arm at her back. Always the gentleman, Eliot left the door open, but moved her inside his bedroom suite.

"Here—these—I want your opinion. Too much?"

Eliot showed Lara several newly acquired oil paintings, beautiful seascapes painted by a famous artist. He'd scooped up at an auction in Newport, Rhode Island.

"What do you think?" He watched as Lara's eyes swept over the details of the spectacular paintings.

"These are amazing, Eliot. They're perfect for the décor here."

Eliot moved closer to her. "Yes, like *you*, stunning, incredibly beautiful."

Lara dropped her glass of Champagne disturbing his cozy moment with her.

"Oh gosh, I'm sorry." Lara murmured. She found a towel in the master bathroom and dabbed the expensive Persian carpet. "I'm so sorry, Eliot." she repeated on her knees now in Eliot's reading room.

"You don't have to do that. It's only Champagne. Raphael will take care of it."

He took Lara's hand and brought her to her feet. She stood directly in front of him, close enough to smell the Ralph Lauren cologne he wore, close enough to see his soft brown eyes as his pupils dilated slightly. Eliot's hands were now holding hers and the towel dropped to the floor.

"You're not really *seeing* this Keegan guy, are you?"

She averted his gaze. "He's a *good friend*, that's all."

"He's not with you for Christmas?"

"He's returning from a business trip tomorrow."

Eliot was now close to her face and he lowered his voice. "And he's pursuing you, isn't he? He wants more than friendship, I'm guessing."

"If you mean *am I sleeping with him*, no. I'm not like that, Eliot. You know me better than that—at least I hope you do. I have principles."

"Oh, no—I'm sorry." But his words were too late. He managed to anger her, and that was the *last* thing he'd wanted to do. She already started down the stairway and by the time he got down to the first floor, she was moving through the crowd. He caught up to her in the hallway as she searched for her coat.

"Lara—please forgive me. I'm meddling where I shouldn't be. I'm sorry."

She turned around and faced him. He could tell she was furious with his earlier question about Keegan. He'd hit a raw nerve—so, he assumed he was right. He quickly pivoted and changed the subject.

"Lara, please—let me introduce you to some wonderful clients. They came here to meet *you* tonight—they're interested in the new creative genius I have on my team. Please?"

He knew her pride was bruised, but he also knew the splendor of his mansion filled with potential clients interested Lara. She was thirsty with ambition and he took her hand and introduced her to numerous couples—all excited to meet her. Eliot noticed how she carefully worked the room shaking hands, smiling, getting the clients to talk—then, she'd intersperse a word here or there. She was very good at making small talk. By the end of the evening, Eliot figured she'd made good use of the opportunity. The folks attending Eliot's parties were multi-millionaires and exactly the potential client pool she wanted to tap into.

A couple of hours later, she said goodbye to Eliot. He watched as Lara slipped into the Bentley for the ride home. He knew she belonged in this world—of elegance, opulence—she wore it well. As Eliot returned to his guests, the rest of the evening was a bore for him. Once she had left the party it lost any sense of excitement. The vision of Lara in the green velvet dress was on his mind for the rest of the evening and the next day. He couldn't wait to be with her again.

In the back of the Bentley on the ride home, Lara yawned. It was tedious being with so many people all at once. When she got back to her condo, Lara climbed the stairs and Einstein was doing his happy dance.

"Aw, I've got to take you outside, buddy." She kicked off her heels and slipped into sneakers quickly—and secured his leash. As she walked the dog down the street a short distance, she stood and watched a shooting star. She closed her eyes and made a wish—that Ben would be home soon, safe and sound.

CHAPTER 19: *Christmas Eve*

Lara decided tonight would be fun, even if she was alone—but she wasn't completely alone. She had Einstein. She brought the dog to Ben's condo and turned the TV to an old movie channel. Ben would be home the day after tomorrow and she planned on cleaning his place—and leaving some freshly baked Christmas cookies in the kitchen for him with a note. Just being in his living quarters made her feel closer to him. She laid upon his bed and thought about the time he comforted her when she most needed it. Einstein cuddled against her back and she enjoyed the warmth of the bed and closed her eyes.

When she woke, she realized she had slept eight hours in her clothes. While brushing her teeth, she realized it was Christmas Eve! Einstein was whining to go outside, so she quickly slipped into her winter coat brought him outside. It was so cold, even Einstein wanted to come back in. Her phone chimed with a text from Ben saying simply: *Miss you*. Lara whispered, "Oh Ben, you have no idea how much I miss *you*." She felt like texting, *by the way, who are you really?* But she didn't. She sent a message back to him: *I miss your voice*. Five minutes later he called her. He was somewhere between the Iraq and Israel. She was thrilled to hear his voice on the phone and her heart ached missing him. He could not say exactly where he was or what he was doing, but he did tell her that he missed her--and he said something else. She heard him say her name, but her cell phone dropped the connection before she could reply.

Don and Olivia Henderson had invited Lara the farmhouse for Christmas Eve brunch. Olivia was standing in the doorway with the December sun shining on her gray hair and she was smiling when Lara arrived.

"It's so good to see you, Lara." Olivia gushed as she hugged her in the hallway. "Come in and get comfortable."

Don was sitting at the table and stood to hug Lara as she stepped into the room. Lara gave them a beautiful Christmas centerpiece for their farmhouse table. It instantly made the kitchen smell like Christmas.

"What have you been up to? You are glowing." Olivia asked.

Lara smiled. "Dog-sitting Einstein, Ben will be home tomorrow."

"Ah, yes—I was just going to ask about him." Olivia smiled.

Lara sat at the table across from Don. "Merry Christmas, big guy."

Don smiled. "Merry Christmas to you, grasshopper." He stood up and hesitated, then limped forward.

"You've gotta try this eggnog, Lara. It's delicious!"

"You're limping. What happened?"

"Aw, nothing—my leg gives me some trouble now and then." A Vietnam vet, and former Green Beret, Lara knew Don had a few old wounds. Once in a blue moon, he'd talk about his time there, but it was rare. Awarded the Bronze Star, he had broken bones in one leg that never healed properly. However, he was not one to complain. Olivia, the consummate housewife, loved all things domestic and feminine. She often had long talks with Lara about clothing or make-up.

Olivia smiled. "Brunch is almost ready. It's your favorite, Lara."

"Oh goodie. Roast beef with gravy!"

It was always great to see Olivia and Don for Christmas. She loved them so. They were the best friends she had, besides Rusty. Don surprised Lara by giving her a Christmas gift, a simple white envelope. "Open it when you get home."

"Oh, one thing—I need to ask you, Olivia. Did you give Eric a green cashmere scarf?"

"No, why?"

"I found one at my house after the Thanksgiving meal. No worries. It might belong to my mother."

Lara knew Eric was a blowhard and now she suspected he might be a liar. So, she chalked it up to that and thought nothing more of it. After a couple of hours of football, Lara waved goodbye to Don and Olivia as they stood in the doorway. Driving home in the Fiat, Lara wished Ben had been with her. She opened the white envelope from Don. It was a year of free lessons at the dojo. Just what she wanted.

As Lara climbed the stairs to her condo, her phone vibrated. It was a text from Ben that said: *Miss you. Facetime me.* As she got inside, Lara felt a wave of relief flood over her. Ben was still all right. Only one more night alone: Christmas Eve. Then on Christmas Day, Ben would be home.

"Keegan." When he answered, his face was there, and he looked tired.

"Ben, oh, it's so good to *see* you."

She could hear him exhale. It was amazing to see his smile complete with dimples on her phone. "Thank you for calling, you made my day, or my night. You look fantastic, darlin."

She missed his face, his voice—everything about him. For the first time she realized his accent was incredibly pleasant even when he answered *Keegan* in his business-like way. Ben usually spoke with measured tones, but today he had a hint of excitement in his voice.

"Lara, I have something serious to discuss with you tomorrow."

She wondered what that could might be but did not press him for details. Ben seemed to be in a lighthearted mood. Lara kept the conversation cheerful on the phone.

"I hope you didn't get me some extravagant Christmas gift."

Ben smiled, "Don't set yourself up for disappointment. I'm a last-minute shopper and a cheapskate, at that." Then, suddenly, the conversation took on a serious note and he spoke tenderly. "Before this damned phone cuts out, I want to say Merry Christmas and to tell you, in case you didn't get the hundreds of texts from me in the past few days, that I miss you. I can't wait to get home to see you tomorrow. I love you, Lara."

She whispered, gazing at his image on the phone. "I can't wait to be with you, Ben."

Lara couldn't tell if Ben's phone cut out or if her cell phone connection died, but the call dropped. The image of Ben on her phone only served to make her miss him more, if that was possible.

"Christmas Eve is going to consist of baking cookies and watching old Christmas movies on television with *you*, buddy." Einstein wagged his tail.

"Will you help me make cookies? Yes, of course you will."

Her original plan for this evening was to go into the bedroom to slip into her comfortable pajamas. She would spend a quiet night baking with Einstein. Padding around in wool slippers, with Einstein at her heels, she wondered how she'd lived this long without a canine companion. He certainly was good company, especially when food was involved.

CHAPTER 20: Christmas Morning

Early on Christmas morning, Lara rolled out of bed to take Einstein outside. The morning was cold, and a snow squall had left a two-inch dusting of snow. The sun was rising over a frozen white landscape. She shivered in her coat while waiting for Einstein.

"Come on, buddy—we're going to freeze here." Lara's teeth chattered.

Once back inside, she couldn't wait to open the white mystery box that had arrived with few markings on it. Could it be something from Ben? Maybe it was. She would wait to open it. She put the small package back on the table and decided to take a shower.

While in the hot, steamy water, Lara focused her attention on Ben's arrival. She thought about the first time Ben touched her hair and how he ran his fingers through it—and how much she longed for his touch. A sense of urgency filled her as she busied herself feeding Einstein. She absent-mindedly ate a piece of toast as her phone vibrated with a text from Ben. He expected to arrive home at 10 AM and would catch a cab from the airport.

Dressing in the soft red sweater she had selected on her shopping trip, she hoped Ben would like it as well seeing it the second time. An hour passed as Lara brewed a fresh pot of coffee. Einstein was whining, and his tail wagged a moment before she heard the cab pull up. She watched from the parlor window as Ben jumped out and approached the porch heading directly for her staircase. Lara's pulse quickened. She ran down the stairs to the porch door to unlock it as a gust of freezing cold air swept in with Ben.

He hugged Lara so tightly he lifted her off her feet.

"Oh darlin, I've missed you so much." He laughed. "You look great in this sweater, haven't I seen this before?"

Einstein cried out for his master. Ben crouched and hugged his devoted canine. He was in a good mood. They ran upstairs to get out of the drafty hallway and into the parlor near the fireplace. Ben was now before her, so incredibly handsome. He embraced her with tremendous strength and kissed her passionately. Then, he buried his face in her hair.

"Oh Lara, I've missed you so much. You have no idea. I love you, darlin."

His words filled her heart with warmth. She knew he was emotionally invested, but when he said he *loved* her, a shot of pleasure coursed through her veins. What surprised her even more was—she never expected she would fall so hard for him. This was unchartered water for her.

She inhaled his familiar scent as tears formed in her eyes. "I missed you, too, Ben." But, she couldn't say the words he longed to hear. She pulled away to get him a coffee. As she placed the steaming mug in front of him, he grasped her hand.

"I couldn't stop thinking of you, Lara." His eyes met hers and she realized how much she missed him.

"What's this?" His hand touched the small white package on the table.

"I don't know. I thought it was something you sent to me."

"No, I didn't send it. Maybe it's something from your mother."

"Well—I'll open it and find out." Her fingers tore the thick white shipping paper away and the name of a jewelry store appeared on the side of the box. "Hmm—jewelry?"

She opened the box and lifted out the sea glass pendant, and a small piece of paper fluttered onto the table. She picked up the piece of paper and immediately crumpled it.

"Who's it from?" Ben was curious now.

"I don't know *why* this person sent this to me."

"What person?"

Ben unwrinkled the paper and read the note aloud.

"Something beautiful for the most beautiful woman in the world—love, Eric." Ben's eyes met hers and she turned away.

"*Love*, Eric?" Ben asked, dripping with sarcasm.

As he sipped his coffee, she noticed Ben's eyes scanning her apartment. She sensed he was looking for something— anything—to justify what he'd just read. Abruptly his demeanor changed.

"Eric—that's the guy who was here with Don and Olivia for Thanksgiving—right?"

"Yes."

∗∗∗

Ben wondered just how friendly Lara had been with Eric in his absence. He was protective when it came to Lara. She was *his* girl and everyone in their circle of acquaintance knew this as an unspoken rule. But, Eric was *not* part of their world. Ben's first reaction was anger. It wasn't a blow-up in your face type of anger, but he felt a simmering rage beginning.

"So, have you been *seeing* this guy?" Ben was now in interrogation mode.

"No. I have no interest in the idiot."

Clenching his teeth, he let the fury take over. It was as if he couldn't stop himself. He continued pressing her.

"*Why* would he give you a Christmas gift? *Why* would he write *love, Eric*? There must be some reason, Lara. He thinks he has some sort of *chance* with you."

"I have no idea. Ben, why are you asking these things?"

He was now tuned into every movement Lara was making. He was trained to detect lies by reading body language. Lara glanced momentarily at the pendant on the table and avoided his eyes, was she keeping something from him?

"Okay, he gave you a necklace. And, you are telling me this guy is just an acquaintance? Oh god, Lara, you've got to wake up. Eric is trying to have *more* than a friendship with you." Ben was seething inside and hated the feeling in his gut. The fact that Lara was not making eye contact was not good. Ben pressed her further not able to stop himself.

"So, has this guy been pestering you? Has he been hanging around here? Has he been calling you?"

Lara sat in the corner of the sofa and completely avoided Ben's piercing stare. Suddenly, Ben realized he had gone too far. He had no right to interrogate her. He loved her beyond reason and had just spent the past week obsessing about their reunion today, Christmas Day, and how *happy* it would be. It had gone terribly wrong. Lara now had tears in her eyes.

Finally, beaten, overcome with jealousy, Ben sank into the sofa next to Lara with his head in his hands. Einstein came to him and nuzzled him for affection. Ben's large strong hands gently massaged the dog's ears. The room was silent. Finally, he spoke without looking at Lara. He struggled to get the words out. "You are right, Lara. I have no claim on you. Eric is a young single guy and he is doing what any young single guy would do. I have no right to tell you what to do. I have no right to be filled with envy and resentment. I'm sorry."

Turning toward Lara, Ben gently scooped her into his strong arms. He stroked her hair softly for a moment waiting for her tears to subside. Then he held her at arms-length searching her face intently and spoke from his heart. "I have been working twenty-four hours a day for the past week, all the while obsessed with the thought of spending Christmas Day with you—Lara. I wanted *you* more than anything for Christmas. And, I find out about this Eric guy who gave you this gift and this note. I thought you *missed* me. I said *I love you*, Lara—and you can't say the same words to me. Why?" There was an awkward pause as he struggled to articulate his deepest feelings for her.

Finally, Lara spoke. "You know why."

Ben felt like he just received a kick in the gut, then spoke in a calm measured voice. "I'm working on the divorce. While away on the trip, I was on the phone with my attorney day and night attempting to get the divorce agreement finalized. In the meantime, I was meeting with secret operatives in five different countries. It was my original intent to hand you the final divorce decree today, asking you to give me a chance—to allow me to *really date you*. However, the divorce paperwork is still pending Sienna's signature. Throughout the trip I just got more frustrated while Sienna held up the process. I'll be honest. I worried that you might forget about me. You know that old saying, *out of sight, out of mind*. I know you spend time with Eliot Stone and I don't know anything about this Eric guy. I wanted more than anything to come here on Christmas Day and tell you that I'm free of Sienna, legally divorced. I thought about you constantly while away. I had an opportunity in Israel to search in a few small shops between meetings and I came upon this. I knew it was right for you."

There was a pause, as he handed Lara a small silver box. She looked at Ben, then back at the box in her hand, unable to comprehend for a moment. "Please open it, it's a Christmas gift." Ben insisted. He seemed to be holding his breath.

Gasping as she opened the box, Lara could hardly believe what she was seeing: the most exquisite circa 1900 diamond Edwardian cluster. With a large perfect 1.5 carat vintage diamond in the middle with smaller diamonds surrounding it, the design created an old European flower motif, a one-of-a-kind antique ring.

"It's beautiful!" Lara whispered breathlessly.

"I hoped you'd like it." Ben exhaled. His words were genuine, and Lara sensed the pain Ben was experiencing as he held her so tightly she could hardly breathe. His face was now buried in her hair, his breathing irregular. Lara knew he didn't want her to witness the feelings overpowering him. Remaining in his strong embrace she clung to him as he heaved and coughed.

Feeling guilty, Lara realized she had just ruined this highly anticipated homecoming for Ben. A few minutes passed, then he gently pulled away. Ben's beautiful blue eyes lit up when he stared into hers. "I'll get the divorce, I promise." he said with his Irish brogue. There was a glimmer of hope in his eyes. As he tenderly embraced her, Ben's blue eyes closed as his lips lightly brushed hers, tentatively at first. Lara's lips slightly parted. Taking his cue, Ben teased Lara with an intimate kiss that sent a rush of heat through her entire body. Her heart was racing. Ben slipped the ring onto her finger as a silent tear of joy slid down her cheek.

How did he know her ring size? How did he know her style? No one else in the world would have a ring like this one.

"I have insured it for you." Ben smiled with dimples. "It's worth a pretty penny."

Just as he said that, she handed him the gift she had purchased from Rupert. He opened it and held the ancient coin in his hand. "Oh god, Lara, I love it." The coin depicted a Celtic god. She imagined it was Ben in another life. The detail was amazing. The facial features and locks of hair were raised giving it a three-dimensional texture. The ancient gold was thick and heavy.

"This has great meaning for me. I will carry it with me always as a talisman."

He smiled and turned the coin over in his strong hand.

"Merry Christmas, my love." Lara said softly as she kissed his cheek and she finally whispered the words she knew he was longing to hear -- "*I love you.*"

***

Elated, Eric had a wonderful Christmas Day. In Boston, he downloaded all of Lara's personal texts and a Facetime with Ben. The app was proving to give him much more than the flash drives. Keegan was working as an operative for someone, and he assumed it was the CIA, but not certain. He tucked the small sticks of information away for a rainy day. He might need to use them against Keegan. Meanwhile, he played with the wording in Lara's texts—then sent them off to someone who'd be very interested in them.

He knew Lara would be surprised when she opened the tiny box holding the pendant. He suspected she would assume it was from Ben and open it in his presence.   He'd heard the reaction from Keegan over her phone and smiled. The mystery gift did exactly what he wanted—it sowed doubt in Keegan's mind. Eric smiled when he heard the tension between them. Ben didn't trust Lara—he had issues about that. And, Lara was fearful of giving herself over to Ben. Eric would take advantage of the wall that remained between them. Ben was still married and unavailable. He knew Lara would not give herself to a married guy. It was against her rules. This made Eric want her even more. He felt he had made great strides in the last few days. Keegan was obviously involved in something nefarious and most likely dangerous. Eric felt he was more deserving of her affection, but he had to gain her trust. While driving to Uncle Don's farmhouse, Eric was formulating the plan in his mind in detail. He would not give up. Eric prided himself as being that guy—who would not take no for an answer.

Ben was exhausted, and Einstein was already comfortable in Lara's parlor. The best part about Christmas day was the incredible happiness Lara felt in her heart. Ben was home safely from his overseas journey. Breaking the quiet din of the low television noise in the background, a text message chimed on Lara's phone. A quick glance told her it was from Sienna, Ben's wife. The message included her phone number, inviting Lara to call her. Stunned, Lara looked at the words again, wondering *why* Sienna would contact her on Christmas Day. A chill ran down her spine. She didn't want to disturb Ben. He had fallen into a sleep coma on her sofa with Einstein. Lara pondered sending a reply to Sienna. She instinctively messaged back: *I will call you.*

Later in the day, when she looked at her phone there was a voicemail message from Sienna. Lara listened to it. Sienna's voice was calm and soft in the recording. She invited Lara to talk with her before getting too involved with Ben. It sounded like a warning. Lara played Sienna's voice message three times before she got up the courage to make the phone call, while Ben was napping.

Sienna answered on the second ring, her voice feminine and sweet. "Thank you for calling me, Lara. I know this isn't easy to do. I know Ben is involved with you. What I am going to tell you about Ben is strictly for your own benefit. First, you should know that Ben has never been a husband to me or a father to William. He never had time for us. He was too busy being a Navy SEAL. And, when he started his own business, I thought things might change but it only got worse. I just want you to know going into a relationship with him, it is a lonely life to be married to this guy. Think long and hard before you jump in. He's handsome and sexy, but women throw themselves at him constantly wherever he goes. You'll spend your life alone, feeling lucky to get a phone call from him. You'll never be able to hold him for long. He's a wild man."

Lara responded. "We are only friends. It's not what you think. I am not one of the women chasing Ben. I'm holding out for marriage. Yes, I know I'm considered a freak in today's world, but I'm *not* sleeping with your husband. Your marriage and divorce— that's *your* business. I'm sorry to see anyone's marriage end— believe me. I had nothing to do with his decision to divorce you. He was well into that long before I met him. Ben and I are neighbors and I'm a designer. He hired me to do his office at the university." Sienna listened intently. "That's interesting—actually, I have someone texting me, and telling me a *different* story and I have received more than that."

Lara was shocked. Who was texting her? And what else had they sent?

"That's strange. I don't know who is sending you text messages. But, I'm telling you the truth." Lara declared with conviction.

Sienna seemed to hesitate; maybe she wanted to believe Lara. "I need to hang up now, someone's at the door." Lara had a feeling there would be more phone calls like this.

As Ben continued napping, Lara slipped into his apartment to make sure everything was in place. She had shopped and stocked his fridge a few days before and placed fresh flowers in every room to make the place smell wonderful. Lara wrote a note to Ben on his kitchen chalkboard:

Missed you terribly but got what I wanted for Christmas - you!

All my love, Lara.

Sienna's words burned into her brain: *you'll never be able to hold him for long.* She hurried back to her apartment. Ben and Einstein had not moved. They were both snoring. Lara snapped a photo of them with her phone. They looked so innocent sleeping on the sofa together. Einstein was so happy to be with Ben. And, Ben looked peaceful. His black hair was slicked back, and his skin was slightly red—either sunburnt or windburned—she wasn't sure. His sleeping face had an innocence that melted her heart. Lara could not stop herself from wondering what their child might look like. Ben was sprawled awkwardly on the sofa and Lara watched his chest rise and fall. To make him more comfortable she gently placed a soft pillow beneath his head. With his beautiful blue eyes closed, she noted how black his brows and lashes were. He hadn't shaved for days.

As Lara removed his shoes and socks he did not move. His six-foot two-inch frame was lying before her and she contemplated what he looked like without clothing. She carefully unbuttoned his shirt examining his chest and torso. He did not have a tattoo on his chest, but he had plenty of scars. She couldn't stop herself from running her hand over his powerful chest. Her fingers traced his torso, skimming over his solid core. She placed his dangling arm upon the sofa. He briefly stirred, but he was out like a light.

She had an overwhelming desire to lie upon his chest and listen to his heartbeat. She slipped his shirt off one arm and then the other, admiring the defined elongated muscles in his biceps and forearms. She ran her finger over the Celtic cross tattoo on his right bicep. Her hands followed the curves and contours of the muscles of his arms, admiring scars and all. Even his wrists had muscles. She felt him move slightly as she removed his shirt, but he was out cold. She scrutinized the wounds that covered his chest and arms, curious, but afraid to know what caused them. The scars fell into three categories: bullet wounds, lacerations, and burns. The tissue had healed leaving pink disfigured flesh and pock marks and she lightly caressed each one with her fingers.

Carefully, she unbuttoned and unzipped his pants. He stirred but did not wake. She noticed he wore snug-fitting boxers and had a knife tucked inside his waistband. She gently slipped his pants off. She did not touch his legs fearing she might wake him. She studied the contour of his perfectly formed thighs, knees and calves. Even his ankles had scars. Feeling she had already gone too far, Lara took a cotton blanket and covered the sleeping warrior. For a long moment, she remembered what Harris had told her— *he had been captured twice, tortured for days.*

Being a realist, she knew there were serious impediments to having Ben as her husband. Top on the list was Sienna. She also sensed Ben's dislike of Eliot Stone. But, an ever-looming barrier might be Ben's secret life and his dedication to Dark Horse. His frequent absences could eventually take a toll on any relationship. She knew she had to tell him about the conversation with Sienna.

An hour later, Ben woke from his nap and could not help but smile.

"Hey what happened here, my shirt is off, and my pants are gone...."

Lara was laughing as she confessed. "I was curious, and you were sound asleep."

Ben smiled with his whole face, responsive to the idea.

"Hey, let's do this exploration when I am *awake*. I think it would be much more enjoyable for me that way."

Lara wrinkled her nose. "Not just yet."

Ben was treated to a perfectly prepared Christmas dinner, planned by Lara especially for him.

"This is the best tenderloin I've ever had." He smiled as he ate voraciously. She loved watching Ben eat. He enjoyed food and was not shy about expressing his pleasure. His favorite dessert waited in her kitchen, fresh berries and whipped cream. As they fed one another, she playfully dabbed whipped cream on his nose, then on his lips. He placed whipped cream on Lara's lips with his finger and she playfully licked it off. Ben took a deep breath and let it out slowly.

"Be careful, young lady, you are in dangerous waters right now."

The power nap and wonderful dinner was exactly what he needed to restore his depleted energy. Lara had a way of knowing what he required, sometimes before he did. When he woke from his nap, he was more than surprised that Lara had removed most of his clothing. There was no doubt in his mind she was becoming interested in him physically. He imagined her examining him as he slept and smiled to himself. He only wished he could have been slightly awake to have observed her reaction.

With regret, Ben replayed the outburst he delivered earlier. He was insatiably jealous with the thought of Eric, or any guy, receiving Lara's affection. Just knowing Eric was in her apartment drove him crazy, but the gift pushed him over the top. Ben savored every moment with Lara. He had waited two long years to meet her. His recent trip seemed like an eternity while he was away from her. There was no doubt Lara was the woman he wanted to marry. Even though she was an incredible beauty, it was Lara's mind, personality and soul he was in love with. She was sharp, witty, intelligent, sensitive, charming, and trustworthy and could keep up with him on every subject. Although she had been defensive and careful at first, once she trusted him, he found her to be gentle and kind. Lara exceeded his expectations in every way. He sometimes felt he wasn't worthy of her. He knew he loved her more than any other guy possibly could. He reminded himself of his mission: to marry her.

***

Lara's phone rang. After glancing at it, she shut the ringer off and ignored it.

"Aren't you going to answer that?"

"Not right now. I need to tell you something. I've been having conversations with Sienna."

"Oh no!" His face changed from relaxed to angry.

"Please don't get upset. During these calls, Sienna talks and I listen. She unloads a lot about herself. Actually, I think it has been a positive outlet for her."

Lara held her breath as she waited for Ben's reaction.

"Why the hell is she calling *you*?"

"I think, originally, she was trying to run you down and interfere with our relationship. But, lately the calls have been different. She talks more about her life and fear of losing William. I think she feels very much alone."

"I don't like the idea; however, I can't stop you from talking with her. But, you've got to promise me one thing."

"What…"

"You have to be bluntly honest with me—if these conversations suddenly change to threatening—you've *got* to tell me. She's good at that, Lara, believe me." Ben appeared to be struggling with the thought of Sienna talking with her. "Please, take into consideration her frame of mind if she says anything negative about me."

"I don't view this as a burden or intrusion. I am genuinely concerned about her welfare. After all, she is the mother of your son. If it gets out of hand, I'll let you know. In fact, I will tell you what the conversations are about. I can record them, if you'd like."

Ben nodded. "I'll leave that to you. But, keep me posted. I won't get too worried just yet."

Night was approaching, and Ben seemed ready to crash at Lara's, but she convinced him that his place was bigger, more comfortable, and ready for his return. Lara agreed to come with him. Walking into his condo Ben's face lit up with surprise. His laundry had been done, kitchen cleaned and stocked with fresh food, and the rooms filled with flowers. But, it was the note written on his kitchen chalk board that touched him.

"Lara, you are spoiling me." he said with pleasure. "Do you know which words mean the most to me in that message? *All my love.* That's what I want, Lara, *all your love*." She was thrilled to make him joyful for that moment. Simultaneously she was thinking the same, that's what I want, Ben, *all your love. You need to get that divorce before I can give you all of myself.*

Gingerly, Lara delved into the delicate subject of his secret employment, asking about his recent trip. Ben worked long hours, morning, noon, and night.

"So, can you tell me what you're doing, or would you have to kill me?" she asked jokingly.

"You're not far off, saying that." He continued to be evasive when it came to this subject.

Lara had to find some way to engage him. "Just exactly what *is* it that you do?" she finally asked point blank.

Ben wrinkled his brow trying to avoid her direct question. Then he drew a deep breath. "Lara, I really cannot give you details because what I am doing is classified."

Not satisfied, she pressed him further, "Ben, I am your confidante. Whatever is spoken between us will remain between us."

He still dodged the subject. She sensed he was squirming inside, trying to find a way to change the subject, and that's exactly what he did.

"I'll tell you this, Lara." he said with a wink and a smile. "If you let me take you to a faraway place on a white sandy beach for spring break, I will tell you *everything* you need to know. In fact, I will let you torture a confession out of me."

She smiled. "What did you have in mind, Ben?" She noticed the excitement in his voice. "I'm so glad you asked. I have a little tropical bungalow, really the closest thing to heaven on earth, and would love to take you there with me." He left the room as he searched for his laptop. Ben returned and tapped on the computer until he located the photos he wanted to show her. He adjusted them, and they filled the computer screen. Lara viewed a stunning slide show of a small bungalow on a white sandy beach at St. John Island in the Caribbean. Happily, Ben scrolled through scene after scene, explaining the rare beauty of the place.

"This island isn't overdeveloped, most of it has been left in its natural state. I especially love the outdoor shower. You would love it, Lara, and I would be so excited to have you there with me."

Lara wondered if other women visited the St. John bungalow with Ben. Did Sienna ever go there? She tried to suppress those thoughts.

Instead, she tilted her head. "How about first-class seats on the plane?"

Ben smiled. "Consider it done." He was pleasantly surprised that Lara agreed to go. Ben excused himself momentarily and signed into his webmail account, sorting through new mail and responding to some messages quickly. He then shut the machine down and put it on the table.

CHAPTER 21: *Make Me a Match ~ New Year's Eve*

New Year's Eve arrived, and Lara needed to put her plan into action for her mother and Rusty to share an intimate evening together. Ben loved the idea of Lara playing cupid. Rusty and her mother both thought they were coming to a party. It wasn't completely a lie—it would be a party for two. She had carefully decorated her tiny apartment for New Year's Eve and laundered the sheets on the bed, and the sleeping bag, and extra robes that guests used for overnight stays. A delicious dinner was prepared and left in the kitchen warming in the oven. A cold bottle of Champagne chilled in the ice bucket.

Soft music played, as Lara rushed downstairs to answer her buzzing doorbell. Rusty stepped through the porch doorway and followed her up the creaky staircase. Rusty got comfortable in the parlor as Lara placed a hot mug of coffee in his hands.

"Where are the other guests?" he asked.

"She will be arriving in a few minutes."

His eyebrows raised, and she felt Rusty studying her for a moment. The doorbell buzzed, and Lara escorted her mother up to the tiny apartment. As always, she looked wonderful; her black and silver hair pulled back with a feminine barrette, dressed in a white wool suit, her green eyes clear and bright.

Mother and Rusty sat in the parlor enjoying coffee and catching up.

"When will your other guests arrive, Lara?" her mother queried.

Finally, Lara had to tell them the truth. She sat in the

parlor and calmly explained they would be spending New Year's Eve getting to know one another better. The dinner was all cooked and waiting, champagne chilling, and they would both sleep here in the apartment. Rusty could use the sleeping bag for the couch; mother could sleep in Lara's bedroom.

"It's all been arranged." she said with finality. Their eyes were riveted on Lara as she spoke. They seemed to be amazed at the level of detail, planning and deception that it took for her to pull off this arrangement. *But, it worked.*

"I will be staying at Ben's tonight." As she left her apartment, Lara heard them talking and laughing again. She felt as if she had done a good deed.

Secretly, Lara was excited to have a legitimate excuse to spend the night in Ben's apartment. As she entered his condo it was dark, and Einstein happily welcomed Lara when she turned on the lights. She busied herself with dinner preparation while Ben finished working in his office on campus. Another phone message from Sienna was waiting on Lara's phone. Lara made the decision to contact Sienna again, at a convenient and quiet time.

At that moment, Ben bounded through the door. Einstein rushed to greet him.

"How did everything go?" he asked about the New Year's Eve arrangement.

"Perfectly." Lara smiled as a vaguely sensuous light passed between them.

"Just think." Ben raised his eyebrow. "Your mother could be falling in love just a wall away from us." Ben scooped her into his strong arms embracing Lara with agility and he whispered the phrase again in her ear. "Falling in love, yes."

Nestling his face into her neck, he caressed her softly, and explosive currents raced through him. Ben let his breath out slowly.

"Lara, this is a special night for us, too. We're having a sleepover." He nibbled her neck, in an effort to make her laugh; it worked. He knew that part of her reveled in his open admiration of her. But she managed to keep him in check, for the moment.

"Ben, you know the rule, no intimacy until you are *legally* divorced."

"Hey, come on—we've already slept together here—and I behaved myself, right?"

Her face was full of strength, shining with a steadfast and serene peace.

Ben had lost round one, but that didn't mean he would

give up the fight. She allowed him to caress her neck. He felt the warmth of her skin and inhaled the delicious scent that was Lara. His mouth covered hers hungrily. Then his lips seared a path down her neck, to her shoulders. How he wanted her. He felt her hand on his chest and immediately knew he was setting her aflame, the intimacy was getting to her. She wanted him, he knew it. As he released her from the snug embrace, he smiled.

"I need to go take a cold shower."

He hesitated as he stood in the doorway, "Can we at least sleep in the same bed tonight, if I promise to be a gentleman?"

Lara tilted her head and smiled. "I'll think about it."

Ben laughed. "So, will I-- while I'm in the shower."

Ben's eyes lingered on her, soaking in every detail. He wanted to embrace her and cuddle close. Sex wasn't the *only* aspect of a physical relationship. Maybe he could explain to Lara that touching her, in any way, brought him a sense of closeness. Tonight, could be the night she would allow him a little bit of intimacy. She couldn't blame a guy for trying.

***

Lara's plan for the evening was to distract Ben from his physical advances with something shiny. She was at Rupert's shop again and came upon an incredible 11th century coin minted in Dublin Ireland. She had it made into a pendant for him. The coin had a Celtic cross on one side and the word *Dublin* on the other. The unique artifact was no longer shiny but was pure bronze with a dark gray-blue patina. Lara's motive was to prompt Ben to reminisce about his roots, hoping the ancient coin would stir something in him. After dinner, she would spring it on him.

New Year's Eve proved to be a good night to stay inside as the wind was howling and the temperature fell into single digits. Ben emerged from the shower wearing a black T-shirt and running pants. Lara's eyes followed him; her heart quickened as he gently embraced her. He smelled of lavender and sandalwood soap.

Arriving at the table in the candlelit dining room, his blue eyes met hers. "Ah, now I see why you love this place, the atmosphere is wonderful, especially with *you* in it." He had the sound of contentment in his voice. Lara served a simple salmon dish with roasted vegetables and a lemon meringue pie.

Watching Ben eat, Lara noticed he made fast work of it. He always had an insatiable appetite. She wondered if he had the same appetite in the bedroom and sensed that he did. Lara had to stop entertaining these thoughts. She was already finding it difficult to fend off his polite advances. But she had to remain true to herself. In the back of her mind, there lurked the possibility that Ben might *never* get divorced. He could go back to Canada to his wife and son, leaving Lara behind broken-hearted. She had seen this happen to other women and wondered how they could be so stupid. She had to protect herself.

Retiring to the warmth of the parlor, they sat near the fireplace. Lara retrieved the small package for Ben and put it into his lap.

"What's this?" he looked surprised.

"It was hard to top that Christmas present...but I'll try with this."

Ben opened the box and slowly removed the ancient 11th century coin from its purple velvet sack. He felt the weight of the pendant in his hand for a moment; then slipped it on. It looked perfect on his solid chest. Ben's expression became serious as he fingered the coin, his eyes took in every detail. Allowing a moment of silence to lapse between them, Lara waited patiently. She knew Ben was recalling something, and she hoped he would open up and let her in.

His blue eyes met hers. "Lara, there are some things you need to know about me. You somehow knew I had a connection to Dublin. I spent many summers there with my grandparents as a child. It's a magical place to me."

He stopped speaking for a moment as the memories seemed to flood back. His pain was palpable, but he continued. "I especially enjoyed time with Patrick, my older brother, in Dublin. I hope you'll go there with me some day."

Not wanting Ben to stop talking, Lara touched his hand. His beautiful blue eyes locked with hers. "It's as if you *knew*— when you gave me this coin. I love it."

She thought she saw a tear forming in his eyes. He took a

few seconds then continued, "Once I fulfilled my eight years with the Navy, I retired from the SEALs—but only to create Dark Horse Guardians. The work that is performed through my company is called black ops. We gather intelligence for the CIA and other foreign intelligence services abroad, such as the Mossad. I say *we* because there are about thirty of us. It's most important that no one knows who the operatives are in Dark Horse. It would put our lives in danger. We don't want to be looked upon as heroes. We're not doing this for the glory. We don't want the spotlight on us like professional athletes or Hollywood movie stars. *We are the opposite of that.* We need to blend in and live most of our lives in disguise. All my operatives have front jobs. My front job, as you have probably surmised, is the teaching position here at the university. The other guys run used car businesses that I set up. The Dark Horse work must remain secret. We are working to serve justice for those who can no longer speak. It's my life's work to continue the fight against radical Islamic terrorism. September 11th was like a bell ringing inside me for a heavyweight fight. Instantly, I knew what I had to do. I can never bring back those who perished, but I sure as hell can spend my life punishing those responsible."

Lara held his hand as he continued. "I've caused and witnessed carnage in Iraq and Afghanistan that I can never share with you. I have problems with sleeping and hyper-vigilance. The medical diagnosis is Post Traumatic Stress. I'm working on it and have been doing better for the past year. I've worked with a counselor and learned to practice deep breathing, visualization and transcendental meditation. That's why I eat a healthy diet and exercise. It helps me sleep. And, Einstein has been a miracle. For the past two years before coming here, I lived in the cottage on Prince Edward Island with Einstein. It may sound crazy, but the work I'm accomplishing with Dark Horse seems to help. I feel as if I have control over what I'm doing. I'm not under the thumb of the government, putting up with their bullshit. I also feel like I am doing something productive, digging up intel, running back-door missions, eliminating targets. Dark Horse is providing a valuable service, making the world a better place. My work is filled with risk and danger, but I can't change what I do. It defines who I am. The beautiful part of our relationship is that I feel you accept me for who I am. You don't want to change or judge me."

"No, I don't judge you. Somehow, I understand—that feeling—of wanting to make something right."

Ben continued. "When I set up Dark Horse, I knew there was a lot of actionable intelligence in the Northeast quadrant of the United States. Plus, it was a short flight to Norfolk Virginia, where I'd be getting orders. I needed a job that I could use for cover, and the adjunct professor's position at the university was arranged through the CIA and my uncle Harris. *But, the main reason I chose Portland Maine was you.* I studied you for two years before moving here to meet you. Harris arranged our meeting at the recital. I waited that long because I wanted to be sure I was ready to be with someone. I'm full of scars, Lara. Not just the ones you can see."

His hand touched the ancient coin. "This piece is special, Lara. I'll never take it off. It will be a touchstone that will bring me back to Dublin and Patrick, and to you, and my sense of duty."

Lara's heart ached as she listened to Ben. She moved closer and pulled his head into her lap. He curled up and closed his eyes as she stroked his thick black hair. He was silent now. It was obviously agonizing for him to speak about this subject. She had a lump in her throat and choked back tears. Lara felt sadness as she gazed upon the handsome warrior lying on his side. Six years on the battlefield. Even when he had breaks from combat, he was training in work-ups for his next deployment. *He volunteered for it.* She suddenly realized how much Ben had given of himself. Stroking his hair, she watched him drift into slumber. Watching him twitch as he slept, she knew she could never completely comprehend what he had been through. His life experiences were extraordinary, only shared with a select brotherhood of men who were bound by a hardened silence. Knowing all of this only made her love him more. Lara feared losing Ben before ever having him.

When he was sound asleep, she tucked a soft pillow beneath his head and left Ben on the sofa covered with a blanket. She slipped into Ben's beautiful four-poster bed and closed the bedroom door softly. She curled up under the covers and inhaled Ben's scent. She fell asleep and dreamt of walking with Ben and Einstein. In the dream, he turned and kissed her and told her they could get married. He was a free man. His divorce was final. Lara was elated. But, when she woke she realized it had been a dream—a wishful one.

New Year's Eve in Ben's apartment had been a roller coaster ride for Lara. As soon as she opened her eyes she twirled the beautiful ring Ben had given her as a Christmas gift and felt her connection to him was irrevocable. She now understood why he had come to her. It was opportunistic, geographically, but *he specifically came for her*. Ben was already gone when Lara woke in his bedroom. He'd slept on the sofa respecting her boundaries.

She read his note on the kitchen counter. *Thank you for last night. Enjoy the coffee and breakfast in the oven. I'm in my campus office working. Love, Ben.* She detected the aroma of bacon and eggs as she opened the oven door. Pulling out a baking dish, she removed the foil covering it and was delighted to find a full breakfast cooked by Ben just for her. As Lara finished the delicious meal, she touched the phone number for Sienna. Her soft feminine voice answered. "Hello...Lara? Are you available to talk? As I was saying before, there are things you should know about Ben before you get in too deeply."

Lara took the obvious bait. "Like what?"

She listened as Sienna inhaled deeply. "Well, he is a difficult person to have a relationship with. He has been absent throughout our entire marriage. I can count on one hand how many times he has come to see his own son. It breaks William's heart, knowing his father is a plane ride away, but Ben chooses work over everything."

"Go on, I'm listening."

Sienna exhaled. "I don't know what he's told you about me. But, I will tell you this: I always wanted to be his wife. I am nothing but proud of Ben and his military service. I fell in love with him the first night I met him and got pregnant. He married me out of a feeling of obligation. I always hoped he would love me, but now realize he never did. I've finally concluded that Ben may be incapable of love in the way that a husband loves a wife. He has bedded many women, Lara. You are one of many. Being handsome is a curse. Women throw themselves at Ben everywhere he goes. I wish I'd never met him. Falling in love with him screwed up my whole life." Lara could hear Sienna's voice catch and the tears began.

"I'm sorry, Sienna. I didn't realize…"

Sienna regained her composure. "He's never so much as taken William overnight and now he's telling me I'm an unfit mother. I love my son; he is all that I have. I will never marry again. And, there's more, Lara. I suffer from anorexia and bulimia and have since my teen years. I got into modeling in high school. My girlfriends all deserted me at that point. They were envious of my good fortune. Despite my rigorous modeling schedule, I finished high school and went on to university. I graduated with high honors. With a strong work ethic, I made it to the top— modeling for high-end designers at fashion shows. I landed a contract with a French cosmetic manufacturer. I was on the cover of magazines. But no matter how hard I worked, my childhood friends gossiped about me and spread lies. I was ostracized and alone. The other models at the agency competed with me. My agents insisted that I follow a strict diet. Some days I drank gallons of water and ate a handful of almonds. I was seventeen years old and trusted them."

Lara heard her choking up again. "I'm listening."

"You may be surprised to know this about me, Lara, but I don't have *one* friend. The only people in my life are my son, my parents, and a few distant relatives. I live a comfortable life financially, but it's an empty existence. I am alone, and I am dying."

Pain squeezed Lara's heart as she listened.

"I'm glad we talked. Would it be all right if I called you again sometime?"

Sienna said yes. The phone call ended.

Ben's wife was nothing like Lara's preconceived notion of her. Surprisingly, Lara could relate to Sienna's experience with her so-called friends. Lara knew how vicious women could be. Although Sienna was six years older than her, they were two women, detested by other females because they were beautiful and successful. Except for the eating disorder, they had some life experiences in common.

As she hung up the phone, Sienna tried to imagine what Lara thought of her. She gazed into a large full-length mirror and wondered how she'd gotten to this point. She was starving—but it wasn't for food. There was something she'd never had—and it was love. Sienna Pierce Keegan grew up in the wealthy Vancouver Pierce family. Her father and mother both inherited significant wealth. Sienna was an only child and had a nanny from the day she was born. Then she attended boarding schools and the finest university. Her chosen profession was modeling, and her father connected her with the best agent money could buy. Her career was fruitful for as long as it lasted, about eight years. She landed magazine covers and advertising contracts and worked as a runway model at haute couture fashion shows.

However, the life she chose fueled her desire to be thinner—which seemed to be an ironic twist of fate. The thinner she got, the heavier she thought she was. The doctors told her it was a mental disorder, but Sienna fought with them explaining that her thighs were too flabby, her butt was too big, her stomach protruded. In fact, her stomach was pouched out, but it wasn't from eating too much; the bloat was a side effect of starvation. She lost modeling contracts due to health issues and spent much of her time in eating disorder programs and hospitals. She knew she would never get healthy. Everyone had left her, except her son, William. And, now Ben was trying to take him away.

At this moment in time, Sienna was bargaining with Ben through her attorney, Robert Townsend. The one thing she would not give Ben was custody of William. This was the sticking point in the divorce proceeding, plus the fact that Sienna was still in love with Ben. She would never get over him, but she was facing the reality that she never had him. Sienna was resorting to extraordinary measures to hold up the divorce. She knew Ben was seeing Lara and had done a background check on her—clean as a whistle, this Lara Reagan O'Connell. She knew Ben was crazy in love with the dark-haired beauty because pressure for the divorce had suddenly become a top priority for him.

A lonely woman, Sienna felt the only chit she held right now was *delaying* the divorce. Her anger now turned inward. She lived a daily life of starvation and purging. The anorexia had taken a toll on the former runway beauty. Experiencing serious heart problems, she weighed a mere one hundred pounds and she was five-feet eight inches tall. As Sienna looked at herself in the mirror without clothing, she thought she looked pudgy. She was 34 years old and dying. In a final act of desperation, she had reached out to Lara with the hope that Lara would stop seeing her husband. She knew it was a long shot.

Meanwhile, the conversations with Lara had been surprisingly pleasant. She was beginning to believe the things that Lara told her, even the part about not sleeping with Ben.

***

School and work had a way of distracting Lara from the emotional turmoil taking place in her life. Lara's routine was back to the usual hectic pace after the lazy Christmas break. And, she successfully played matchmaker for her mother and Rusty. For the month of January, Lara rushed headlong into classes, projects at the firm, martial arts with Don, shooting with Rusty, and now looked forward to graduating and getting on with her life. Ben was now joining Lara at shooting practice with Rusty every other Saturday and they looked forward to lunch afterward, as Lillian would join them. Rusty was grateful that Lara set him up with her mother on New Year's Eve. Things were progressing nicely on that front.

Lara continued receiving daily e-mails from Sienna in the midst of her busy life. Sienna laid her life bare to Lara in her lengthy notes, describing her childhood, void of love, she told Lara about being shipped off to boarding school at age five. Sienna never knew her parents. She didn't know their habits or their likes or dislikes. They were strangers to her. Her mother suffered from depression and was hyper-critical of Sienna. Her father was never home, traveled constantly, his attention given fully to his profession.

Frequently, late at night, Lara began calling Sienna on the phone and they would talk for an hour or longer. Slowly and systematically, Lara began to understand what made Sienna tick. Sienna had been to many counselors and social workers for her problems, but Lara sensed that Sienna had never given them the full picture. Or, the counselors could have been lacking in the skills to help her. Nonetheless, Lara was beginning to relate to Sienna in a way she never dreamed she could have.

For the first time in her life, Lara began to understand what made her different than the mean girls who excluded her. *It was the rape early in her life that defined her*. Although at the time, she thought it made her weak and vulnerable, it truly served to make her *stronger*. She had never examined the benefits from the experience and how the attack molded her life in a positive manner.

She was also gaining insight into the mean girls themselves—and beginning to feel *pity* for them. Most of them grew up in the same circumstances as Sienna—living lives void of parental love. The loss of family connection served to make them slaves to their ruthless peer group. The persistent bullying, teasing, and downright torture was a gauntlet to be run by young girls in order to fit in. Sienna ran that gauntlet and look what it did to her. *She was dying to belong, but they still excluded her in the end.*

Lara refused to run the gauntlet and ended up better off for it. She was glad that her parents had given her the foundation and the strength to go it alone, to be her own person, to stand up for what she believed in—no matter how unpopular at the time. Lara understood Sienna's pain better than any licensed clinical social worker ever could.

Meanwhile, another person was e-mailing Lara constantly—Rusty McManus. Love was in the air, as Rusty was now dating her mother. Lillian had called Lara and told her how *wonderful* New Year's Eve had been for them. Lara was happy that she arranged the romantic evening together in her tiny apartment. They were in love and Lara was happy for them.

***

Eric was having a heyday with all of Lara's texts and photos that she sent to Ben. The app he put on her phone yielded more every day and he was more than happy to forward them all to Sienna. Today a new excitement ran through Eric—he'd be giving Lara the news of his new job in Portland. He was now heading to the appointment to sign the paperwork for a promotion and a big raise—and, more importantly, a chance to be closer to Lara.

He knew Ben had not been able to obtain his divorce. Eric had been texting Sienna daily filling her in on the most intimate details about Ben and Lara's relationship. Yes, he had to lie about most of it, but didn't someone say *all was fair in love and war?* He imagined the cute selfies of Lara with Ben had to piss her off. Eric knew his communiques with Sienna fueled her rage and kept the divorce from proceeding, thus far. Eric was encouraging Sienna to *get what she deserved* from Ben in assets. After all, it was Ben who left her. She had been a dutiful wife.

Although Lara had refused to go out with him, Eric forgave her, and imagined things would change once Keegan was out of the picture. Today he was moving one step closer to Lara by signing the paperwork for his new job. He remembered that stunning purple Victorian in Portland—the one Lara loved to walk by and admire. He planned to drive by. It was only two blocks away from Lara and had a lovely ocean view, if he remembered correctly.

As she visited Ben's office after a long day of classes and work at the firm, Lara was thrilled to be in his presence. The events through the holiday season brought them closer. Even though their relationship hadn't included sex, they were physically intimate. Lara felt she and Ben shared a bond that many married couples never attained. Ben often held her hand and embraced her. He frequently told her how much he loved her. Always trying to brighten her day, he would do the sweetest things like write her a note or send flowers. Ben had trust in her and shared the most intimate details of his life, except for work. But he was beginning to open up to her and it was the closeness she longed for and treasured so much.

Returning from her afternoon at the architectural firm, Lara was heading to Ben's office to walk Einstein on this late March day. She opened the door to his office and peeked around the edge. "Hello handsome."

Ben looked up from his computer and flashed a dimpled smile, his blue eyes lit up.

"You are the best part of my day. This is my happy hour." He always managed to touch Lara's heart and make her smile. For such a tough guy on the outside, he was sweet and tender on the inside. Einstein ran to Lara's side and she dropped to her knees to rub his ears and kiss his beautiful egg-shaped head. He was ready for his walk. The March sun was higher now and remained later in the day. The walks were extended and more enjoyable.

"I have your fleece jacket." Lara handed it to Ben.

"Where *was* it? I looked everywhere for that thing."

Lara blushed. "I stopped by your office to pick up my books while you were gone. The fleece jacket was draped on your chair and I picked it up—it smelled like you. It helped me sleep."

Ben slowly took his jacket from her hand and smiled. "So, you *did* miss me..."

He grabbed Einstein's leash as they strolled into the fresh air. "It was a fruitful day for me, Lara, how about you?"

She thought for a moment. "I have a new client in Portland. It's a John Calvin Stevens house and they want a complete restoration. It will be huge. I am looking forward to it. The owners are thirty-something and they have two small children."

Ben was observant. "You seem to be a bit distracted lately. Do you have something on your mind?"

Lara had to be careful. He could read her. "Yes, thinking about *you* most of the time." Lara laughed and flirted.

He wasn't buying it. "No, seriously, you seem to be preoccupied, and if there is something I can do to help, please let me know. I have friends in high places you know."

"Can that friend in a high place get your divorce finalized?" As the words rolled off Lara's tongue, she wished she hadn't said it.

Ben surprised her, however. "I have an update on that front. Sienna has agreed to sign the divorce agreement. The kicker is: I will waive all parental rights to my son."

Lara walked in stunned silence for a moment.

"You mean if you get the divorce you'll have *no* visitation rights with your son?"

Ben looked somber. "I will have a strictly limited visitation schedule. I will only be able to see William in Canada, on her turf, until he turns eighteen. That's ten years away."

Lara searched his face for any sign of Ben's feelings about this arrangement. He seemed to have accepted it. She had to ask the obvious question.

"Ben, are you all right with that? It's an awful price to pay for your freedom."

He looked at her and squeezed her hand as they walked.

"I will do whatever it takes to wrap this up, so I can be with you. I will admit, I'm not thrilled about *that part* of the divorce agreement, but I have given this a lot of thought, Lara. It is what I need to do to get Sienna's cooperation."

She looked at Ben, hardly able to believe he was really walking next to her saying this. They were now in front of the purple Victorian that Lara loved, and they stopped. Ben's blue eyes met Lara's with an intensity that almost made her turn away. He embraced her and whispered in her ear. "Soon, we will be living in that house. I want to give you everything you want." Lara whispered back, "*I only want you.*"

CHAPTER 22: Secrets

A sixth sense, that's what they called it—and Ben had it. He felt certain something was bothering Lara but couldn't put his finger on it. He hoped it wasn't that jerk, Eliot Stone, and she did not dare to tell him about it. Whatever it was, he would find out. He knew Lara was getting close to graduation and the firm might make a job offer. He also knew he'd seen Eric Henderson's black Infinity drive by the house a couple of times. He wondered if that jerk was pestering her. Those things could be weighing on her mind, but usually she would talk openly about situations like that with him. He knew Lara was planning her mother's and Rusty's small wedding ceremony, but she had spoken about that frequently. But, he sensed there was something else.

Ben wanted Lara's life to be happy. She deserved a husband who gave in to her every whim—and he wanted to be *that* guy. He wanted to pamper her. He constantly thought about the upcoming trip to St. John, swimming together, relaxing on the beach. He was preoccupied with kissing her, making love to her. He went through the scene over and over in his mind. He knew she was new to the world of intimacy and it was important for whatever she experienced with him to be romantic and meaningful. These were things other guys laughed about, but Ben had tremendous admiration for Lara's serious attitude toward guarding her heart. There were few women who had the guts, determination, strength and self-respect to hold out for marriage. He was grateful that she was his. He didn't just love Lara, he adored her. Ben felt he was so close to marrying her. If Sienna would just sign the divorce agreement he would be the happiest man on earth.

***

A phone message from Eliot Stone asking Lara to attend an important meeting piqued her curiosity. The subject matter of the meeting was not made known to her, and she did not like walking into a room without knowing what the purpose of the meeting was. She made a phone call to Eliot's secretary, Nancy, to fish for information. Nancy told her the meeting would be in Eliot's conference room and could possibly have the personnel director there, so she thought it may have something to do with a job offer. Then she said not to assume that or let anyone know she said it. Lara hung up the phone with a feeling of anticipation mixed with dread. She dressed carefully in a gray suit with a white shirt. She was five minutes early for the nine o'clock meeting. She did not fidget but spent time breathing and getting centered.

Lara stepped into the conference room at the appointed time, but no one was there. She made herself comfortable as she tried to imagine exactly why Eliot wanted to talk with her. Just as she started flipping through the most recent Architectural Digest magazine, Eliot walked into the room and closed the door. Slightly tanned from being outside, his brown eyes met hers with unbridled delight as he sat across the table from her.

Lara set the magazine aside and smiled. "Good morning, Eliot, what's up?"

Eliot got comfortable in his seat unbuttoning his brown tweed jacket. He slipped a pen out of his pocket and had an envelope in his hand and he placed both on the table in front of her. "Lara, I want you to accept a position here at the firm. I am impressed with how you have handled your projects during your internship. I don't want to let you graduate and get away—I mean—get another job offer from a competitor. So, I am making this offer to you *now*, before you graduate."

Lara was a bit surprised she was getting an offer without the personnel director in the room. "Thank you, Eliot. I'm flattered and interested to hear what you have in mind."

Relaxing, Eliot smiled and waited as she opened the envelope. Her eyes scanned the offer. It was a generous salary, full benefits including health insurance completely paid in full by the firm. Also, there were six weeks of paid vacation in the offer. Lara read the fine print and hesitated.

"Do you have any questions about the offer? Is there anything that I've left out?"

Lara took a deep breath. "I would like a couple of days to sleep on it. Would that be okay?"

Eliot seemed a bit surprised by her reaction. Lara knew any of the graduates at the university would have jumped at this chance. Offers like this did not come along often. But, the truth was, Lara had thought about starting her own design firm upon graduation. She knew the level of dedication it would take but felt she had the connections to get her one-woman business off the ground. *She did not want to tell Eliot that just now.* After some small talk, Lara took the envelope with the job offer and departed the building. Driving home she thought about talking it over with Ben. Having his input would be helpful.

***

Eliot Stone watched Lara through the window as she walked to her car. She was particularly beautiful today in that tailored gray suit. She was more than beautiful, she was *elegant*. He was shocked that she did not jump at the chance to take the position with his firm on the spot. He wanted her on his team as a designer. The clients loved her. Each one she worked for came to him afterwards and told him he should hire her. They gave her rave reviews—and his well-heeled clients were not easy to please. Lara was an excellent listener and she went above and beyond to satisfy them.

Eliot was also fascinated with Lara's personal life, or lack of one. He viewed her as a lonely workaholic. He knew she spent time at the dojo and hung around with the new professor, Ben Keegan. But Eliot knew Ben was married, and he didn't picture Lara dating a married man. As far as he knew, Lara O'Connell was a single 24-year old woman living alone, and he was interested in pursuing her, whether she took his job offer or not.

Sinking into her sofa, Lara put up her feet on the ottoman and read the job offer carefully. The fine print stated that she would give up any possibility of leaving and starting up her own firm for a three-year period. She could, of course, leave and work for another firm, but she could not start her own firm and if she left, she could not take any former clients with her. Her immediate concern was: what if she took the job at the firm and decided a year or so into it that it was the wrong decision. If she was going to strike out on her own, she would have to do it now. Or, she could choose what seemed to be the safe option and accept Eliot's job offer with its great salary and benefit package.

She stopped at the campus café for a quick bite and headed to one of her classes. It was getting down to the finish line with only a few weeks left. She did not want to stand on the stage at the university in front of a crowd to receive her master's degree. Instead, she arranged to pick up the documents at the dean's office. The pomp and circumstance involved with graduation ceremonies bored her. She wanted to get on with her life. School, in a formal setting, would finally be over. She would celebrate in her own quiet way. The afternoon at the architectural firm went by quickly as she finished the last details of the renovation projects and ran through her checklist for the day.

Her phone buzzed with a text from Ben: *Can you dog-sit Einstein? No walk today. I'll be at your place in an hour."* She messaged back: *Sure.* Her first thought was; he's heading out to Virginia again for more meetings. As she walked up the creaky staircase to her condo, Lara decided a relaxing warm bath was what she needed at that moment. When she stepped out of the long hot soak she heard Einstein snorting at the bottom of her apartment door. Lara had just emerged from the tub, wrapped in her robe. She heard a soft knock and opened the door to Ben. His handsome smile and blue eyes radiated hope and Lara was pleased he'd stopped to say goodbye.

"Lara, I've got to hop on a plane to Vancouver right away to finish the business with Sienna. I'll contact you as soon as I have further news. I'll miss you, darlin."

Lara's eyes met his and she wondered what she had ever done to deserve such a wonderful man. As she embraced him, her robe parted slightly; she felt Ben's glance drift downward. She sighed as his strong hands slipped inside the robe briefly caressing her warm body—and for a split second, Lara reveled in the pure pleasure. She let Ben kiss her and he whispered. "You are amazing." As he turned to leave, he gazed at her and lightly touched her hair as if creating an image to keep in his memory. Then he was gone. Lara crouched and whispered into Einstein's ear. "It's just you and me again, buddy." However, she felt optimistic as she listened to Ben's footsteps going down the staircase.

***

Ben boarded the plane for Vancouver with the hope that he would be able to *finally* get the divorce agreement signed by Sienna. Negotiating with terrorists had been easier than negotiating this divorce. He needed to marry Lara before some other guy made a move. He felt hopeful Sienna would finally sign the paperwork.

Although he was hopeful the divorce agreement would be signed, he also had a sick feeling in his stomach that Sienna might make more demands or change her mind about some detail. *She was so unpredictable*. Confronting her was a chore that Ben detested. Sienna had become a skeletal shell of her former self. She no longer was able to model and was ill most of the time. The bulimia and anorexia had taken a toll on her young body. She was having symptoms of heart failure, yet she continued withholding food from her fragile body. He never could understand how anyone could cease eating or willingly regurgitate food. Sienna's teeth were now eroded from the constant reflux of stomach acid. Her bones were breaking down from osteoporosis. The worst part of their relationship was the fact that she took out all her frustrations on Ben and William, but in different ways.

Sienna was desperately trying to hold onto her marriage to Ben, even though they never had a normal marriage relationship. Ben never made love to her after William was born. He was overseas most of the time. When on leave, they would argue, and he avoided her. That was when he found the Prince Edward Island retreat. Sienna took out her bitterness on William in a different way. She coddled her son to the point of making him embarrassed and uncomfortable. William was ashamed of his mother's angry outbursts when she appeared at his boarding school. He did not want his friends to know she was his mother. Ben knew that William lived a life walking on eggshells around Sienna, as he never knew what might set her off.

The one thing Ben regretted most in his life was not taking William with him when he left. But he physically couldn't. When he left Sienna, he was a SEAL deployed to the Middle East. When he returned, he concentrated on setting up his consulting business, suffering with his own problems. There was never time for William, and it was the biggest regret of his life.

He wanted a chance to start over with Lara. If he was fortunate enough to have children with her, he vowed that he would be an excellent father. As the plane was about to land in Vancouver, the flight attendant smiled at Ben as she asked him to place his seat in the upright position. Vancouver was in a frozen state when the plane landed. Ben wasted no time getting to Sienna's attorney's office. Robert Townsend was one of the top-notch divorce attorneys in Vancouver and his office was a show of wealth. Expensive original artwork hung on the walls and the furnishings were rare antiques. Ben was greeted by the receptionist, and then shuttled into a luxurious conference room. Townsend had told him that Sienna would be at this meeting. Ben's body tensed. He listened to the clock ticking in the conference room as he sat there alone. He practiced deep breathing and meditation. He knew his blood pressure would rise just with the vision of Sienna coming through the door.

Finally, after waiting thirty minutes, Sienna and Robert Townsend entered the conference room. Sienna glared at Ben and sat across the table from him. Townsend sat at the head of the table.

"I'm sorry we are late, Ben, but Sienna has some misgivings about the divorce agreement..." Townsend's sentence didn't end there. Ben slumped in the leather chair realizing this was a colossal waste of time and money. He knew another roadblock was coming.

The attorney continued. "Sienna feels that she should receive more financial security, as she is not modeling any longer. Actually, she is not able to work at all due to her health issues." Ben listened silently, but he really wanted to put his fist through the wall and leave. Here was this woman sitting before him asking for his blood, sweat and tears because she was killing herself with voluntary starvation. Sienna was committing suicide and blaming it on him.

Finally, he asked Robert Townsend to please cut to the chase. "What exactly is it that Sienna thinks she is entitled to?"

The answer from the attorney infuriated Ben. "Sienna wants half of the 17 million you have earned as a consultant." Ben felt he might lose control. Sienna had no role in his business and they had been separated ever since William's birth. He saw this as a ruthless demand to purposefully derail the divorce agreement. Ben spoke with carefully chosen words.

"I'm sorry Robert, but we had a perfectly good agreement and I came here ready to sign it, in good faith. What Sienna is requesting is absurd and I will not agree to it—period."

Ben watched as Sienna's face turned crimson. He knew an outburst was coming. She stood and slammed her enormous designer handbag on the table almost hitting Ben with it. She shrieked at him with outrage saying he was cheating on her. She screamed the divorce was Ben's fault. There was a pattern with Sienna's outbursts. They were short-lived as she had little energy to sustain them. Exhausted, Sienna abruptly collapsed into her chair and Robert Townsend got her a drink of water. Then the attorney held her hand and asked her to calm down.

Ben spoke once more with calm deliberation. "We never had a *marriage* to begin with. After William was born, Sienna and I rarely saw one another. I was deployed in Iraq and Afghanistan for years for god's sake. The reality is my consulting business is *mine*, not hers. It came about because I couldn't deal with government bullshit any longer, so I decided to go on my own. Sienna never had anything to do with my business."

After a pause, Robert Townsend calmly asserted. "However, Ben, you *were* married to Sienna when you created that business venture, thus she is legally entitled to half the earnings."

At this, Ben stood up and stormed out of the room. He couldn't believe Sienna was taking this route. She didn't need the money. Her family had millions and she was the sole heir. She did this only because she wanted to complicate his life. He felt sick to his stomach as he took a cab to the airport and boarded the plane to return to Maine.

Two hours into the flight Sienna sent him a text message.

I love you, Ben. I can't let you go.

Ben closed his eyes. He had been hit with shrapnel in Iraq and enjoyed it more than this. He survived torture and beatings in Afghanistan, but this situation with Sienna gave him more pain. He had to think of a way to shut her down. The first step would be to freeze his assets. If he could not get an agreement with her, he would play hardball. He made a mental note to contact Seamus, his brother in Ireland. He handled his financial stuff and Ben wanted to lock things down.

After several hours of peace and quiet and homework, Lara heard a vehicle pull into the driveway and peered through the parlor window. It was Eric Henderson and he had a huge floral arrangement in his arms. What was he doing here *now*? He rang the buzzer and she ran down the stairs to discuss his spur-of-the-moment visit.

"Eric, what are you doing here?"

Dressed in a tailored black business suit, Eric handed her the bouquet and smiled. "Surprise, I'm taking you to dinner to celebrate!"

Lara was puzzled. "Celebrate *what*, exactly?"

"I haven't seen you for a long time and I have a surprise!"

"And, what's the surprise, Eric?" She forced herself to remain calm.

"Well, I thought it would be a great idea to surprise you and take you to dinner to celebrate my *new job*." Smiling, he remained standing on the porch. "I'll wait while you change."

Lara was confused and stunned. "Well, I don't think I can go to dinner with you."

"Uncle Don and Aunt Olivia will be disappointed. They wanted me to invite you."

"Well, hold on—wait here." Lara moved into the hallway and called Don.

"Eric is here—telling me something about a *new job*?

Dinner? What's this about?"

Don confirmed. "Yes, he's pretty excited. I think he wanted you to come to dinner. It's his way of thanking you for having him for Thanksgiving. You know—he's alone—and excited about this new job. We're meeting him at the restaurant. If you're busy, we understand."

Lara glanced at Eric standing on the porch with the flowers and made a snap decision.

"No. I'm not busy—I'll see you there." She hung up the phone and stepped outside.

"Okay, Eric—but, I'm driving my own car." She took the flowers from him. "Thanks, these are nice. Wait here, I need to get Einstein squared away."

While she ran upstairs and gathered her things, she slipped her pink wool jacket over her black T-shirt and pants. When she returned to the porch, Eric was waiting with a smile on his face. Lara started the Fiat and watched as Eric attempted to start his Infinity. She got out of her car and approached to hear him muttering. "Damn, I need a new battery."

"Want me to call AAA?" Lara offered.

"Sure, But I'll be late for dinner." Eric sighed.

She thought for a moment, then reacted. "I'll give you a lift, come on."

Eric squeezed into the Fiat, barely. They both laughed as Lara drove to a nearby Italian restaurant and they met Don and Olivia. Eric ordered a scotch, and then Don bought a round.

Olivia congratulated Eric. "It's great, you'll be working nearby, and we will see much more of you."

"Yes, maybe I'll see you at the dojo now that you'll be in town." Don smiled.

Soon Eric was having his third drink before dinner came to the table. Lara wondered if Eric was nervous, excited, or just thirsty.

"Don't worry; we will take him home, Lara." Olivia whispered to her.

"I sure *hope* so." Lara answered back.

"I'm celebrating my new job in Portland." Eric slurred his words as he sloppily ate his meal.

"Where are you working, Eric?" Lara queried.

"I'm working at a major investment firm—with a big raise and great benefits. They even gave me a signing bonus. Hey, Lara, will you help me renovate the house I just bought?"

Lara had no idea what he was talking about. After the meal, she, Don, and Olivia helped Eric into their car and she waved goodbye as they took him home. She checked her phone. She hadn't heard from Ben and was hopeful that the divorce agreement was being signed in Vancouver and she would see him tomorrow.

As Lara made her way up the creaky staircase, she was glad Don and Olivia drove Eric home with them. She could not, in good conscience, let him drive—and would've gotten him a cab or an Uber, if needed. If Don and Oliva hadn't been her best friends, she would've thrown Eric off her porch the moment she laid eyes upon him tonight. She didn't like the guy, but he was their nephew and they seemed to fawn over him as if he were their own son.

Ben had never been so frustrated in his life. Sienna knew how to push his buttons and he was most angry with himself for allowing her to put him in this state of mind. He tried to relax and forget about the aborted meeting while flying home, but he kept turning it over in his mind. There was one other way to divorce Sienna in Vancouver. According to provincial law, if he could prove her to be unbalanced mentally, he would not need her consent for divorce. It would be a long and contentious court battle, but it may be his only hope. Sienna would lose custody of William. Ben was concerned about how this might affect his son. But more so, he was preoccupied with telling Lara about the disappointing meeting. He knew she would not allow him to be close to her until he was legally divorced. Although this frustrated him, he also had a deep respect for the boundary she set when she discovered he was married. It was one of the reasons he loved her so much. She held steadfast to her principles. She didn't know, however, how much he wanted her and just how far he would go to have her. He lumbered out of the cab at 2 AM in front of the pink Victorian and stretched. Ben was exhausted from the long flight to Vancouver, then the lengthy return flight home. His eye traveled to the front of the house and he noticed the black Infinity there.

**

Lara was startled by the sound of the cab in the driveway and leapt out of bed. Ben seemed surprised when she met him at the door.

"I'm sorry if I woke you, darlin." Ben exhaled, his eyes bloodshot. He sat down on her sofa as she got him a bottle of water.

"It's okay, I just fell asleep." She yawned.

"Really? You're up late, darlin."

Ben began describing the terrible scene with Sienna. Lara had been so hopeful that the outcome would have been different, especially since she had been communicating with Sienna. She had the impression things were getting *better*, not worse. Ben looked fatigued and hungry as he continued talking about his failed meeting with Sienna. His beautiful blue eyes were fraught with anger and frustration. Lara made a salad for him in her kitchen. She listened as he raved about Sienna and her ridiculous demands. He told Lara there was one way to get the divorce and he would take that route now that Sienna had pushed him to it.

It made Lara miserable watching him twist in mental anguish this way. She felt helpless as she watched him eat the salad. She wracked her brain thinking of how to get him to sleep. An idea came to her. Lara took Ben by the hand and led him into her bedroom, then steered him toward the queen bed. The small bedside lamp bathed the room with a soft golden glow. As Lara faced Ben he looked exhausted and perplexed. She unbuttoned his shirt slowly and Ben smiled, his dimples appeared. His blue eyes met hers.

"Whatever you have in mind, I am all for it."

His smile was full of mischief. He enjoyed the long minute it took her to finish removing his shirt.

"This is what you need." She unbuttoned and unzipped his pants and pushed them down to the floor.

"Yes, this is *exactly* what I need." He happily replied. Ben was now standing before now in his underwear resembling a tired little boy.

"Let me take care of this." Lara said as she pushed him gently face down upon the bed and grabbed a bottle of lotion.

Ben laughed. "Hey, I *like* this idea..."

As she started massaging his upper back, she was mesmerized with the form and fitness of his shoulders. The muscles that made up his neck and back were perfect in symmetry and proportion. Lara heard him laugh and she slapped his rear as she straddled his lower back. His six-foot two frame had elongated musculature, a swimmer's body—a SEAL's body.

As she applied lotion to his back, he did not resist. She could not help but notice Ben was covered with scars on his back, too. His shoulders and arms were littered with wounds ranging from burns to knife and shrapnel wounds. They'd been debrided, then healed leaving hideous patches of mangled flesh. Lara knew she could never comprehend the horrendous things that had been done to his body to produce such scars. She had a powerful longing to kiss each one. Instead she focused on using her hands to smooth his muscles into compliance, gently kneading each section of his neck and back until she felt the tension subside. She finally felt him exhale. His eyes closed, and he relaxed. Soon he was asleep. That was her goal.

She covered Ben with the blanket and kissed his forehead. As she watched his face in slumber, she thought how young he looked yet realized how much he had been through—and the battle was not over. She wanted more than anything to slip into the bed next to him and wake the next day in his arms. She longed to soothe the wounds she knew he carried inside. Instead, Lara tiptoed out of her bedroom as she shut off the light, she closed the door softly. In her parlor, she curled up on the sofa with Einstein.

It was early when she heard Ben stir—he used the bathroom and cuddled beside her on the sofa. Lara giggled.

"I knew you were awake." He removed the blanket. Einstein whined at the door. "Duty calls." He had already dressed. He slipped on his warm jacket and took the dog out. When he returned, however, the smile had left his face.

"Lara—who's black Infinity?"

"Oh, it's Eric's—you know, Don and Olivia's nephew."

"What's *his* vehicle doing here?"

"He popped by unannounced—asked me to join him for dinner with Don and Olivia last night—to celebrate his new job."

"I supposed he gave you those flowers. I wondered about that last night." Ben spoke in a measured but angry tone.

"I can explain everything, Ben."

"Why was his vehicle left here all night?"

She thought smoke was going to come out of Ben's ears at any moment. His blue eyes flashed.

"Okay, this is what happened. We had dinner, that's all. His battery died. I'm sure the tow truck will come this morning to take it away."

Lara watched Ben as he absorbed the details. His hair was messy, and he was standing there trying to piece this together. Lara quickly changed the subject.

"By the way, you never thanked me for that fantastic massage last night."

Ben's posture relaxed. Finally, he smiled. "Oh, you have no idea how great that felt. I only wish..." and he did not have to finish the sentence. Lara could read his mind.

"I wish...too, Ben."

He moved across the room and embraced her. Her arms encircled his back as she nestled her face into his chest with the ancient coin now gracing it. She inhaled the warm sandalwood scent and listened to his heartbeat. Finally, not able to resist him any longer, Lara brought her lips to his. When she kissed him, it was as if tasting a tempting dessert—wanting to devour it, but at the same time wanting to savor it slowly. Ben responded as if reading her mind. His kiss was heavenly and naughty all at once.

***

Ben responded eagerly not knowing *why* Lara was kissing him; but he didn't care about the reason. His desire for Lara had changed from want to *need*. He would take any morsel of affection she would toss his way. If this was how he had to live with her, he would be grateful and love her forever.

Another meeting was coming up in Virginia. He would only be gone for one day, but he hadn't told her yet. He decided to wait until the details of the meeting had been confirmed.

Ben had to assume that Lara had no idea how much he truly loved her. She probably never experienced the devotion of a man in her life. He knew the level of closeness was new territory for her, especially anything in the physical realm. *But she had kissed him this morning.* That was a step in the right direction. Although he wanted more, that was enough for now. He trusted Lara and made a mental note to rein in his jealousy regarding her relationships with other men. But this was the difficult for him. This Eric character had shown up here, given her flowers, asked her to join him for dinner—even though it was with his aunt and uncle. Ben knew he was hanging around Lara because he wanted her.

It wasn't that he didn't trust Lara; it was other men he didn't trust. He knew how they thought. He was thinking the same things. How could any red-blooded man look at Lara and not imagine kissing her, mentally undressing her? But he knew he had to trust her, too. It would be detrimental to their relationship if he did not give her credit for taking care of herself before she ever met him. He knew, deep down, there was a side to Lara that only surfaced on rare occasion when she felt threatened. He knew, physically, she had what it took to bring a guy down. He had to trust her judgment if he was going to marry her.

It was difficult for Ben to put aside his threat assessment state-of-mind and just be Lara's mate. He couldn't stop the overwhelming urge he had to protect her. He wondered if he could ever really stop that instinct from kicking in—it was very much a part of him.

CHAPTER 24: To Have and To Hold

Regularly meeting with Rusty at his place, Lara was pleased to see that her mother had left some of her personal items there.

"Are you guys having slumber parties?" she teased. Lillian was at Rusty's cottage most of the time and it was great to see them happy together. Rusty, Lara and Ben continued their target practice sessions, however Ben was not there today.

Rusty asked Lara if he could speak with her privately after shooting. As they finished the session at the range, Rusty took on a serious tone. "Lara, I want to marry your mother. I hope you approve. I want your blessing."

"You have my blessing." Lara squealed and hugged him. "When is the wedding?"

Rusty took her arm and linked it in his. "You'll be my step-daughter. I always felt as if you were my daughter already. As for the wedding plans, I left that up to your mother. But, I wanted you to be the first to know." He was smiling. Lara thought she saw a tear in his eye.

After speaking with her mother, Lillian said she wanted to get married right there in Rusty's little cottage on the porch facing the water—nothing fancy. She wanted Lara and Ben to be there and, of course, the minister. She said April 2nd would be good timing for her, as she could move out of her condo and have her belongings packed and shipped to the cottage.

"Sounds like a plan." Lara smiled and hugged her. She noticed her mother's skin was glowing. Lara had not seen her mother genuinely happy for several years.

As the wedding night approached, Ben and Lara got dressed and made their way to Panther Pond to Rusty's comfortable cottage on the water. It was still cold, and the pond was covered with a thin coating of ice, but the sun was setting later now. Lara noticed how Ben embraced Rusty, as if they were old friends, athletes going onto the playing field. There was an obvious mutual admiration between the two. Lillian was dressed in a navy-blue suit. Rusty wore a sport coat and tie for the first time since Lara knew him. The minister arrived shortly after. Lillian and Rusty said their wedding vows on the porch facing West just before sunset.

Lara felt butterflies in her stomach as Rusty slipped the golden band onto her mother's finger. Ben squeezed Lara's hand and she thought she detected tears welling in his blue eyes. After the legal paperwork was dispensed with, they shared Champagne and a delicious meal brought by Lara. She also surprised them with a small wedding cake for dessert. It was a romantic and beautiful evening. Lara took photographs. The foursome sat in the Adirondack chairs on Rusty's windowed porch overlooking the water, enjoying the warmth of the wood stove.

"Spring will be here soon." Rusty said as they observed the birds of prey circling over the pond. The sun slipped slowly toward the horizon in a riot of yellow, gold and red. Ben kissed the palm of Lara's hand tenderly. The Champagne produced an entertaining burping contest between Rusty, Ben and Lara. Lillian decided she would be the judge. Lara was certain their uncontrollable laughter could be heard across the pond.

* * *

The next day, the dojo was busy when Lara arrived, and she went into the locker room to change. Emerging near the front desk, she tapped Don on the shoulder.

He turned and smiled, "Fancy seeing you here, where the hell have you been?" Lara hadn't shown up for a week. Don told her he would only be a few minutes and they could get a sweat-inducing martial arts workout underway. She could always lean on Don for support and guidance. In a few minutes, he returned, and they used a small private room to stretch and get ready for some serious grappling and kicking.

"What's up, buttercup?" Don asked.

"Well, I've been to hell and back. Ben was supposed to be getting his divorce agreement signed, and he flew to Vancouver and returned—somehow, the agreement fell apart".

Don whistled. "Sounds like Ben's wife could be giving him the runaround on the divorce and sometimes these things happen, Lara. If you love him, you must exercise patience. Did you hear the good news about Eric? He bought a house in your neighborhood. He told me you'd be renovating it."

"Oh, *did* he? Hmm. I don't remember that conversation."

Don then moved the discussion back to Ben. "Ben will get his divorce, come hell or high water. The guy's in love with you."

Lara furrowed her brow. "But, why is Sienna torturing him like this?"

"Ah, the complexities of divorce. She wants *something*,

obviously."

Lara told him the sticking point was custody of William and financial assets that stalled the divorce. She confessed her frustration about the divorce to Don.

"And, I just got a job offer from the firm. I met with Eliot Stone." Lara added.

"What's the offer? Is it what you want?"

Lara stopped lunging at him for a moment. "I'm really not sure...*what* I want." Then she took the big man off his feet with one quick move. Don hit the mat and she heard him exhale loudly. "You caught me off guard that time!" He then set about to give her some challenging moves that required her complete concentration and she ended up on the mat herself a few times. Bowing and out of breath, they agreed to hit the shower and meet at the smoothie bar out front.

Don and Lara picked up the conversation as if it had never been interrupted with a workout or shower in the middle.

"I'm thinking of starting my own design firm." Lara said tentatively.

"I think that's a great idea. Do it." Don said with complete confidence. "What's stopping you?"

Lara thought for a moment. She could live comfortably on her small stipend from her inheritance, but she would need to stick to a rigid budget. The reality was she needed to make money within a year. She didn't have any start-up money, except for her anemic retirement fund. She didn't have the confidence in herself that Don had.

"Money is my biggest worry." Lara confessed.

Don looked at her and smiled. "Lara, if you end up with Ben, financial issues will be the least of your worries." That comment made her pause. He was right. Ben had a healthy income, but the worries she might have living with Ben would be about something money couldn't buy: safety, security, life itself. Then there was the constant travel. Would she want to live the life Sienna described to her? She made the decision to strike out on her own and start her design firm. She had to come up with a good name. She loved the sound of Dark Horse Renovation.

On the way home from the dojo, her phone rang. It was Eric. He was in Portland and wanted to bring Lara to the house he just purchased. He asked if he could pick her up to bring her there. She made an appointment with him and insisted on driving her Fiat to follow him to the house. Even though she didn't *like* him, he had plenty of money and could possibly be her first client.

The moment she finished the phone call, Ben bounded through her apartment door.

"I've got to run to Virginia for a day of meetings."

Lara was finishing up the last of the details for her master's degree and had scheduled several client appointments plus a meeting with Eliot Stone.

"I have lots to finish up while you're gone. I'll walk Einstein."

She missed Ben when he traveled. He had become a fixture in her orderly world. Her life was not the same without him in it. Ben embraced her, and she could tell he sensed the disappointment she was feeling.

"My darlin." He spoke softly in her ear, then stroked her hair and caressed her cheek gently. "It's only *one* day."

She pressed against the six-foot-two wall of muscles. His arms tightened around her and he slowly pulled her body into his. Parting was filled with melancholy for Ben, and this was his expression of it—an embrace that left her wanting more.

"A kiss goodbye?" he whispered.

She nodded, and his lips touched hers. He always started off kissing her softly, gently, but built to a crescendo that left her breathless, and he never disappointed.

"Oh, Ben, I will miss you so much. You have no idea."

"Just one day." He smiled with his whole face and his blue eyes lit up. "I'll text you on the hour." His hand caressed her soft dark hair as he paused taking her image in, his eyes memorizing everything about her. In a split second he was gone. She heard his truck pull out of the driveway and never felt so alone.

Virginia. That meant he was getting orders for another mission.

CHAPTER 25: *From This Day Forward*

The movers had packed everything up neatly for Eric. Only his personal possessions were waiting to be put into the black Infiniti. He was thrilled to be moving to Portland to start a new career. But his true motive was to move his relationship from friendship to something much more serious with Lara O'Connell. He could not stop thinking of her. She was the one that got away, the one girl he could not bed. He would make her forget about Ben Keegan.

Lara was not just any girl. She would never tolerate a man that drank to excess or one that was unfaithful or unsuccessful. Only the best man could be her suitor. Eric vowed to clean up his life and pursue Lara with renewed purpose and energy. He would have much more time with her as she would be renovating and decorating the beautiful home he just purchased. The time together would be good to get closer to her, forge a romantic connection.

Ben was a major problem for Eric and his plans. It was important that Ben did not get his divorce from Sienna. Thanks to Eric, Ben's divorce was still in a state of turmoil. His wife, Sienna, had been receiving texts and photos telling her all about Ben's life with Lara. No juicy details were spared. Eric had driven Sienna mad with jealousy regarding Lara, and now Sienna *never* wanted to give Ben a divorce.

Feeling quite pleased with himself, Eric packed up the last of his belongings and tossed them into the Infiniti. He started the drive to Maine. He was moving into his new home this weekend and starting his new job on Monday.

* * *

As Ben arrived in Norfolk Virginia, he took a rental car to McLean. It was a direct flight and the time passed quickly. He prepared for the meetings he would be attending. Senator Sam Cohen on the Senate Intelligence Committee requested Ben's presence and sent him 1,200 pages of reading material. Ben read all the material. He marveled at how the U.S. government printed voluminous documents with many words that virtually said nothing.

At these meetings, Ben always did more listening than talking. The last thing he wanted to do was give too much information to any of these guys, even the good senator.

As he exited the rental car he took the sport coat out of the carry-on bag and slipped it on along with a tie. This was required window dressing and he was fine with it. Whatever boosted his credibility he would wear it. He tossed the carry-on bag into the trunk. The only item he carried was his laptop.

After biometric security clearance, his laptop was checked but not scanned. Ben's face was a familiar one at the gate. He made it a habit to be at least thirty minutes early for all meetings. Even if he had to wait, he liked having the chance to see who was coming and going. He did not like surprises.

Walking into the atrium of the CIA, he sometimes paused to look at the 102 anonymous stars engraved on the memorial wall. He felt a special affinity with those who came before him. He reminded himself that he was being paid to decrease and intercept threats to the United States of America—the very same mission those 102 anonymous stars had. He belonged to a uniquely secret group of warriors. Looking at the wall always reminded him of rule number one: *don't get caught.*

The meeting was to be held in the Special Activities Division conference room. In the past, his targets had been rogue arms dealers, terrorists dealing in weapons of mass destruction and scientists who were weapons designers, all working for the wrong team. He made his way to the conference room with plenty of time. The meeting was called by the Under Secretary of Defense for Intelligence. The subject matter was counterintelligence field activity which seemed vague enough— he knew what that meant as a contractor. The CIA didn't want their fingerprints on anything. He would be given an assignment that was something the government didn't want to be tied to. It would be dirty business, most likely high risk.

Sam Cohen arrived first. "Good to see you, Chief." They shook hands and others began filtering into the conference room. There were twelve people in all. Ben knew ten of them. After the meeting, Ben broke into a smaller meeting in a different room. That's where the details of the mission got worked out. Sam Cohen had to leave early to attend another meeting but said he would touch base with Ben about this subject.

In the smaller room, Ben met with one familiar face, the Director of the Special Activities Division, Kip Larson, and was given the outline of the mission. Both men took precautionary measures. Kip Larson waited as Ben swept the room for listening devices and set up a jammer, just in case. Kip Larson used a wand to check Ben for a wire. Everything was verbal. Ben used an encrypted program on his computer to take notes.

This would be a big complex mission for the CIA. The

bottom line was: the government needed specific information on sleeper cells operating in the United States. The top brass had executive orders to pull the trigger for a drone strike—if and when the cell was targeted.

However, they needed eyeballs on the target. Ben and his operatives would be the eyes and ears on the ground in the Northern New England sector. The payment would hinge on whether the mission was successful. There was no room for error. The mission had to remain top secret. There could be no collateral damage, and no one could know about the strike. There was huge money on the table. Ben verbally accepted the contract, with certain conditions, for Dark Horse. The hunt was on.

Now there would be a series of tactical meetings in the coming weeks to iron out the details. If Ben or any Dark Horse operative ever got caught or killed, the government would deny their existence. Payments were made via cash drops and no record was kept of this meeting. This was black ops.

At the firm, Lara caught Eliot Stone's attention in the hallway and asked if she could speak with him privately.

"Of course, Lara. Come in." Eliot smiled as he held his office door open.

Lara sat in an expensive ultra-modern chair created by a famous designer made of transparent plastic. Wearing a deep burgundy suit with a patterned scarf and her favorite diamond earrings, her dark hair was loosely pinned into a French twist.

"First of all, Eliot, I want to thank you sincerely for the wonderful job offer. I have given this a tremendous amount of thought and have decided to decline it."

Eliot's facial expression changed from excitement to dismay. "I must confess, Lara. I am a bit surprised."

Lara knew she had to play her hand carefully with Eliot. He was a powerful entity in the small world of design in New England, and she preferred to stay on his good side, if possible.

"This may come as a surprise to you, Eliot, but I have aspirations to start my own company. I know it will be difficult at first, but I have confidence in my abilities, thanks to you, to go forward with the dream of owning my own firm. I was lucky to have the experience of working for you as an intern. Without your tutelage, I never would have thought this possible."

She hoped by laying on the compliments he would at least respect her determination. Eliot's brown eyes seemed deep in thought. Lara anticipated he would try to sweeten his offer and that's exactly what he did.

"If I gave you a bigger salary or better benefits, would you reconsider?"

Lara looked down at her hands on the table holding the job offer. Without looking at him she slid the envelope toward the middle of his desk.

"I can't, Eliot." Lara stood to leave his office. Walking around his desk she faced him and extended her hand and spoke with genuine kindness. "Thank you, Eliot. I won't forget all that you have done for me."

Eliot's brown eyes met hers and she felt the warmth that emanated from them. He grasped Lara's hand with both of his and smiled pleasantly. "I shall miss you, Lara."

She sensed there was more.

"Lara, would you consider having dinner with me?" She was blindsided by this. She never thought Eliot would ask her out, especially at this moment. "Well, I am seeing someone right now."

Eliot was still holding her hand and finished her sentence. "Ben Keegan."

Lara felt embarrassed for a moment. Removing her hand from his, she felt a bit awkward. "Yes. It's Ben Keegan."

She felt Eliot studying her face closely, and Lara felt her face warm.

Then, he surprised her. "If you are going to start your own firm, I want to give you some advice regarding going on your own. There will be things like liability insurance and contracts that will protect you in client relationships. It may shock you, Lara, but I want to see you *succeed*."

At this, Lara smiled. She knew Eliot would be an important ally.

"That's very kind of you, Eliot." Lara exhaled. "Give me a call and we'll schedule it."

Eliot Stone watched Lara walk across the parking lot from his office window. He was stunned by her beauty in the burgundy jacket today. He imagined what her hair looked like when it was loose. She always tied it up at work. He was more than surprised she turned his offer down. But he felt a sense of freedom now to *really* pursue her—actually, it would be much easier for him to pave the way for a personal relationship with her now that she *wasn't* an employee.

Very few women ever turned Eliot down in business or in pleasure. He had admired Lara for two years now, remembering the day he talked his father into hiring her for the internship. He knew the first time he met her that Lara's beauty alone would attract clients, but she also had a magnetic personality and was highly intelligent. She wasn't full of herself, but confident and bright—there was a difference. Lara was also a hard worker and she made a good deal of money for his firm.

He was confident she would be successful starting up her own firm, this much he knew. Lara would also make a perfect wife and mother. Eliot wanted a wife and family, sooner rather than later. His thoughts turned to winning her over. He knew impressing her would be difficult. She was not dazzled by his wealth, as other women were. He knew he would need to impress Lara in other ways. He planned to give Ben Keegan a run for his money.

Taking a deep breath as she got into her Fiat, Lara thought the meeting with Eliot had gone better than planned. She went about her day of classes and worked on wrapping up design projects. Driving into the pink Victorian's driveway her phone chimed, it was a text from Ben. He was on his way home from his meeting in Virginia. In his message, Ben told her he was taking her to dinner. She got into a hot shower to prepare for Ben's return. In her bathrobe, as she was brushing her teeth, the doorbell buzzed.

Wondering if Ben had arrived early, she looked through the parlor window. Eric's Infiniti was in the front driveway. She ran down the creaky staircase quickly to warn him that Ben was on his way home.

Eric had a big smile on his face when she opened the door.

"Hi Lara, I am all moved in and want to bring you over to my new place to talk about renovations. Can you come take a look?"

Lara felt desperation sweep over her as she expected Ben to arrive at any moment.

"Eric, you need to leave *right now*, I have plans. You can text me and we will set up a time to go over the project."

Just as she spoke the words, Ben's truck pulled into the driveway and he saw Eric on the porch with her. She could tell by the way Ben jumped out of his vehicle that he was seething with anger. Here she was in her bathrobe talking to Eric on the front porch. She couldn't imagine what was going through Ben's mind at that moment, but she knew it wasn't good. As he strode purposefully toward the porch, Lara feared the inevitable.

Ben walked directly toward Eric and stood within an inch of his face.

"What the hell are *you* doing here?" he asked the question with a quiet fury.

In shock, Eric backed up and looked at Ben as if he'd just seen a ghost.

Once he got his footing, Eric said rudely. "I'm talking with Lara about renovating my new place. What's it to you?"

Ben glanced at Lara. "Is this true? Are you going to renovate *his* house? Tell me this is some sort of joke."

Lara had to separate the two of them and fast. Shouting, she asked Eric to leave. Grabbing Ben by the arm she pulled him into the hallway and closed the door in one swift move. As they walked up the stairs, Lara heard the Infiniti driving away.

***

Ben could not contain his exasperation with Lara. She was talking to this Eric character again and he was furious.

"What is *he* doing here? Am I missing something? Every time I leave, this guy ends up here."

Ben watched Lara as she got into a defensive position. Her arms crossed and her green eyes pierced Ben with an unwavering stare. At the end of his diatribe, there was an uncomfortable silence.

Her gaze was intense, filled with frustration.

"No. You're *wrong* about that. He bought a house. He's a *client*. He will be paying me to do a huge renovation for him. I'm starting my own company. Eliot Stone offered me a job, but I turned it down. I'm striking out on my own—starting my own firm. You will need to put a lid on your jealous outbursts. I can take care of myself. I did quite well before I met you, and if you leave, I'll be just fine. I don't need you looking over my shoulder telling me what to do every minute of my life."

Her words were harsh, and Ben felt the sting. Maybe he had it coming. But he had an instinctive feeling about Eric Henderson.

"Oh, and one more thing." Lara added. "Eric is working at an investment firm in Portland. That's why he purchased the house here."

Ben felt his heart sinking. He had to state the obvious.

"He's moving *here*, Lara, to be closer to you. *Can't you see that he is stalking you?* He's obsessed with you."

But, Ben never saw the next arrow coming.

"Like *you* stalked me, Ben?"

He never thought he would hear Lara say that. But he could not challenge her words. Technically, Ben *did* stalk her.

"I'm sorry, Lara. You are right. I investigated you for two years. I couldn't wait to meet you. I thought we had something—special."

Lara had tears in her eyes. "Ben, you are *still married*. I want a relationship with you, but I need to protect myself. Do you know how many women have fallen madly in love with a married guy, only to be dumped a few months or a year later? I always thought: how could they be so stupid? *But now I understand how it happens. And, I don't want it to happen to me.*"

Those words really stung. Ben had to differentiate himself from those *other guys*, and fast, and convince her that he was not the typical married man looking for a fling. He moved closer to her to argue his case.

"That's *not* me, Lara. I am *not* that type of guy. And, if you think that's what I'm about, you couldn't be more wrong. If you tell me you don't want me around, I'll go. I'll respect your wishes. I always have."

Lara had tears of anger in her eyes. "You don't trust my judgment!" She slapped him across the face. Stunned for a split second, Ben didn't move. He realized being a gentleman at this moment was the best course. The more he begged her, the worse the situation became. She wanted her freedom. He wanted her mind, body and soul. But, he had no *right* to insist on *anything*. He was still legally married.

Ben walked slowly down the creaky staircase and into his condo and closed the door. Einstein was waiting for his walk. For the first time in eight months, he took his dog on a walk alone. It wasn't the same without Lara. Even Einstein missed her. Ben took Lara's favorite route past the purple Victorian. As he approached, a sense of resentment filled him as he saw the black Infiniti parked in the driveway. Eric had purchased the purple Victorian that Lara loved, the one Ben had promised to buy for her. Eric bought it, and that sneaky bastard was hiring Lara to renovate it.

CHAPTER 26: More Trouble

Eliot Stone did not waste any time. "How about a quiet dinner at my place tonight? He dangled the invitation in his impromptu phone call. "We can talk about setting up your new design firm."

Lara was silent for a moment. She had been sobbing prior to his phone call.

"What time would you like to have dinner?" Eliot asked. "I'll send my driver for you. I have a great bottle of wine and Charles is cooking seafood tonight. How about 7 PM?"

Lara thought she could pull herself together and regain her composure by then. "Yes, Eliot, that would be fine." She hung up the phone and splashed cold water on her face. Her eyes were swollen and red. She was shocked and still reeling from the argument with Ben. How had it gotten so out of control? She couldn't believe she slapped his face—she had never done such a thing. What came over her? It was like all her frustration spilled out at once, and she could not stop.

As harsh as her words were, they did ring true. Ben *did* stalk her. He wanted a total monopoly on her affection. She wanted to give him all her affection more than anything in the world. But she couldn't have a romantic relationship with him until he was divorced. She could not tolerate his angry outbursts every time she was in the company of another man. Ben acted possessive and treated her like a child. He wanted to be in control, calling the shots. But Lara had the same personality. This may be the one thing that would destroy her relationship with him.

She decided tonight, with Eliot, she would focus on starting her new business. He was willing to help her, and she wanted to keep him as a friend. After washing her face, she used eye drops to soothe her red eyes and applied a fresh coat of lipstick. She dressed in conservative attire wearing a button-down navy-blue shirt with a long matching skirt and boots. She left her hair loose tonight. The April night air was chilly, and she cinched the hot pink wool jacket around her waist as the driver pulled up in the Bentley.

She glanced up at Ben's window, but his condo was dark. Lara listened to classical music in the Bentley as she treated herself to a tall glass of chilled champagne. The driver had opened the bottle just before picking her up, so it wasn't too fizzy. Lara had little experience with alcohol. She tried it when she turned twenty-one, but never developed a taste for it and didn't like the thought of being out of control. But this champagne tasted a bit like ginger ale and she had a second glass.

As the Bentley coasted along Route 88 in Falmouth Foreside, Lara stared out of the window as she swept past multi-million-dollar homes. The car pulled into the long smooth circular driveway and parked in front of the Tudor style mansion. Soft golden lamplight radiated from within. Manicured shrubs and flower beds were lit by outside lanterns mounted at a hand-carved wooden door. The driver took Lara into the foyer and Raphael removed her jacket. Then the small Italian servant escorted Lara to Eliot waiting in the luxurious parlor deep within the mansion. She passed through the library and an outer reception room before she got to the arched mahogany door of the parlor.

As Raphael opened the door, Eliot was seated in a

comfortable chair wearing a V-neck sweater and khaki pants. No tie tonight.

His brown eyes lit up when he saw her. "Lara, I'm so happy you could come tonight."

He rose from his chair to greet her taking both of her hands into his. Without the business suit, he appeared rugged and youthful. His thick brunette hair was usually tousled but tonight it was combed. His smile was genuine, and she detected the scent of an expensive aftershave. An outdoorsman, Eliot always had a slight tan. Being an avid sailor, he had lines forming on his forehead and crow's feet at the outer edges of his eyes. Lara never thought of him as being handsome, like Ben. Even though he was not a rough and tumble type of guy, he was a sailor and had masculine qualities. For Lara, Eliot's most important attributes were his kindness and patience.

Lara sat in the quiet parlor with Eliot for an hour and had a third glass of champagne. It tasted good and seemed to calm her nerves after the earlier scene with Ben. Lara felt Eliot's eyes on her. Even when she looked down, she sensed he was observing every detail. She wondered if he could sense her somber mood. She tossed her hair aside with her hand.

"I'm sorry for staring, but I've never seen your hair like this."

Dinner was served in the formal dining room filled with flowers and candlelight. It was lobster and tenderloin; everything was prepared perfectly. Lara ate with a voracious appetite. "I'm sorry, Eliot, but I forgot to eat today, and this is so delicious."

Eliot seemed to enjoy her enthusiasm for the food. "It's a

compliment to the chef if you enjoy the meal." He smiled, and his brown eyes met hers. Lara was trying not to be impressed with her surroundings, but it was difficult to ignore the opulence Eliot lived in.

"I really appreciate your help with getting my new firm established. I was going to call it Dark Horse Renovation, but I thought I'd get your input. What would you suggest?" Lara waited for Eliot's opinion.

"I like Dark Horse Renovation; that's a beautiful name. Or, you could just use your name, O'Connell and Company. But there's something about Dark Horse. It is unique. I can envision the website already. I asked you here tonight because I think I have your first big client, even if you don't have a name for your firm just yet."

Lara's eyes were fixed on Eliot's face with anticipation. "Who is it?"

Eliot grinned. "I was thinking of asking you to take on a big renovation project—here for me—this place. What do you think?"

Lara paused for a second, a bit surprised, but interested at the same time.

"What renovations are you thinking of doing here?"

He went through a long list of items, but the main renovation would be the kitchen, parlor, several bathrooms, and his master bedroom suite. The discussion led to a detailed discussion about her new firm, contracts, liability insurance, and start-up capital. As they moved into the library for dessert, Eliot schooled her in all the details of setting up her new business. He helped her map out a business plan. Lara took notes. He shared his knowledge and expertise with her freely.

As dessert arrived, Eliot sat across from Lara. She perched on the velvet settee facing the fireplace and he on a smaller upholstered chair facing her. Raphael served them cheesecake with fresh blackberries. Lara was bathed in soft firelight and she sensed Eliot drinking in every detail of her face and person.

There was a lull in the conversation as they finished. Then, Eliot started talking about his personal life, or lack of it. "I spend too much time at work. I'd like to see you, Lara, as a friend, if you would be comfortable with that."

Lara managed a smile. "I can always add another friend to my roster—and you'd be a good one." She tried to keep it light.

"Lara, I don't know if you have noticed, but I really enjoy being with you, on a personal level. I have never said this to you before because, as an employee, I did not want you to feel uncomfortable. But, now that you are going to be my equal, I feel I can be honest with you."

Lara was grateful for his kind words and a little bit drunk on Champagne.

"Eliot, I'm flattered. I would be fine with having dinner with you. But you need to understand that I'm involved romantically with someone…." Or, *was* she? At this moment, Lara wasn't sure if she was still seeing Ben. She twirled the antique ring, Ben's Christmas gift, nervously on her finger.

***

He instantly knew when Lara agreed to see him, there was

a fissure in her relationship with Keegan. Eliot caught just the slightest suggestion of that while they ate dessert. She never brought Ben Keegan up once. She gave her full attention to Eliot, for the entire evening and, he loved it. He found Lara delightful in every way. He could not stop staring at her tonight. She was sexy wearing a buttoned-down navy shirt with a few buttons opened at the top. He suspected she didn't wear a bra. He'd been staring at her in the firelight for a long while. It was surprising to him. For two years she worked in his office and he never knew this. Her beautiful eyes were expressive when she spoke about ideas for her new firm. He could not take his eyes off her sensual full lips. He fought to maintain composure. If she could read his thoughts, she would know he was excited and planning his next move.

As Eliot walked Lara to the Bentley, the April air had a chill and he put his arms around her. Lara made him feel younger, athletic, and strong. She had just enough Champagne to let him embrace her. Holding her close made his heart race. She backed away blushing and disappeared into the backseat of the Bentley.

Her beautiful face peered up at him. "Thank you for the nice dinner, Eliot." At the last minute, Eliot decided to slide into the backseat of the Bentley to accompany Lara on the ride home. He slipped off her glove and held her hand in the Bentley.

"Tomorrow?" he asked. He had to confirm another meeting with her. But, Eliot was disappointed as she pulled her hand away and slipped on her glove. It was as if she didn't want to give him the impression this was anything beyond a business relationship. As he helped Lara out of the Bentley, he could tell she was beginning to feel dizzy.

***

Ben watched Lara get into the Bentley at little after 6 PM. He knew she was with Eliot Stone tonight. She told him earlier that she would be talking with him about setting up her new business. However, Ben was stunned she ran off to see Eliot so soon after the blow-up she had with him. He surmised that Eliot called her for dinner right after he left her condo, and, in a weak moment, she'd accepted. He knew Eliot was seriously attracted to Lara. Ben even mentioned it to her once or twice, but she dismissed it out of hand. But, being a guy, Ben saw the way Eliot looked at her the few times he dropped by the firm to pick her up.

Ben got the feeling that Eliot thought he was superior to him. In Ben's mind, Eliot Stone was just another spoiled trust fund brat who lived a pampered life. A well-known playboy at the Falmouth Yacht Club, he lived off his family's wealth, and now he was moving in on Lara. The thought of this gave Ben heartburn. Then he realized the stomach pain wasn't heartburn but gnawing hunger since he hadn't eaten all day.

Earlier, right after the dispute with Lara, he'd taken Einstein on his walk and came home to feed the dog. Then Ben sat by his parlor window in the dark and watched as Lara got into the Bentley. He was still waiting for her to return. He drank water for five hours at the window. Finally, at midnight, she arrived home.

Ben peered from the darkness in his condo just in time to see Eliot Stone kissing her. It was just a peck on the cheek, but he didn't like the way it went down. Ben thought he saw Lara push him away. He continued watching as the driver escorted a wobbly Lara to the pink Victorian porch. He never knew her to drink, but she was obviously compromised. He could faintly hear her walking up the stairs and listened as she clumsily latched her apartment door.

He stayed in the dark parlor on his sofa listening for her movements a wall away from him. He suppressed the urge to run to her and embrace her. He knew that would only make matters worse. He had to give her space and time to think. And he would use this time to get his divorce finished, once and for all. He sent a text to Sienna asking her to speak on the phone in the morning. There had to be some way he could convince her to sign the divorce paperwork and get it over with. He was willing to do anything.

She had not been drunk like this, *ever*. Tonight, with Eliot Stone she'd had one too many glasses of champagne. She was mildly surprised by Eliot's behavior tonight. He was helpful with the start-up of her business and even offered to back her financially. The shocker was the kiss as she exited the Bentley and she realized that Eliot had a strong physical attraction for her. *Ben had been right all along.*

It suddenly occurred to her that Eliot had possibly been ogling her for two years and she was too stupid to notice. She thought about how Eliot presented himself tonight. Looking back on the evening with him, he started out as the consummate gentleman. When he spoke from his heart about his intentions to see her on a personal basis, she knew it would be a delicate balancing act to keep him as a friend. She made a mental note to reinforce that the next time they met.

She kicked off her boots and stripped off her clothing leaving everything in a trail on the floor. Washing her face in the bathroom sink she felt as if the room was spinning. She didn't like the feeling. As she slipped between the covers in her bed, she thought of Ben on the other side of the wall. It was quiet over there. She imagined he was probably sleeping. His truck was in the driveway out back next to her Fiat.

She replayed the argument with Ben in her mind. She regretted saying those horrible things and slapping him. Lara had never lost control like that before. But, she felt he was putting pressure on her, while not holding up his end of the bargain. He wanted her to be exclusively his, but he could not commit to her completely. *No matter how much she loved him, he was still a married man*. She lay quietly in her bed and pictured Ben sleeping on the other side of the wall. She missed walking Einstein. She missed Ben's voice and hearing about his day. She wondered if he was working on getting his divorce finalized or spending more time at the roadhouse. She woke in the middle of the night sweating and crying, another bad dream.

Lara did not have to wait long to hear from Eliot. Her phone rang the next morning and he wanted to take her to dinner at the yacht club. It was casual. Lara liked the yacht club and had an interest in sailing. She was totally ignorant on the subject, but willing to learn. She had plenty to keep her busy today. She had to finish up class work and polish her master's project. Her final day at Stone and Associates happened to be today. She was distracted in classes, and when she passed Ben in the hallway, she avoided his eyes. She did not even acknowledge him. When the appointed time for Einstein's walk rolled around, Lara did not show up in Ben's office.

She walked home to the pink Victorian and got ready for dinner at the yacht club with Eliot. Searching through her closet, she chose a red silk dress and a pair of low heels. Looking in the mirror she decided to wear her long hair up tonight and pinned it carefully into a loose twist leaving some strands undone. She remembered Ben loved her in red. As she was applying the scent of Sexy No. 9, she thought of Ben and wondered if he was burning the candles in his bedroom, thinking of her. Her reverie was interrupted when her doorbell buzzed. She looked out and saw the Bentley ready to pick her up for the yacht club. She grabbed a black wool coat and her leather bag and floated down the stairs to the driver waiting on the porch. She glanced at Ben's condo, but the lights were not on. She wondered if he was gone to Virginia on another mission?

At the yacht club, Eliot was there at the door to meet her. The sun was setting and the view of Casco Bay from the windows was breathtaking. Eliot pointed out his vessel on the mooring in the harbor, a beautiful 40-foot Hinckley sailboat.

"I put her in early this year. I cannot wait to take you sailing, Lara, you will love it."

As they entered a private room at the yacht club, Lara was speechless as she was eye-to-eye with all the employees from the firm.

"Surprise!" They all shouted in unison.

Eliot had set up a wonderful going away dinner for her. She sat at the head of the table with him. He handled everything, including a heartfelt speech announcing Lara's start-up of her new firm. She blushed as he spoke appreciatively of her internship and hard work at Stone and Associates. After dinner the guests stopped to congratulate her. Then after dessert, they said goodnight and drifted off one by one.

Eliot and Lara were now alone in a private corner booth with an ocean view. He had a bottle of her favorite French champagne brought to the table.

She hesitated. "Do you really think we need more Champagne?"

"It isn't every day you start your own business!"

She agreed. It was a time to celebrate. But she would only have *one* glass tonight.

"Here's to your new venture, Dark Horse Renovation." He raised his glass enthusiastically and said he had a little something for her. He slipped a check into her clutch telling her not to look at it until she was home.

"Oh Eliot, I cannot accept your financial help..." But Eliot insisted. He would not take no for an answer. Eliot was positioned close to Lara in the booth and at the opportune moment he leaned in and gently slipped his arm around her shoulders. She leaned back and laughed at his funny sailing stories. Eliot could be entertaining, at times, and quite humorous.

Several club members stopped by the table to congratulate Lara on the start-up of her new business. As the hour got late, Eliot whispered in Lara's ear.

"Let's go."

Parking well away from the building in the corner of the parking lot, Ben could see directly inside the yacht club. He forced himself to bring the high-powered binoculars to his eyes as he viewed the well-lit scene inside. The whole waterside of the building was wall-to-wall windows.

Slouching in his truck, Ben observed Lara as she sat in the private booth with Eliot. He watched as she tipped her head back laughing at whatever he was saying. He couldn't be *that* funny, the prig. He saw Eliot slip his arm around her. Instinctively, at that exact moment Ben's fists and jaw clenched simultaneously and he felt a knot in his stomach. He was compelled to turn away. The pain was too great. She was *his*. But it was clear to him that she enjoyed Eliot's embrace. Ben took a deep breath and continued his observation.

As Lara came out of the building, Ben watched her get into the Bentley with Eliot. Ben followed from a safe distance in his truck. The Bentley drove to Eliot's mansion, and he waited until it disappeared past the thick landscape surrounding the long driveway. Then he parked on the roadside a good distance from Eliot's house and walked up to the hedgerow.

He took a moment to scope out the security cameras. He spotted them and was careful to stay hidden in the cover of the lush landscape. Crouching and moving with caution, Ben made his way around to the backside of the Tudor. The large three-paned arched window of the library was well lit, and the drapes were open. Ben hid behind a grove of mature trees and watched with binoculars as Eliot brought a bottle of Champagne to Lara. Surprised, he watched Lara take the long-stemmed crystal glass filled with the sparkling liquid.

She was laughing again at whatever Eliot was saying. She looked stunning in the red silk dress. Ben had never seen it before. Her long dark hair was pinned up revealing the alluring nape of her neck. Lara was disarmingly feminine, difficult for any guy to resist. And he could see that Eliot was drawn to her. In fact, all night Ben noticed Eliot could not keep his eyes off her.

Ben was enraged to think of another man kissing and touching her. Even though he knew he had no right to feel this way, he could not stop the deep love he felt for Lara, nor the urge to protect her. Eliot was kissing her neck and his hands encircled her waist. Then stealthily, Eliot's hands slid down to her shapely bottom.

Ben, filled with self-hatred as he watched, knew it should have been *him* caressing Lara that way. Unable to continue watching because he felt physically ill, Ben made his way back to his vehicle and drove home in silence. He felt frustrated, enraged and heartbroken all at the same time. But he knew there was *nothing* he could do—or, was there? As he hopped out of his truck in the driveway at home, he tapped Sienna's phone number. He would speak with her tonight on the phone and *beg* her, if necessary, to agree to the divorce. *He would give her anything*.

While she was trying to escape the grasp of Eliot Stone in his library, Lara heard her cell phone chime. She pulled away telling Eliot she had to take the important call. Thank God, her phone rang at that moment. She excused herself to use the powder room. Looking at her phone she saw the message from Officer Bettencourt and listened to it. He asked her to stop by the police station tomorrow. He wanted to talk with her personally. His deep voice sounded ominous.

She called the cell number and he instantly picked up.

"Bettencourt."

"Hi, I'm returning your call—it's Lara O'Connell."

"Yes, Miss O'Connell. I wonder if you could come by the station tomorrow. I'd like to fill you in on some details regarding Bill Stephens."

Lara froze. "Sure, I'll be there in the morning. Would 8 AM be all right?"

"Yes, I'll see you then."

She felt something foreboding in his tone. Whatever Officer Bettencourt had to say to her, he wanted to relay it in person. She sensed he didn't want to go into the details on the phone. But, she had the impression this was on his to-do list, even though it was after hours.

She returned to Eliot in the library and made an excuse to leave. She thanked him profusely for the lovely going away party and the champagne. Eliot was disappointed that she could not stay longer. Lara had to get away and regretted coming to his home tonight. Eliot was making her uneasy. He got his hands on her bottom when he kissed her neck earlier, and she didn't like the idea of this friendship blossoming into something more.

Eliot walked her to the Bentley and embraced Lara tenderly.

"When can I see you again?"

Lara remained non-committal.

"Give me a call and we'll go over business."

She slipped into the Bentley and closed the door. She knew Eliot was expecting something more, but she was not going to comply. Ben was on her mind as the Bentley pulled in front of the pink Victorian. She noticed his condo was dark as the driver walked her to the porch.

In her condo, she slipped out of the red silk dress and unpinned her hair shaking it loose. Her cell phone rang, and it was Sienna.

"Lara, I hope this isn't a bad time to call you. It's late."

Lara said. "I'm here alone, doing nothing."

Sienna's voice sounded different. "It's just that Ben has been particularly brutal lately in our divorce negotiation. He called me again tonight. A few weeks ago, he was threatening to have me declared mentally ill, so he could take William away."

Lara heard Sienna sobbing for a moment, then she stopped. "But, now he's had a change of heart. He told me he *won't* demand custody of William."

Lara listened intently. Although she felt sorry for Sienna, she felt she had to stand up for herself.

"You think *I'm* responsible for all of this, don't you, Sienna?"

There was a pause and then Sienna surprised her. "No. I don't blame you any longer, Lara. At first, I did. *But now I realize Eric has been lying to me in those texts.* Now the argument with Ben is about assets. I want half of his earnings from Dark Horse. And, if he takes William from me, I will kill myself. It will be the end for me."

For a moment, Lara didn't know if she heard the words correctly.

"Did you say the texts from *Eric*?"

Sienna paused. "Yes, Eric. He's the guy that sent the photos of you and Ben and told me all about your relationship." Lara's heart stopped beating for a moment. Eric, had been sending the texts and photos to Sienna. *Why would he do such a thing?* She had to process that for a moment.

"I'll tell you this, Sienna, I am not dating Ben and the only relationship I ever had with him was as a friend, neighbor and a designer. And, if you want to believe the lies someone named Eric is making up, then you go right ahead. But, you're being lied to. I wish you the best and sincerely hope you can work out an agreement that gives you peace. You said Ben is willing to give up custody of William. That's what you wanted all along—at least, that's what you told me."

Sienna did not respond right away. "You're right. Thank you, Lara. You've given me a lot to think about." The phone call ended with a sense of shared camaraderie between the two women. But, now Lara had to find out *why Eric was sending lies and fake photographs to Sienna*. She had a sick feeling in her stomach and suddenly realized why he might do such a horrible thing.

The next morning Lara arrived at the police station precisely at 8 AM and Officer Bettencourt met her at the front desk. The big man towered over her as they walked down the hallway to a private consultation room—the same room used to photograph her bruises. He pulled out the chair for her to sit and took the seat next to her. Placing his hat on the table he pulled out a folded piece of paper.

When he spoke, it was in a low serious tone.

"You need to be aware that Bill Stephens has a long record of violence against women. I'm not supposed to do this, but here's a copy of his arrest record."

He pushed the folded paper toward Lara.

"When he attacked you, he was held at the county jail. The next night he was bailed out by his attorney, but he was picked up driving while intoxicated. He's now behind bars. The county sheriff's office contacted me the next day with a tip that Stephens had a lot of child pornography on his computer. I got a warrant and we searched his place and, sure enough, he's now being held for that charge as well. You can keep the restraining order in place, but I just wanted to let you know Stephens is behind bars without bail. With the additional assault charges, the

DUI, and the porn charge, I expect he will be in the Maine State Prison for a long sentence."

She opened the folded sheet of paper with the arrest record of Bill Stephens and her eyes began to read line after line of violent acts. Multiple charges of aggravated sexual assault were printed on the page before her. "I'll sign the paperwork for the restraining order." she finally exhaled. Officer Bettencourt prepared the paperwork for the judge.

Lara felt a sense of relief as she looked into Bettencourt's serious brown eyes and his handsome somber face. His hand automatically touched hers lightly, as he slipped his official business card to her. It was as if he wanted to say *I'm here if you need me*. She turned the card over in her hand and noticed his cell number was written in block numbers across the back.

"Keep this on you. Program my cell number into your phone. Don't hesitate to call me. I'm available 24/7." There was something kind and sensitive about his eyes. Then he walked Lara to the parking lot.

"You don't know how much I appreciate this." It was the first time she saw him smile, and she realized at that moment that he was youthful, kind and sensitive.

"You take care, Miss O'Connell." Before she got into the Fiat, she felt an overwhelming curiosity. "Military background?

She had Randall Bettencourt's attention. "How'd you know?"

With a slight smile, Lara said. "It's just the way you carry yourself and the level of professionalism you bring to the job.

Iraq?" she probed.

"Actually both, Iraq—then Afghanistan." he answered.

"Navy SEAL?"

Bettencourt's brown eyes narrowed. "How'd you know?"

"I just had a hunch." She couldn't help herself. "Do you know Ben Keegan?"

Bettencourt smiled. "Chief? Hell yeah! We were in the same platoon." Lara also learned that Ben and Randall Bettencourt knew one another from the roadhouse. Again, she thanked him for his help and for his service.

Randall Bettencourt tipped his hat. "Thank you, Miss O'Connell."

The April sun was sliding behind a very dark cloud. Rain was threatening any moment, but she didn't want the weather to affect her excitement. Now in the midst of launching her new firm, Dark Horse Renovation, Eliot had connected her with the best web designer north of Boston. Things were progressing rapidly. In fact, Lara had five clients, including Eliot, on her schedule for the month of May.

April brought a mixture of warm temperatures mixed with occasional inclement weather, but now it was in the form of rain. The yellow Crocus pushed their green chutes out of the warming earth. Then, Tulips and daffodils emerged from their winter sleep. By mid-April, flowering trees started to bloom. The oaks and maples hadn't unfurled their budding leaves just yet, but that would be coming in a week or two. Spring was a gradual process in Maine, but it always had the same effect on Lara, filling her with hope that better days would come. She couldn't imagine missing the majesty of spring, watching the birds return and the Forsythia blooming brightly against a stark landscape of dried mud and naked trees. Early spring always made Lara feel rejuvenated.

The sky opened with a sudden spring rain storm as Lara pulled the Fiat in front of the printer that was preparing her business cards and brochures. Although her presence on-line was paramount, she needed to have print media for those who wanted to hold a glossy brochure in their hands to look at the stunning pictures of her design portfolio.

She picked up the printed materials neatly packed in boxes and slipped plastic wrap around them. Then she ran through the rain to stash them into the back of her Fiat. As she did so, cars backed up at the traffic light creating a long procession next to her vehicle. Out of the corner of her eye she caught sight of the black 1940's Indian, with Ben straddling it. He was idling next to her car, three feet away, waiting for the light to turn green. At the sight of him, she ceased breathing momentarily. Rain soaked, Ben lifted his goggles. Her eyes met his, blue and filled with pain. Lara abruptly closed the trunk and got into her car. The light turned green. She watched as Ben pulled ahead on the motorcycle and was swallowed up in a mass of traffic.

At that moment, Lara felt her heart breaking. She wanted nothing more than to be on the back of the motorcycle with Ben, feeling the warmth of his solid body and experiencing the overwhelming sense of security that infused her just from touching him.

She knew Ben had been busy at the campus. He had left

town briefly a few times. She surmised that he traveled to Virginia. He worked constantly, either teaching classes or in his office on the phone, buried in his computers with Dark Horse. Lara had no appetite for food. She purposefully kept her apartment quiet so that she might hear Ben on the other side of the wall. She watched him drive away on the Indian and longed to be with him. She watched as he ordered mulch for the flower garden out front and shoveled it into the garden wearing a T-shirt. She couldn't help admiring his muscled arms as he expertly prepared the soil. She cried herself to sleep every night missing Ben and Einstein more than she could have imagined possible. Seeking distraction, she threw herself into her business plan with Eliot's expert help.

The Dark Horse Renovation website was launched. In a couple of weeks, she would officially have her master's degree tucked away in her filing cabinet. She needed to focus on being self-sufficient, building her own life, but thoughts of Ben constantly invaded her mind every minute of every day. She thought about running to him as she watched him coming and going in his truck. She would stop by Professor Harris' office occasionally hoping to get information about Ben. Rusty and Don Henderson told her Ben stopped by to see them and shared whatever information they had. She even thought about going to the roadhouse but didn't. She steeled herself every time she had these thoughts. Ben would remain off-limits until he was single. It was too painful to be in love with Ben. The distance kept her safe from getting a broken heart, or so she thought. It seemed her heart was breaking anyway.

But, she had a score to settle with Eric Henderson. She would meet with him today about his renovation and the rotten texts and photos he had been sending to Sienna. Her blood was boiling, but she fought to maintain composure. This would go down on *her* terms.

The past four weeks were the most desolate Ben had ever experienced since the loss of Javier. Losing Lara crushed his spirit. He spent many hours in solitude. Occasionally, he took a motorcycle ride to the roadhouse to meet up with the guys. But when he arrived there, they asked about Lara. *She was setting up a business, too busy to see him. That's what he told them.*

He missed talking with Lara, being in her presence. He watched her every move from his condo and at the university. He observed her visits with Professor Harris. He would go into Harris' office after she left to find out what she talked about. He secretly followed her as she made trips to Eliot Stone's mansion or went anywhere. He followed her to the purple Victorian and watched from afar as Eric Henderson answered the door. She now went there frequently with her own intern, Monique.

Ben continued making visits to Rusty's and Don's, hoping to bump into her at the shooting range or dojo. It helped him to talk to the men in her life. It made him feel as if he was still connected to her. Plus, he felt Rusty and Don were on his side. They were always supportive and sympathetic, rooting for Ben to get his divorce finalized.

Ben knew that Lara *could* live without him. She was a strong independent woman long before he came into her life, and she could easily make her own way. It was one of the attributes that attracted him to her in the first place. He second-guessed himself over and over about not trusting her with Eric. He berated himself every time he watched her walk out of her condo and drive away in the Fiat. He cursed himself every time he saw her in the hallway at the university and she avoided his eyes. Even

Einstein was showing signs of depression. Ben focused like a laser beam on the divorce with Sienna. He would give up William if Sienna would leave his assets alone. He felt he was very close to getting resolution. He was on the phone with Sienna daily begging her.

CHAPTER 27: *Satisfaction*

As Lara stood before the front door of the beautiful purple Victorian house that Eric purchased, she knew exactly what she had to do and say. She had thought long and hard about it. Expecting her visit, Eric greeted her at the door with excitement.

"Come in. Let me get you a glass of champagne."

Lara forced a phony smile.

"How about coffee?"

She walked with Eric through the lovely rooms of the incredible Victorian home instantly knowing the place had tons of potential. But her *real* business was to take place in the kitchen at the table with Eric.

"Let's sit down." She started slowly.

Eric made coffee and they sat across one another at the simple wooden table.

"You have a lot of nerve, Eric."

"What do you mean?" His eyes were fixed on hers.

"This shit—that you sent to Sienna!" As she spoke she opened the portfolio on the table. It contained a copy of every text and every photo Eric sent to Sienna, undeniable evidence.

"Where the hell did you get *that*?"

"I think the question is: Why did you do this to me and to Ben and to Sienna?"

Lara's voice was now low and deep, with an insistent tone. Eric stood and turned away from the evidence on the table. He ran his hand over his face and Lara knew he was searching for another lie to tell her. But it was futile.

He instantly switched into apology-mode.

"I'm sorry, Lara. I didn't mean any harm. I was jealous. I wanted you to like *me*, not Ben. I made a big mistake."

Lara thought he looked like the proverbial boy with his hand in the cookie jar. But, she wasn't going to let him off so easily.

"You have no idea the damage this has done. It has created problems for Sienna, and her young son. It has created problems between Ben and me. But the person affected most negatively is *you*."

Eric was backing up as Lara's spit hit his face—she was that close to him.

"Lara, I'm sorry. I wish I could take it back. I don't know what I was thinking."

Lara looked at him coldly. "I *do* know what you were thinking. That's the problem, Eric."

She tossed the sea glass pendant onto the table and swiftly grabbed him around the neck shoving him against the kitchen wall. Every nerve in her body came alive as she brought her knee sharply into his groin. Then, surprising herself, she drew her right hand back and punched him with great force just below his rib cage. Her left hand was still pinning him to the wall cutting off his oxygen. She held him there for a moment, as his face turned purple, his arms flailing at her, then she let go with her left hand and punched his face hard with her right. Blood spurted from his nose and she tossed him to the floor like a rag doll. Then, she realized she had better stop or he could press charges for assault and battery.

She kicked him while he was on the floor coughing and choking. She tossed a pen and a contract on the floor in front of him.

"Sign it!" She ordered.

She watched as he scribbled his name and snatched the paperwork away from him. As Eric cowered, she turned and strode down the hallway and through the front door. Driving away in her Fiat, she exhaled a sigh of relief. She now knew what Eric Henderson was all about. Her company would renovate his house, but she would charge him *double*; he had just agreed to it. And, her design intern, Monique and some burly contractors, would be at her side every step of the way.

Ben had been right about Eric all along. She owed Ben a huge apology. At this point, she wondered if he would even accept it.

***

The next morning in his office, out of the blue, Ben received yet another phone call from Sienna. But this wasn't just *any* phone call. She agreed to the terms of the divorce—just like that. She would maintain custody of William, Ben would have visitation in Canada only, and she would release any claim on his Dark Horse earnings. Ben could hardly believe what he was hearing. He was instantly flooded with happiness. As he hung up the phone, his first impulse was to call Lara. But this was something he wanted to discuss with her face-to-face, if she would have him. His first thought was to get to Vancouver as quickly as possible to seal the divorce deal while he had a verbal agreement from Sienna's own lips. If he could get the divorce, he would be free to pursue Lara. He intended to do so as soon as possible. He had waited long enough, dreaming of holding her, kissing her, making a life with her.

He would have to take the chance, go to her now, this minute, and tell her the news. He only hoped she would forgive him for all that went before. What would he do if she gave him the cold shoulder like she did the other day when he saw her on the street? She was three feet away when he was next to her on the motorcycle. She had stared at him and turned away. What if she had a better offer from Eliot? What if she was dating Eliot? Ben's mind was racing in a hundred directions as he locked everything up in his office and placed the leash on Einstein. He walked straight to Lara's residence, hoping she would be there.

Lara had just stepped out of the shower and slipped into her robe. She finished combing her damp hair and was applying lipstick as she heard her ancient doorbell buzz. She wasn't expecting anyone, and when she looked out front there was no vehicle. In her bathrobe she slowly walked down the creaky stairs to peek through the porch door. She caught sight of Ben through the wavy glass. Her heart was pounding. She could hear Einstein snorting under the door. As Lara opened the porch door, her eyes met Ben's as he stood silently before her. Einstein, wild with excitement, wriggled around her legs. Her eyes filled with tears as she dropped to her knees and rubbed Einstein's thick bull dog body. The dog whined with happiness. She held Einstein's face in her hands.

"Oh, my baby, I've missed you."

Her legs felt weak as she stood facing Ben with tears streaming down her cheeks. Ben swept her into his muscled arms and held her so tightly he lifted her off the floor. She sensed strong emotion was traveling through him. No words were spoken; it seemed he could not release her.

***

Ben was overcome with a multitude of feelings. He held her face with his broad hands and tenderly kissed her, tasting a mixture of mouthwash and tears. Without saying a word, he took Lara into his arms and carried her up the creaky stairs into her condo. Standing in her parlor, he felt her arms move around his waist and her fingers moved across his back. He closed his eyes as he buried his face in her neck inhaling her scent.

All he could manage to say was. "I'm sorry, I'm sorry." He knew he sounded like a broken record but couldn't help himself. Lara was sobbing uncontrollably. Ben felt responsible for her tears. He held her for what seemed like twenty minutes. When they separated, he gazed into her beautiful hazel eyes moist with tears. "I can't live without you. I have news about the divorce. It's over."

He couldn't physically release her. He had waited weeks, longing to talk with her, to touch her, to smell her. He had followed her movements daily, watching as she enjoyed meetings with Eliot Stone and as she walked into the purple Victorian to meet with Eric. For the last few weeks, Ben felt he was dying from a broken heart. He didn't want to release her from his embrace. He knew he couldn't live without her.

***

Lara was trying to understand exactly what Ben was telling her.

"The divorce is over?" She whispered.

"Yes. There's only paperwork to be signed, but she has agreed to it. I know it's finished." Ben sounded confident. "Lara, I need you to fly to Vancouver with me. I want you there with me."

Lara took a long deep breath. She wanted to go with Ben but was filled with anxiety. She had never been on a plane. She was terrified with the thought of flying. Ben assured her he could help her work through it. On his phone, he made arrangements for two round-trip tickets to Vancouver, then booked a hotel room and made arrangements for Harris to take Einstein.

Lara cancelled her upcoming appointments and packed a small carry-on bag. Ben got a stand-in professor for his classes. He had a bag packed in five minutes and a cab waiting to take them to the airport. Frightened and exhilarated at the same time, Lara's first time on an airplane was terrifying. As she stepped through the tunnel-like covering connected to the plane, she shivered— the air was cold. The moment her feet stepped over the steel plate onto the aircraft, she realized she had no control over what would take place for the next ten hours.

The distance flown from Portland to Vancouver was about 2,500 miles; they landed in New York as more passengers boarded. Lara felt panicky again as the plane took off; it felt like the load was much heavier. The flight seemed to take forever. The air was cold and dry at 35,000 feet. She drank lots of water. Ben was attentive to Lara's every need. He showed her how to use the bathroom. Too nervous to eat, she sipped water and tried to sleep. Lara's heart raced. The only time on the plane when she was not in panic-mode was when Ben whispered in her ear saying crazy things to divert her attention. His commentary in her ear was filled with risqué and sensual things he wanted to do with her, and it worked for a while because she couldn't stop laughing. He nuzzled her neck and never stopped touching Lara throughout the entire flight, even sleeping with his arm around her.

As nerve-racking as the take-off was in Portland then New York, the landing in Vancouver was even more terrifying. Lara watched as they flew over what seemed to be hundreds of miles of city. The slowing of the aircraft was evident and the clicking of the landing gear was noticeable. She clutched the arms of the seat, trying to control her breathing. After what seemed like an eternity, moving from one runway to the next, the plane finally taxied to a full stop. After ten hours of flight, they landed in Vancouver.

Although she felt exhausted, Lara knew she had to be strong and supportive for Ben during this tumultuous time. Ben checked them into a beautiful five-star hotel in Vancouver. He attended to Lara's every need, arranging for a spa visit and spoke to the concierge to make sure every detail was carried out as he intended. Ben quickly showered and shaved. When he emerged, his face was filled with concern.

"Sienna has been taken to a hospital not far from here. I just got a phone call while shaving. Not sure what's going on, but I am going to meet her there. I will text you as soon as I have further information." He looked so handsome, even when serious. He seemed to brace himself as if he were going into battle. His expression became solemn as he kissed her goodbye.

Having flown through a time zone or two, Lara felt hungry and tired. Room service brought her brunch, but it was really dinner in her body's time. Fresh flowers were delivered with a note from Ben, with a note scrawled in his handwriting, *I love you*. They were her favorite blossoms, a mixture of white and pink peonies. She arrived at the spa at the appointed time. As she stretched out on the massage table, Lara enjoyed the relaxation and a complete hour to daydream about Ben. She decided she could never be without him again, no matter what happened now.

Arriving back in the room, she received a text from him. Sienna was being force fed in the hospital; she was weak and heavily sedated, as she fought with the doctors constantly. Ben seemed discouraged and could only see her briefly alone. He literally begged her to sign the divorce paperwork that he brought with him. Sienna was unresponsive to his request and he left the room, hopeful she would be stronger tomorrow. He said in the text message he was stopping to see his son. William was staying with Sienna's parents. He would text Lara again later. Lara's heart broke as she contemplated the anguish Ben was going through. She wondered what his visit with William would be like. The thought crossed her mind that Ben may need to take physical custody of William if Sienna's health did not improve. She recalled the many conversations she had with Sienna and how she described her love for William. Lara felt a deep sense of sorrow sweep over her, followed by a strong instinct to meet with Sienna in person.

She awoke with Ben's hand touching hers, not sure what time it was. As Lara opened her eyes, she thought she saw tears in his eyes but wasn't sure. Still groggy from sleep, she listened as

Ben spoke.

"I hope you have been comfortable here today." His first thoughts were of Lara's comfort.

"Ben, I'm fine. How are *you*?" His blue eyes looked tired and he dropped onto the bed, his body lying next to hers, as he stared at the ceiling. Lara listened as Ben unraveled the events of the hospital visit.

"Sienna is in and out of a drug-induced state. Even if she signed the divorce document, it might not hold up in court because she is not of sound mind. I need to wait until she is a bit stronger, at least able to speak with me. Then, I visited William at Sienna's parents. He is staying there with them and doing well, despite the circumstances. I tried my best to tell William that Sienna had anorexia before I married her. It even affected her pregnancy and delivery of him. The doctor advised she would never be able to have more children as her heart was too weak from her deliberate starvation." Ben heaved a sigh and continued. "I wish I had never left William in her care. I am a terrible father."

Lara noticed tears filling Ben's eyes. Wrapping him in her arms, she told him he was not responsible for Sienna's disease. It didn't assuage his feeling of guilt, however. He said he could have handled the situation differently and the outcome could have been better for William. Lara knew he was flogging himself emotionally, filled with blame and guilt. She held Ben and softly consoled him.

Driven by a strong sense of instinct, Lara requested Ben to arrange a meeting between her and Sienna. At first, Ben thought the idea was not a good one. But, Lara told him she felt strongly about it. She wanted to speak with Sienna privately with no one else in the room. Room service arrived with dinner and they ate quietly.

"What will you talk about?" Ben asked.

"I know her, Ben. She has poured her heart and soul out to me on the phone and in emails for months now."

He seemed to trust Lara's insight. He phoned Sienna and told her she would have a visitor tomorrow; someone named Lara. Ben and Lara started out sleeping in separate beds, but during the night Ben woke and slipped into Lara's bed. She felt his body against her back and his breath on her neck as he snuggled against her. Lara knew he was concerned that Sienna might die. Of more concern, however, was his young son's reaction, should that happen. When morning came, they prepared themselves for the hospital visit. Ben brought Lara a hot coffee and croissant with fresh fruit while she was in the shower. Then, hailed a cab for them outside of the hotel.

Sienna was improving in the hospital, but her progress was slow. At least she was out of the intensive care unit. The feeding tube was now removed. Oxygen was being administered to her weakened body and she had been moved into a private room. Cardiac experts were in and out on a regular basis. Lara sat in a small waiting room at the end of the hallway as Ben made the initial pilgrimage to Sienna's bedside to let her know Lara was waiting to visit with her. From the end of the hallway Lara watched and listened as Ben left her room. He reported that Sienna's heartbeat was stronger, and the feeding tube got her past the point of danger. She was now sitting up in bed, looking like death warmed over.

Sienna seemed surprised to see Lara appear in her room, but her expression soon turned to a warm smile.

"You came to see me? I can't believe it..." she could barely speak.

Lara wanted to assure Sienna that she wanted the best for her and William.

"We have a lot in common, you and me." Lara started. "I am thankful that we had those long conversations. I understand what drives you. It's your love for William."

Sienna's large brown eyes lit up as she examined Lara's face and she listened.

"I want you to know that I am on your side. I believe William should be with you, his mother. And, I confronted the jerk that sent you those awful texts and photos. He did it because I rejected his advances. Eric was jealous of Ben. I met Ben though other people at the university and was hired to renovate his office. I also want you to know I have never gotten involved with a married man. To be honest, I have never even had a boyfriend."

Sienna smiled as Lara continued. "I'm here because I wanted to personally thank you for making the effort to get an agreement and put the divorce behind you. It is the best thing for you and Ben, but more importantly, the best thing for William. Would it be all right with you if I met William?" Lara placed her hand on Sienna's as she spoke, a simple gesture of kindness.

"Of course, Lara, I would love for you to meet William. He's quite a young man, you know. I am so proud of him." Her eyes never left Lara's. "I will sign the divorce agreement. I just want William. After talking with you for months, I finally came to the realization that Ben never loved me from the beginning. He married me out of a sense of duty. That's part of who he is. But it was never a real marriage. Through talking with you, I recognized I was clinging to my *fantasy* of Ben, not reality."

Sienna paused to sip ice water from a straw as Lara held the cup for her. "And, you are right, Lara. My opinion of you has changed completely because of our conversations. You are nothing like I first imagined. In my jealous rage, I pictured you as some sort of hussy. I thought you were playing around with Ben. But now that I know you much better, I recognize you are deeper than that. And, whether it's with Ben or some other deserving guy, I wish you happiness, because you are a good person."

Speaking for this length of time seemed to exhaust Sienna. Lara squeezed her hand and thanked her. "Rest now, Sienna. You need to get strong for William. He needs you." As Lara left the hospital room, her eyes brimmed with tears. She wasn't sure if Sienna was going to make it. Lara now wanted to meet William.

Ben was standing in the small waiting room at the end of the hallway. He watched Lara as she emerged from Sienna's room wondering what the two women could have talked about. He was completely perplexed. As Lara came into the small waiting room, Ben saw the tears streaming down her face and quickly embraced her.

"I'm sorry, Lara. I hope she didn't say anything to upset you."

Lara could not speak as she stared at the wall, attempting to rein in her emotion, as tears slid silently down her cheeks. Ben stroked her hair softly with his hand as he held her face close to his chest.

"I'm fine, really." Lara declared softly. "We understand one another and that's all that matters. Is it possible for me to meet William today?"

Ben was silent for a moment. He peered into Lara's eyes. "Are you *sure* you want to do this now?" Lara was resolute. "Yes. Please arrange lunch with him. I need to meet him today."

At the restaurant Lara's heart was in her throat, but she maintained her outward composure as Ben walked William toward the table. William was a slightly built blonde boy with a confident air about him, dressed in a buttoned-down shirt with a tie and a navy-blue sport coat.

William was eight years old, but small for his age. As Ben arrived at the table with his son, he introduced Lara. "William, I want you to meet Lara."

William looked directly into her eyes, smiled and extended his hand. "I'm pleased to meet you, Lara." His brown eyes studied her with curiosity. His handshake was strong and firm. Lara felt an overwhelming need to know William. She immediately learned that William was not shy. He was bright and inquisitive.

"What do you do, Lara, for a living, I mean?" She explained her architectural training and internship. Then said she was just starting her own design firm. She expressed her love for architectural design, especially historical details. She showed him photos on her phone of the old pink Victorian and photos of his father's office at the university. "I was the decorator." She showed him the Dark Horse Renovation website with photos from her portfolio. William asked questions about Lara's childhood and if she had ever been married. Lara told him about her life as a young girl and her first jobs in high school. Lara told him she was an only child, too. William listened with rapt attention and seemed to enjoy the personal information she shared with him.

After the meal came, Lara asked William questions about his life. He talked about the strict protocol of boarding school, but said he liked it there. He had close friends and knew what to expect every day. He enjoyed the routine. William seemed older than his eight years, especially when he spoke of his mother's illness. "I have been studying anorexia and I know it is not just a physical illness, but mental, as well."

He spoke poignantly about his concerns for Sienna's deteriorating health. He also made loving remarks about his grandparents, Sienna's mother and father, who had stepped in to help raise him. Ben added a few remarks throughout the meeting but acted mostly as a conduit between Lara and his remarkable son.

After the two-hour lunch, William and Lara knew one another quite well. When they parted, William shook Lara's hand, and thanked her for caring about his dad. "I hope you marry him." Lara felt a lump in her throat and feared she might cry as the trio made their way to the waiting cab to take them to the hospital and Sienna's bedside. William slid into the cab beside Lara. Ben was quiet, but Lara sensed his satisfaction with the conversation during lunch.

The three of them walked down the long hallway to Sienna's private room. Ben and Lara waited in the small room at the end of the hallway.

William insisted on visiting his mother alone. He had purchased a large floral arrangement in the hospital gift shop and carried it into her room. The door was left ajar and Lara and Ben could hear his youthful masculine voice.

"Mother, I hope you are feeling better. I miss you and hope you can come home soon. I'm on the chess team now at school and I'm taking violin lessons." Sienna seemed to be listening intently to her son's words.

William cleared his throat. He was a boy on the threshold of becoming a young man.

"I had luncheon today with father. He's looking quite well. He's happy in America. He's not a heartless monster, not in my eyes. I love him."

Sienna responded, and it sounded as if she said she wanted William to love his father. William continued. "I met Lara today at luncheon." The room was silent. "She's very nice, I think, mother. And, I think father loves her. He didn't *say* he loved her, but I could tell just by the way he looked at her. She would be a nice step-mother. Are you going to agree to the divorce?"

Lara heard Sienna's response. "Yes, William. It's the best thing. And, your life will not change. You will stay at the same school and I will get strong and be home soon." After a few minutes passed, William emerged from the room and joined Ben and Lara at the end of the hall. "I'll wait with you here, father." Ben made the phone call.

Sienna's lawyer arrived twenty minutes later in her hospital room. Sienna lifted her claw-like hand and scrawled her signature on the document handing it over to her attorney. A nurse acted as a witness. At the end of the hallway, Ben embraced his son briefly with tears in his eyes. Ben felt it was an act of kindness that William shared this difficult moment with him.

His son had grown up without a father in his life. But, at eight years old he was mature enough to understand Ben's situation and wanted him to be happy. It was a selfless gesture. At that moment he began to view his son differently. Ben wanted to thank Sienna before leaving and William went with him. When father and son emerged from Sienna's room into the hallway, they both glanced Lara's way. She met them at the elevator, and William smiled at Lara—it was a genuine smile of relief. They made their way to the lobby. William's car service had arrived at the front of the building. There were tears in Ben's eyes as he embraced William and watched him drive away with the chauffeur.

A cab was hailed and within minutes they arrived at Ben's attorney's office. Ben took Lara's hand and said, "You know what this means -- don't you, Lara? We can get married."

She had hoped and wished for this moment for so many months, she couldn't believe it was really happening.

"Ben, I love you." It was all that she could manage to say as tears of relief streamed down her face. She felt Ben's strong arms around her as he kissed her tears.

"We will be married as soon as possible." He whispered in her ear, his voice filled with excitement. Sitting in a cab in Vancouver with her Navy SEAL Lieutenant, Lara felt her heart might swell and burst. The turn of events stunned her. Ben was kissing her softly and tenderly in the cab as he told her he wanted to get married as soon as possible. Lara wondered if she should pinch herself. They pulled up to the Baird building that housed Ben's attorney. Ben tipped the cab driver and the vehicle disappeared into the mass of traffic.

Vancouver in April was covered with melting snow. Ben held Lara's hand as they stood in front of an enormous glass and steel skyscraper. He expertly guided Lara toward the elevators and pushed the button for the 22nd floor. There were people in the elevator, but Ben kissed her again, and she blushed. He was like a child at Christmas eager to open his gift. They traveled through several hallways to a great mahogany door.

Ben opened the door and was greeted by a cheery receptionist. "Oh hello, Lieutenant Keegan!" she could not take her eyes off him.

"Hi Nora." Ben said in a hushed tone. "I don't have an appointment, but I have something important, we need to see John Baird right away."

The receptionist excused herself and in a quiet tone checked with someone behind her. "Mr. Baird is in his office. You can go in, Lieutenant Keegan." She smiled sweetly at Ben ignoring Lara.

Ben took Lara's hand as they walked into John Baird's ultra-modern office. Baird was a dignified white-haired gentleman, probably fifty years old, athletically built, expensive suit. The attorney rose as Ben and Lara entered the room and his eyes lit up. "Ben, great to see you." He placed one hand on Ben's shoulder as he shook his hand.

"John, this is Lara Reagan O'Connell." The attorney shook her hand and looked Lara over slightly narrowing his blue eyes.

"The divorce papers have been signed, here they are." Ben announced as he plunked the thick envelope on Baird's desk.

"My god, man, how did you accomplish this?" Baird asked appearing amazed.

"It's a long story; suffice to say that Lara and William had a hand in it." Ben smiled.

Baird removed the paperwork and put on his reading glasses. "Sit, please, coffee?" Ben and Lara sat in black leather chairs in front of his glass desk.

"No coffee thank you, but I do need to know how soon I can marry Lara."

The attorney peered at Ben over his glasses and then he peered at Lara. "As soon as these are processed through the court; I'd say sixty days."

Ben asked if the process could be accelerated. Baird said he would attempt to push the court date up and would get back to him.

"I will await your call, John, and if you can accelerate it, I'll make it worth your effort." Ben said jotting his cell number on a post it note and handing it to Baird.

Ben grasped Lara's hand. "It's just that I don't want her to get away."

The attorney nodded. "I understand, Ben. You don't need to explain that to me. If I had a beauty like her, I'd hasten the process along, too. You'll hear from me."

They exited the office and rode the elevator down 22 floors. Ben passionately kissed Lara on the elevator and the small group of people in it started to applaud. As they stepped off the elevator, one woman squealed. "When's the wedding?" Smiling with dimples, Ben looked into Lara's green eyes. "The wedding will be as soon as I can arrange it."

Lara felt Ben exhale a long sigh of relief as they got into the cab to go to the airport.

"We are going home, Lara. And, I have one question to ask you: Will you marry me?"

Lara embraced Ben and she spoke with breathless excitement into his ear. "Yes."

She'd never experienced such a flood of emotion. She wanted to laugh and cry at the same moment. All the tension of the past few days melted away in Ben's strong arms. She never wanted to let him go. She suddenly felt overcome with exhaustion. The turbulent events of the past few days drained her. The plane ride home was a connection through Pittsburgh. They finally arrived after midnight at the pink Victorian. Ben left her briefly to retrieve Einstein from the professor's house. While standing in Ben's apartment alone, the thought of being his wife became real to Lara. When he returned, Einstein was delighted to see her, and she rubbed his doggy ears.

"Stay with me tonight." Ben softly requested. Too tired to shower, they curled up together in the big comfortable four poster bed and immediately fell asleep.

When Lara woke in Ben's bed, she was filled with a feeling of anticipation. Ben was already up, and she shyly joined him in the shower. She washed his thick black hair and kissed his face as the hot water pummeled them. Ben soaped her body, slowly and sensuously. She thought she might die from wanting him. He washed her long hair, rinsing thoroughly and kissed the nape of her neck as he finished.

She knew Ben wanted her and she sensed this would be

the moment they had long awaited. Stepping out of the shower, he towel-dried her body slowly and then combed her long, wet hair methodically. He blotted her hair with the towel, wrapped her in it, and embraced her.

"I know you've not done this stuff before. I have lots of patience." He was gentle and understanding with Lara. She realized how wonderful intimacy could be with the one special man meant for her. For the first time in her life, Lara felt honored and respected. Ben was worth the wait.

He prepared breakfast and they took Einstein for a brief stroll. Lara felt she was walking on air. Ben's mood was one of contentment. They walked by the purple Victorian and stopped for a moment admiring its beauty in the morning light. Eric's black Infiniti was in the driveway.

"It's beautiful, just like you, Lara." Ben whispered in her ear as he kissed her. Sadly, Lara would be renovating the purple Victorian for Eric. But they both decided it wasn't meant to be their home.

"There's something better in store for us." He smiled, and his blue eyes lit up with mischief. Lara believed there was something better, too.

She had contacted the landlord and moved her things into Ben's apartment. Her condo was now on the market.

"When's the wedding?" the landlord asked. "Ben's planning it." Mr. Walsh smiled. "What a great love story."

Four days later the phone call from Ben's attorney, John Baird, confirmed that the divorce was legal. Benjamin Aiden

Keegan was a free man. Lara had never seen Ben smile so much. Lara had almost forgotten about the trip to St. John. Ben was plotting and planning the late April vacation in his office.

"Just take a small carry-on bag." he advised Lara. "We'll buy everything we need when we get there. That's how we roll."

CHAPTER 28: Spring Break

Ben was secretive about the details of the St. John vacation. He wanted the fine points of the trip to be a surprise for Lara. He knew she had never traveled south of Boston. As she bounced through the doorway of his office one April afternoon, Ben was engrossed in his computer while he spoke softly on the phone in Hebrew. He no longer wrapped up calls quickly or minimized the computer screen when Lara entered. Ben was at ease with her.

He waved her in. As soon as he finished the phone call, he turned his attention to her. "The travel plans are all set. We leave on April 13th and return on the 20th. Here's the paperwork you need to sign for your passport." Ben slipped the paperwork in front of Lara with an X where she was to sign. It was fun to watch Lara's excitement about the St. John trip. Ben knew a vacation would give them time to process all that had occurred in the last few weeks, and a chance to be alone. He could not hold back his happiness. The last time he smiled this much was when he touched down on American soil, and he kissed the tarmac. *It was that kind of feeling.*

They had a direct flight from Portland to Miami. Ben had secured first class seats. From there they took a smaller plane to St. Thomas, as St. John did not have an airport. This flight was not as terrifying as her first one. Lara watched as they flew over what seemed to be hundreds of miles of ocean. Finally, a tiny spot of land thirteen miles long and four miles wide appeared as a sand-colored dot in the turquoise water, St. Thomas. The slowing of the aircraft was evident, and she listened for the familiar click of the landing gear. Clutching the arms of the seat, Lara tried to control her breathing. Ben sensed her anxiety and wrapped his arm around her. She felt safe and secure, even though it seemed she was hurtling through the air at 200 miles per hour.

Lara watched through the window as the plane came closer and closer to landing. It felt like they were touching down so fast they might run out of pavement before they stopped. She envisioned the plane missing the runway and crashing into the ocean. When the wheels of the plane touched the pavement, she felt the familiar bump, and they were finally in St. Thomas. Lara exhaled. Ben kissed her as the plane taxied to a full stop. St. John was located about four miles from St. Thomas' east end and they took a ferry to their destination.

Having never traveled out of New England, Lara felt like she had just landed in the Garden of Eden. The ecosystem of St. John was vastly different than anything she had ever seen. She had only viewed pictures of places like this. The island was lush, green and tropical. Filled with hills and valleys and relatively few flat areas, the island encompassed 20 square miles of breathtaking scenery. A small island, the highest point was Bordeaux Mountain at 1,307 feet and the island's coastal areas consisted of beautiful white sand beaches in protected bays. The major harbor was Coral Bay; however, Cruz Bay housed the main town and harbor. More than two thirds of the island was protected by the National Park Service.

Ben's little bungalow was tucked into a private cove, Caneel Bay, with rocks and trees surrounding the beach area. There were no islands in the distance. They were facing west. The turquoise water was eighty-five degrees and a light trade wind was blowing.

"You *own* this place?" Lara asked incredulously.

"Yes, I have a good man who takes care of it when I'm not here. This is my hideaway and I can't wait to share it with you."

Ben pulled her toward the white sand beach. "Now let's get into the water." He instantly removed his clothing with the efficiency of a Navy SEAL and plunged into the warm tranquil ocean. Lara had never been on a beach naked in her life and felt a twinge of modesty in the bright sunlight. Ben was waving to her and yelling. She rummaged through her bag and found a swimsuit. "I'll be right back." She waved as she stepped inside the cottage and changed quickly.

Ben was happy when Lara finally plunged into the warm water wearing a one-piece swimsuit. He teased her relentlessly swimming underwater and grabbing her legs. Although she feigned escape, Ben sensed she was enjoying his touch. Ben was at one with the water. He embraced Lara as they stood up to their necks in the turquoise water. His eyes searched her face, reaching into her thoughts—and he instantly knew she was happy. It felt like they were on another planet alone.

With his strong arms, Ben dragged her to the warm wet sandy shore and collapsed upon it with her. He enjoyed watching the sun glistening on her smooth skin. He sensed Lara was self-conscious, but she seemed to be enjoying the warmth of the water, the smoothness of the sand.

"Someone might see us."

"Oh, let them look. They will need powerful binoculars and if they do, they'll be terribly jealous." Ben was natural and comfortable without a stitch of clothing. Lounging in the ocean water triggered memories of the times during BUD/S training when he was forced to swim in wet clothing with boots, weighing him down. He would run in the water for hours on end and roll in the sand until his skin would bleed. That experience made him appreciate *this* one so much more.

Ben focused on Lara's beautiful long legs and shapely bottom as she laid prone in the shallows. He rolled toward Lara as he placed wet sand on her bottom. He spent a long time admiring the shape of her back, then placed his hand on her bottom.

"Do you think you can ever swim without the suit?"

"Maybe. I've never done that before; maybe at night?"

He never wanted the sun to set so much. He gently spanked her. For an hour they stayed like that, side by side, allowing the warm waves to tantalizingly roll over the lower halves of their bodies then recede. He could not stop smiling. When her eyes met his, Ben felt she was not only basking in the sun, but in his admiration. He listened as she described with child-like excitement the events of the past twenty-four hours.

"Just this morning we were getting into a cab and it was thirty degrees in Maine. By the end of the day, we are naked in an eighty-five-degree tropical paradise. I can't believe it."

It had been more than eight months getting to know Lara, and he had often wondered what she looked like without clothing, but he'd settle for this swimsuit. Ben savored this moment, wanting to memorize every inch of her shimmering in the sun. The need for food and drink forced them inside temporarily. Drying off with towels they slipped their travel clothes back on.

"Come on," Ben beckoned her toward an outdoor café around the corner and up a hill. "You won't believe the food here, Lara. It's spectacular." He knew she would enjoy this place. The restaurant was a tiny French café. They ordered a delicious salad and a warm slice of freshly baked bread.

"We need to get to the shops before they close." Ben said abruptly. Catching a shuttle bus, they rode to the Cruz Bay downtown area. They had about an hour to get the necessary items: clothing, toothbrushes, and shampoo. Ben purchased a few white shirts and white cotton pants. Lara found beautiful long skirts and feminine tops.

"Oh, we must come back tomorrow." Little did she know, he intended to pamper her for the next few days, shopping and devoting every minute to whatever pleased her.

"There are jewelry shops and hand-made clothiers that I would love to explore." Lara bubbled with excitement. Ben found it exhilarating to be with her, having fun, being spontaneous, and enjoying one another without the business of Black Horse, the university, or Lara's new work venture.

As they arrived at the bungalow, they dropped their shopping bags inside.

"Ah, we are just in time for our appointment." He knew he caught her attention with that statement but would not reveal what they were going to do. Ben knew she would be expecting something dramatic like parasailing from her former military man. But, he enjoyed the astonishment on Lara's face when he led her into a cabana set up on their little private beach. Inside were two massage tables and two white robes and cold bottled water. One whole side of the cabana was open to the ocean waves rolling onto the beach—a tranquil and quiet scene.

"You couldn't have chosen a more beautiful setting." Lara whispered. Two masseuses awaited their arrival and left the cabana briefly, so they could remove their clothing and get onto the tables underneath a white cotton sheet. Ben knew by Lara's expression, this was a treat she had not expected. The massage was exactly what they both needed, especially after the long day of travel. Ben glanced at Lara a few times out of the corner of his eye. They did not speak during the hour-long session, but he listened to her soft breathing and the waves on the beach. Ben had never seen Lara in a state of complete relaxation and made a mental note to massage her like this at home.

After the session, he led her back to the bungalow in preparation for their evening meal. "Don't dress for dinner, just shower and wear that robe. It looks perfect on you."

"Aren't we going to a restaurant to eat?"

"No, I've arranged for our meal to be served here tonight." He gestured toward the charming dining room just off the kitchen of the bungalow.

Ben encouraged Lara to slip into the outside shower, something she had never experienced. She ran the steamy hot water and lathered up. Meanwhile, Ben busied himself at the blender. To serve her, he opened the shower door.

"I have a virgin colada for you, Lara. I will put it here." He set the tall drink on a metal table near the outside shower.

She stopped soaping herself and stood looking at him. His gaze traveled over her face, then her body. He was taken aback by her sheer beauty; her long wet hair draped over her breasts covering her almost completely; Ben felt as if he was viewing a sexy mermaid. He stood mesmerized for a moment, then slipped his robe off to join her. Taking Lara into his arms, his lips pressed against hers, then gently covered her mouth. Throttling back his eagerness was not easy as his legs trembled, his heart pounded, he wanted her more than anything ever and lost track of time. It was as if all his fantasies had come true for that one moment as his lips caressed Lara's, and his hands moved over her soapy body. She was relaxing with him now and enjoying his touch. Lara soaped Ben and they enjoyed the simple pleasure of rinsing one another.

As they dried their bodies with towels, Lara replayed the afternoon swim on the beach with Ben earlier. For eight months Lara had a close relationship with Ben, and often caught herself in the fantasy of wondering what he looked like in the buff. Her dark tresses fell to the middle of her back and Ben combed her hair methodically. Lara slipped into the robe. She was thirsty, and the virgin colada was exactly what she needed.

Ben stayed in the outside shower area a bit longer and emerged in his robe with his face clean shaven.

"My goodness!" Lara said with surprise. "You're a new man!" Lara thought he looked even more handsome with a clean shave. Normally, Ben wore a two or three-day scruff of beard.

"I did it just for you." She thought she knew what he had in mind as there was a mischievous quality to his smile.

Ben hired a local chef and the meal served to them in the bungalow's dining room was exquisite. They were hungry and ate quickly, laughing and talking excitedly.

"Oh Ben, I love it here." Lara said with delight.

"I can see it in your eyes, Lara. You are like a kid in a candy store." Ben smiled. He ordered dessert to be served later. They sat together in the cushioned porch glider on the terrace as they drank cold Perrier and watched the sunset. The sky became a wild burst of pink, gold, and red as the sun slipped gradually toward the turquoise horizon. Ben put his arm around her and drew her close.

"Lara, I have dreamt of being here with you so many

times." She placed her finger on his lips and he stopped talking. She wanted the pleasurable experience of kissing him without the stubble. Lara thoroughly enjoyed clean-shaven Ben. Parting her lips, she raised herself to meet his kiss. His mouth was soft, sensual and skilled. Lara was on the verge of being swept away with passion. She sensed Ben wanted nothing more than to carry her into the bedroom and work off all the frustration he carried over the past few months. But she knew he was taking it slowly because she had no experience.

Before they retired to bed, dessert was served to them on the terrace. They sat in the porch glider enjoying a delicious cheesecake with fresh raspberries.

Ben had an intensity in his eyes as they met hers. "Are you *sure* about marrying me, Lara?"

She didn't expect such a serious moment after the lighthearted fun of the day. But she instantly responded. "Yes. Ben, there could never be another man for me."

He smiled with his whole face, then kissed her passionately. Burying his face in her hair, he whispered. "I don't just love you, I'm crazy about you, darlin."

In the morning, Lara awakened to the gentle sound of waves washing upon the beach. She inhaled the aroma of freshly brewed coffee. Ben was sitting in a chair next to the bed, observing her.

"You're awake already?"

"Coffee, my darlin?" He asked as he watched her eyes open. "I like watching you sleep. You're incredibly beautiful and

I'm madly in love with you. But you know that, don't you?" He leaned down and kissed her lips sweetly.

He had slept with her in the comfortable king-sized bed last night; they cuddled until sleep overtook them. But not before Ben got to first and second base, and very close to third. Lara hoped it would always be like this between them—passionate, fun, exciting. It was as if Ben could read her mind and she could read his. Every moment with him was meaningful, even when they sat silently in the porch glider holding hands or reading a newspaper. But, she sensed he wanted more than sitting in the porch glider this morning. His eyes lingered on her figure beneath the sheet.

"Let's go swimming." Ben offered with dimples. Lara stretched lazily and got out of bed. Taking a quick shower, she brushed her teeth and applied sunscreen. Then, she placed a croissant, fruit and coffee on a plate and sat on the terrace. Watching Ben toss his robe on the sand and enter the water took her complete attention. He lingered just long enough on the beach in the sunlight, so she could examine his muscled form. It was as if nothing else on earth existed except watching Ben move before her eyes. The beautiful symmetry of his muscles took her breath away. She studied his neck, arms, legs, knees and feet; all perfect in every detail. The scars on his body stirred a primal urge in her to caress each one. The one thing that made him most attractive, however, was how oblivious Ben was to his own good looks. He didn't focus on what he wore or how he looked. In fact, he rarely looked in the mirror or shaved. He was a bare bones type of guy, brushing his teeth, washing his hair, and showering with that sandalwood soap. Small things didn't bother him. He took life in stride, living each day to the fullest with a quiet confidence she not only loved, but admired.

She could tell Ben was aware that she was watching him. He turned and playfully smiled at Lara before disappearing underwater. When he emerged, he relaxed in the wet sand. Her eyes took in every gorgeous detail.

Finishing the croissant with fresh raspberries, Lara tossed her robe on the sand and joined him in the water. Ben swam to her and wrapped his arms around her body in the turquoise warmth. She felt his chest against hers, and it was a delightful feeling of freedom. Ben kissed her for what seemed like an hour. He told her she tasted like raspberries.

The morning consisted of long sensual kisses in the warm sunshine. Lara swam away repeatedly, but he would dive under and catch her causing her to laugh. They played a game of water tag with child-like pleasure. Lara had to admit, it felt much better to swim au natural, with the added bonus of no tan lines. They finally pulled themselves onto the wet sand exhausted. It felt good to soak up the sun. Ben played with Lara's long hair. "Don't ever cut this, I love it." He said with affection. And, he kissed her again teasing her, making her want him.

St. John seemed to be a tonic for Lara, and she'd never seen Ben so calm and happy. Lara felt it was a miracle that she felt so relaxed and free of anxiety. As they swam each day, Lara marveled at Ben's physical abilities, and she was taken with his boyish charm. But living with Ben she learned he had a dazzling mental acuity, too. Above all, Lara's favorite attribute was his sensitivity and patience, especially with her. As they lounged in the surf naked, Ben kissed her neck and whispered in her ear. "I'll wait until we are married -- I just wanted you to know that." Lara blushed and kissed him.

***

Enthralled with her feminine trappings, Ben examined Lara's items attempting to understand everything about her. Finding her favorite hair brush, he used it to untangle her long tresses. Using the Sexy No. 9 lotion, he massaged her shoulders before bedtime. He noticed the smallest details about her. He loved how she stirred her coffee and sipped it in a feminine dainty way. He observed her as she cut up fruit into tiny bite-sized pieces on her breakfast plate. One night he gazed into the outdoor shower and watched with rapt attention as she shaved her long legs. She was civilized but not pampered; feminine but athletic and graceful.

He couldn't wait to accompany Lara on a shopping trip. He knew few men would make that statement. But he genuinely enjoyed every moment with her, even shopping. They took the shuttle to the town lined with tiny shops filled with jewelry, clothing and unique art.

Ben insisted that Lara try on clothing as he sat in a comfortable chair. He thoroughly enjoyed watching her as she gave him a personal fashion show. She must have donned twenty ensembles, and she looked prettier in each one, as she did a runway strut just for him. It wasn't the clothing he focused on, but her demeanor. It was the first time Ben had seen Lara carefree and happy. He wanted her to feel like this all the time. But, life had a way of intervening posing unforeseen challenges and decisions. He wanted to be the guy she turned to for every challenge and every decision.

She popped out of the dressing room with a white halter top and long soft pink cotton skirt that floated to her ankles. The skirt was embellished with multi-colored beads. She looked angelic. For a moment his heart nearly stopped beating as he was struck by her extraordinary beauty. She twirled with the grace of a ballerina, her long dark hair and skirt flying softly around her. Lara's skin had color and her eyes were even more beautiful today.

"Yes, that one." Ben said. Lara squealed and put it in the pile. Ben paid for everything with a wad of cash and carried her bags as they moved into the jewelry shops. She loved the handmade pieces created by the local island artists. Ben bought her whatever she wanted.

Both laden with bags, they hailed a cab back to the bungalow. Ben told her before they landed in St. John that he had a surprise planned for her that would blow her mind. She had assumed it was the vacation itself; then the massage, or the shopping trip, but he told her there was something more.

She begged for a hint. All he said was that he was taking her dancing tonight at Danny's Love Shack, a short distance from the bungalow. It was known for great food and a fun dance crowd. Ben dressed in a comfortable white cotton shirt and matching pants.

Lara asked him which outfit he wanted her to wear.

"That last one you tried on, the pink skirt with the white top." Ben smiled.

When she emerged from the bedroom in the white halter top and pink skirt she took his breath away. To Ben, she was the picture of feminine beauty in the soft full pink skirt. Lara was a beautiful woman with a touch of innocence. Ben wolf whistled.

"Every guy is going to wish they were *me* tonight."

***

About a mile into the walk along the ocean, Lara noticed a lovely pergola set up on the beach covered with white flowers. There was a large group of people dressed in white.

"Look, Ben, there's a wedding taking place right here on the beach."

As Lara got closer to the group, she recognized her mother and Rusty, Don and Olivia, and a group of young men and women.

She ran to embrace her mother.

"Have you figured it out yet?" Lara's mother asked with tears in her eyes. Rusty hugged her tightly. "I'm giving you away." he said with a shaky voice. Lara's eyes were filled with surprise.

"Oh gosh, it's us! We're getting married, aren't we?" Lara could not believe what was happening as she turned to Ben.

Don and Olivia embraced Lara. A cabana off to the side of the beach had a full bar set up. Ben took her hand and led her to meet his brothers, the Navy SEALs he had spent the past decade of his life with.

Lara said hello to Tom Wilson and his wife Amanda. "Do you know what you're in for?" Tom joked. "Actually, Lara he has been a changed man in the past eight months. We can't keep him focused on work. He talks non-stop about you." Amanda smiled.

At this, Lara blushed.

Tom's step-brother, Jake, shook Lara's hand. "Welcome to the family. You're even more gorgeous than the pictures he showed us!"

Then, Ben introduced Lara to his brother Elvis, who once carried him to safety in a very bleak moment. Another dark-haired SEAL, Elvis Shaw was six feet tall. He described himself as a Ninja SEAL, as he had a fourth-degree black belt in mixed martial arts. His black hair was longer than the others and he wore it slicked straight back. He bore resemblance to Elvis Presley. His wife, Jessica smiled. "Elvis has some funny stories to tell you about Ben."

Then Nate pushed Elvis out of the way and introduced himself to Lara. Nate O'Neal looked so much like Ben they could have been from the same family. He had Irish roots with black hair and blue eyes. Smaller than Ben, Nate stood only five nine and was lightweight compared to the others. "I'm his little brother!"

Gus took Lara's arm and introduced his wife, Linda. Gus Jorgenson was a six-foot two former football player and solid. With blonde hair shaved close to his head, he was incredibly handsome. His wife, Linda, was six feet tall and a former professional volleyball player. Gus had kind brown eyes. "We are all so happy for both of you. You're getting a pretty boy here, Lara, but he has a lot of scars, too."

Lara smiled as she listened to their colorful descriptions of Ben. His brothers were accurate in their portrayal of him: *a pretty boy with a lot of scars*. She sensed she would learn so much more about Ben through them and looked forward to future meetings.

These men did not resemble the preconceived notion she had in her head. Before meeting them, she had a myth in her mind that Navy SEALs were big, narcissistic, loud, obnoxious guys, sort of like the ones on the football team in high school. She couldn't have been more wrong. These men were polite, friendly, warm, engaging, and humorous and they came in all shapes and sizes. She felt like she was at a family reunion and they were graciously accepting her into their clan. There was one thing that all these men had in common: a quiet dignity. They carried themselves a certain way. It wasn't cockiness. They exuded confidence, responsibility, masculinity, strength, intelligence, and a sense of duty.

Lara was led by Ben to meet the patriarch of his family, now 65 years old, his father Jonathan Keegan. Tall, dark and handsome with more silvery hair than black, Jonathan Keegan had those amazing blue eyes. Lara immediately recognized the origin of Ben's genes. It was as if she was looking at a future version of Ben.

Jonathan Keegan embraced Lara with affection. His voice was identical to Ben's with the same Irish inflection. He introduced his wife, Catherine. Ben's mother was a pretty blonde with soft brown eyes. She spoke quietly as she introduced Ben's four sisters, Grace, Anna, Mary, and Megan and their respective husbands. Then, Ben's one surviving brother, Seamus, gave her a hug. All of Ben's siblings were older than him. The girls all had blonde hair and brown eyes. Seamus was dark, like Ben, but had brown eyes. Ben's family was thrilled to meet Lara and immediately made her feel accepted.

After about thirty minutes of meeting and greeting, Ben led Lara to a separate cabana on the beach. He closed the curtain and took her hands. "We have some business to finish."

With tears streaming down her face, Lara threw her arms

around Ben's neck. She could not stop weeping. She couldn't believe this was happening. There was a government official in the cabana, and Lara provided her passport photo as the man handed Ben a document.

"Our marriage license, you signed for it in my office over a week ago. They needed a photo identification to make it legal, and now it is." Ben peeled off several hundred-dollar bills and the official left.

Ben turned to Lara. "You need to change into your wedding dress." A smile crept over his face as he gestured behind her. There stood a tiny Asian woman in the cabana behind a table with the most beautiful wedding dress lying atop it.

"Oh Ben, it's beautiful." Lara choked up.

"One more thing." Ben said as he handed her a black velvet box.

"What's this?" Lara asked with disbelief."

Ben nodded. "This is for you, darlin."

Gasping as she opened the box, her eyes fell upon the most beautiful vintage engagement ring she had ever laid eyes upon. It was a two-carat oval cut Victorian diamond, set in antique gold.

"Don't cry now, you can save that for later." Ben soothed her. He left her alone in the cabana with the Asian woman. Lara slipped into the off-the-shoulder chiffon gown with a fitted bodice and beaded accents. The gown had been handmade for her, selected by Ben, the Asian lady explained. It fit Lara perfectly. Then the woman placed a flower in Lara's hair with a few diamond hair pins.

Lastly, the small woman handed Ben's wedding ring to her. "Keep this safe. You need it for the ceremony."

Lara applied a fresh coat of soft rose lipstick. She still couldn't believe this was happening. Ben wasn't kidding when he said he was going to blow her mind.

As Lara emerged from the cabana, Rusty was waiting and took her arm. Choking back tears, he guided her to Ben standing beneath the pergola with a priest. The anxiety melted away as Lara faced Ben and their eyes met. Ben smiled with his whole face.

The fragrance of the blossoms was intoxicating as a soft trade wind blew over them. Everyone was dressed in white. The guests were seated in white chairs on each side of the pergola. There were two photographers. The backdrop was the beautiful turquoise ocean and the sun as it moved toward the horizon. The priest said a prayer and read traditional wedding vows. Lara gazed into Ben's blue eyes as she slipped the wedding band on his finger. She was not nervous. There was no anxiety as she said, "I do." She kissed Ben with great enthusiasm.

Nothing in her life ever felt so right. The sunset spread along the horizon into a blend of gold and pink. The whole group, barefoot in the sand, walked a short distance down the beach to Danny's Love Shack for an evening of dancing and fun.

***

Danny's was a mid-sized place, more intimate than most. Ben arranged ahead of time for the food, which was particularly good, and accommodations for the wedding party. Ben and Lara sat at a table often reserved for honeymooners. The group of family and friends surrounded them. Ben held Lara's face and kissed her, as Nate made a heartfelt toast to his SEAL brother.

Lara was a vision of feminine loveliness in the gossamer wedding dress. As his eyes met hers in the candlelight, Ben thought her face was exquisitely framed with her long dark hair. He could not wait to finish the meal and hold her in his arms on the dance floor. The food was delicious, and Lara allowed Ben to slip a bite or two between her lips a few times during the meal. Photographs were taken. Ben's brothers tapped their forks to the glassware beckoning the groom to kiss the bride again and again. Ben was enjoying this.

Ben expertly swept Lara onto the dance floor once the music started. He tenderly placed his strong arms around her as they moved to one of his favorites, the Tim Halperin song, *Think I'm in Love*. Lara rested her beautiful head on his chest and all was right with the world. Ben was filled with pride to have her in his arms. *Lara was now his wife*. He sensed the eyes of every man in the place giving her the once over. Good. Let them gawk. Even he was amazed that he had this stunning beauty in his arms. The trade wind blew Lara's dark hair and he drew in a breath inhaling the soft scent lingering on her skin. Ben wanted to remain suspended in the moment for eternity. He closed his eyes attempting to keep the image of Lara at that instant in his memory.

After dancing for two hours, they finally stopped and enjoyed the wedding cake. Family and friends stayed at a nearby resort and as the festivities ended they drifted off to their respective rooms, promising to meet at the bungalow for breakfast and a swim in the morning. Ben and Lara took a cab back to the bungalow and decided to enjoy a late-night swim. Ben was eager to get back into the warm tranquil water with her. He loved swimming at night, but especially on *this* night. It was dark and deserted on the beach. The water had cooled to eighty degrees. In the bungalow, Ben unzipped Lara's beautiful chiffon wedding dress slowly. They silently slipped into robes.

Ben took Lara's hand and they walked down to the water's edge. The couple simultaneously dropped their robes in the sand. The water felt deliciously warm and sensual as they entered, and the heat of the day melted away. Light from the terrace and stars above illuminated their bodies with a soft glow. Taking the lead, Lara wrapped herself around Ben's naked body beneath the tranquil warm water.

Ben was beaming. "We're married!" He could not restrain his happiness. He ran his hand through her thick dark hair shining in the moonlight. His blue eyes met Lara's. "At last. I have you exactly where I want you." With unbridled enthusiasm, Ben kissed her as a happy groom would kiss his new wife. They innocently swam in the warm water and ended up on the wet sand at the water's edge. Ben slipped a towel beneath her body. Lara relaxed as Ben's body covered hers. He felt the warmth of Lara's wet skin against his, the water moving over them, between them. Ben's tongue probed the seam of her lips as his hands caressed her body. A trade wind whispered across their skin and Ben drank in her beautiful form in the moonlight. He was captivated and focused on one thing: making love to his wife. Thoughtfully, putting Lara's wants and needs before his, Ben did not rush into intimacy. It was most important for him to create a feeling of complete trust and relaxation for Lara.

Lara's body quivered with a desire she'd never felt before. Seeing Ben there in the moonlight made her tingle from head to toe. She realized tonight was the night she could freely explore and caress every inch of her husband. She watched Ben as if spellbound. Although she only caught a glimpse of him naked, the moonlight reflected on his muscled form and Lara could think of nothing but pleasuring him. She longed to pin him on the wet beach sand and make mad passionate love to him. But she had no idea how to go about it. Gazing at Ben stirred a feeling of desire in her that was wild, sensual, and instinctive. Her anxiety had melted away, now replaced with a delightful sense of freedom.

Lara moved so she was on top of Ben as he lay on the wet sand. She kissed him with a hunger she seemed unable to control as her silky hair tumbled upon him. Then she did something she'd dreamt of—caressed each scar, one by one, on his chest, his arms, his torso, and his legs as Ben fell into a trance of pleasure.

She heard him murmur, "Now, it's my turn."

***

He moved above Lara and set about to replicate the tantalizing kisses from head to toe. His hands and lips moved proficiently over her body, sensing exactly when to stop and when to move further. Ben exercised patience. This was Lara's wedding night and he wanted her to delight in every moment. His mouth seared a path down her neck and shoulders. When he gently caressed her breasts, she whispered, "I love you." Ben was barely able to control his desire and she was caught up in the heady stimulation. When he expressed his love for her in this way, he felt her back arch. There was no restraint now. Ben moved his hands over her thighs and felt her push against him, welcoming his touch. He felt her breath hot against his face.

As he roused her passion, his own grew stronger. His lips traced kisses over her breasts, down her belly and he felt her hips move upward toward him. Moving her legs apart his tongue moved along her inner thigh, then along the soft petals of skin, now moist and warm. He felt her moving and his tongue dipped in, gently at first—then with a rhythm that brought her to a shuddering ecstasy. He pulled away and gazed into her half-closed eyes. He knew she was in a hypnotic trance of pleasure.

"Are you ready?"

He heard her exhale a faint, *yes*, her breathing labored. Lara's long dark hair surrounded her on the white sand in the moonlight. The rest of the evening was filled with instinctual pleasures. Ben made love slowly and gently at first, looking into her eyes, reading her mind, fulfilling her needs over and over, delaying his own enjoyment. He never wanted to stop. He'd waited so long for this moment—so very long—and it felt so damned good.

***

Lara watched as he lost control and she soared with him to a crescendo of pleasure never- before imagined. Love flowed in her like warm honey. They remained entwined in one another's arms for an hour in the wet sand with the warm water washing over them. In bed that night, they made love again. Then, they both slept soundly from sheer physical exhaustion.

The next morning Ben joined Lara in the outdoor shower. No words were spoken. He covered her mouth with his and moved his soapy hands over her body. Lara found herself wanting him again. Slowly and carefully, he moved her body against the wall and brought her legs gently around him. Then he cupped her bottom with his hands and he moved in rhythm with her as rolling waves of pleasure engulfed them. She heard him cry out and she felt his body shudder. "Oh Lara." It was all he could manage to say as his breathing was labored and he held her close. Gasping, breathing heavily, he whispered. "I love you."

Finishing the most wonderful shower in the world, Ben served her breakfast on the beach. Now in swimsuits, they were lounging on the towel near the water's edge, knowing family and friends would be arriving any time now. Lara was not aware that she was getting sunburned. Ben found her sunglasses, sunscreen, and hat. He slowly applied the cream on Lara's legs and arms. They were sitting facing one another on the towel as he dabbed the sunscreen on her cheeks and nose. With his face so close to hers, he sweetly kissed her.

Suddenly, there was the sound of car doors closing. Lara realized they had company. Nate and Elvis were yelling. "Last one in the water is a loser!" All the brothers and their respective wives arrived at one time. As if synchronized, they jumped into the water together, laughing and splashing. Ben's sisters and their husbands joined in, too. Ben's parents sat with Lara's mother and Rusty in lounge chairs on the beach. Ben had arranged for the chef to cook breakfast on the terrace of the bungalow.

"Best wedding ever." Ben's brothers shouted from the turquoise water. Lara's mother sighed. "It was so romantic, Lara. Perfect." Ben and Lara jumped into the fray. The women sat on the shoulders of the men tossing a beach ball back and forth. The swimming and laughter was great fun. It seemed they had all become child-like within a few minutes.

After an hour of boisterous swimming games, breakfast was served on the terrace and the men split off from the women. Lara overheard bits and pieces of the conversation from the men. The gist of their conversation was that most people would think they were crazy because they didn't want to leave Iraq and Afghanistan – they *wanted* to be there – to finish the job. The decision was made to pull out too soon. The U.S. spent trillions building an infrastructure and military bases and soon Iraq and Afghanistan would have the black ISIS flag flying over the U.S. bases. America only served to be the most expensive building contractor on the planet. The military bases filled with equipment too heavy to transport were spectacular -- and now would be occupied by the enemy.

"We gave them a gift all right, but it wasn't the gift of freedom. We built the infrastructure and bases for the enemy to reunite and fight us with more ferocity." The warriors clearly felt by pulling out early the United States was allowing everything they had accomplished, all the blood and treasure sacrificed, to be trounced upon by radical Islamists chomping at the bit to rule with their barbaric laws. And, now the dedicated veterans being sent home, that fought so valiantly, losing limbs, suffering from PTSD, and brain injuries, were being pushed aside, waiting in long lines for their well-deserved veteran benefits, medical care or a job. These veterans returned to a 70 percent unemployment rate. And worse, there was a 25 percent suicide rate. For every veteran killed by enemy combatants, 25 veterans kill themselves. That's 22 deaths each day, or one every 65 minutes. And it's possible these numbers were being *underreported*. Not only was integration into civilian life a challenge, these warriors fought for ten years to make progress in Iraq and Afghanistan. It saddened them deeply to see it all trickle away. It was hard to take.

She heard Ben. "Yeah, the real kicker is, President Karzai just let 65 terrorists out of prison. *These are the guys we took months to capture.* We set up recon on those terrorists for days, weeks. You can bet your ass those vengeful bastards will be coming to the United States to mete out their retribution." The group was concerned that the U.S. military was going to be reduced to levels prior to World War II. They clearly felt the number one responsibility of the U.S. government was to *protect American citizens*, as the Constitution clearly stated, but it seemed those in power had their priorities upside down.

Lara spent the day getting to know each one of Ben's brothers. She saw Ben in his element, with his unit. She now understood the men he trained with, served with, and fought with. These men were his family. She sat with the wives, as they clustered together to discuss family matters. There was little discussion of their husbands' occupations, although the women demonstrated special reverence for these men. In the forefront of Lara's mind, she realized that Ben was part of this secret brotherhood and always would be. It wasn't as if he would wake up some morning and move on. There would be days when he would be quiet, sullen, and distant. There was a patriotic passion, raging like a storm inside of him. Lara joined the women as they lovingly watched the elite band of warriors once again rough-housing in the surf.

It was unspoken, but the wives had the knowledge that these men had suffered together, beyond what the human spirit was intended to endure. They had medically treated one another, saved each other's lives, killed enemies together, endured recon missions that lasted forty hours barely moving. They had starved together, been sick together; fell into swamps, climbed mountains and broken bones together. On missions, they slept fitfully, often waking to strafing and rocket propelled grenades. As they traveled together, carrying 60 pounds of gear on their bodies, they knew every bump in the road could possibly be an improvised explosive device. These men were tortured together and cared for one another through parasitic infections and hypothermia and profuse bleeding. They were sandwiched into armored Hummers and Blackhawks not bathing for a week. They shared the inconsolable loss of many brothers, SEALs, just like them, on the battlefield. They held their dying brothers with tenderness as they bled to death in their arms. They risked their lives to double back and retrieve a sacred warrior's body.

Lara was starkly aware that she was in the company of elite shadow warriors who were responsible for protecting the freedom of the country. Ben once said to her about his fallen brothers, "I can never bring them back, but I sure as hell can spend the rest of my life punishing those responsible." She now understood why Ben was not involved with the acquisition of things; he acquired relationships, people. Everything else was window dressing.

Lara also began to understand why Ben never had a normal life. As a Navy SEAL, he could not expect a woman to care for him in a deep and committed relationship. He knew a relationship would never survive. He was gone non-stop. First, he spent four years in the U.S. Naval Academy. But, becoming a SEAL changed him in a fundamental way. For eight years, failure was not an option. Any misstep could cause death or injury to his brothers. The environment he lived in was foreign to Lara. For the last decade, Ben's world in Iraq consisted of desert as far as the eye could see, living in constant dust, extreme desert heat, squalid urban areas, and the hypothermic cold of the 10,000-foot mountains and lack of oxygen in Afghanistan. And, when he wasn't physically there fighting he was working up for deployment five months at a time. Traveling the country for special training, learning new methods, testing new combat equipment, running, lifting, staying in shape for the next deployment.

Lara had always seen Ben as an impulsive, spur-of-the-moment nomad. But she couldn't have been more mistaken. SEALs had to be prepared for a mission to go wrong, so they were expert planners. And, now she saw that Ben was truly a fanatical planner. These guys not only had a plan B, they had a plan C, and a plan D and a plan E. Ben had the skills of a linguist, mechanic, paratrooper, communications expert, medic, breacher, sniper, advanced demolition specialist, communications and high-tech guru, and diving expert. But the physical skills were only half of it. It was the mental toughness that bound him to his brothers. The moment he earned his trident, Ben's life became the SEAL platoon. His family became the SEAL platoon. Ben's reason for existing became SEAL principles: love, honor, commitment, loyalty.

All of Lara's life, she had worked on restoring beautiful antiques and historical buildings to their former glory. She now accepted the fact that Ben would never be one of her restoration projects. She could never remove the scars or change him in any way. But she also recognized *that was the very reason she loved him from the beginning*. Just as she admired the beautiful patina on the ancient coin that graced his chest, she appreciated Ben's scars. It was because he was unchangeable, unwavering, and steadfast in his principles that she loved him so much. Those were the very traits that attracted her to him and now made her admire him even more.

***

Ben was being ruthlessly teased by his brothers asking if he would be setting up a new business as a wedding planner. There was energetic laughter and rowdy behavior among the group of men. Ben missed their companionship more than he realized. Joking and drinking beers on the beach, they swapped stories and caught up with one another. Ben sensed that Lara was not yet aware that these men were Dark Horse operatives. The men in the group had frequent contact, but not often in person out in the open like this. Whenever Ben met with his brothers, it would be a private meet somewhere out of the way. Eventually, Lara would get to know them all and love them as he did.

He had already broached the subject with his brothers about bringing Lara into the company. At first, he met a wall of resistance. No woman could have the stomach or tenacity to do the work. And there was the concern about her being killed or captured. But over time they began to see the value of having a woman as an operative. Lara could go into places and do things that a male could not. She was young and healthy and partially trained. Ideas started forming and, one by one, the brothers gradually started warming up to the idea of having Lara involved. But, they all agreed, there would need to be intensive training, and Ben would be responsible for that. The only issue that got in the way for Ben was the risk and danger involved to Lara if she agreed to work with him. He knew he wanted her to be part of Dark Horse. Her performance at the gun range had been exemplary and her martial arts skills had improved exponentially. He was now weight training with her and running. Lara was a good apprentice and he relished the extra time with her.

Leaving St. John was bittersweet. However, Lara was leaving with the happiest memories of her life. She even managed to relax enough on the plane ride home to fall asleep with Ben. Every so often the thought would come to the forefront of her mind: *I'm married to Ben. I'm his wife.* She never felt such unbridled happiness. She had an irrational fear that if she reveled in this joy too much that someone or something may take it away from her.

She overheard Ben on the phone before they left the island. Someone had broken into his university office—it was Randall Bettencourt on the phone. Lara only caught bits and pieces of the conversation and hoped Ben would tell her about it on the plane ride home. But, nothing was said.

CHAPTER 29: Black-op Life

The end of April in Maine was still cold and rainy, but the sunny days that Lara enjoyed were a welcome respite from winter's grip. She still could not believe she had experienced such a magical wedding on the beach in St. John, and it had all been planned by Ben. It was the high point of her life. Ben made everything so exciting. A simple breakfast with him was filled with current event discussions, or some days a quiet meditation on the porch holding hands. On sunny days, the two would go for a ride on the Indian motorcycle. Sometimes they would visit with Rusty and Lillian. Lara celebrated her twenty-fifth birthday and in a couple of weeks her university degree would be finished. Setting up Dark Horse Renovation, was well underway. She had client meetings lined up throughout the month of May and the projects would keep her busy for the summer, possibly into autumn.

Lara was thrilled to be Ben's wife. Living with him day-to-day, she was beginning to know him on a deeper level. She was learning that Ben was an open book in many ways, but when it came to Dark Horse, he was careful with sharing details. He had the unique capability to compartmentalize his life, and Lara knew this came from the way he had always lived. This would not change. Lara concentrated on integrating her life with his in a way that made both comfortable.

Lara and Monique drove to the new renovation job on the West End of Portland. The home was an historical beauty and Lara had the plans ready to show the owner. As Lara pulled up to the stately brick mansion, Monique exhaled. "Wow, this is amazing." Lara asked Monique to come along as it would be a learning experience for her as a new intern.

The homeowner, Diana Farrington, met them at the door. "It's so nice to deal with people who are on time." She ushered them into the enormous parlor of the 1800's John Calvin Stevens colonial revival home. Lara, Monique and the homeowner went over every design detail. The meeting took about ninety minutes.

Lara was only now learning about Ben's SEAL brothers, Javier Mendoza and Sam Clark, who never made it back from their last mission in Afghanistan. Always wondering why Ben drove the ten-year-old Dodge Ram truck full of dents and scratches, Lara never asked the question. Although Ben lovingly took care of the truck mechanically, he never repaired the scratches and dents on the outside. Ben told her it was the perfect vehicle for the harsh Maine climate. Lara frequently rode in Ben's truck. As she observed small things about it, she came to the realization this vehicle was not originally Ben's. He owned it and it was registered to him, but she noticed small things that made her think differently.

One day as she waited for him to come out of the bank, she fingered a pair of dog tags in the console. She had always assumed they belonged to Ben. Upon closer inspection, when she turned them over in her hand she noticed the name *Javier Mendoza* on them. Another time when she was folding his laundry, she came across a shirt with the name *Mendoza* on the back. She later found out it was Javier's BUD/S graduation shirt. It had been given to Ben and he wore it from time to time. Lara found Sam Clark's boots, the exact same size as Ben's, and Sam's SEAL harness in Ben's closet. He never spoke about Sam or Javier with her and she knew better than to ask.

***

The Holy Grail for Ben was to find out the name of the Taliban bastard that took out Javier two years ago. And through many months of careful intel, he finally had a name and photograph of the Afghani drug lord who attacked them on that fateful day. Not only did Ben have the name of the drug lord, he had the name and photograph of the henchman, Muhammad Akhtar, who put the bullet into Javier's head.

It was amazing how these guys turned on one another for the right type of bait and a slice of revenge. Akhtar was now trying to muscle out the drug lord above him. Thus, he wanted to intercept the next load of munitions for his own little army of killers. It was frequent for these animals to brag about killing an American soldier. Akhtar's chest-beating and bragging served Ben well. The next step would be to set up the careful execution of him. There was no room for error.

Ben was working every day obsessed with surveillance reports on the ground in Afghanistan. He received intel that Muhammad Akhtar was planning a trip to Pakistan. He was waiting for more information. The meet had to be carefully structured, so he could trap the insect in his web for the execution. He contacted his Pakistani cohorts and through several sources got the time, date, and place of the meet. It was to take place with a tribal leader, an arms dealer. He now made arrangements through Moshe to formulate the details of the meet.

* * *

It was Memorial Day weekend and Lara was hoping to spend time with Ben and some of his military friends. She suggested a cookout. But today was Sunday, never a day of rest for Ben. She felt him tossing and turning last night in bed and sensed something was going on in that beautiful head of his.

He would only tell her things when he was ready. On this morning he was awake earlier than usual and showered. While he was in the bathroom, Lara made coffee and breakfast in the kitchen. He was startled at the sight of her sitting in the kitchen with eggs and toast for him.

He smiled as his eyes met hers. "I'm sorry I woke you, love. I hoped you'd sleep in. It's Sunday, your day of rest."

He kissed her and smiled, but his blue eyes looked tired. Lara whispered, "When you're ready I know you'll tell me."

Ben pretended to be casual. "Don't worry. It's just a routine thing. I have something going on in Pakistan. Need to get on the horn with a buddy of mine. But, I'll be back shortly. If not, I'll text you. Or, you can stop by if you'd like." He ate quickly and was out walking Einstein toward his campus office. Lara noticed the satellite phone on him and sensed he was expecting information. She knew this could be a long day.

She spent a few hours doing laundry and decided to visit Ben in his campus office. She knew something was up when she walked through the doorway. When she slipped into his office, Ben was on the satellite phone with Moshe speaking Hebrew. They were going back and forth with details, coordinates, times, descriptions. Lara knew that meant serious business.

She hoped that Ben would not fly to Pakistan; it was a particularly dangerous place. Once he hung up the phone, Lara spoke. "I suppose you will not clue me in on any of the details."

Surprising her, Ben spoke freely. "Yes, I will tell you. I'm going to have a guy executed who took out my best friend, Javier Mendoza. It has taken me two years to find out who the son-of-a-bitch is, but I'm going to have a bullet put through his skull. And, don't try to stop me, Lara, because this is personal."

Lara had never seen his blue eyes flash so intensely, and she took a deep breath momentarily taking in what he just said. She knew better than to try to stop him. Lara walked home with Einstein and waited, busying herself with household chores and waiting for Ben to send her a text. He was always very thoughtful about that. He would let her know if he was coming home for dinner, or not.

***

Ben was watching a satellite feed on his computer screen giving him real-time movement in Pakistan on the ground. He had a front row seat. Moshe's men were there, and the meet was set up. Arrangements had been made for a cache of weapons to be at their disposal upon arrival. There were operatives in the area that Ben and Moshe trusted, and he was confident the plan would be executed flawlessly. He wouldn't be participating in the mission if he didn't trust the details from those on the ground.

Arriving in Pakistan, Moshe and his men were picked up by two Suzuki Cultus, mid-sized SUV's fitted with armor plating and bullet-proof glass making them drive like tanks. They rendezvoused with one up-armored Chevy Suburban. The eighteen men made their first stop at an operative's bunker, an underground living quarters, to hide and rest, then get armed properly for the coming high-risk meet.

Ben was informed every step of the way. For the first two hours in the hidden bunker they were almost comfortable, but Moshe and his men did not rest until every detail of the meeting had been scrutinized many times. Where would the target enter? How many people would be in the vicinity? Everything was discussed right down to swapping out security guards, the weather report, jamming cell phones and disabling security cameras. *There could be no mistakes.* Finally, after eating, Moshe and his men slept. Ben worked in his office but left the screen up for viewing. He set his cell phone to alert him and he fell asleep for several hours at his desk. He sent a text to Lara. *Sorry, working late tonight. I won't be home for dinner.*

Ben's alarm woke him at the appointed time and he noticed Lara standing next to him with a sandwich and milk. She stood in the room for a few moments and he knew she was gauging where he was in the mission. He didn't realize she had left the room. He was focused on the screen before him, listening to his men.

Ben was back in touch with Moshe. It was pitch dark in the remote region of Pakistan. Communication systems were tested. Weapons examined and double checked. The Suzuki and Suburban brought them to the location for the high risk meet and Moshe's team entered the building surrounded by razor wire and guards. No one questioned their presence at the meeting. Prior to their arrival, the guards were quietly captured and killed. Different guards dressed exactly like them took their places. There was no time to waste.

As Akhtar entered the room, Moshe stepped from behind the door. Akhtar spun around and for a split second looked Moshe directly in the eye. The suppressed 26mm Glock was trained on Akhtar's head with a laser. Moshe whispered, "This is for Javier." He pulled the trigger quickly putting one bullet in Akhtar's head and one in his chest for good measure. "Enjoy your virgins, you bastard."

He quickly stepped over the body, as he and his crew calmly exited the building. The Suzuki and Suburban swept Moshe and his men to the airport and they journeyed back to their secret location, exhausted but satisfied with their mission. It was perfect, and Ben observed the satellite feed as it happened, but he couldn't see inside the building. He waited to hear from Moshe. Ben received the confirmation on the satellite phone a few minutes after midnight in his office. It was Moshe's voice. "The target was successfully eliminated."

Ben smiled when he heard the mission was successful. Javier's service was honored. It was Memorial Day.

* * *

It was after midnight. Lara was sitting by the parlor window reading as she watched Ben stroll into the driveway. His stride and cadence told Lara his mission was accomplished. She heard his footsteps as he came up the back stairs and Einstein whined with excitement. She ran to the door to embrace him. He looked tired but satisfied. That was all that mattered. He kissed her passionately. She whispered in his ear, "It's Memorial Day, and I want to thank you for your service, my handsome Navy SEAL Lieutenant."

Ben pulled her into his chest. "And, just how do you plan to thank me?" He was teasing now with his Irish brogue. Lara's eyes met his. "In a very personal way."

~THE END~

Thank you for reading, A Sense of Duty. I sincerely appreciate each and every reader.
If you enjoyed this book, please leave a review on www.Amazon.com for me.
As a self-published author, reviews are one of the only marketing tools I have,
thus I appreciate them greatly.

Book 2: "Encountering Evil" is next in this series.

Wall to wall action, you will follow Ben's black-op missions as he tackles some of the most frightening terrorist elements imaginable lurking in sleepy New England towns. Meet the other former SEAL operatives, Dark Horse Guardians, in Ben's New England unit. As Lara starts her own design firm, Dark Horse Renovation, she gradually she learns more about her husband's black-op world and struggles with evil forces in her own life.

Made in the USA
Columbia, SC
14 October 2018